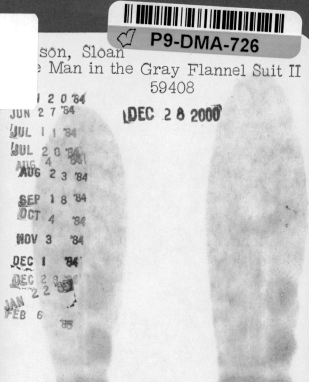

...son, Sloan
...e Man in the Gray Flannel Suit II
59408

1 2 0 '84
JUN 2 7 '84
JUL 1 1 '84
JUL 2 0 '84
AUG 4 '84
AUG 2 3 '84
SEP 1 8 '84
OCT 4 '84
NOV 3 '84
DEC 1 '84
DEC 2 8
2 2
JAN
FEB 6
'85

DEC 2 8 2000

THE NORFOLK LIBRARY
Norfolk, CT 06058
542-5075

INTER FOLIA FRUCTUS

1. Books may be kept two weeks and may be renewed once.

2. Each borrower is held responsible for all books drawn on his name, and for any damage or fines on such books.

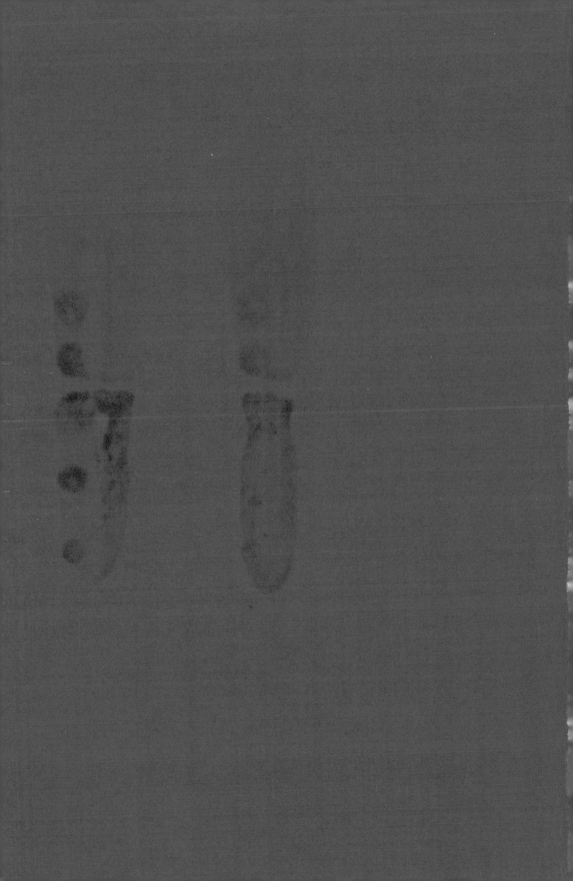

THE
MAN IN
THE GRAY
FLANNEL
SUIT III

ALSO BY SLOAN WILSON

THE MAN IN THE GRAY FLANNEL SUIT II

SLOAN WILSON

ARBOR HOUSE
NEW YORK

To my darling daughter, Jessica,
with my usual plea—be careful!
S. W.

This novel is a combination of highly subjective memories and imagination which can truly be called fiction.

—S. W.

1

MY NAME IS Tom Rath. There have been times when that name sounded better to me than it looked on paper because wrath in various forms was boiling up in me so hard that it seemed natural to be named for it. At roll call in the army when I was a raw recruit in World War II, the sergeant used to bark, "Rath?"

"Here," I'd growl, and there I was, angry as hell at almost everything, as most young soldiers have a perfect right to be.

So my name is anger, I used to think, and I was strengthened by the sound of it when I was a paratrooper dropped over the German lines like, I liked to imagine, an avenging angel. Self-dramatization is, I think, a necessary part of war, because if a battle has no thunderous meaning, why risk one's life in it?

Later, when I changed my army uniform for a gray flannel suit, I learned that anger has to be carefully camouflaged in civilian life. Men in gray flannel suits are supposed to speak softly and carry a big pencil, but I still wryly thought of myself as the last angry public relations man. There was still, of course, plenty to be infuriated at in the world, but young executives were supposed to keep smiling. Sometimes I thought I should change my name to Tom Bland.

In any case, I soon became a minor assistant to Ralph Hopkins, the president of the United Broadcasting Company in Rockefeller Center, New York. Sometimes I admired this vastly successful man and sometimes I hated him. What I actually saw was a surprisingly mild, affable man who did almost nothing but work all the time, exhausting whole relays of assistants. Over the years he had won vast wealth and power, but neither seemed to interest him much as far as I could see. He lived an apparently ascetic life alone in a house on East Sixty-third Street in New York that his wife had had furnished with fine antiques before she started spending almost all her time in another place they owned out in Connecticut. Even the most malicious gossipers could not make rumors of Ralph Hopkins having a mistress or homosexual lovers sound believable enough to last long. He was, though, a strangely asexual man who spent at least twelve hours a day trying to keep the United Broadcasting Company ahead of the other networks in the ratings, and he gave the rest of his time and energy to the job of running countless charities, including his favorite, the National Foundation for Mental Health, which he had headed since its beginning. Some of the wiseacres on his staff called him a workaholic and found irony in his devotion to the cause of mental health, but a lot of people praised him, and I suspected that maybe this was a kind of approval he needed.

Whatever the reasons for his unremitting labors, I hoped that he would not quit soon. I was one of the highly specialized assistants who were assigned almost exclusively to his charities. My main job was, as the saying went, "helping him to write" the many speeches he gave on mental health, education and his theories on "the role of mass communications in the modern world," a subject with which he wrestled a good deal. Sometimes my job seemed dead end, but as I got into my forties I began to realize that I could look a long, long while before finding a position that would pay a decent salary for my skills, which consisted mostly of my ability to write in Hopkins' deliberate, understated style on deadly serious subjects which bored almost everyone to death.

My worry over Ralph Hopkins' retiring wasn't helped by him seeming old and unwell to me when I first went to work for him in 1953, and as the years wore on he grew even more pale and thin despite the fact that he still seemed to burn with energy. In the late fifties he appeared to be slowing down a little, but when President Kennedy was elected in 1960 he seemed to be rejuvenated. Never before had he shown any open interest in politics, and I'd always assumed that like so many big businessmen he was a conservative Republican, but President Kennedy's father was a friend of his and he had known "Jack" since he was a college boy. Hopkins became one of those elder business statesmen the young president often consulted, and soon after the inauguration began spending a lot of time in Washington and receiving frequent telephone calls from the White House when in New York. This connection to a power greater even than his own obviously pleased him, and he began assigning me to work on speeches in which he praised the new president's policies.

I WAS NOT too surprised, then, when Ralph Hopkins called me into his office on a cold Friday afternoon in September of 1963 and announced that President Kennedy had asked him to serve as chairman of a White House Conference on Mental Health.

"That's quite an honor," I said.

"I suppose, but it's also the kind of thing that could turn into a fiasco if we don't run it right. Many a businessman has gone down to Washington feeling cocky and has come back with his tail between his legs. It's an easy place for a man to make a damn fool of himself."

"It's a great opportunity . . ."

That's the kind of language Hopkins liked—*positive.*

"That's the spirit," he said. "We'll have to put together a team to help me carry the ball on this. It's a rush operation for a project as big as this one. The president is aiming for early next summer."

"We can do it," I said. "As far as the mechanics go, we can take Eisenhower's conference on education as a model."

Hopkins had played a small part in that affair, which had been run by his old friend Neil McElroy, the president of Procter & Gamble, and I knew he admired the results, which had actually helped make McElroy secretary of defense.

"That's it exactly," Hopkins replied. "We'll set up a similar organization. How would you like to be my right hand on this, at least in the initial stages?"

"I'd like that very much," including, I thought, the higher pay that should go with it.

"If all goes well maybe I can make you staff director when we get the thing put together. Of course that will be a congressional appointment and I can't promise it, but I'll want somebody I can work with closely and I think my recommendation will be taken seriously."

"Yes, sir, that would be great."

Like many men of real power, Hopkins was always careful to define the limits of his strength and to avoid promises, but he was good at holding out bait.

"I'm afraid that right from the start you're going to have to spend most of your time in Washington if you work with me on this," he went on, "and there will be a lot of other travel if we set up state committees. You won't see much of your home for almost a year."

Leave my wife and three children for a year? "With a project this important, I guess we'll all have to make some personal sacrifices," I forced myself to say, and wondered how my wife Betsy would react when she heard about this.

"Now, the first order of business is for you to set up an office down there—our Washington bureau will fix you up. And tell Ed Banks in personnel to hire a good assistant for you. We've got to get cracking right away on a whole mass of detail. And all of this is top secret, of course, until the president announces my appointment. Try to get down to Washington by the middle of next week and meantime, give me a list of people you think should be on our steering committee. Jack wants my ideas on that."

"I'll have that ready for you Monday."

"That's the spirit," he said, repeating one of his favorite phrases, and got up from his chair to signal the end of the meeting and to bid me farewell with his usual habit of almost exaggerated courtesy. "I'm glad to have you with me on this, Tom," he said, taking my hand and giving it a quick but firm shake. "We may run into some thunder and lightning, but at least we'll be on the side of the angels." He tried to smile. "After all, what's more important than mental health?"

2

ON THE TRAIN out to South Bay, Connecticut late that afternoon I tried to sort out my feelings about my new assignment.
There was a good deal of excitement in the notion of working for
President Kennedy and the top people he would enlist. There was
also relief from my worry about finding myself without a job when
Ralph Hopkins retired, but the thought of being away from Betsy
and my children . . . All my life I had been deeply susceptible to
loneliness, and I needed my family at *least* as much as they needed
me.

When I came home from the army after World War II I thought
that in peacetime most civilians just worked from nine to five and
spent worry-free nights and weekends at home. Promotion to high-
paying positions, I thought, depended mostly on intelligence and
maybe a little charm and luck. I was one of those young veterans
who had perhaps been more worn out by the war than they realized, and my ambition was to earn enough money to buy a decent
house where Betsy and I could make love, raise children and enjoy
ourselves after four years of being apart. We kept telling ourselves
that money didn't matter much.

In those days, when all the young soldiers were coming home,
it wasn't easy for a man without any special training except a liberal
arts education and whatever he had learned in the war to get a
good job, and I counted myself lucky when one of my grandmother's friends, Dick Haver, offered me a minor position with the
Schanenhauser Foundation, an outfit that distributed the dwin-
dling funds of a long-dead millionaire to scholars and scientists. It
was a low-keyed outfit, and it took me some three years to realize
that I was never going to make enough money there to meet the

needs of my growing family. So I found myself a job at the United Broadcasting Company that promised much more pay, but the hectic pace of Rockefeller Center was something of a shock.

Anyone who expected to work from nine to five at the United Broadcasting Company couldn't rise above the rank of elevator operator. The competition of the executives with each other and with the other networks was so intense that a man had to devote his mind, heart and soul to it if he had any serious desire to win out. The result was that all the top executives, not only Ralph Hopkins, seemed to me to be more than a little crazy. Betsy and I talked about this and made what seemed to us to be a sane decision. I would try to get to a position of middle rank in this vast corporation and wouldn't enter the race to see who could work himself to death first.

It was a good deal easier to make this nice philosophical choice than to put it into action. Executives at United Broadcasting either moved up or out—there was little chance to stay long in one place treading water. My position as a special assistant to Ralph Hopkins was unusual. Because I became, in effect, his ghost writer, he sometimes involved me in discussions of high policy that were closed even to most of the company's vice-presidents. Also, my experience with the Schanenhauser Foundation had equipped me to help him set up the National Foundation for Mental Health, his first excursion into the world of big-time charity. After working hard on his speeches half the night, we would sometimes have a drink and talk almost as friends, in spite of the vast difference in our wealth and rank.

"What are your plans for the future?" he once asked me. "What do you really want from this business?"

It was then I told him about my great philosophical decision. It was a touchy conversation because I was actually saying that I didn't want to become a workaholic like him. I was as tactful as possible, and he congratulated me on being a sane young man. The only trouble was that I soon found myself restricted to a job of working exclusively on his charities at a level a good deal lower than I'd hoped for. The raises in pay came very slowly after that and I realized that I had no one to blame but myself.

Among other things I hadn't planned on was the increasing cost of raising a growing family and the resurgence of my own ambitions as I grew bored with the same old job year after year. I was lucky that when my grandmother died she left me her big house in South Bay, but she also left no money with which to maintain it. For a while we thought we could sell some of the land around it, but zoning restrictions finally outlawed that and we found ourselves stuck in the curious position of living in a large house in a wealthy suburb with barely enough money to pay the bills, never mind saving for life insurance, a college education for the children or emergencies. A white elephant.

Our position was made more difficult and in a special way by a situation I still find difficult to talk about without a rush of shame and a curious reverse feeling of stubborn pride. The fact is that I was one of hundreds of thousands of veterans who had fathered an illegitimate child while overseas during World War II. Most who did this probably never even knew it—often they were moved on by the tides of war before they were sure their girl was pregnant, and even if they did find out there was rarely much they could do about it. My case was different because my girl, Maria, whom I'd loved very much during a leave in Rome, had been able to get in touch with me through an old army friend who had married a cousin of hers. Maria had no legal claim on me whatsoever, but she did write to say that she had borne my son and asked me to send whatever financial help I could manage. I could hardly ignore that, but it was impossible to send her even the most modest monthly check without telling my wife where the money was going. Which, not surprisingly, precipitated the worst crisis of our marriage. We'd been married shortly before I joined the army, and she had believed that I had been as faithful to her as she had been to me, a youthful assumption—or maybe presumption—that had seemed natural to her at the time. Betsy was too good a person to tell me to refuse to help a destitute child in Rome that I'd fathered, but her pride and idealistic notions about us were badly shaken. Though she soon said she forgave me, her resentment—and who could blame her?—never really died—it was pretty damn hard to forget when every monthly bank statement showed the amount I'd sent to Maria through a lawyer, no matter how impersonal he tried to keep the transaction. During times like Christmas, when our own bills were piling up and I had to ask her to economize as much as possible, it was understandably hard for her not to remind me that we had some peculiar expenses which weren't exactly *her* responsibility.

Still, in spite of this shadow from the past, Betsy and I had achieved a kind of contentment with each other and our own three children that struck many of our Connecticut friends as enviable —we were, I believe, known as an unusually happy couple. We did not fight much. If Betsy needed relief from the duties of a house-wife in the many parties I didn't much like, I couldn't blame her any more than I could blame myself for sometimes wanting to escape the unvarying routine of commuting to the static job I'd created for myself in New York. We made the best of it as cheer-fully as we could, and it really wasn't so bad . . .

But now that I was going to be away from home for most of a year, much of this would have to change, I told myself as I rode that train out to South Bay. The excitement of working with Presi-dent Kennedy and a lot of stimulating people on an important project would be all mine while Betsy would be left with the job of taking care of the kids and the big house alone. And as a sort of temporary widow she might find it difficult to give and to attend the parties that gave her a release from routine. Since she was sensible enough to realize that I couldn't refuse this new assign-ment without giving up all hope for promotion, or even keeping the job I had, she probably wouldn't make too much fuss, but I knew that I was asking her to make a big sacrifice for distant gains. I didn't look forward to giving her my big news.

IT WAS DARK and very cold for September when my train pulled into South Bay that night. The mud in the station parking lot had turned to icy ruts which caused the commuters to pick their way carefully to their cars. Betsy was waiting for me in our well-used Ford station wagon. In the glare of passing headlights I could see that she had bundled herself up in ski clothes that made her look like a schoolgirl, but her face looked harried and she was shivering.

"The damn heater won't work," she said as I climbed into the seat beside her. "The man at the garage said it's completely shot and he thinks it's a shame to sink more money in this old wreck."

"He's always trying to sell us something new," I said, and leaned over to kiss her on the cheek. "We can get the heater fixed."

"I'm sorry to give you such a tale of woe," she said as she joined the parade of traffic crawling away from the station, "but Janey has another cold and everything's been so damn hectic . . . What kind of day did you have?"

Obviously this was not the time or place to break my news, but I didn't know how to avoid it. The best I could do was to give her the sunny side of the situation first.

"Hopkins has a big new project," I began. "It looks like it will be good for me . . ."

"What is it?"

"President Kennedy has asked him to head up a White House Conference on Mental Health. Hopkins says he wants me to be his right hand setting up the thing, and there's a good chance he'll make me staff director."

"Will that mean a raise?"

"Probably in the long run, but you know how Hopkins is. First you do a new job well, then you get the raise."

"A White House conference . . . does that mean you'll have to spend a lot of time in Washington?"

"I'm afraid so, but—"

"How long will you be gone?"

"On and off, most of a year—"

"A year! And you're not even going to get a raise?"

"We have to keep thinking of what this will do for us in the long run—"

"I don't care! I know I should be big about this, a marvelous, understanding wife, but damn it, I just can't. Damn that bastard Hopkins. Why can't you just tell him to go to hell?"

"Because where else would I get a job half as good? One thing I like about this new deal is that it will give me a chance to get known outside of Hopkins' office. I won't be so dependent on him anymore—"

"Damn him, he's wrecked his own family so now he has to wreck ours—"

"Betsy, he pays me pretty well—"

"How can you *say* that? Plenty of people make a lot more than you do right here in South Bay. They don't even have to go to New York, never mind Washington."

"There's no way I can do my kind of work out here and you know it."

"Why not change your kind of work? I bet Bert Andrews could get you into selling real estate. He says that things are just beginning to boom out here—"

"I'm not a real estate man, Betsy. I'm going to have a fairly important job. It could mean something—"

"It will be just like the war. 'Good-bye dear, I'll be back in a year . . .' "

"I'll probably be able to get home a lot of weekends—"

"*Marvelous*. We'll write each other a million letters."

Silence as she concentrated on negotiating a sharp curve in the road.

"I might be able to talk the company into getting me an apartment big enough for all of us in Washington. Would you like to go with me?"

"And take the kids out of school?"

"There are schools in Washington."

"You can't just shift kids back and forth like that. No, that's *okay*, I'll stay back here and keep the home fires burning. Give me a few minutes and I'll get used to the idea."

She turned into our driveway. Light was flooding through our downstairs windows, making yellow squares on the frosty lawn, and there was the sound of Barbara practicing scales on the piano. The old house suddenly looked so warm to me, so friendly and safe, that I thought I must be crazy even to think about leaving it for so long. Except what was the alternative? Real estate, courtesy of Bert Andrews?

When we went inside, Barbara got up from the piano in the living room and gave me a perfunctory kiss on the cheek. She was sixteen years old then, almost seventeen, a very pretty girl who looked much as her mother had when I first met her. More than the symmetry of her face and figure was involved in that resemblance—there was a special combination of recklessness and vulnerability that made me worry about her in spite of her frequent insistence that "I'm no longer a *child*, daddy, I can take care of myself." Sure . . .

"Do you want a drink?" Betsy said, taking off her knitted ski cap and parka. Alongside Barbara she looked a bit heavy and worn, but there was still a kind of rebellious eagerness in her eyes. At forty-two Betsy was often angry at herself for gaining weight, but she was still full of vitality and would never let herself go into doughy, middle-aged sexlessness.

"In a minute," I said and went upstairs to see Janey, who was huddled in her bed doing her homework. Only a year younger than her sister, Janey had a weight problem, but a sweet face and a depth of emotion that made me feel close to her. She gave me a bear hug while turning her face away to avoid giving me her cold.

Pete, my thirteen-year-old son, was peering through a microscope on the desk in his room. He was a thin, oddly mature-looking boy who sometimes appeared withdrawn and solitary, but he was devoted to his schoolwork and had already announced that he wanted to be a "scientist." He greeted me with a casual wave of his hand and continued to draw in his notebook.

When I went downstairs Betsy was in the kitchen mixing a martini.

"Sorry I was bitchy," she said as she handed me my glass. "I realize you have to do what you have to do. Actually I guess I should congratulate you on your new assignment . . ."

I kissed her my thanks for that, but she was not very responsive.

"Drink up, but don't forget that we have to go out tonight," she said.

"Where?"

"The Richardsons' party. Don't you remember? I reminded you about it this morning."

"Oh, I guess I forgot," I said. "I was hoping we could spend the evening with the kids—"

"Tom, I have spent every day and every night all week with them. You can stay here if you want, but I'm going to this party."

"I'll go with you."

"There's no need. Besides, I have to start getting used to going to parties by myself, don't I? I sure as hell am not going to spend every night at home for a year."

"You don't have to begin tonight, Betsy. What time are we supposed to be there?"

"Any time—it's one of those bashes. Alice always has a buffet, so we won't have to eat here. Are you hungry?"

"Not too."

"Then I'll go up and change. You can go as you are unless you want to put on a fresh shirt and a sport coat . . ."

I was too tired to bother with that. One good thing about a gray flannel suit is that one can wear it almost anywhere. I sat in the living room sipping my drink and then I mixed one more before Betsy came downstairs. In a new black cocktail dress she was transformed into a much younger woman than the one who had met me at the train. Her brown hair had been brushed until it shone and makeup smoothed the lines around her eyes and mouth. The dress was quite low-cut, but she was full enough to make it attractive, and she'd nipped her waist in to make her figure quite startling. I thought the kids looked a little embarrassed when they kissed her goodnight.

"I know I must look sort of wild," she said to me as we got into the car, "but damn it, I feel sort of wild tonight. If we don't kick up our heels once in a while we won't even be able to pretend we're young much longer."

I nodded.

THE RICHARDSONS HAD recently moved to South Bay from Long Island and had built one of those huge modern houses of glass and stone. Ben, about my age, was vice-president of a big advertising agency, flying at higher financial altitudes than I ever expected to reach. He was a tall, fat man who gave the impression of being lighthearted, not work-driven at all, but he had already had two heart attacks, his gaunt wife, a former model, had told Betsy. In spite of his illness, Ben and Alice gave lavish cocktail parties.

"There's just no way to slow Ben down," Alice often said.

Now they were standing just inside the front door of their crowded house, warmly greeting their guests.

"Betsy, you look marvelous!" Ben said, and gave her a little hug before kissing her on the cheek.

"You too, Ben, and you, Alice! You two are even better-looking than your house."

Betsy sometimes tended to pass out compliments like pieces of fudge. Their intent was to please, which I thought sort of got out of hand at times. We entered the big, high-ceilinged living room, which was so packed it was difficult to make our way to the buffet and bar. I saw no close friends of mine . . . did they exist? . . . but several men and women waved to Betsy, called to her or pushed through the crowd to give her an affectionate embrace. As a girl Betsy had always been the belle of the ball, and she still played that part nicely. To her any big party was a sort of return to her youth, and her eyes sparkled with pleasure at the familiar ambience of it all . . .

We'd just succeeded in reaching the bar and buffet when we saw Bert Andrews, an old friend, sort of. Bert was short, bald and in his mid-fifties; he was also energetic, bright and charismatic, to use a word which was popular in the Kennedy era. He had just filled a plate with ham, turkey and salad for himself, but when he spotted Betsy he handed it to her and hurried to get her a glass of wine.

"Bert, I'm so glad to see you," she said, "I've been feeling down and you always cheer me up . . ."

"What's the matter?"

— 20

"Tom has to go to Washington and work there for almost a whole year."

"What's up, Tom?"

"I'm not supposed to talk about it yet." Big deal, Tom . . . who are you trying to impress? Your wife, Bert, both . . .?

"That sounds great . . . And don't you worry, Betsy, we'll keep you plenty busy right here in South Bay. I have a project I've been wanting to talk to you about."

"What kind of project?"

"Ever heard of the Thespian Society?"

"They put on awful amateur plays, don't they?"

"It has been a pretty stuffy little group, but a lot of new people are taking it over. They're planning to put on *Streetcar,* and they've asked me to direct it."

"Are you going to do it?"

"I will if you'll help. How would you like to try out for Blanche?"

"Me? I haven't done any acting since school . . ."

"I bet you'd be marvelous . . . you're going to need something to keep you busy while your old man's away. You can't just stay home knitting . . ." And turning to me, he added, "You wouldn't want her to do that, would you, Tom? She'll have to have something to keep her occupied—"

Good old Bert . . . the lonely lady's white knight . . . "What do you think of the idea, Betsy?"

"Well, truth to tell, I've always had, as you know, a kind of hankering to act and I've always loved that play—"

"Let's go into the dining room and talk—it's less crowded there. You don't mind if I steal her away from you for a few minutes, do you, Tom?"

Hell no, Bert, old buddy . . .

They headed toward a large double door where a few couples could be seen at a large table drinking and eating. I did feel left out, but it had never occurred to me before to be jealous of Bert Andrews, he'd always seemed much older than we were . . . Still, the thought of his taking charge of Betsy while I was away did bother me, face it, and after getting myself a martini and a plate of food I stood in a corner where people couldn't jostle me and thought some on Mr. Bert Andrews.

Like me he'd been born and brought up in South Bay. His mother had been a teacher and his father had often been unemployed during the Depression. While in high school Bert had done odd jobs like mowing lawns and putting up storm windows for people like my grandmother, in whose house my mother and I lived after the early death of my father. While I was growing up I admired Bert yet also disliked him . . . my grandmother was always holding him up to me as an example of an older boy who did everything just *right*. In high school Bert was good enough as a scholar and track star to win a scholarship to Columbia, and worked his way through law school. Afterward he married a plain but well-to-do girl whose family owned a brass foundry in Bridgeport and moved back to South Bay, where he started his law practice. Everybody said that Bert would go far and he did, both as a lawyer and as a shrewd speculator in real estate.

In some curious way, I thought of Bert as a member of my parents' generation, not as a person only twelve years older than myself. A heart murmur he attributed to his early exertions as an athlete had prevented him from going to war, and for some reason he and his wife had no children. He also got bald early, and so my image of him was a hard-working businessman who had none of the pleasures and worries of my age group.

About five years earlier, when Bert and his wife Paula were about fifty years old, they surprised everybody by getting divorced. Some people said that Bert's blossoming financial success had gone to his head and that he had been running around with younger women, a notion which at the time I found hard to believe because he had always seemed so respectable even when he was young. Paula, who had never made many friends in South Bay in spite of her husband's popularity, moved back to Bridgeport and Bert began to play carefree bachelor. He bought a red Mercedes roadster and one of the showiest houses in South Bay, an ancient gristmill on a small river which had been restored and expanded by a series of wealthy owners. In a huge living room with a terrace overlooking a waterfall he began to give parties for his old friends and for new ones who drove in from Westchester and New York, including a good many attractive young women. Bert seemed to enjoy a good deal the gossip he stirred up.

I never really was able to blame him for trying to make up for so many dull years with an autumnal fling and who was I to judge anyway? Betsy and I enjoyed his parties, which were considerably less stuffy than most in South Bay and which sometimes included minor celebrities; Bert cultivated actors, musicians, writers and painters, some of whom made livelier conversation than most of the businessmen and housewives we knew.

I guess my feelings about Bert were, as they say, mixed. When I found it hard to pay my bills I envied, even resented his financial success, remembering that he had at least begun it during the years when I was in the service and real estate in Connecticut was cheap. He had married a dull woman for money, I thought, had used her capital to build his little empire and then had dumped her when he no longer needed her. I also realized that this cynical and jealous interpretation of his life was lopsided. Of course I had no idea what his attitude toward his wife had been, and it was wrong to assume that he had been a draft dodger. He was, at least superficially, a sunny, energetic man of considerable charm who had been lucky in some ways and unlucky in others. Although I had hated the war I was still damn glad I had experienced it, and I was certainly grateful that I had spent most of my life married to Betsy, not Paula. I had three fine children, and though I sometimes . . . too often . . . expressed my love for them more in worry than in enjoyment, I felt sorry for people who were heading toward a childless old age. So there was really no logic in envying an aging playboy or worrying that my wife would be romantically attracted to him while I was away. The mere fact that the thought was in my head made me angry at myself. It demeaned both Betsy *and* me, while attributing powers to Bert that probably existed only in my imagination . . .

Bert's conversation about *Streetcar* with Betsy seemed to be taking a long time. When she finally rejoined me she sounded excited.

"Bert's trying to do something, not just a little amateur production. He has a friend who's directed on Broadway and he's going to help us. A pro is going to design the set."

I hoped Betsy had some notion of the time, effort and strain involved in the part of Blanche in *Streetcar,* but it seemed mean-spirited to dampen her enthusiasm . . . half-joking, true, but she was already beginning to work up a southern accent.

3

WHEN WE GOT home about eleven we were surprised to see
two battered cars parked in our driveway. Loud rock music was
coming from the house, although at first we could see no lights.
They flashed on when the kids heard us approach.

"They appear to be having a party of their own," Betsy said.

I still wasn't used to leaving the children without a sitter, in spite
of the fact that both Barbara and Janey were old enough to work
as sitters themselves. When we walked in the front door we saw
about a dozen teenagers tangled together on the couch and in easy
chairs, drinking beer. They jumped up when they saw us, and
Barbara said, "Some friends just dropped in, dad. They brought
their own stuff . . ."

She turned off the music. In the abrupt silence a tall, thin young
fellow in sneakers, blue jeans, a dirty T-shirt and a black cowboy
hat said, "Would you like a cold beer, sir?"

His manner was almost smirking and he was a little drunk.

"No *thanks*," I said. "It's getting late. I'd say it's time to call it
a night."

"But tomorrow's *Saturday*—" Barbara said.

"Sorry to be old-fashioned, honey, but I just don't like unsupervised parties in my house. And most of you kids here aren't
even old enough to drink—"

"Oh, *daddy* . . . I'm sorry, guys, that's just the way he *is*."

They looked at her with head-shaking commiseration, then hurried out to their cars and roared off . . .

"I hate you," Barbara said in the time-honored fashion of
daughters to fathers who humiliate them in front of their friends,
and ran up the stairs.

"We weren't really doing anything wrong," Janey said. "I didn't even drink any beer."

"Where's Pete?" I asked her.

"In bed—he slept through the whole thing."

And she too went upstairs.

"Janey's right, Tom . . . I don't think they were doing anything so wrong," Betsy said. "You embarrassed Barbara in front of her friends—"

"I *know* that . . . but, damn it, do you think they should be giving parties here all by themselves—"

"No, but sometimes friends drop in—"

"I hope this won't go on while I'm gone."

"Tom, I'm not going to be able to stand guard here twenty-four hours a day. I think I trust Barbara. Don't you?"

"A sixteen-year-old girl still needs some supervision, probably more than ever."

"Well, maybe so, but it's damn hard to do these days. Chaperones are out of date. Barbara will do what she pleases when she goes out with her friends, so we're better off having her see them here."

"We don't have to set the scene for trouble—"

"Why are you getting so upset?"

"I guess because you seem to be taking all this so casually, a bunch of kids necking and drinking in our house—"

"Nobody *necks* anymore—you're pretty out of date, Tom . . . well, goodnight, I'm going to bed."

I cleaned up some, collected the beer cans and wine bottles. When I got upstairs Betsy was sitting at her vanity table in a white cotton night dress and blue robe rubbing cream into her face. Message sent and received.

AT BREAKFAST I explained to the children that I would have to spend a good deal of time in Washington during the coming year. Barbara was still angry at me and I thought I heard her whisper under her breath, "Good!"

Janey asked whether she could visit me and I told her it might be possible some weekend. Pete wanted to know all about the White House Conference on Mental Health.

"What's it supposed to do?" he asked.

"Help crazy people," Barbara answered for me. "They're going to get millions of crazy people together down there in Washington and daddy's going to straighten them out. Isn't that right, daddy? You'll read them all the riot act."

"Don't be rude to your father," Betsy said.

"Who's being rude?" Barbara said, and excused herself from the table. In a way I had to admire her performance . . . maybe she would be the actress Betsy wanted to be.

"What's it really supposed to do?" Pete said.

"Raise money for better hospitals and research on mental illness," I said.

"How did you get tied up with that?"

That was a question I did not want to try to answer and I was glad when Betsy said, "I've got to get started with my shopping— I have a million things to do. What are your plans for today, Pete?"

"I've got to do some digging. Will you help me, dad?"

"What kind of digging?"

"I want to cut out a cubic foot of earth."

"What for?"

"I want to bring it inside and study it, see how many insects I can find with my microscope. I read where there's supposed to be hundreds of kinds of life in one cubic foot of earth."

"Wonderful," I said, and thought I was having enough trouble with the human varieties of one family of five.

FROST HAD HARDENED the ground, and it took considerable effort to chop out the block of soil Pete wanted. After he had carried it upstairs in a washtub, I watched him take a few grains from the top and fix them to a glass slide.

"I can observe this all winter," he said. "I'll keep the dirt watered and in the sun so nothing dies . . . I wish I had a better microscope, though. How much would a really good one cost?"

Everything, it seemed, came down to a question of money, and my familiar guilt and annoyance at not being able to supply it in unlimited quantity. When Betsy returned shivering from her shopping trip I took the car down to the Ford garage to have a new heater installed, and while that was being done an attendant rightly pointed out that we needed two new tires to replace the bald ones. In Washington I'd at least be on an expense account with a per diem that would even allow me to save a little money if I didn't eat and drink too much. My straining waistband told me that a diet was overdue. Maybe I should ask Hopkins for a raise before accepting this new assignment—hell, I was working for a multimillionaire, no good reason why I couldn't buy a good microscope for a brilliant son, or why I had to make my wife drive a car old enough to quit on her at any moment. The only trouble was that asking Hopkins for a raise was like trying to stab a billiard ball with a knife. He tended to look on such requests from subordinates as impertinent, bad manners. If Hopkins felt a man proved himself worthy of more money, he prided himself on paying it without being nudged, and didn't much like having his judgment questioned. . . .

That was a strange "last weekend," as Betsy called it, a little like the last of a ten-day leave during the war when she and I had wanted everything to go just right, and the strain made spontaneity impossible. We talked about money and budgets and whether Barbara should be allowed to take a train to New York with her friends to explore the city, her latest request. I, predictably, I'm afraid, voted no and Betsy voted yes, resulting in a long debate during which I finally backed down.

When we went to bed that night it was clear that Betsy felt under an obligation to make love. She did not rub cream on her face and put on a beige negligee instead of her cotton nightgown. We didn't really feel emotionally close to each other and our first kisses were forced. There were times when making love seemed a difficult test that I worried I might fail, and especially when I was going away I didn't want to leave behind a memory of sexual disappointment, even though we both counted ourselves mature enough to accept the fact that such matters are unpredictable and uncontrollable for much-married husbands and wives. It wasn't so much that Betsy and I were bored with each other or bored with sex, but we seemed somehow afraid of each other or put off by the anger in ourselves that so often left us exasperated with each other, no matter how much we were still tied together by a long-standing affection and, of course, the prosaics of marriage. Sometimes I wished I couldn't remember the intensity of our lovemaking when we were younger and surely didn't need to read the books on the subject that Betsy had recently brought back from a store in Stamford. On this night I was grateful at least to find that our bodies were able to satisfy each other, even though at times we still seemed to grapple more like enemies than lovers. Afterward we told each other how great the lovemaking had been, turned away to our familiar sides of the bed and escaped into sleep.

4

MONDAY MORNING I had in mind that Ralph Hopkins had told me to hire an assistant. I got off the elevator at the twenty-sixth floor to see Ed Banks, the director of personnel. Ed was a tall, handsome, I guess, man who looked as though he had been hired to advertise the appearance of an ideal executive at United Broadcasting. He was as silver-tongued as he was silver-haired when conducting his business with strangers, but in private with friends he showed a rough, raunchy manner that was, I supposed, his own form of rebellion against the corporate world we lived in. He thought of me as a friend because we had both been paratroopers during the war, a fact he had discovered while going over my record when I was hired, and though we had never met in the army he considered this a bond. It's possible that he also valued our acquaintanceship because I was close to Ralph Hopkins, who seemed a remote and mysterious force even to many of his vice-presidents. Whatever the reason, Ed often asked me to have a drink with him after work and seemed to enjoy giving me all the latest company gossip.

Now he said, "I hear you're going down to Washington with Hopkins. Congratulations."

"I'm not sure you shouldn't be giving me sympathy," I said. "It's going to be a long haul, maybe a year."

"It'll be better than jumping out of an airplane with a gun. That's what I keep telling myself every morning when I come here."

His richly furnished office, which was decorated with prints of fighter planes and a photograph of Ed as a colonel standing alongside General MacArthur, didn't seem to me to be such a bad place to make the fat salary I guessed he earned, but I let that pass.

"Mr. Hopkins wants me to hire an assistant," I said. "I thought maybe we ought to talk about the kind of person we're looking for."

"If you're like everybody else looking for an assistant around here, you want a girl with a high I.Q., a good college education and great tits. You like blondes or brunettes?"

"I'm not particular, but this person is going to have to work closely with Hopkins and all kinds of big shots. It's partly an executive secretary's job, but there will be some research and public relations work."

"What you want is a good bright girl who's not afraid to work her ass off. They're hard to find these days and not many around here want to go to Washington. Let me go through my files. How much rush is there on this?"

"You know Hopkins. I'm supposed to go to Washington tomorrow or next day. We have a job to do and the sooner I can get help, the better."

"I'll sound around inside the company first and see if anybody good wants a job like this. I'll be in touch."

"Mr. Hopkins and I will be grateful," I said with a smile . . . A touch of the whip, but in his case I sort of enjoyed flicking it.

"I'll give Hopkins what he wants, but I'll keep you in mind too, old buddy," Ed said with a retaliatory smile. "I can't guarantee D-cups, but I won't send you a dog. We old jump boys have to look out for each other, right?"

I knew I was still New England stuffy, but this kind of badinage made me uneasy. I hurred to my office and began to draw up a list of possible members for Hopkins' steering committee which, with some bravado, I'd promised to give him this day for submission to President Kennedy. Although I was familiar with the names of the key people in the National Foundation for Mental Health and its state chapters, the thought that I was making recommendations to be considered by the president of the United States tended to slow me. A committee of this kind had to be balanced in many ways. Each member had to have a big reputation of his or her own, but mavericks who would rebel too much against Hopkins' leadership had to be avoided. A man who appoints a committee pretty much determines the results of its meetings. For a beginning I wrote down the names of a half dozen directors of the Foundation for Mental Health that Hopkins most admired and trusted. All were big businessmen, and I needed a representative of labor, a couple of women and some prestigious physicians to round out the committee. For two hours I studied the files, drawing up a list that was much too long before studying each name, trying to decide which to cut out.

I was interrupted by a telephone call from Ed Banks. "I think I have the right girl for you," he said. "I'm taking her right out of my own department, so I know she's good."

"Many thanks."

"Look, she's not as experienced as she should be for this job, but nobody has experience in anything like this Washington thing. I figure you need someone who can deal with top people, learn fast and work hard. This girl fits the bill."

"She sounds great."

"She's also kind of cute in her own way, even if she's only about a B-cup. I sure wouldn't mind spending a year in Washington with her. When do you want me to send her up for inspection?"

"Right now, if it's convenient."

"Okay. Her name is Ann McSoaring. If you don't like her, send her back. I have a big fat lady down here with horn-rimmed glasses who's just dying for the job. Now there's an X-cup for you if you're interested in sheer quantity."

Paratrooper or not, Ed was also pretty damn boring.

Five minutes later Ann McSoaring walked into my office. I don't know what I had expected, but it wasn't a girl who at first glance reminded me of my daughter Barbara. As she came closer to my desk she looked somewhere in her late twenties, but she was so short and slender that she seemed younger. She had dark, curly brown hair cut just below her ears, high-cheekboned features with almost no makeup, a tentative smile. She was wearing a navy-blue businesswoman's suit with a short jacket and a loose-fitting white silk blouse—altogether an outfit almost nunlike in its simplicity. My first impression was not exactly of a beauty so much as of a person with vitality and poise.

She put on no airs, but she also was not in the least nervous. "Mr. Rath, I'm Ann McSoaring. Mr. Banks said that you might have a job for me."

Her voice was educated, neutral, no hint of class or regional origin, but there was a nice sort of lilt to it. I got up to greet her and asked her to sit down in a chair at the corner of my desk.

"Thank you for coming up on such short notice. Did Ed Banks tell you anything about this job?"

"He told me it's in Washington and has something to do with Mr. Hopkins—he said you'd tell me the rest."

"President Kennedy has asked Mr. Hopkins to head up a White House Conference on Mental Health. I'm Mr. Hopkins' assistant on the project and I'm looking for someone to give me a hand. Right now this is all supposed to be confidential."

"That sounds exciting." She had large brown eyes, which now looked amused. "But I must say that I don't know anything about mental health. If you're looking for an expert in the field I'm afraid I'm out."

"We won't get involved in anything technical. A White House conference is kind of like a big convention of experts. They listen to speeches, hold a lot of committee meetings and try to agree on some recommendations for government action. Our job will be to stage-manage it. Yours would be an executive secretary's job with some P.R. work and research thrown in."

"I can handle the secretary part and I like P.R. work, but I've never tried research."

"The kind I have in mind isn't too difficult. Mostly it involves a search for people who should be invited to an affair like this. Eisenhower's conference on education involved some two thousand delegates . . . We just work with lists of names and check biographical materials. Eventually we'll have a staff of twenty or thirty people to help us. Our immediate job is just to help Mr. Hopkins get this thing started."

"Mr. Rath, this may sound cheeky, but what's the purpose of all this? Does President Kennedy really need two thousand people to come to Washington to tell him what to do about mental health?"

"A good question, a lot of people will ask it. A conference like this can bring the president a lot of information, but it also can stir up public interest in the whole question of what the country should *do* for better mental health. To put it bluntly, I think we're selling mental health the way Neil McElroy sold public education for Eisenhower. That's why presidents pick men like McElroy and Hopkins to head up these things—they want great salesmen."

"So we're to be salesmen of mental health," she said with that amused look in her eyes again. "I must say, it's a good product, but will we have to *demonstrate* it?"

"As best we can. If we want legislation for better mental hospitals, medical research and all the rest we have to sell the program to Congress. And if we want to do that, we have to sell it to the people. Those two thousand delegates will come to Washington to give their opinions but they'll go home as salesmen of a program they helped to shape."

"What kind of program?"

"Don't know yet. I'm sure the president will have recommendations which he will try to sell to the delegates and they'll have recommendations that they'll try to sell to him. Some sort of report will be hammered out that a majority will agree on."

"Will they vote?"

"That's a touchy matter. The president wouldn't want to hold a conference that could vote against everything he wanted."

"Is mental health so controversial?"

"Socialized medicine is, and that's always on the edge of government programs for mental health."

"If they're not going to vote, how are they going to find out who wants what?"

"The delegates listen to the president's ideas and record their opinions for his consideration. Some people will call this evasive, but what would a vote from two thousand delegates mean anyway? The man who picks the delegates can determine the outcome of the vote. The only vote that means anything is the vote of people at the polls in regular elections."

"You really believe in all this . . ."

"Yes, I do believe in it. I'd also rather be selling mental health than booze or cigarettes."

"So would I, and I'd love to work on it if you think I'd be useful."

"You've already gotten closer to the basics than most people who work on it ever do. You're hired. When can you start?"

"I'm afraid I'll need a few days to sublet my apartment and wind things up here. Would a week from now be okay?"

"I've got to go down to Washington sooner, but I'll just be trying to establish connections at first. Did Ed talk to you about salary, other arrangements?"

"He said my regular salary will continue until I prove myself, and then it will be up to you and Mr. Hopkins. I understand I'm to get an expense account and that our Washington bureau will find me some place to live."

"They'll probably put us in a hotel and give us a per diem—it's not a bad deal. The bureau will give us office space until Congress passes a budget for this thing and makes it a government operation."

"Will we be working for the government then or for Mr. Hopkins?"

"I'm not sure. We're going to have to play it by ear."

"I don't mean to sound gushy about this, but I am excited. I can't help feeling something special about President Kennedy. He's the first president who ever really seemed to me to be part of my own generation."

"I admire him too. And I think it's a plus neither of us is cynical about this . . . Mental health may be kind of a trite phrase, but it's a damn good cause, as such things go."

Her smile was merry. That's the word that came to my mind.

"I've always needed a cause," she said, "and anyway, I'm sick of New York. Can I just report for work to you Monday morning at the Washington bureau?"

"I'll be there with a desk full of paperwork for you," I said, standing up as Hopkins always did to say good-bye to people. "I'm looking forward to working with you."

"Me too," she said, giving me a small but strong hand to shake. "I think I like you, Mr. Rath."

5

I DID NOT have time to think much about my new assistant because Ralph Hopkins called to say he wanted my suggestions for his steering committee. I finished up my list fast, had it typed and went up to his office.

"This is a good start," he said, penciling out some of the names and adding others. "We're under even more time pressure than I thought we'd be. The news about my appointment is leaking. Jack is going to announce it at his news conference tomorrow."

"In some ways that may make things easier," I said.

"Maybe. He wants me to be on hand. I'm going to fly down there at eight tomorrow morning. Want to go with me?"

This of course was an order, Ralph Hopkins style. I said I'd be delighted to go.

"TOMORROW?" BETSY SAID when I told her the news that night while driving home from the station in South Bay. "I thought we'd have another couple of days . . ."

Strange, genuinely not wanting to leave each other, yet also in conflict much of the time we were together. Somehow I felt she was making me feel guilty for going to Washington to do my job, and I resented that—I wanted her to help me celebrate my new stature, my emerging into the limelight at Ralph Hopkins' side. And my annoyance at her built my already well-developed sense of guilt . . . a wife about to be left by her husband for so long a time of course has a decent reason for some complaint. No doubt I'd be resentful and even suspicious if she *didn't* complain . . .

"Betsy, I don't think I've made clear the real meaning of all this for us," I said. "Up till now I've had no real sense of security, my whole future has depended on one man—who's more anonymous than a ghost writer and personal assistant behind the scenes? We both know that. Well, now this new job can help make me my own man, an administrator of a highly public event. I may be put in charge of a large staff. Hopkins has already given me an administrative assistant—?"

"What kind of assistant?"

"What do you mean?" I knew very well what she meant.

"Oh, I was just wondering if this assistant were male or female . . ."

"Ed Banks assigned a woman from the personnel department—"

"You're going to take her down to Washington with you?"

"Betsy, I'm going to need all the help I can get. I have to line up some two thousand delegates from all over the country—"

"How old is she?"

"What? I don't know . . . Thirtyish, I guess. Betsy, what the hell difference—?"

"What does she look like? I hear looks make a difference." And she gave me one that could kill.

"She's a little woman, nothing special, but Ed says she's hardworking and capable—"

"Well, Ed would certainly know . . . When can I meet her?"

"You can come down to Washington and visit me any time you want. She's supposed to report to work in about a week. When you see her, you'll stop worrying about whatever it is that's on your mind," knowing damn well what was on her mind. Was she entirely wrong . . . ?

"I'm sorry, I sound like a ridiculous bitchy wife, but . . ."

And I knew that she was thinking about my romance in Italy during the war, my only infidelity in twenty-two years of marriage, but one that was understandably impossible for her to forget . . . "Well, I've got to admit that I've been having some less than noble thoughts too," I said. "They have to do with good old Bert Andrews—"

"Him? Tom, he's just an old friend. You can't be serious—"

"I don't know about old Bert," I said, warming to the subject, to the role. "He seems to have to prove himself quite the ladies' man these days, and now with this play, he's going to get you involved with a new crowd. A woman alone is always kind of a target—"

"I've never given *you* any reason to worry about me . . ."

I, of course, knew what she meant. Italy again.

"We're both being too touchy," I said quickly. "We've had our problems, but we've got a marriage. A real marriage. We've got the years and the kids to prove it." And it seemed the natural thing to do to pull her toward me and give her a loving kiss.

THAT EVENING WE all really tried to give each other a good last night together. Sitting in the living room around the fire Barbara actually talked to me about *The Red Badge of Courage,* which she'd just read in school. The fact that I had felt obliged to play the cop who enforced all the rules had created strain between us for a long while, but we seemed to find a sort of truce and meeting ground in books.

"Was the war you saw as awful as the Civil War?" she asked.

I'd never tried to tell my kids or even Betsy, for that matter, much about the war—it was a part of my life I found near-impossible to explain, and I figured that the whole thing was put behind me. But I thought it would be wrong to be evasive with Barbara now.

"I guess that fear is about the same in all wars, honey."

"Were you scared?"

"Sure was."

"That's hard for me to imagine."

I guess she meant that as a compliment, but I thought it also showed how little a father and daughter can really understand each other. My God, truth to tell, I'd been running scared nearly all my life, and not just in the war . . . I was scared right now of not making it in my new assignment in Washington, and I was full of fears about Barbara herself, who seemed to me to be moving into a dangerous time in her life without much sense of what could happen to her. Okay, so she didn't understand me, but who said a daughter is supposed to understand a father? Doesn't she have a right to be protected by a calm, self-confident man? And doesn't a father have the obligation to see that she is? Yes . . . in the best of all possible worlds. But this was the land of mortals, fallible mortals in a place called South Bay, Connecticut . . .

"Everybody is scared some of the time," I said. "And maybe that's not so bad . . . sensible fear can help keep you going, avoid bad trouble . . ."

She didn't, of course, want to hear that, and sensing that a lecture was imminent she buried her face in her book.

Janey had overheard this conversation and it struck me that she knew all about fear and perhaps even sensed mine. Janey, overweight, her round face sometimes looking so stolid, was by far the most sensitive of the children to other people's moods and feelings. Like Barbara and Pete, though, she turned from me when I tried any serious conversations. Parents didn't do that . . . Now she was saying she wanted to knit a sweater for me while I was away and began to show me samples of yarn Betsy and she had bought. For a minute I thought I was about to cry.

Which wouldn't have been so terrible. I loved my children. It was a deep gut-feeling stronger than any fear, but nowadays it seemed increasingly difficult to express. When the kids were younger we hugged, snuggled and kissed a lot, and I could still feel the warmth of them in my arms, but once they reached their teens they seemed to shrink away from my touch, a perfectly natural phenomenon but still an unsettling one. Affectionate words seemed to embarrass them. Sometimes it seemed the only emotions we were able to show each other were irritation, worry and anger.

I often blamed myself for this lack of communication, but tried to excuse it some by reminding myself that because my own father died when I was only five I had no clear idea of how a father was supposed to act and had to invent the role as I went along. When I sometimes worried that my children actually did not seem to show much affection for me I remembered the love I continued to feel for my own father, even though he'd been too sick to pay much attention to me, and I also reminded myself that fathers are at least a permanent part of their children's lives, even if they often can't or don't do much to deserve such immortality. One way or another we were all bound together, and I found strength in that . . .

Pete now asked me to play chess, and I was so preoccupied with my thoughts that he beat me three games straight, which pleased him greatly.

"Were you really trying?" he asked.

"Sure I was."

"I didn't know I was so smart," he said, and went happily upstairs to his microscope.

WHEN BETSY AND I went upstairs to bed I sensed that she had been disappointed by the quality of our lovemaking on Saturday night and wanted to improve on it as a kind of final going-away present. She kissed me that way, and I did my best to respond with equal enthusiasm.

"Let's take a bath together," she said. "We haven't done that in ages."

In truth we hadn't attempted such a revel in years and we had both—me especially—gained enough weight since the last time that it was not easy to fit ourselves into my grandmother's old-fashioned tub. A sense of the ridiculous is death on passion and I tried to escape it, but the damn faucet was digging into my back and there wasn't room for her legs to wrap around my waist. Still, we laughed a lot and when we dried each other, I felt such tenderness for her and her desire to be young again that I was once more moved almost to the point of tears. Realizing that I would be alone in a hotel room for a long time, I was grateful for her when we got into bed and she did everything possible to give me a fine time, and I did the same for her. Well, if that wasn't at least a show of love, of caring . . . what was?

BETSY WANTED TO drive me to the airport, but I was afraid our Ford would break down on the parkways and insisted on taking an early train to New York and a bus to LaGuardia. I was carrying two heavy suitcases with enough clothes for my expected long stay in Washington. I knew that Hopkins would be taking his company plane, a luxuriously outfitted DC–3, and waited for him in a small lounge maintained for V.I.P.s. As always, Hopkins was on time. His chauffeur was lugging the big briefcase he carried papers and books in for study on airplane trips and handed it to me before returning to his limousine. Since I already had all the luggage I could handle, this was awkward, but I tucked the weighty case under my arm and struggled along toward a distant runway where our plane was waiting for us. Empty-handed, Hopkins walked beside me, chatting pleasantly about the weather, which happened to be good. He was not the kind of man who would, as a privilege of rank, carry no bags while his assistant carried three. He simply did not really see me any more than he might have observed a waiter bringing him his food. This was a kind of warning, I thought. Hopkins was always elaborately courteous to subordinates, but he was really unaware of them as people. He never did anything for the sake of an employee and could fire one as casually as he might drop a faulty pen into a wastepaper basket.

_ 38

The cabin of the DC–3 was not pressurized, and perhaps because my ears had suffered some damage during the war I felt sharp pain in them when the plane gained altitude. Which made it difficult for me to concentrate when Hopkins said, "Have you roughed out anything for me to say when the president introduces me to the press?"

He hadn't asked me to write such a speech for him, but one thing I'd learned with Hopkins was to think fast.

"I've given a lot of thought to that, sir," I said. "I think it's just the wrong time for you to give a speech."

"Why?"

"President Kennedy is so articulate and witty at those press conferences, it would be hard to compete with him, and the schedule is always crowded. I suggest you keep your remarks very short. Something like, 'Thank you, Mr. President. You have given me a great honor and I will do my best to live up to it.' "

"Is that all?"

"That's all. I think this is a case where brevity is the best policy. Can you picture President Kennedy standing at his own press conference and listening to someone else giving a speech?"

"No, it's his show, you're right about that. Thanks a lot, Tom. I know I can always rely on your judgment."

But could I always be so lucky . . . ?

I HAD ASSUMED that Hopkins was going to take me to the White House with him and I was looking forward to seeing President Kennedy in person, but shortly before the plane landed Hopkins said, "Jack wants to talk to me a few minutes before this thing starts. No need for you to hang around. I think it would be a good idea for you to get settled in an office at our bureau here. We're going to get a lot of calls and mail as soon as my appointment is announced. We've got to be ready to handle them."

A company limousine was waiting for us at the airport and drove Hopkins to the White House before delivering me at the bureau. I had seen the White House from the outside while being with Hopkins during the Eisenhower conference on education, but my first glimpse of it now still awed me. That rolling lawn, still green in September, with the white portico of the old mansion and its long wings sparkling in the morning sun looked so grand that it was as though George Washington or Thomas Jefferson in powdered wigs and knee britches still lived there, not a brisk young president in a modern business suit. A guard at the gate had been informed of Hopkins' arrival and waved us through. When Hopkins got out of the car at the front door, he looked more nervous than I had ever seen him. If he succeeded at this job it was quite possible that a cabinet post would follow, and who knew what other ambitious dreams the old man was keeping to himself?

My part in all this at the moment, however, consisted mostly of taking care of his briefcase, which tended to temper any grandiose notions I might have. I took the briefcase with me to the office building near Capitol Hill where the Washington bureau of United Broadcasting occupied two floors. John Blake, the manager, had been told I was coming and had a big if sparsely furnished room ready for me, complete with three telephones and secretaries to stand by them. A television set stood in the corner, and I turned it on to watch the news conference. The first shot showed President Kennedy striding to a lectern emblazoned with the Great Seal of the United States. He looked marvelous, a young prince, graceful, at ease, self-confident. I had mixed feelings about him, as did many people who had witnessed his career from the start. At Harvard, where he had been a senior when I was a freshman, I had had him pointed out to me as Ambassador Kennedy's son, a glitteringly rich kid, and at the same time, a rebel of sorts against the Boston establishment. His rise was meteoric, propelled by a father who had achieved a reputation as a ruthless businessman, womanizer and apparent apologist for the Nazis at the beginning of World War II, but all that was forgotten now when I saw this almost boyish man stand up and begin by discussing the "hot line" which recently had been established to reduce the risk of accidental war with Russia. I had a sudden sense of identification with him, of imagining myself in his shoes. How did he handle the awesome responsibilities of the presidency? I, after all, often couldn't get to sleep at night from worrying about such comparatively pigmy problems as paying my bills. How did *he* sleep at night with thoughts of Russian missiles racing through his mind?

He looked remarkably serene now as he went on to give his reasons for sending military advisors to Vietnam and to describe current civil rights legislation. It seemed a long while before he got around to Ralph Hopkins, and after the important issues he had been discussing, the announcement of his plan to hold a White

House Conference on Mental Health came as something of an anticlimax. He said he was glad to name Ralph Hopkins, the president of the United Broadcasting Company, as chairman of the committee to organize the conference because of Hopkins' long association with the National Foundation for Mental Health. Then he introduced Hopkins, who walked out from behind a curtain to the microphone, looking small and rather faded beside John F. Kennedy.

"Thank you, Mr. President," he said into the microphone. "I consider this appointment a great honor and a great responsibility. I will do my best to live up to it and to find the best brains in the country to help me."

There was polite applause from the rows of reporters, and President Kennedy took over the microphone to open the meeting for questions. Most were about Russia, Vietnam and civil rights. One female reporter asked about the White House Conference on Mental Health.

"What's it supposed to accomplish?" she asked.

"I hope it will bring me information that will help me propose a program in this important field for submission to the Congress," the president replied.

"Has Congress appointed funds for this conference?" the woman persisted.

"That's the next step," Kennedy said. "We have to start by drawing up a blueprint for the conference, and that will be Mr. Hopkins' first responsibility."

Mine too, I thought, and immediately asked the head of the bureau to have a researcher get transcripts of all the beginning documents of the Eisenhower conference from the government files.

"I don't have any researchers to spare. I thought you were going to bring your own assistant with you."

"She won't be here until Monday and we have to get cracking. Do you want me to ask Hopkins to straighten this out?"

"No, no, I'll find you somebody, but everything's coming down on us at once around here. We're trying to get together a special on Vietnam."

I was amazed how quickly the telephones began ringing. The news conference had, of course, been broadcast coast-to-coast, and immediately on hearing it a lot of eager beavers demanded more information. Hopkins had already arranged to have these calls routed from his office in New York to this one.

Some of these early calls were pathetic. A woman in Ohio said she'd been unable to get any help for her husband, who'd been diagnosed a depressive by his family doctor but couldn't afford a psychiatrist. He just stayed in his room all day and wouldn't talk to anyone. Could Mr. Hopkins help?

"I'm afraid that we're just in the initial stages of—"

She hung up. Who could blame her? Another call was from a man in California who said he could show Hopkins how to organize group therapy sessions in churches. I took his name, said we'd be in touch.

When Hopkins came in later that day I told him about the calls.

"That's the trouble with getting into this whole mental health thing," he said with a straight face. "You have to deal with all kinds of nuts."

He was, I thought, sincere in his desire to help solve "mental health problems," but he thought of them entirely as questions of fund raising and legislative programs, not aid to "crazies" that he wanted to keep away from as much as possible. Even psychiatrists were suspect, with all their peculiar theories. The important thing was to raise dollars "the experts" could spend as they liked. There was a certain rough pragmatism, even a form of humility in this, that tended to endear him to the very doctors he avoided. Everything came down to a question of money, and Ralph Hopkins was a man who understood money.

Before going back to New York that afternoon, he told me that a White House aide named David McKay would be in touch with me.

"Don't worry too much about the mechanics of this thing," he said. "The president's men will take care of them. What we have to worry about is the substance."

Whatever that meant . . . he then assured me he'd keep in touch and rushed off to his plane.

The Washington bureau had rented two rooms in a residential hotel, the Westminster, which was within walking distance of my new office. It was a second-class establishment that seemed to cater to retired military men and out-of-office politicians—the lobby looked like an old people's home. My suite offered a kitchenette that wasn't much more than a wet bar with a two-burner electric stove hidden under a sliding counter. The furniture was early Grand Rapids and the view from the windows was of an alley beside a garage. After I had unpacked my two suitcases I stood looking five floors down at a cat that was exploring a group of trash cans. Except for the whir of distant traffic, my rooms seemed unnervingly quiet. At home I had often objected to the music played by the children, their arguments and their constant running around, but I was used to family life in a house, not this deathlike silence. The thought that I was going to have to live like this for a year gave me something like a panic of loneliness. I supposed I'd eventually make some friends in Washington, but I didn't want just friends . . . whatever our problems, I needed my wife and children.

My old inability to endure solitude, being alone, loneliness, was a kind of affliction. Maybe I could blame it on the fact that as a child, I had often been left alone in my grandmother's house and had developed a kind of terror about noiseless rooms. One reason I'd rushed Betsy into such an early marriage was my need for someone to fill an emotional vacuum, and except for my years in the army I'd looked to her to fulfill needs I'd never had satisfied when I was young, as well as those of a man. Not too manly a thing to admit, but why else would I feel so panicky every time I left home for a few days? Of course I'd survived four years as a paratrooper, but in the army no man was ever alone, which maybe was one reason I got along with less complaining than most. My nightmare was not being killed but having to live alone day after day for an eternity.

Trying to explain myself to myself didn't solve the problem of getting through this evening. I wanted a drink. The hotel bar was full of people who sat staring into their glasses. I couldn't even get the attention of the bartender, who was stirring up martinis for the regulars and never looked in my direction. I knew I was being dramatic, but I had a sensation of being a ghost, condemned to wandering the earth without receiving even a glance from anyone. Leaving the bar, I walked for what seemed a long while, looking for a more lively place. Daylight was fading, and the faces of people waiting for buses looked gray, tense and as uneasy as I felt. I hurried on until I found a bar emblazoned with neon lights. This one was crowded with young people, secretaries and minor government employees probably, who were laughing and draping their arms around each other as they drank. I felt even more out of place there, and after one martini went back out into the gathering darkness. I was angry at myself for feeling like a forty-three-year-old abandoned kid, and when three young black men stepped around a corner and menacingly asked me for a dollar, I abruptly refused them and found to my astonishment that I hoped they'd start a fight, but maybe they knew a man in a crazy mood when they saw one and melted away into the shadows. I was suddenly sobered by my own absurd pugnaciousness. Mental health man, heal thyself . . .

I walked slowly back to my hotel. The crowd at the bar had thinned out and I got my second martini. A tall, sensitive-looking man of about thirty, wearing a white turtleneck sweater under a yellow linen coat, sat down next to me. "I haven't seen you here before. Are you new to Washington or just to this bar?"

It was a relief to talk to someone, and I told him a little about the White House Conference on Mental Health. He seemed interested and asked some intelligent questions. We chatted for half an hour before his eyes turned sort of sly and he asked me up to his room, where he said we could be more comfortable. Jesus. His smile tightened when I said I was sorry but I had to telephone my wife and kids. At least I wasn't alone in the world the way he appeared to be as he slid off his bar stool and moved on.

Back in my room I lay down and telephoned home. Barbara answered. "Mother is at Mr. Andrews' house reading for the play. She left me her number. Do you want it?"

I said no, I didn't want to interrupt her. In the background I heard laughing young voices and music and guessed that some of Barbara's friends had dropped in for the kind of unsupervised party I didn't like, but there was hardly any point in making long-distance complaints. For a few minutes I talked to Pete, who was briskly cheerful, and to Janey, who sounded the way I felt and very hoarse.

"When can I come down and visit you?" she asked.

"Any weekend's fine for me," I said. "Just figure it out with your mother."

"I'll have to wait till my cold is over. The darn thing seems to be getting worse."

Feeling less than inspired by these calls to home base, I went down to the small, ornately decorated hotel dining room, which was almost empty by this time, and ordered my third martini and a steak. After dessert I had a brandy with my coffee because I couldn't think of anything else to do. When I started toward the elevator to go to my room I realized I was quite drunk, and that scared me. My first night away from home and loaded? What kind of shape would I be in after a year?

6

THE NEWSSTAND IN the hotel offered morning papers from several major cities, and at breakfast the next day I sat reading the press coverage of Hopkins' appointment. The New York *Times* and the Washington *Post* ran Hopkins' picture at the bottom of the front page with brief noncommittal stories, but one syndicated columnist asked why a man whose chief occupation was presiding over "the great wasteland of television and devising programs filled with sex and violence" should be asked to head up a conference on mental health. This kind of criticism had dogged Hopkins since he had started his charitable activities, and he always ignored it.

David McKay, Kennedy's aide, did not telephone that day and there was some delay in getting me copies of the records of Eisenhower's conference. The only thing I had to do in the office was to answer more telephone calls from people who expected Hopkins to help them find psychiatric care or who were job hunting. That night and several following I read a lot and went to the movies. On Friday the first stacks of letters, the equivalent of the telephone calls, started to arrive, and to stem the flood I spent the weekend dividing them into categories and devising form letters for answering them. With all the work, I was anxious for my assistant, Ann McSoaring, to arrive.

SHE WALKED IN about ten on Monday morning, towing behind her an enormous suitcase on a rack with wheels that had various hat boxes and satchels strapped to it, a movable pyramid of luggage. She was wearing a gray woolen jumper and looked even younger and more attractive than I remembered.

"I'm so glad to *get* here," she said. "And what a nice office. I'm sorry to be so late but I'm gung-ho to go to work."

"Wouldn't you like to get settled in your hotel—?"

"I don't even know what hotel I'm supposed to go to—they said they'd tell me here."

I called the bureau manager and found that she too had been booked into the Westminster. "It's just a few blocks away. If you want to call a taxi I'll give you a hand with your luggage."

"Thanks, but I might as well get settled in here first. Do you have a desk for me?"

I showed her to a large one near mine and across the big room from a row of smaller desks where I'd set three stenographers to work typing and addressing form letters. She glanced at the stacks of unopened envelopes piled all over the place in wire baskets. "I figured that all that publicity would bring us a bunch of mail. This is one kind of operation I understand, Mr. Rath. We should order in some automatic typewriters. They can cut the work by more than half."

"I'll try to get the bureau to find us some."

"I'll take care of that. Can I flaunt Mr. Hopkins' name?"

"Flaunt away."

She sat down at her desk, picked up the telephone. I brought her a cup of coffee with packets of powdered milk and sugar.

"Black is fine," she said. "*Thank* you, Mr. Rath—I never had a boss who brought me coffee before."

Her smile was something special, delighted in spite of the tired lines around her eyes and mouth, but in those sparkling dark eyes there was also that glint of wry amusement, a little as though we were both playing parts in a situation comedy, which·pleased her. At our first meeting she had made that surprisingly open but really not flirtatious remark, "I think I like you," and her manner now seemed to continue that feeling. It would have been nice to believe that I was being singled out, but I suspected that this was her attitude toward anyone who treated her halfway decently. Maybe she was that rare bird, a genuinely sunny person. It certainly seemed so when she introduced herself to the rather grumpy and overworked stenographic staff. Her cheerful enthusiasm appeared so genuine that she soon had those stolid faces smiling.

I went back to my desk to go through the mail, looking for letters that should be brought to Hopkins' attention. In short order three stock boys arrived pushing automatic typewriters on wheeled tables from other parts of the bureau. Apparently Ann McSoaring had flaunted Hopkins' name to good effect.

At twelve-thirty the secretaries went out to lunch.

"Would you like to go out for a bite?" I asked Ann.

"Oh, that's very nice of you, but they fed me on the plane and I'm not really hungry. I'd like to start going through this mail to get the feel of it."

I went out for a hamburger, a little miffed because I was tired of eating alone and, face it, had looked forward to getting to know her better. What was our relationship going to be, anyway? Would she be wonderfully friendly in the office but keep to herself after hours, even if we were staying at the same hotel? What else did I have in mind? Maybe a sort of surrogate daughter-figure, a nice paternal friendship to take the curse off the loneliness without running the risk of an entangling alliance? All nonsense, of course. Whether it was a weakness of mine or a natural phenomenon, I'd never maintained a platonic friendship with an attractive woman in my life—my efforts to preserve my marriage had steered me away from any woman who offered any real temptation.

Maybe Ann McSoaring and I would develop an all too accurate copy of my real father-daughter relationship—good feelings but a gulf between us. Whatever, if I wanted someone to help banish loneliness, it wasn't a daughter I was looking for, and I had better stop kidding myself . . .

When I returned to the office Ann showed me some letters she'd found that she felt should go to Hopkins. She had a good eye for recognizing important names and questions that deserved individual answers.

"From now on, you can leave all the mail to me," she said. "You must have a lot more important things to do."

At the moment I didn't, but I hoped I soon would, and I was grateful to her.

At four-thirty we closed the office and I insisted on helping with her luggage. The taxi we'd ordered by telephone didn't come and at that time of day we had little chance of flagging one down. Still, the cartlike arrangement on her baggage worked well and it was no trouble for me to pull it the few blocks to the Westminster Hotel. She walked along beside it, steadying the small bags on top. All her suitcases, I noticed, were of battered leather in old-fashioned shapes and covered with yellowing Cunard Line labels, some of which showed pictures of high-stacked ships that no longer existed and customs stickers from all over Europe. I wondered if she'd been to all those places in her childhood . . . her background was impossible to guess . . .

It was a warm September afternoon in Washington, with none of the chill we had left behind in New York. As I lifted the wheels up curbs crossing streets I took off my suit coat, folding it on top of the luggage, where she kept a hand on it. Service was not exactly a strong point at the Westminster. No bellman appeared to help us after she had registered, so I wheeled the luggage into the elevator myself. "What floor?"

She glanced at her key. "Five."

Her room was diagonally across the hall from mine, only a few steps away. Her baggage truck was too big to go through the door so I muscled her big suitcases in while she took the small ones.

"You remind me of my father," she said as I wrestled her biggest piece of luggage upon her bed.

I must have looked stricken . . . I sure as hell felt that way.

"Oh, but I meant it as a *compliment*. My dad's big and strong, like you."

I wasn't accustomed to flat-out compliments like that. There followed an awkward moment during which I was tempted to hug her, she made me feel so good . . . Instead I said, "If you want that stuff lugged to the top of the Washington Monument I'm your man." Not exactly Cary Grant, but the best I could manage at the moment, and I meant it . . .

She laughed and I reluctantly moved toward the door. "Do you plan on eating here in the hotel tonight?" I asked.

"As far as I know."

"Would you mind if I joined you?"

"I'd love it, I hate eating alone."

"I'm in the same boat. What time . . . ?"

"Give me an hour or so to get settled in and clean up. Is there a bar where I can meet you?"

SITTING AT THE hotel's unlovely bar an hour later, sipping a martini as I waited for Ann, I certainly felt much better than I had for the past week. For several weeks. All right, I wasn't one for platonic relationships with attractive women, but this time I couldn't run from temptation as I'd always done in the past (except in Italy). Ann, I figured, was somewhere around twenty-eight, fifteen years younger than I was, not young enough to be my daughter, too young for any other kind of relationship, unless I was going to turn out to be an aging playboy like Bert Andrews, a very unwise idea for the father of four children who could hardly pay his bills as things were . . . Of course it was premature . . . foolish . . . even to think of things like that, so stop thinking then, I instructed myself . . .

When Ann came into the bar I saw that she'd changed into a fairly low-cut summer dress, a flowered print of red and green silk. As she came toward me through the semidarkness her petite figure with its slender waist and modest but well-proportioned bosom made her look like the kind of girl I used to take to prep school dances, the sort who made me tremble while I helped them pin a gardenia to their first evening gown. Betsy had looked this way when I first met her, when she was seventeen and I was eighteen, and Maria had when she'd first worn a new dress I had bought her in Rome. Ann even seemed to look like my daughter Barbara, for God's sake, when she was going out to a high school prom . . . Ann was all kinds of images of youth, no question. I may have been trying to insulate myself, I'm not sure, when I complimented her on her dress and told her she reminded me of my sixteen-year-old daughter. Whatever, it didn't work.

"I'm glad the lights are so dim in here," she said. "The last time I applied for a modeling job the art director told me to come back when I was five years younger, before the plaster had begun to crack."

"Do they really talk like that?"

"Some of them. I tell you, administrative assistants get treated a lot better than aging models."

". . . Do you want to have a drink here or would you like to go into the dining room right away?"

"I'm kind of hungry and if I start drinking, well, I won't stay on my diet. Believe me, if I remind you of your daughter even in this dim light, it's because of my famous iron will, not my tender years."

WE WENT INTO the pretentious dining room, where we were seated under a chandelier of fake crystal and handed a menu printed on fake parchment. She ran her eye over the entrees, which were listed in fractured French. "Oh, my, they have *le red snapper.* Doesn't that make you feel downright Parisian?"

"No . . . damn near takes away the appetite . . . Where did you work as a model? From all those labels on your suitcases it looks like you've done a lot of traveling."

"Are you asking for my life story?" She smiled when she said it.

"Absolutely. I want to hear how a well-traveled former model became an administrative assistant who knows all about handling heavy mail and—"

Before I could ramble on further in this fairly inane fashion the waiter came to our table. Ann ordered le red snapper with a green salad, no other vegetables or potatoes. I followed her sterling example.

"If I hang around you maybe even I'll learn how to diet."

"You're tall and wide-shouldered enough to carry your weight," she said, "but maybe for the sake of your health you should drop a few pounds. I'm afraid I'm something of a nut about diet and exercise. I want to live forever."

"I don't think I've ever heard anybody say that."

"It does sound silly, doesn't it? I should be getting ready to grow old gracefully, but frankly I hate the whole idea." She paused before adding, "My mother never grew old. She got cancer when she was only thirty-nine. One of the last things she said to me was, 'Hell, I always hated the idea of turning forty anyway.' "

"My mother died young too."

"It makes you grow up fast, doesn't it? My mother left me some grand memories. She never felt sorry for herself. Just about everything went wrong for her but she was a great romantic. I think she always thought of herself as the heroine of some wonderful romantic novel."

"Sometimes I think my mother played Camille for most of her life," I said. "I'm not criticizing her . . . when things are rough it helps to think that your life is at least dramatic."

"My mother's life really was. She was a professional dancer, no big star but she loved dancing so much that she was willing to starve for it, and one thing it did for her was to get her the hell out of Brooklyn . . ."

Ann paused.

"Mom's people were Italian. Her real name was Rosa Minelli, but I guess that seemed pretty unglamorous so she gave herself a stage name, Carmen, and most of the time she actually worked as a Spanish dancer . . ."

Ann's face softened with the recollection of these memories.

"Actually, she had a very good time, compared to most working girls. In her day it wasn't hard for a good dancer to get jobs on ocean liners, not just cruise ships but the big transatlantic vessels. Mom loved it. Fact is, that's the way she met dad—he was the second engineer of the *Britannic,* a handsome young Scot. She loved to tell me about their great romance."

Annie laughed gently. "I heard that story so often when I was a little girl that sometimes I think I actually saw my parents meet. During a whole ten-day voyage, dad watched mom and her partner do their Spanish dance. I imagine that mom was quite something with her black lace shawl, her mantilla and her castanets. On the last night dad couldn't stand it any longer. After her act ended he went up to her on the stage and introduced himself. He spoke in such a thick Scotch burr that she could hardly understand him. His first words were, 'Me name is McSoaring and I canna dance a step, but I admire you very much and would be pleased to buy you a drink.' "

"That must have taken some courage."

"You bet it did, because he was really very shy, and there was trouble because mom's dance partner thought he was just a drunk from the way he talked and tried to get her away from him. Dad didn't have to push or shove. He just said, 'Now let the lady get to know me and make her choice.' "

"And so they were married . . ."

"Oh, that took a long time, but it sure was the beginning."

"It's a nice story."

"Mother told it in different ways sometimes, but that was the gist of it."

"Did you ever take any trips with your father?"

"No. All that happened just before the Depression, and it wasn't long after before he lost his job. He moved from Glasgow to Brooklyn and tried to get jobs in the shipyards. They had a bad time."

"The Depression was rough on a lot of people—"

"Not for me, really. I had a wonderful grandmother in Brooklyn who took care of me while my folks traveled around looking for work. It wasn't long before mom showed me how to get jobs as a child model and taught me to dance. I learned typing and short-hand in high school, so from the time I was sixteen I could always find some kind of work even when mom and dad couldn't."

"That must have been a pretty hard way to grow up—"

"But it wasn't! Think how proud I was. It was terrible for dad sometimes, but everybody kept telling me how great I was. My ambition was to be a real dancer and when I was in my late teens I did get a lot of nightclub engagements."

"I wish I'd seen you."

She smiled. "Oh God, I loved dancing, but when I got good enough to understand that I didn't have a big talent, I just did it for money when I could, modeled when I could, and went to business school. I never especially wanted to starve for art—I'd seen too much of that. As soon as I could, I got a job at United Broadcasting, and the little I'd learned about show business helped. Ed Banks was good to me right from the start."

"No reflection on your acting talents intended, but Ed has an eye out for a pretty girl—"

"Oh, he has his pick of them . . . A lot of people have helped me but no one has ever really given me a rough time. I've been lucky right from the start."

I found myself wondering if she had ever been married or come close to it, but although she seemed very open about her background she had a kind of dignity that discouraged such personal questions. When the waiter brought the food, we ate hungrily and talked little. For dessert she ordered coffee and a bowl of fresh fruit, which didn't sound as good to me as the French pastries, but again I doggedly followed her noble example.

"Now how about *your* life story?" she said as she deftly peeled an apple. "No fair asking without telling, you know."

My own history, the way I looked at it, was so dark compared to hers that I really didn't want to go into it . . . "Mine's nowhere as interesting as yours," I said, "and I'm not being modest. I'm not even sure how my parents met. I've got a rather conventional background but we have something in common—mostly my grandmother brought me up."

"What happened to your father?"

"He had a bad time in the First World War. He was gassed and had what they used to call shell shock. He never really got better and was killed in an automobile accident when he was only twenty-eight. My mother never got over that shock. She was an invalid after that and died when I was sixteen."

"*That* is what I would call a rough childhood," Ann said.

"Well, my grandmother was very strong and she had some money. She sent me to college. I got married when I was only twenty-one. Then there was the war . . ."

"You were a paratrooper like Ed Banks. He told me."

"Yeah, I made a few jumps in what they called the European theater and a few more in the Pacific theater. You know, it suddenly strikes me as strange to call a battleground a theater, but a lot of people did seem to think the war was show business."

"I can't imagine anything more terrifying than jumping out of an airplane."

"There's a kind of limit to fear, just like pain. Shock takes over. I went through a lot of it in a daze."

"You must feel a good deal of pride to have survived all that."

"Survived . . . well, in a way I didn't have anywhere near as bad a time as my father did. We never got pinned down in trenches for months at a time. Except for a few scratches I never was officially wounded. After the war I came back to Connecticut, got a job, bought a little house and started to raise kids. That was the proper happy ending—it seemed that all my troubles were over. Most of us thought that way . . . ."

"Were they? The troubles, I mean."

"Not exactly. I woke up a little late to the fact that it's not so easy in civilian life either. Actually much tougher, beginning with making the kind of living we considered I was supposed to make."

"How many children do you have?"

Whenever I was asked that question, I thought four and said three, excluding my son in Italy, and I automatically did that now. I had never acknowledged the existence of Mark to anyone but my wife, my lawyer and one old army buddy who knew Maria. I was tempted, though, to tell Ann about him, but this was not exactly a time for true confessions.

"Three!" she repeated. "I envy you. That's something I regret —no kids."

"You still have plenty of time—"

"Not really. I'm glad you think I look like some sort of teenager, but I'm going to be thirty any day—"

"There's still plenty of time . . . ."

"But after a while time stops working for you. I'm beginning to get set in my ways. Not many of the men I meet are dying to start a family, and I get more and more choosy anyway. I'll probably end up being one of those women who finally buys a poodle and drives it crazy, fussing over it."

"I doubt that."

"Anyway, in the meantime I like my work—I really do. If I had a bunch of kids I'd probably be sitting out in some suburb with a wandering husband, watching television instead of having dinner here with you . . . Do you think we'll ever actually meet President Kennedy?"

"We'll get to see him at least, I guess. I'm waiting to hear from one of his aides, David McKay. Probably this thing will really begin to roll when he calls."

After we had finished our coffee and signed the check there was an awkward moment. I hated the notion of spending the rest of the evening alone, but the hotel lobby was too noisy for conversation, and I didn't feel I could ask her up to my room. Since she didn't drink there was no point in suggesting a bar.

"Would you like to go to a movie?" I finally asked, not sounding too enthusiastic.

"No thanks," she said with a smile. "I've had a long day and I still have some unpacking to do . . ."

We walked to the elevator. Riding up together, it was impossible not to sense the tension—the fact that we were living in the same hotel in rooms only a few yards apart . . . obviously that offered possibilities that couldn't be kept entirely out of mind, anyway out of my mind. I'd no idea she shared such wayward thoughts. When we arrived at our floor she actually thanked me for having dinner with her, as though I'd done her a big favor, said she'd see me in the morning and went through her door without a backward glance.

I lay down on my bed, and after a few minutes called Betsy and the children. No one answered—had they all gone to a movie or some event at the school? It was silly to think that something bad, like an automobile accident, might have happened—my constant expectation of disaster was a damn bore. I chose a fat paperback novel by Herman Wouk and lay back to read myself to sleep . . .

About an hour later there was a knock at my door. Could it possibly be that Ann might be as restless and lonely as I was . . . ? It was only a maid who said, "Just checking," a mysterious phrase that I had often heard in hotels but never understood. Why did hotel maids have to keep prowling around at all hours, opening doors and saying that? What were they *checking* for? Illicit lovers, thieves, guests who had died in bed?

I finally slept and had erotic dreams about Ann which, of course, made me feel properly guilty when I woke up. What man can keep his dreams under control, I instructed myself, but good old New England Protestant guilt would have none of such logic.

7

AT NINE-THIRTY the next morning David McKay called me at my new office.

"I'm sorry it's taken me so long to get in touch," he said in a Massachusetts accent that sounded very much like Kennedy's. "The president is very interested in this project and had been giving it a good deal of thought."

"That's great . . ."

"We've got the program we want pretty firmly in mind and a good many of the details worked out. Can you stop in to see me about two this afternoon? The lower level of the White House, Room Thirty-two B. One of the attendants will show you the way and I'll make sure that the guards at the gate have your name."

"I'd like to bring my assistant, she'll help me take notes—"

"Fine. What's her name?"

"I CAN'T PRETEND I'm not excited about this," Ann said when I told her about the appointment. "I'm going to the White House! That's something I can brag on to my grandchildren, if I ever have any."

Then she hurried off to ask questions of some of the old Washington hands in our bureau, consulted reference books and in less than an hour she had typed up a brief biographical sketch of David McKay for me:

"Mr. David M. (for Murray) McKay does not have a big public reputation as a top White House aide, but our correspondents say that he has the president's ear and is often assigned to his favorite projects. He's cast very much in the Kennedy mold—born in Boston (1919), he's the son of Arnold K. McKay, an investment banker. He went to Milton Academy and Harvard, class of '41, and was a lieutenant in the navy during World War II. He was working in a Boston advertising agency when he became a volunteer worker in John Kennedy's first campaign for Congress and was hired as a full-time aide a few years later. He married Virginia Stillwell in 1947 and has three children. His hobby is sailing."

I too was in the Harvard College class of '41. I'd been almost a recluse and hadn't known many of the thousand or so men in my class but I had some dim recollection of David McKay as one of the golden boys, not a leader with the luster of John Kennedy but one of those quiet men who considered Harvard a natural extension of home and treated the best debutante parties as family events. Betsy had been on the edge of that inner circle when I had first met her and might have danced her way into it if I hadn't come along, a possibility which it seemed to me she sometimes, not altogether unreasonably, remembered rather wistfully.

I thanked Ann for preparing me for the meeting and she hurried back to the hotel to change for the great event, though she looked just fine to me as she was. I could hardly argue, though, with the stylish beige linen suit she showed up in.

I figured that my all-purpose gray flannel suit would see me through this meeting, as in its fashion it had through so many others.

At one-thirty we took a taxi to the White House and arrived so early that we walked up and down Pennsylvania Avenue outside the iron fence in front of the great mansion for about fifteen minutes. It was a fine sunny afternoon, but a brisk September wind was blowing leaves on the rolling lawn, which still was summer-green.

"Do you know that this place was called the Palace in the original plans?" Ann asked.

"Where do you learn that?"

"The encyclopedia. I always look everything up. George Washington picked out this site, but John Adams was the first president to live here. The building is actually made of gray stone. It wasn't painted white until after the British burned it in 1814, and Teddy Roosevelt was the first president to make the name White House official. I'm glad, aren't you? If it weren't for Teddy, we might be trying to plan the Palace Conference on Mental Health."

I told her I was indeed duly grateful. The blue-uniformed guard at the gate glanced at a list on a clipboard when we gave him our names and without asking to see identification, directed us toward the colonnade at the public entrance on the east end of the mansion. Another guard met us there, ushered us through a chamber that looked like a plush museum of early American art, through a side door to a busy flight of stairs and a corridor that led to an area full of utilitarian offices that looked more like the editorial section of a magazine than part of a palace. David McKay's room was so small that his big desk, three chairs and a filing cabinet crowded it. I recognized him the moment I saw him—he was a ruddy-faced, hawk-nosed man with a big athlete's body turning to fat. He wore no coat. His sleeves were rolled up, his collar was open.

"Tom Rath!" he said, leaning back in his swivel chair and extending a hand in a rather lordly gesture. "It's been a while . . ."

I was surprised that he remembered me and even more so when he went on to reminisce.

"You're the one who married Betsy Hewat, aren't you? I never forget a pretty girl. How is Betsy these days?"

"Just fine," I said . . . "This is my assistant, Ann McSoaring."

He nodded at Ann, his big, sensual face almost too appreciative, and suddenly he was all business. "Sit down," he said. "The president has approved Mr. Hopkins' suggestions for the steering committee and has added a few more names. Now the first thing we have to do is to hold a meeting here in Washington and get agreement with all these people on a statement of purpose. That's the key document."

I really didn't understand what he was getting at.

"Now we can't expect a big committee like this to work out a clear statement of purpose at one meeting. The best way is for Mr. Hopkins to write out what we want and submit it for approval to all the members of the committee in advance of the meeting. Then they can think it over and ask for whatever specific changes they want. I'll tell you what we're hoping for . . . if we do this thing right, Mr. Hopkins will come up with a real rafter-ringer, a statement so strong that the committee will approve it unanimously and get off to a gung-ho start without a lot of tiresome debate."

"That might be tough with a diverse group of people like this—"

"We have to lift their sights, take them where they can see the whole forest, not just the trees. We're hoping for a conference that will finally do something constructive about mental health. We want this to be more than an exercise of private fund-raising or requests for congressional appropriations. If the public isn't told what the money is for, what can be done with it, no purse strings will be loosened, private or public."

His New England twang rang with enthusiasm, but I sensed that it was secondhand, that he was parroting phrases he'd heard from the president himself, and that sounded better coming from the president. I got no signals from Ann, who was busy taking notes on a pad she held against her purse on her lap.

"Of course, we're all laymen here, not psychiatrists," McKay went on in that voice which sounded so much like the president on television. "The trouble with us laymen is that we don't really know what we're talking about when we get into questions about mental health, and the trouble with most psychiatrists is that the public can't understand them and most of them get so lost in the trees, even in the damn underbrush, that they never see the forest anyway. Now, President Kennedy knows one psychiatrist who can give us a real mountaintop view with no jargon. His name is Clifford Harbringer. Have you ever heard of him?"

"I've heard of the Harbringer Clinic," I said. "It's somewhere out in Ohio, isn't it?"

"Windsor, Ohio, not far from Cleveland. We suggest you get Dr. Harbringer and Mr. Hopkins together. We hope the two of them can work out the kind of statement we need."

"I'll try to set up the meeting as soon as I can," I said.

At that moment a stout man I recognized from newspaper pictures as Pierre Salinger appeared in the door, and behind him I was astonished to see the comparatively slight figure of President Kennedy himself, who looked so startlingly like his photographs that I felt I was looking at a movie that had suddenly been projected onto the wall of the corridor.

"Dave, come upstairs as soon as you get a chance," Salinger said, and the president gave McKay a smile with a casual little wave before he and Salinger continued down the hallway, talking together. Without thinking, I went to the door to get a look at them. Ann joined me. President Kennedy looked so elegant, so jaunty as he strolled along, talking to his big rumpled press secretary. Of course any president of the United States tends to inspire a kind of awe when glimpsed in the flesh, but Kennedy seemed to be a rather dazzling mix of idealism, power, intellect and grace. If any man ever seemed to glitter, he did. When he turned to go up the

stairs Ann and I glanced back at McKay, embarrassed by our tour-
istlike reaction to the president's appearance.

"Sorry . . ."

McKay smiled. "I've seen some of the most powerful men in this
country stand on chairs to see him."

WHEN ANN AND I got back to our office we were especially
eager to go to work. McKay had made the conference on mental
health sound more important than ever before.

"Laugh if you want," Ann said, "but I really feel as though I'm
working for the Sun King, and now we're being sent off in pursuit
of a wizard. How come he's in Ohio, not Tibet?"

OF COURSE THE next step was for me to call Hopkins and tell
him that the president wanted him to meet with Dr. Harbringer.

"I've heard of that guy," Hopkins said. "I get the impression
he's kind of wild-eyed."

"My assistant took notes," I said. "Would you like to hear exactly what Mr. McKay said?"

Ann got on the telephone and read from her shorthand pad.

"This fellow McKay is certainly trying to sell Harbringer to us,"
Hopkins said when I got back on the line, "and that of course
means that Jack wants him . . . It's strange that Jack didn't say
anything to me about him. If he wants me to head up this thing
but is going to pressure me into doing everything Harbringer's
way . . ."

"Let's find out first just what Harbringer's way is."

"Yes, but I don't want to see him right now—I don't like con-
frontations. You go out and see him. Find out what he wants. Take
your assistant with you. I want to hear exactly what the man's got
on his mind before I get mixed up with him."

Ann immediately called Harbringer and found that he was in
England and wouldn't be back until the middle of October, two
weeks away.

"It's like the army: hurry up and wait," I said.

BUT THERE WOULD be plenty to keep us busy in Washington
until Harbringer returned . . . the mail, speeches for me to write
for Hopkins in his new role as chairman of the conference. That
evening I telephoned Betsy, who was delighted to hear that David
McKay remembered her as a pretty girl.

"I danced with him a lot at parties and I think he was getting ready to ask me out when you and I started going together," she said, and I couldn't blame her if she was wondering how different her life would have been if she had married that handsome Brahmin.

"How's the play going?" I asked.

"We're actually going into rehearsals. I was scared to death at first, but Bert is very encouraging. *He* really thinks I have talent."

"I'm sure you do," I said, although to tell the truth, I wasn't.

"I have a little bad news, though . . . the car is acting up again. I'm having trouble starting it and the motor conked out the other night when I was coming home from a meeting. Bert looked at it and says we're crazy to put any more money into it—"

"Does Bert have any ideas about how we pay for a new one?"

"Matter of fact, he does. Do you know he's part owner of the big Chevy garage in Stamford?"

"No, that one escaped me."

"Look, Tom, he can get us a practically new station wagon, a demonstration model at cost, only eighteen hundred dollars. Isn't that a terrific buy?"

"It is if you have eighteen hundred to spare."

"They'll allow us something if we turn in our old wreck and we can pay the rest on time. If only for the safety of the kids, I think we should do it."

"Go ahead," I said, although I knew that monthly payments would make it harder than ever for her to live on my current salary. "Let me talk to the children."

"Barbara's out on a date and Bert has taken Pete over to Dr. Pemberton's office."

"What? Is Pete sick?"

"No, Bert found out that Pete needs a better microscope. Bert and Doc Pemberton are old friends so Bert asked him how we could get a secondhand one. It turns out that Doc Pemberton has an old one he used in medical school. Bert's taken Pete over to see it. I think Doc Pemberton is just going to give it to Pete. Not a bad deal, wouldn't you say?"

"Bert sure seems to be the problem solver."

"Tom, how can you possibly get mad at him if he gets your son a free microscope—?"

"I can't." (But I could.) "Can I speak to Janey?"

"In a minute, but I want to explain something. She'd love to see

_ 62

you for a weekend but she's afraid of flying alone and she doesn't want to admit that to you."

"She can take a train."

"She's afraid of *traveling* alone, getting lost in the stations and all that. She really is a very apprehensive child. Bert . . . I mean, I think maybe we should try a psychiatrist."

"Does Bert have one available at cut-rate?"

"How can you joke about a thing like that? Janey really is very depressed a lot of the time. I worry about her—"

"So do I. Take her to a therapist if *you* really think it's a good idea . . . Can I talk to her now?"

I heard Betsy calling and soon Janey got on the phone.

"Hello, daddy. I wish I could come down and see you but this terrible cold hangs on—"

"That's okay, honey . . . I'll get home to see you pretty soon."

"Aren't you lonely down there? It must be awful to be away so long."

"I keep busy, honey."

Of course feeling guilty because I hadn't felt lonely at all since Ann had arrived.

"Have you seen President Kennedy yet?"

"I sure did. He looks just like he does on television, only better."

"I wish I could see him with you . . ."

She sounded so awfully *sad* . . . it did worry me . . . "Janey, it's not so bad to feel bad sometimes. When I was your age, I felt lonely and scared of almost everything—most people go through that. It's part of growing up—"

"I know," she said and then she seemed to brighten, as though trying to reassure *me*. "I'll be okay . . . my school work is going a little better . . .

"That's great."

"I got an *A* on an algebra test."

"That's better than I ever did."

"And I may be starting to take riding lessons. Uncle Bert has a friend who owns a horse . . ."

Oh, shit, is what I almost said, but bit my tongue in time . . . "Who's going to give you the lessons?"

"Uncle Bert. He's done a lot of riding, did you know that?"

"No, I guess that Bert has all kinds of skills I don't know about. Well, have a good time, baby, and try to be careful."

"You too," she said.

"UNCLE BERT" INDEED! What made me maddest about Bert Andrews was that I was supposed to be *grateful* to him for helping out my family while I was away. Who could be a truer friend?

8

DURING THOSE GOLDEN October days in Washington I worried about my family in Connecticut a great deal, worry that I think was at least a form of love. I also worried that Hopkins and President Kennedy both had such strong personalities that it was going to be hard for them to work together on the conference. If President Kennedy pushed his own ideas or those of Dr. Harbringer, whatever they were, too hard, I sensed that there was a danger that Hopkins might quietly resign "for reasons of health," and my chance of having a part in this national project would go up in smoke.

Waiting for Dr. Harbringer to return from England, Ann and I got into the habit of having dinner together. The restaurant in the hotel was expensive, and since we both wanted to save money on our per diem arrangement she suggested that we buy groceries and do our own cooking in the kitchenette in her apartment.

We were in a damn curious situation, no question . . . almost living together but maintaining a careful sexual truce. The pressure was considerable. I was taken with Ann more and more every day, she seemed to look prettier every time I looked at her . . . but I also kept reminding myself of the thousand or so reasons why I should keep this platonic . . . assuming I had an option. I was, I told myself, too old . . . she would be properly disenchanted if I turned out to be just another lecherous middle-aged married boss on the make for a cheap adventure. And even if I could interest her, a fling with me . . . noble fellow that I was . . . couldn't do her any good, and I still knew myself well enough to realize I wasn't one for a lighthearted affair to be forgotten as soon as I went home. If I weren't careful, it would be damn easy to fall in love with my assistant.

The idea of a forty-three-year-old man who could barely support his wife, three children and one illegitimate son "falling in love" with a woman fourteen years younger than himself was, I told myself, unrealistic sentimentality. It would be more honest to say that I felt tempted by a strong sexual pull . . . Ann's willowy figure, the dancer's grace with which she moved, the warmth in her eyes stirred up feelings that were almost adolescent in their intensity. This awakening should make me grateful, I thought—at least it proved I wasn't as far gone as I'd often felt . . . and it was true that I found myself enjoying, looking forward to each day more than I had in a long time.

Maybe it was permissible for me to fantasize about Ann in bed, but to remind myself that if it happened it would destroy the fine working relationship we had already established . . . And once again I told myself I had no reason to believe that I was tempting her the way she was tempting me . . .

So I tried to relax and enjoy the situation as it was, without, at least consciously, trying to change it. I also tried to get to *know* Ann. Although she was much younger, she apparently dreaded old age even more than I did, which was one reason why she clung so tenaciously to her regime of diet and exercise. She was aware, she said, that the "falling apart" of her face, as she put it, was much less under control than the condition of her body. Usually her features showed warmth, a wry maturity, not the self-obsession of youth; but sometimes, after a hard day's work or thinking about something that troubled her, her mouth would tighten and the little wrinkles around her eyes gathered, and something like despair would cross her face before her expression re-formed into a sunny mask. Such moments of self-revelation were brief. They ended when she wearily rubbed her face with her right hand, as though she were deliberately erasing everything written there, shook her head and looked up with a determined smile that quickly softened if she caught me glancing at her.

Between quitting time and dinner she liked to take long walks, and in spite of my habitual dislike of exercise in any form, I always accepted her invitations to go with her. Walking briskly beside me while I strode along trying to keep up with her on my much longer legs seemed to revive her, brought back her usual, youthful mood of gaiety. I'm sure that people who caught a glimpse of her must have figured her about eighteen years old. Men of all ages, high school boys, old codgers, let their eyes linger on her. When a crew of burly construction workers greeted her with loud wolf whistles, she gave them a flashing smile.

"Thank you, boys, you've made my day," she called before hurrying on.

Unlike me, usually absorbed in my own thoughts, Ann noticed everyone and everything around her, and her face often mirrored the mood of passersby, breaking into laughter as we passed a group of skipping girls, saddening at the sight of a blind man tapping along the sidewalk with a white cane. Although she almost never bought anything, she loved window shopping and zigzagged across streets to inspect mannequins displaying the latest styles, new cars, bookstores, even hardware emporiums. She loved parks and often gave me a chance to catch my breath on a bench while she admired babies in perambulators or struck up conversations about the weather with old women or men feeding pigeons. Once while we were sitting on a grassy knoll at the foot of an equestrian statue of some old general waving his sword at the sky, a Frisbee came sailing from a ring of children and flopped at our feet. She jumed up, grabbed it and skimmed it back to them. One of the kids returned it to her with a smile and she was soon playing with them. I guess I was getting carried away, but once when she leaped up to throw with an outstretched arm she seemed almost to follow the Frisbee into the air, and I thought her name McSoaring was especially apt. At that moment it was impossible for me not to love her.

Not long after we continued our walk we passed a sidewalk cafe with umbrellas emblazoned with the word CINZANO. We sat down at a table, and breaking her rule against sweets, we ordered dishes of brightly colored Italian ices and espresso coffee.

"I love Italian food," she said. "Mother never cooked it—I think she thought it was kind of low-class, and dad hated it, but when I was about fifteen she took me to Italy. I loved it. From dad and his people I think I'd got the idea that Italians were no good compared to the Scotch, but what did Scotland have that could compare to Rome? It's such a magnificent place . . . have you ever been there?"

"Yes."

"When?"

"During the war."

"How long did you get to spend there?"

"About a month."

"Was it a good time for you or did the war ruin it?"

"Well . . . there was an Italian girl . . ."

I'm not sure why the urge for confession came over me then . . . maybe partly because I couldn't imagine Ann judging me, or anybody else for that matter, maybe because I was feeling guilty about having such a good time away from my wife . . . but whatever, I blurted out, "We had a child, a son. I don't know why I told you that, I don't usually go around spilling my guts this way . . ."

"I hear that wasn't too unusual during the war," she said, waving away my apology. "Have you ever seen the boy?"

"No . . . I send some money every month, not much, I'm afraid. Probably not enough. He's nineteen now, a student in a Catholic seminary, a sort of college. His name is Mark."

"I should think you'd be dying to meet him—"

"I'd like to, but it would be very hard on Betsy . . . I had to tell her about him, of course . . . With my salary you don't send even a hundred dollars a month off somewhere without explaining it."

"She couldn't possibly resent a thing like that—"

"Why not? We were married before the war. She was faithful and I wasn't. Also, it's hard for us to save enough money to send our own kids to college."

"I know, but still . . ."

"What would we do if we brought the boy over here? I've seen photographs of him, he looks like me. Betsy is a New Englander, all this isn't easy on her. Never has been. To have to see the boy, be nice to him in her own home, even for a short visit . . . it's asking a lot . . ."

"I'm sorry, it's none of my business, but what about *your* feelings . . . ?"

"Well, Betsy's very good about me sending off a monthly check. I can't blame her for wanting to keep the whole business at arm's length. It's not her fault, after all—"

"Why don't you go to Rome?" she said with some impatience.

"Betsy would know why I was going, it would upset her. She's even been known to imagine I want to go back to the boy's mother. When she gets mad at me, or I at her . . ."

"Do you?"

"Go back to her? After all these years? Hell, Maria has married, been widowed and remarried. She has at least a half dozen kids by her husbands. If we met on the street we probably wouldn't even recognize each other."

"Did you love her?"

"I think so . . . I thought so. When we met I'd been through two years of the war in Germany and Italy. I was headed for Japan. I was a paratrooper. I didn't think I had a chance of surviving the war, and by that time I didn't really give much of a damn. Most of us didn't. Maria gave me a new reason for wanting to survive."

"Was she beautiful?"

"To me, she was. But remember, she was only eighteen, not much older than my daughters are now. She was a child, more a waif, I guess. She came from a little village where her whole family had been wiped out. I met her in a bar, she was trying to cadge money or food from the soldiers. She wasn't a prostitute. It was just the way things were then . . ."

"She was lucky she met you. How many soldiers ever sent any money to all the kids they left behind?"

I shrugged. "Most of the guys never even knew if their girl had a child—we hardly ever spent more than a few weeks in one place before we were shipped out. I only learned about it because a sergeant in my company married one of Maria's cousins and brought her over here as a war bride. I ran into him five years after the war and he told me about Maria and Mark."

"Did she make a legal claim on you?"

"No, she didn't ask a thing for herself, never has, but she asked me to do what I could for the child. Who could blame her for that?"

"No one, but a lot of men would never have answered her."

"Don't hang any medals on me . . . I just didn't like the idea of a son of mine starving and dancing for pennies on the streets of Rome. Hell, any man wants to take care of his own if he can—"

"I don't know about that"—her face had gone tight—"my father wasn't so hot at that . . ."

Somehow I'd guessed that her romantic version of her mother's and father's story had glossed over some pain.

"Of course it was the Depression," she added quickly. "He couldn't get a job in New York. He ended up by going back to Scotland and then got jobs on tramp steamers that went all over the world. Sometimes we didn't hear from him for years at a time."

"That must have been rough."

"Not always. Whenever he actually did show up he was flush and treated us to expensive dinners, and he *was* so handsome . . . I used to make him walk with me around the neighborhood and to school. I wanted all the kids to see I actually did have a father . . . and such a handsome one at that . . ."

"But you still blame him—"

"My mother always said he did the best he could, but they did have some awful fights . . ." The muscles in her face tensed at the memory.

"Mom always told me to marry the first really reliable responsible man I could find, even if he was only three feet tall. I was about twelve when she first said that and I thought she meant it literally. I had this picture of myself marrying this earnest midget. The whole idea seemed horrible, but I was determined to do it if mom thought I should."

"I'm glad that wasn't necessary."

"Don't speak too soon. All the really good reliable men I've ever met were already married . . . like you. Who knows . . . somewhere out there may be that earnest midget waiting just for me."

"I'd say there's better than that, by a long shot—"

"I'm not so sure . . . Something about me attracts the dingbats, or maybe I turn good men irresponsible. Actually, it's probably simpler than that. One look at me and any sensible man knows he's not going to keep me vacuuming his house for long. Maybe I'm more like my father than my mother. I'd love to have a child, but if the price is housewife . . . I don't know . . ."

"You don't seem to have too high an opinion of marriage."

"I'd like to, but I hardly ever see any happy marriages. Tell me about yours. I need to know about one that works."

Was there a note of irony in her voice? If there was, I couldn't detect it. My suspicion, I suspected, was more my own problem than hers . . . "Oh, mine hasn't been so bad," I said. "We have three good kids. Betsy and I more or less go along with each other . . ."

"Except that she doesn't want you to see your son in Rome."

"Like the man said, nobody's perfect."

"Look, Tom, like I said, it's not my business, certainly not to criticize Betsy, but . . . well, I just got this idea . . . if you ever *want* to bring your son over here, he could stay with some of my mother's people out in Brooklyn. If he wants a job, I bet we could find him one . . ."

"You'd do that?"

"To quote Tom Rath, don't hang any medals on me. But really, it would be no big deal. We've brought several relatives over here. And things aren't so good in Italy right now, I hear."

"That's still one hell of a lot to do for a boy you've never met, and a man you haven't known very long . . ."

She shrugged. "Tom, I love you for sending money to that boy, is it all right for me to say that? Don't answer. I'd *like* to help. When we get back to New York after the conference, let's work on it. Okay? And no strings attached."

"I don't know how to say thanks—"

"Yes, you do—my God, you say it all the time. I've never *heard* a man use the word so much."

"Is that bad?"

"No. It's nice, a refreshing change. You're big, handsome, charming and God knows, *responsible.* The only trouble is, you're well-married, just like every other good man I meet."

"I'm also too old for the likes of you—"

"Old? You're younger than President Kennedy, and everybody goes around saying how young he is."

Things were shifting, and neither of us was an innocent in what was, seemed to be, happening. "Do you know how good you make me feel?"

"Maybe," she said, touching my cheek with her fingertips. "You make me feel good too."

"You know, I don't think I've had the guts even to say I like you."

"You don't have to say it. I sort of figured it out when we started eating three meals a day together . . . I hated the idea of coming down here to Washington alone."

"So did I."

Our faces were drawing closer together as we sat at that little table. Our lips had just touched when she drew back.

"I'm afraid this isn't exactly the way to keep on being *responsible.*" Her face was serious.

"One little kiss couldn't hurt," I said.

"Famous last words."

9

SHE EVEN SUGGESTED we go to the top of the Washington Monument. I told her I definitely was not up to climbing all those stairs, never mind the noble purpose, so we took a long, brisk walk instead.

That night I had a terrible time getting to sleep. I still tried to laugh at myself for thinking about so-called falling in love, in my situation. But I also had to face the fact that something like that was really happening to me. Well, a lot of people, I realized, might not find that so surprising. Magazines and newspapers of the day frequently ran articles on "the midlife crisis," "the male menopause" and "the dangerous years." Somehow these phrases infuriate me. Hell, most of my life had been a series of "crises," from the early death of my parents to my struggle to win Besty away from all the other boys in the stagline, and on to the affair with Maria. Why denigrate middle-aged passion with a condescending term like that? "Male menopause" was even worse. It wrote off love as a disease or symptom of the inevitable disintegration of the body. As for "dangerous years," well, the war had already given me four of them, so I didn't really feel myself in such deadly peril now.

There were, I supposed, several ways to look at a situation like mine, or at the one I thought might develop. I knew people in South Bay who boasted about their lighthearted affairs on business trips and who would think me hopelessly square for giving a second thought to such an opportunity, let alone worrying about how to avoid it. After all, we were supposed to be in the middle of a sexual revolution and nobody was required to feel guilty anymore. If the fates or whatever had put me in a situation where I was practically living with an attractive young woman who appeared to like me very much, why not just enjoy, without all this self-questioning? According to the gossip of the time, even President Kennedy and his brothers didn't carry New England puritanism too far. Many men considered discreet extramarital affairs a part of the pursuit of happiness.

All well and good . . . but, as I've said, I just wasn't built to be casual. And, even assuming Ann would go along and I could, as they say, cut the mustard, what about after the conference was over and we returned to New York? If we had any sense we'd force ourselves to say good-bye . . . which would be less painful than meeting on the sly while I tried to play loving husband and father during the nights and weekends in South Bay. Divorce? Support two households when I couldn't even afford to send my kids to college? And Ann obviously wanted a child of her own . . . I could end up with two women and five children to support. And now I switched to Betsy and Bert . . . what if Betsy actually did get involved with Bert Andrews and *she* ended up wanting a divorce to marry him? She'd certainly take the children with her, I'd lose them . . . Much as I might love Ann I couldn't stand the thought of walking out on my kids . . .

My head, my thoughts were spinning . . . rushing ahead from reality to fantasy, from fact to rationalization. One fact I faced now was that as much as I felt myself falling for Ann, I still felt possessive about Betsy, even jealous when I thought of her having anything to do with Bert Andrews, never mind marrying the old s.o.b. and getting my children. Was I a male chauvinist pig? Aching to have an affair with Ann, furious at the idea of my wife doing likewise? Wasn't I still a disciple of the double standard, not acceptable to enlightened women in this supposedly enlightened year of 1963? Face it, I was . . . and I was in trouble . . .

I looked at my watch on the bed table. Two A.M. Get some sleep, forget all this. I couldn't. Not yet. I thought about Maria . . . what if we had been less innocent, or careless, there wouldn't have been a child to cause so much heartache over the years, but there also wouldn't have been that month I spent with her, not to mention the existence of Mark, whom I now really wanted to meet . . . It was undoubtedly the war, but the days and nights with Maria had been the most intense I had ever known before or since—something I of course had never admitted to Betsy, even though I suspect she long ago suspected it . . . and resented it . . .

In some ways Ann even reminded me of Maria, as I dimly remembered her—they were both slight and dark-haired, full of vitality . . . oh, come off it, don't tell yourself Ann is some spiritual reincarnation of Maria, sent to give you a second chance at the grand passion and so forth . . . couldn't I leave it that we were mature enough to commit ourselves to the present without hope for the future? Wasn't half a loaf better than none?

On that profound and original question I *finally* fell asleep a little before dawn. At seven my alarm clock woke me. Feeling groggy from too little sleep and too damn much stewing, I quickly showered, shaved, got dressed and walked across the hall to Ann's room. I tapped on her door. When she opened it I saw through bleary eyes that she was wearing a tweed skirt and a brown sweater, which made her look like a college girl. She had set the breakfast table and a coffee pot was heating on the stove, filling the room with its fragrance. Bright sunshine was flooding through her window, spotlighting her as she stepped back from the door.

"Good morning," she said. "It looks like we're going to have another beautiful day. I wonder how long this Indian summer will last . . ."

She didn't usually chat about the weather and I noticed a new briskness in her manner, a kind of restraint in her expression as she bustled about the room, pouring the coffee, putting bread in the toaster, slicing a melon.

"I've been thinking," she said as we sat down at the table, "we'll probably be going out to see Dr. Harbringer next week, won't we?"

"It looks that way . . ."

"Things will probably be even busier when we get back. I guess that this would be a good time for me to take a weekend and go back to New York. My grandmother isn't well and I have some friends I'd like to see . . ."

It seemed I wasn't the only one who'd done some thinking during the night . . . very sensibly she'd decided to get away from me for a while. If I could find any comfort there, it was that maybe she at least felt something strong enough about me to need to back off a bit and give it some thought. Of course that was the instant interpretation that was most flattering, and therefore acceptable, to me . . .

Well, I ought to go home too and try to get my bearings on reality . . . When I telephoned Betsy and told her I would arrive at LaGuardia at six o'clock Friday evening she said that would be great, that she was having a few people in for dinner and it would be so much more fun with me there . . . I told her I was hoping for just a quiet time, with her and the kids . . .

"I can't call this thing off—I've already invited everybody. It's just the theater group and they've done so much for me . . ."

"Okay, okay."

"I wish I could meet you at the airport but people are coming at seven and we'd never get back in time—"

"*Okay.*"

"But I'll come down to the station and pick you up whenever you get in—just call."

"Sure . . . thanks, I will . . ."

"I'm so glad you're coming home, Tom. The kids are dying to see you and . . ."

Well, what did I expect? She couldn't very well call off a party at the last moment. And after all, I'd only been gone three weeks. Did I expect to be received like a soldier returned from the wars?

ANN AND I shared a taxi to the five o'clock shuttle plane to New York. It was raining lightly. She looked dashing in a tan trench coat and matching wide-brimmed hat, but she seemed preoccupied and withdrawn. The plane was so crowded with businessmen we weren't able to find seats together. I sat across the aisle from her. Her face looked tense as she put her head back and closed her eyes. The thought . . . I suppose it was inevitable . . . came to me that maybe she was going back to New York for a reunion with a lover, and I promptly felt as jealous as I had when I worried about Bert Andrews. Maybe some men whose affections get tangled up with two women also doubled their pleasure, for a while at least, but what I seemed mostly able to do was to double my miseries, perhaps a just punishment for a would-be errant husband . . . at least I could see some humor in this . . . here I was, guilty about my feelings for Ann and so far I had never even succeeded in giving her a proper kiss, for God's sake. Clearly I was something of a genius in winning for myself the worst of several worlds, guilt without the pleasure of sinning, jealousy without knowing love before it was lost. If anybody needed better mental health, it was me. I had better get cracking and get that conference started. I was likely to be a prime beneficiary.

IT GAVE ME no pleasure to see that my worries about Ann were justified as we stood in line together waiting to disembark from the plane in New York,

"An old friend is meeting me," she said. "Can we give you a ride into the city, or is your wife meeting you?"

"My wife is meeting me," I said quickly, surprised by my own lie, but I sensed that Ann didn't want me to intrude on her reunion. I also had no desire to be on hand for it. Her "old friend" turned out to be a tall, thin man about thirty years old, in dungarees and a leather jacket, who now shouldered his way through the crowd at the gate and clasped her in a warm embrace.

"Annie, you're a damn sight for sore eyes . . ."

She seemed a little embarrassed by this display in front of me and quickly turned to introduce us.

"This is Harry Comstock," she said. "Harry, this is my boss, Mr. Tom Rath . . ."

"Glad to meet you," Comstock said, but he didn't look or sound it. He had a craggy face and piercing blue eyes that seemed to challenge me as he looked me up and down.

"Come on, Annie, I'm parked in a bad place," he said and put his hand on her arm to hurry her off.

"I'm going to take the eight o'clock shuttle Monday if you want to meet here," she called over her shoulder.

"I'll try to make it," I said, and then she disappeared with her friend into the crowd.

He wasn't good enough for her . . . how predictable of me . . . she could do better than this character in dungarees and leather jacket. Still, Harry *was* about her own age . . . apparently the reason she'd spent so much time with me in Washington instead of going off with younger friends was she'd been waiting to go back to this Harry Comstock . . .

The truth was that I appeared to myself to be a faintly comic figure as I climbed onto a bus headed for Grand Central Station, the tired husband and would-be lover heading home. Except laughing at oneself, while perhaps chastening, can also be bitter pleasure. I was glad to find that I had enough time for a drink before boarding my train for South Bay.

The splotched blue upholstery of the New Haven car I sat in was so familiar I felt as though I were sinking back into my old commuter's routine, almost as though I'd never been away at all. The acquaintances who had ridden with me for years on this run nodded casually—obviously they hadn't noticed my absence during the last three weeks. Nothing, it seemed, had changed, I decided, as I peered through the rain-streaked, dusty windows of our train crawling out of the station . . .

It was pouring by the time we got to South Bay. I called Betsy, and she soon arrived in a new station wagon that looked so elegant I assumed it belonged to someone else until she waved and called out to me. As I walked toward her, she surprised me by getting out of the car in the rain and running to give me a hug. Being away from someone you're very familiar with lends a sort of objectivity at first reunion. She had thrown on an old blue raincoat to protect her party dress and had covered her head with a red scarf, but in spite of this garb Betsy was a handsome woman as she splashed toward me in the glow of the station lights.

"Where's your coat? Get in the car or you'll be drenched." We ran for the shelter of the station wagon.

"It wasn't raining much when I left Washington and it's still so warm down there that I forgot all about coats," I said.

"We've been having a wonderful Indian summer here, but this looks like the end of it. What do you think of this car?"

"Very spiffy."

"Bert really did give us a good deal. Try to be nice to him—he's at the party now."

"Sure . . ."

"He's not the kind of man you think he is."

"What do you mean?"

"Oh, I don't know what you think, but at heart he's a very lonely man, in spite of all the parties. He really seems to love kids—it's a shame he never had any of his own."

I'd never exactly thought of Bert as a frustrated family man.

"He's kept his nose to the grindstone all his life, but now I think he's getting bored with it, and with all the parties. That's why he enjoys putting on this play so much—it gives him a chance to get out and work with people, it's better than drawing up contracts or drinking cocktails."

"I suppose . . ."

"Maybe he's just been going through a sort of midlife crisis. He's been running around with all kinds of women . . . *I'm* not a target, in case that's crossed your mind . . . he seems to think of me sort of as the daughter he never had." She smiled when she said it.

77 —

Was it possible that Bert was going through the same convolutions of thought about Betsy that I'd been afflicting myself with over Ann? Could be . . . could damn well be . . .

"Anyway, he's been a real friend," Betsy went on. "Especially these last few weeks with you away."

I wished we had been able to find something beside Bert Andrews to talk about during these first minutes together. When she finally asked how things were going for me in Washington I felt a little jolt, but didn't have time to say more than "just fine" before she turned into our driveway, which was crowded with cars, including Bert's red Mercedes roadster.

Our living room was crowded with middle-aged women in low-cut cocktail gowns and graying men in colorful slacks and jackets —the theater group dressed less conservatively than most people in South Bay. Bert, standing near the door, was the first to greet us. He was wearing black slacks and a cream-colored cashmere sportcoat. In spite of his baldness, short stature and relatively advanced years, he seemed to give off a sense of strength and self-confidence, with no hint of alleged loneliness so far as I could tell. But then even my own daughter thought that I'd never known fear.

"Tom, I'm glad you're back," he said, taking my hand in his firm grip. "I can tell you, your whole family has really missed you. I wished somebody cared as much about me when I go away."

I tried to smile, but it felt like a rictus. Maybe looked that way too. "Thanks . . . and thanks for that car deal, Pete's microscope . . ." I hoped my face didn't crack.

"Not at all. The microscope was a present from Doc Pemberton anyway—"

"Excuse me, Bert, I want to go upstairs and see the kids."

My three children met me in the hall at the top, and there was a satisfying group hug. They could not possibly have grown much in the three weeks I had been away, but perhaps I had been remembering them as younger than they were and the first glimpse of them now brought me up to date. Despite whatever mistakes I might have made in my own life, I was decidedly blessed with two fine daughters and a handsome son whose voice had begun to change to a manly baritone. Barbara's delicate beauty had lost the angularity of adolescence—no man, including her father, had a right to treat her as a child anymore. Although she was overweight, Janey's smile and large brown eyes made her beautiful to me in some special, almost heartbreaking way.

"You're all wet, daddy," she said. "You ought to go and change before you catch your death of cold."

She was right. In our bedroom I found Betsy changing her stockings and shoes, which had also got drenched. Since she had taken off her raincoat, I could admire the wine-red party dress she was wearing.

"You've lost weight," I said. "You look . . . great."

"I've been dieting for the play. Whoever heard of a fat Blanche DuBois? Say, you've lost a lot of weight too. Congratulations."

"I've been on a sort of health diet."

"You see, when we get separated we just fade away," she smiled brightly—"but don't lose any more—you're looking a little gaunt."

I nodded. What other response was possible?

For years I'd had a habit of putting things like return airline tickets, my wallet and loose change in a drawer in my bedside table when I came home and changed clothes. As I opened that drawer now I was startled to see a small pearl-handled automatic pistol lying there.

"What's this about?" I asked.

"Oh, I guess it's silly but I got nervous about spending the nights here alone. There was a scare in the papers about people coming out from the city to rob houses in the suburbs. They killed an old couple in Westport—"

"Do you know how to use this thing?" I picked up the weapon and pointed it out the window while I checked it over.

". . . Bert showed me. He lent it to me . . . it's his."

"Do you know it's loaded?"

"Bert said there was no use having a gun unless it was ready to shoot—"

"Have you ever actually shot this thing?"

"No, he just showed me where the safety catch is and how to cock it. I really don't want to fire it, unless I have to."

"I don't think it's a very good idea for you to keep this thing here."

"Why?"

"A whole lot of reasons. Especially with kids in the house, a gun should be kept locked up."

"The kids don't come in here—"

"Some of their friends might when you're away. If you're going to keep this thing I should take you to a range and teach you how to handle a gun."

"Well, Bert says all I have to do is point it at the thief and pull the trigger—"

"Is that what Bert says? Well, sometimes that's not so easy. You can't hit anything with this at a distance of more than about fifteen feet. Even if you hit a guy, this wouldn't stop him unless you hit a vital spot. If you're going to have a gun you should have one that will stop someone from shooting back. This thing isn't much more than a toy."

"Bert says it's a good gun, he collects pistols—"

"There are a few things I know more about than Bert does, and guns are one of them. I don't even want to have this thing in my house. It's useless as a weapon and dangerous to leave around. Tell Bert to put it back in his collection."

"What do you propose I do if I'm lying here alone and hear someone breaking in downstairs—?"

"Call the police—"

"They'd never get here in time. Don't you care about your kids—?"

"I *care*, but you're more liable to get in trouble with that damn gun than—"

"Say it, you don't trust me. You just think I'm a fool. Why not . . . you always have—"

"That isn't true, damn it—"

"It's worse than that. No female should have a gun, right? You think all women are damn fools—"

"I *think* that anyone who hasn't been trained to use a gun shouldn't have a gun. Betsy, it's less than ten minutes since I got home and we're fighting."

"*You* started it."

"Because that stupid little gun scares me—it's a dangerous thing to leave loaded in an unlocked drawer. Dangerous to you and the kids . . ." I took the ammunition clip from the pistol and checked to make sure the chamber was empty. "I want you to give this thing back to Bert, or do you want me to do it?"

"Tonight? He'd be insulted—"

"All right, not tonight. I'll lock the damn thing in my tackle box."

"How can I give it back to him so his feelings won't be hurt?"

"Is he all that touchy? Maybe it'll help if I give him a few facts about guns—"

"How tactful, when he has a huge collection of them."

"Tell him I bought you one of your own. Matter of fact, I'll give you my old service pistol—it's somewhere up in the attic—"

"I can hardly lift that old thing."

"We'll go to a range and I'll show you how to use it."

"You don't really want to, do you?"

"I do if you really want to learn. But it will take a while."

"You'll deliberately make it complicated—"

"Guns are complicated, Betsy. Why are you doing this? I'm just trying to protect—"

"You're trying to make me feel stupid, as usual."

Before I could answer . . . and make things worse . . . she marched to her closet, put on a dry pair of shoes and almost ran toward our bedroom door. Pausing, she said, "At least try to act pleasant when you come downstairs. I don't want all my friends to think we fly at each other's throats the second you get home. Even though we seem to . . ."

I thought I saw tears in her eyes as she quickly turned and went out the door.

10

THE PARTY THAT night was a nightmare. Betsy and I acted out the parts of a happily reunited couple while this undefined anger kept building in us. Bert was much quieter than usual, barely talked or danced. With the image of Betsy's tears still fresh, I began to berate myself . . . maybe Bert *was* a sincere friend of the family who'd just been trying to be helpful while I was away. Betsy and he, thrown together by this play thing, could have developed a genuine affection for each other that was bothering their consciences . . . the way it was with Ann and me . . . Whatever, Bert and I avoided each other that evening and he went home at ten saying he had an early golf date the next morning. Our other friends must have felt the tension in the air, or knew more about what was going on than I did, because the party broke up early, toward eleven.

I drank too much—and have only a fuzzy memory of going to bed with elaborate courtesy, pleading extreme weariness as an excuse for avoiding any lovemaking, a natural way of making up. When I woke up bright sunshine was streaming through the window, I had a headache and Betsy's side of the bed was rumpled, and empty. While I was getting dressed she came in with a cup of coffee for me. She was wearing a cotton housedress, looked briskly efficient but friendly.

"Tom . . . I'm sorry I made such a fuss about that damn gun last night—"

"And I apologize for making such a big thing of it."

"Shall I tell you why I got so upset?"

"Why don't we just let it go—?"

"I think we ought to talk out things like this. I felt you were

_ 82

treating me like a child. You didn't leave it up to me, what to do with the damn gun . . . you just took it and locked it up because you didn't think I was fit to handle it—"

"I know, I was high-handed . . ."

"I really have been scared, spending nights alone here with the kids. There have been a lot of robberies around here . . ."

"Look, I understand your fear, you'd be foolish not to be worried. But please try to understand mine too. A loaded gun in a bedside table usually creates more danger than it prevents. Most thieves are smart enough to break into houses when no one is at home, right?"

"I guess . . ."

"They often look for pistols because they're easy to sell, and the most obvious place to check is in a bedside table. So you've armed your thief. If you happened to come home while he was still in the house, he could shoot you with your own gun. That's happened more than once . . ."

"So where should I keep it?"

"Maybe in my tackle box in the closet, someplace where you can get it quickly but where it's not likely to be easily found."

"Bert doesn't hide his guns, he has a lot of them in a glass case in his study."

"If he's smart he at least hides the ammunition or takes the firing pins out of the display guns."

Bert again . . . still, wasn't there an innocence in her constant references to Bert? If she'd been having or contemplating an affair with him, wouldn't she pretend that she never thought of him? . . . I never mentioned Ann . . . "You know, maybe one difference between Bert and me is that he sees guns as collector's items, and I look at them as things that kill . . . In the army they taught us that there are only four reasons for touching a gun: to clean it, practice with it, carry it or kill somebody with it. You don't pick it up to play with it or to try to scare someone—"

"All *right*, take me out and teach me how to shoot the damn thing."

"I'd like to take the kids too," I said. "If we're going to have a gun around, they ought to have some basic understanding of it."

The children seemed startled by the idea, but Barbara and Pete showed some enthusiasm. Janey said she didn't want to have anything to do with guns but she'd come along to watch. I took them to an abandoned gravel pit that was often used for target shooting

by the local rifle club. I took along Bert's automatic, my old Colt
.45 and a sack of empty beer cans left over from the party.

It was a bright October day with a nip in the air, but the gravel
pit, which had been used as a trash dump and had been flooded
by the previous day's rain, was kind of sinister-looking. Janey, who
occasionally displayed a macabre sense of humor, said it looked
like a good place for bodies to be buried and she wouldn't be
surprised to see fingers sticking up through the dirt. I picked out
a spot with some high sand bluffs as a backdrop and propped a
beer can on a branch of a sapling. Backing off about thirty feet, I
demonstrated the mechanisms of both guns before firing one shot
from Bert's automatic. It made a sharp crack but didn't hit anything or even make a spurt in the sand. After putting Bert's piece
back in the car I held my service Colt in both hands and blasted
away, making the beer can disintegrate into shards of shiny aluminum. I was, of course, showing off one of my few skills. My reception was mixed. Pete and Barbara were impressed, Janey looked
horrified as she stood there with her hands clasped to her ears.
Betsy laughed nervously.

I looked at her.

"Just nerves, I guess, and you looked so sort of fierce . . ."

Without saying anything, I put another beer can on the tree.

"Come and try it," I said, returning to insert a new clip into the
Colt.

"I'd rather shoot the small one. It looks easier to handle."

I brought the automatic from the car.

"Try it. You'll see that nobody can hit anything with it."

After fumbling with the safety catch she pointed waveringly at
the target, squinted and fired with her eyes almost closed. Nothing
happened except the noise, but she kept on pulling the trigger
until the four remaining shots in the only clip Bert had given her
were exhausted.

"Now try the Colt," I said. "Hold it in both hands."

Closing her eyes tightly this time, she blasted away, kicking up
a lot of sand around the tree.

"Seeing I can't hit anything anyway," she said, "I might as well
stick with the little gun—at least it doesn't scare me so much."

"The difference is that you can learn to be accurate with the big
one," I said, trying not to sound as exasperated as I felt.

"I hate the darn thing—let the kids try it."

Pete was businesslike but not very interested after he had hit a beer can. Barbara surprised me by taking pleasure in shooting and quickly learning to do it well. She didn't stop until we had used up all the ammunition.

"It looks, dear, as though you can have a career as a police-woman," Betsy said.

"Why don't you really try to learn, mother?" Barbara said. "Why do you always have to try to make a joke of everything?"

"Please don't be rude, dear," Betsy said. "If I wasn't cut out to be a stormtrooper, can I help it?"

Sometimes Betsy's flip manner got to me, but over the years I came to realize that the light touch she tried to give so many things was a cover-up . . . the thought of burglars at night scared her and shooting guns scared her almost as badly. And on top of it Barbara's easy proficiency showed her up. Who could blame her for trying to make jokes? I took her arm to steer her around a puddle as we returned to the car.

"Thank you, dear," she said. "Now if we can find our way out of this dump, let's go home, lay down our arms and find something more civilized to do. Maybe you'd like to help me rehearse my part for the play. I have Blanche down pretty well, but I still need someone to follow me with the text and tell me when I mix up lines . . ."

I was less than thrilled by the prospect, but went along to the living room, where I sat on the couch while she paced up and down spouting the tortured lines of Tennessee Williams. It's difficult for a person from Boston like Betsy to get a New Orleans accent right, and Betsy was in such good health that it was doubly hard for her to portray the wasted vulnerability of a Blanche DuBois, but I give it to her that she did capture the spirit of the character, and I could see why Bert figured she'd be good for the part. Both ladies were free spirits of a sort, both had an attraction for fantasy . . . trying to make life conform to a dream.

Since I'd met Betsy at the first Boston coming-out party I ever attended I was attracted by her ability to create an illusion and determinedly try to live it. On our first date she never really saw me as a tense, lonely teenage orphan who probably would have fallen in love with the first pretty girl who smiled at him—she took me for a big brain because in her eyes she found me moody, gloomy, romantic. Her own father and mother, who were so sternly puritanical that they never complimented her on her blossoming good looks, seemed to her the perfect parents, even when they told her they couldn't understand what on earth she saw in me as "husband material." As soon as I joined the army after Pearl Harbor she saw me as a stainless steel hero and imagined me fighting the war without a trace of fear or a glance at the native girls wherever I went, a misconception that contributed to her shock when she finally learned about Maria and Mark. After I got out of the army and took my first job with the Schanenhauser Foundation in New York, she just assumed that before long I would become a great success and we would all be as rich as her parents had been before the Depression—wealth to Betsy seemed the only normal way of life, with brief spells of hardship to be bravely endured when things mysteriously and temporarily went wrong. Why save for a rainy day when the sun was always sure to come out before long anyway?

This wasn't exactly my experience, and I must say her kind of optimism had often struck me as a little nutsy—but it was also a kind of courage, it seemed to me now. Her confidence that I would soon become a great business success had allowed her to work with reasonably good cheer at the job of raising three children with little money in a small development house for years before my grandmother left us this Victorian manse. The thought that we weren't saving enough money to send our children to college didn't bother her as much as it did me; she was confident that somehow the good Lord in his wisdom would provide even if, by some wild stretch of the imagination, I might fail her. She was so good at looking on the sunny side of the street that just possibly Bert did appear to her as nothing more than an old and loyal friend who sought out her company during her husband's absence just because he loved children, was lonesome himself and wanted to be helpful. She probably wouldn't see any advances from Bert as the opening gambit in a round of suburban adultery . . . more likely she would picture herself as the heroine of a great romance, of a dramatic triangle in which three essentially nice people could all feel for each other without doing any harm. If there was danger of any real human wreckage it could easily be avoided, the way a fear of burglars breaking into her house could be overcome by the acquisition of a useless gun that she really didn't want to learn how to shoot anyway.

Regardless of my own fantasies about Ann, I did still love Betsy, at least in my fashion. And maybe I'd been too close to her for too long really to *know* her . . . I suspect that happens in more than a few marriages . . . maybe she was nowhere near as wide of the mark on important issues as she seemed to me to be when confronting small ones. In any case, just now my main feeling about her was that she needed to be protected (never mind that maybe *I* was the one who needed a keeper, the way I was carrying on in *my* fantasies). Bert Andrews, who had got her involved in *A Streetcar Named Desire*, also struck me as a kind of aging Connecticut version of Stanley Kowalski, a wrecker of illusions and delicate sensibilities. Polite, effusive as Bert was, he was a tough cookie who so far as I could see had mostly been out to win revenge against the world for his early poverty and probably wasn't finished yet. And winning Betsy could be part of his ongoing campaign to get even and get what he figured was owed him. He'd admired Betsy ever since I'd brought her to my grandmother's home as a radiant bride. Maybe she'd stayed in his mind as some sort of symbol of the unreachable, but now that he was so rich and I was away for long periods she might appear to be very attainable—and even fair game.

Of course I had probably always been jealous of Bert, resented him for getting rich and being independent while I struggled at United Broadcasting, worrying about every damn bill the mailman delivered. I'd figured him for a damn draft dodger, his alleged heart murmur never having kept him away from golf or tennis . . .

That afternoon Bert drove up to our house in his red Mercedes roadster. At least, I thought self-righteously, he could have given me a weekend alone with my family, but he was too full of news about an unexpected disaster . . . the woman who had been preparing to play Stella in *Streetcar* was threatening to drop out of the cast and he wanted Betsy's help. He seemed unusually upset. Perhaps it was absurd of me to suspect that he had got himself so emotionally involved with Betsy that he had to *invent* some excuse to break into our privacy and see her . . . maybe he was as jealous of me as I was of him . . .

Whatever the reason, the three of us were visibly ill at ease together in our living room as Bert described what to me seemed like a nutty situation. Dottie, the woman who had been preparing to play Stella, was married to the local Presbyterian minister, Roger Marshall, and he had recently received intimations that the elders of his church disapproved of their minister's wife playing such an earthy part on the high school stage, where the rehearsals had started. Roger was already in some hot water with the elders

87 —

on account of his liberal political views, and there was some danger that Dottie's emergence as an actress in a Tennessee Williams play would be the last straw. Roger was idealist enough to risk his job for his wife's right to be in the play and was telling her not to quit, but she said she couldn't sacrifice her husband's career to her hobby and was determined to resign.

"I think the whole community is involved here," Bert said. "We're not in the Dark Ages, the church elders can't be allowed to get away with this—"

"Of course they can't," Betsy said, eyes blazing excitedly. "Those people are insulting *all* of us. Just who are these so-called elders of the church anyway?"

Bert said that Wilbur Cartwright, an elderly banker, was the head of the committee that hired and fired ministers at the local Presbyterian church.

"I know old Wilbur," Bert said, "and I think he can be talked to. I think we ought to beard the old devil in his den and ask him outright whether he thinks the church should be opposed to freedom of expression. If he thinks we'll make a public issue of this I bet he'd back down."

"Bert, I totally agree," Betsy said.

"I think we ought to take action right away," Bert said. "The more people take sides on this thing, the harder it will be to solve, and everybody's talking about it."

"What do you want to do?" Betsy asked.

"I think that three of us—you, me and Olivia Cousins—should make up a delegation and call on old Wilbur this afternoon."

"I'll be glad to go," Betsy said. "Don't you think it's a good idea, Tom?"

"Any Presbyterians in the crowd?"

"We're Christian! This isn't a denominational issue, Tom."

"Maybe an old Presbyterian elder wouldn't look at it that way. You just might make things worse for Roger."

Bert's blue eyes gleamed brightly behind his steel-rimmed glasses. "There could be some danger of that if I didn't feel I knew old Wilbur Cartwright so well."

"To know him is to love him?"

"No, but as a banker he's just as much in the real estate business as I am, and he doesn't want to lose my good will, especially now when some new developments are coming up. Olivia Cousins and her whole family do a lot of business with his bank and he doesn't want to lose her either. Of course he couldn't allow business considerations to affect a church decision and no one ever gets anywhere with threats, so Olivia and I will just sit there holding our big sticks while Betsy gives him a good dose of moral indignation. By the time we get through with him he'll say the whole business of Roger Marshall being fired was only a rumor. We'll make that old s.o.b. come see our play and clap."

Betsy seemed impressed. "Bert, thank God you're on the side of the angels."

Whatever side he was on, Bert succeeded in whisking Betsy away for more than an hour that afternoon to visit Wilbur Cartwright.

"It worked just the way Bert said it would," she announced jubilantly when she got home. "One thing about Bert, he gets what he wants."

11

As THOUGH THE tension I felt with Betsy and Bert weren't enough, I managed to get in trouble with both my daughters that weekend. On Sunday morning Gordy Morphet, the tall, thin boy who habitually wore a black cowboy hat, roared into our driveway on a motorcycle and wanted to take Barbara for a ride. This I briskly forbade on the grounds that all motorcycles were dangerous and I of course cited a string of statistics to prove it. Barbara, unconvinced, asked me why I bothered to come home at all, then ran up to her room in tears.

"I'm sure you're right about motorcycles," Betsy said, "but do you have to be so abrupt with her?"

"A long drawn-out no is worse than a short one," I said like the sage of the ages.

My disagreement with Janey hurt me even more because we so rarely had a difference of opinion. She asked me to drive her to a barn owned by some friend of Bert to show me the horse he'd given her a riding lesson on. Of course I couldn't afford horses and had no connection with the horsey set in South Bay, and hardly felt at ease when we drove into a lavish estate. The owner, a tall, well-turned-out man in English riding clothes, was practicing jumps on a chestnut mare in a ring bordered by a split-rail fence near the barn. Janey insisted that we get out of the car to watch, and before long the owner trotted his horse over to us.

"Hello, Janey," he said, "are you and Bert planning to take a ride today?"

"Not today, Mr. Osmond . . . this is my dad . . ."

"Your daughter really seems to like horses," Osmond said. "When she gets a little more practice I'll give her all the riding she wants—I have two Morgans my kids don't use enough and they always need exercise."

"I'll be here every afternoon after school," Janey said happily.

After that we went to the barn and Janey showed me the Morgans, which looked sleek and restless but held still while she fed them handfuls of grass, patted their heads and kissed their noses.

"I think they already know me," she said. "Oh, daddy, I just love horses . . . don't you?"

"They sure are beautiful," I said, but then I made the mistake of going on to give my horse lecture, which my mother and grandmother, both good horsewomen when they were young, had given me when I was a boy on summer vacations in the Adirondacks, where we used to do a lot of riding.

"Horses are beautiful, but if you're going to be around them you have to learn to understand them. No matter what you see in the movies, horses are not very intelligent and not really affectionate, compared to a dog, for example. They're susceptible to panic, and when they're scared they run. A horse is a very big natural force, honey. It takes a lot of strength and skill to control it, and if you don't have those, and know how to use them it can kill you—"

"Oh, *daddy*, you take the fun out of *everything*," she said, not unreasonably. "All you ever see is that everything is dangerous—"

"I'm trying to teach you to be careful—"

"I already am careful, in fact, I'm already so scared of everything I'm almost afraid to leave my room, and you keep making it *worse*."

"I don't mean to do that—"

"Uncle Bert teaches me how to ride but *he* doesn't try to scare me to death."

Bert's name made my mouth tighten, which didn't escape Janey. Janey seemed to understand everything. I think she sensed even before Betsy and I did that the emotional currents running through our family were deeper and more threatening than guns, motorcycles or horses, no matter how much we tried to pretend that everything was just fine.

And pretend Betsy and I did all that weekend. Betsy's talents as an actress seemed to serve her better when she played the part of loving wife than when she played Blanche DuBois. And if part of her role was to prove her love for her difficult husband, to herself as well as to me, when we went to bed on both Saturday and Sunday nights, then I was grateful for it, especially after three weeks of celibacy. I was also angry at myself for feeling that it was all an act. How damned churlish, ungenerous . . . What in hell did we really want from each other anyway? Unqualified admiration without anger? In all honesty we didn't have that to give. We both wanted understanding but didn't read it in each other's eyes. Or perhaps the contrary was true, and we understood each other all too well . . . We both kept hoping that the physical acts of lovemaking would bring us closer together, and when we still felt apart, no matter how close our flesh, we knew that we were somehow cheating each other, ourselves too. No matter how many climaxes we managed, sex left us with a sense of failing, which we tried to cover up with murmured reassurances, apologies and protestations of love.

With Maria it had been different . . . after so many years I shouldn't have been remembering that. Maybe the difference had been in me, not in the two women—maybe the war had somehow blasted away my inhibitions . . . tomorrow we die, and so forth . . . or I'd impressed Maria in a way I never did Betsy, and her uninhibited enthusiasm for me had helped free me from my usual old constraints. Whatever, I'd been very young and hungry for a woman's affection in a way, I suppose, I would never be again . . . it was wrong, unfair, to compare an idealized memory with the actuality of a twenty-year-old marriage. It was probably even less fair, or accurate, to compare what Ann had stirred in me and the fantasy affair I'd built up with her to the reality of a wife's effect after a typical married day of cooking and caring for the kids, taking care of the house, and so forth . . .

MONDAY MORNING I woke up at five, remembering that Ann had said she would meet me at the gate for the eight o'clock shuttle to Washington. I figured she'd spent her weekend with Harry Comstock, which no doubt would make her forget about me, if she ever was going to remember. As for me, I was almost schoolboy-anxious to see her again.

Betsy stayed asleep as I got dressed. The damn problem of the guns still had to be solved, and I found an answer of sorts by putting both pistols in my steel tackle box, locking it and storing it on the top shelf in my closet. I put the key in the drawer of the bedside table—I would have to trust Betsy to handle the situation as best she could after I left.

When I woke her up to ask her to drive me to the train, I showed her where I had put the key and the tackle box.

"That seems sensible," she said sleepily. "Now we have the new car, why can't I drive you right to the airport?"

"That's a lot of trouble, isn't it? You wouldn't get back in time to help the kids get ready for school . . ."

"They're plenty old enough to find their own clothes. I'll wake them up and tell them . . . they'll want to say good-bye to you anyway."

We had a leisurely breakfast together in the kitchen. In their pajamas Pete and Barbara gave me sleepy hugs before going back to bed, but Janey stayed with me till the last moment, sipping coffee and looking quite grown-up in her rumpled blue bathrobe.

"I'm sorry I got mad at you about the horses," she said. "I know they can be dangerous . . . a boy I know was killed on the bridle trail near here last summer when his horse bolted. His foot caught in the stirrup and he got dragged. It's just that sometimes I wish—"

"I know, hon. Sometimes you wish your father would come down from the lecture platform. I'll try, I promise . . . by the way, do you have riding boots?"

"Not yet . . ."

"Please buy her a pair, will you, Betsy? Good ones have fairly high heels that make it harder for them to get caught in a stirrup . . ." All right, all right, I was lecturing again, but damn it, how else to make sure my daughter was protected . . . ? Betsy was so involved with that damn play she needed to have it mentioned, impressed on her . . .

Betsy made a passing comment about the expense of good boots, threw on an old parka over her cotton dress to ward off the October chill and I drove the station wagon on the Merritt Parkway toward LaGuardia. I tried not to remember that good old Bert had been largely responsible for the new Chevy.

"It's a nice car," I said nicely, also trying not to spoil the drive by giving voice to my worry about the payments. I needn't have tried, because Betsy brought it up.

"What kind of shape is the exchequer in?" I asked.

"Not so hot . . . Janey saw Dr. Richter and he thinks she ought to come twice a week. He charges less than a lot of psychiatrists, but that will still come to something like two hundred and forty a month."

"Whew! Well, of course, if he's doing her any good . . ."

"Dr. Richter says it's too early to tell yet."

"We'll just have to economize every which way we can."

"I'm *trying*. I admit I spend more on parties than I should, but after rehearsals our theater group meets at the house of one member or another and I can't very well keep going to other people's houses without doing my share."

"Well, we've got to write out a budget and stick to it. I've said that before—"

"I told you, I'm trying! After all, we do have some unusual expenses . . ."

Obviously she was referring to the monthly check I sent to Mark in Italy. I was being dispatched on what the kids would call a guilt trip.

"Betsy, it's a fact of our lives—"

"So are the bills piling up that you're so worried about . . . This is going to set you off but I'm going to mention it anyway . . . hold on, because it involves Bert—"

"Jesus . . . does he have to get involved even in our personal finances—?"

"He suggests that the cheapest way to get money is to borrow on life insurance. If we do that we can pay back the loan for the car and we wouldn't have to keep collision insurance. It would mean a big saving."

"How much do you want to borrow?"

"Two thousand for the car—the radio and a set of snow tires were extra. Then while we're at it I'd like to borrow another two thousand to see Janey through her treatments and clean up all the back bills."

"Four thousand dollars?"

"The interest rate is very low . . ."

"We should be saving these days, not borrowing. Year after next Barbara will be in college, and the next year Janey . . ."

"You'll be getting a raise pretty soon, won't you?"

"I've got a good chance, but it's not in the bag yet."

"What do you *want* me to do?"

"Borrow if we must to get over this hump, but we better sit down and figure out why we can't get by on twenty thousand a year."

"With four children to support that's not so much—"

"Plenty of people raise more children on a hell of a lot less."

"Not in South Bay, Connecticut, they don't, and not in a big house like ours—"

"Then maybe we should sell the damn house and move to someplace we can afford, maybe somewhere farther out in the country where everything is cheaper. I wouldn't even mind a longer commute if it would keep us solvent—"

"How can you say that? I think I'd die if we left South Bay—"

"Betsy, that's a pretty silly statement—"

"Silly? Yes, you always think I'm silly, don't you? I'm silly about guns and silly about the play and silly about parties, about everything—"

"I've never said that—"

"The hell you haven't. If you think I'm so damn silly about money why don't *you* take over the checkbook and see how you handle the bills?"

"I can't do that very well while I'm in Washington—"

"Have your *assistant* do it. You have one, don't you? How is she working out?"

"Pretty well, but she's not hired to take care of our personal finances. Anyway I don't criticize the way you handle bills *after* they come in, it's the spending that's got us in a hole—"

"I'm not a scrimper and saver. I confess. I do my best, but it's not my nature. If you wanted the big economy model, maybe you married the wrong girl."

You could be right, I almost said, but somehow managed to keep my mouth shut. Actually, I suppose the ensuing silence said it all for me, spoke volumes, as it were . . . The tires hummed on the highway at an increasing pitch, and I forced myself to slow down.

"Tom . . . we're really not very happy anymore, are we?" she said suddenly. "And it's more than the money, isn't it?"

"What? Well . . . right now my main worry is money, petty though that may seem—"

"But you're not happy at home . . . don't you think I can tell that?"

"Maybe you better speak for yourself," I heard myself say with some amazement.

"Do you want to know the truth?"

"I'm not sure," I said honestly.

"Well, Tom Rath, I'm *tired* of your moods. You make every little thing into such a big damn *problem*. I get a little gun because I'm afraid of burglars, but you can't let it go at that—you have to make me feel like an idiot if I don't want to learn how to fight World War Three. Barbara wants to ride around the block on her boyfriend's motorcycle, and you can't think of anything except terrible accidents. Janey gets into horses, you scare her to death about them —as though she weren't already scared enough about too many things. We get behind in our bills, you make me out a spendthrift."

"Wait a minute . . . I may overdo it, I admit, but I'm *trying* to protect my family . . . that's my responsibility and—"

"There's not much joy in you, Tommy—too much worry. You don't seem to have much confidence in anyone or anything, maybe including yourself."

"There's some truth in that . . ."

"All right, you had a rough childhood, fought a tough war, but you can't just go on forever expecting the *worst* to happen. It's bad for you and it's bad for all of us . . ."

"Maybe you're exaggerating just a little? I do have some high hopes about my job—"

"Are you happier in Washington than you are with us?"

"I miss you and the kids . . ."

"We miss you too, but when you come home why does everything have to be so . . . so awful? Is it Bert? You seem to bristle every time you see him."

"Do you have any idea how often you mention his name?"

"Tommy, I'm not in love with Bert. I'm not sleeping with him. Only you could imagine that I was."

"I believe you, but he seems to have been playing an awfully big part in your life, in my life . . ."

"I like him. Is there anything wrong with that? He's cheerful, is good at solving annoying problems, isn't a worrier—"

"Just the opposite of me . . ."

"In some ways, yes. He likes me, Tommy, even respects me—"

"And I don't?"

"You always thought I was kind of shallow upstairs . . . after all, I never went to college, never saw a war, never had a job—"

"Those things don't have anything to do with intelligence."

"Stop hedging. You also think I've lost my looks."

"I never thought that. Don't I keep telling you—"

"Oh, you're very good with compliments, but I honestly don't think you've ever forgiven me for getting to be more than forty."

"That's crazy . . ."

"I agree, but it's the way most men are, isn't it? You keep remembering the way I was before I put on weight, before my tits began to head for the ground—"

"Do we have to talk like this?"

"Why not? I'm trying to face the truth, like you say I should do and never want to."

"A truth is that we're both getting older."

"But middle-aged men still like younger women. I accept that as natural. But one thing about Bert, he thinks I'm young and I am compared to him."

Something jolted in me. I not only thought it, this time I said it. "Betsy, do you want Bert?"

"I *told* you, I'm not in love with him, and I doubt if he'll ever want to get married again. But he does admire me, maybe even loves me a little, in a nonserious way. Can't you see how I might need that?"

"Just how nonserious?" I said, avoiding her question.

"Nothing for you to worry about. It's funny that you're still so jealous—that seems to be the only part of your love for me that you still hang on to—"

"You're painting me as quite a monster. Do you think that picture of me is one hundred percent true?"

"It's not too far off, and I think that if you weren't afraid to admit it, the picture you'd paint of me wouldn't be much prettier . . ."

We were getting into serious waters, and I think we both knew it, but it was like some invisible hand was pushing us toward the edge. Funny, but I felt an almost icy calm as I said now, "If you really believe that, what do you think we should do about it?"

"There aren't many alternatives, are there?"

"No."

"We can try to live with these pictures we've painted of each other, we can both try to change, or . . . or we can get a divorce."

There it was . . . it was actually *said.* God knew, we'd had our arguments, but that was the first time either of us had ever used that word.

"I'd say that about covers it."

Silence for a while, then . . . "Right now we're driving each other crazy and I doubt we can change . . . I don't know, maybe this year you've got in Washington is a blessing . . ."

"Maybe."

"I'm not *scared* of divorce, if it comes to that. Are you?"

"Yes." And I was.

She almost seemed to be talking to herself now . . . "I don't think it would bother Peter and Barbara too much, and Janey might be better off if she got away from all the tension . . ."

"Has it really been that bad?"

She was silent a moment . . . "Haven't you *felt* it?"

"A few weeks ago we were happily married, now I come home to find you wanting a divorce—"

"Tommy, the trouble between us has been building a long time, you must realize that. Your going away just put things into perspective."

"Is that what we've got things in now?"

"I didn't say I *wanted* a divorce—I said it was one alternative . . . we've got time, almost a year, to think it over—"

"I can't believe this . . ."

"You mean you've never thought about it?"

"I *mean*, you're so matter-of-fact, cold-blooded about it."

"Would you like it better if I screamed?"

"I don't know. To tell the truth, I feel like screaming."

"Try it if you want."

"God damn it . . ."

"Tom, I think we've both been lonely for a long time—lonely when we're apart and somehow even lonelier when we're together."

"Maybe we expect too much . . . the Constitution talks about the pursuit of happiness, not catching it."

"Tommy, that's a smart phrase, but it doesn't help . . . I'm not old enough to settle for what we've got. Are you?"

"I'm also not for throwing out the baby with the bath water . . . Sorry . . . there I go making smart phrases again . . ."

A long silence then, during which I realized that if I'd thought her criticisms of me were completely undeserved they would have been much easier to take, but I had, in spirit if not in the flesh, been a runaway husband for a long time and I shouldn't really be surprised to find that my wife had gotten lonely and restless in my absence . . . Still, damn it, this wasn't entirely my fault. If I had retreated from Betsy, I'd had some realistic grounds too . . . she'd been more involved with parties, with Bert and her play and—oh, to hell with it . . . Here we were, driving a nice new car on a bright October morning through the flaming foliage of Connecticut and Westchester County, a man and wife with more blessings than ever came the way of most people, and what were we doing? Building cases against each other.

The same thought, more or less, must have occurred to both of us, because as we neared the airport Betsy said, ". . . Tom, I'm sorry, I didn't want to make such a big thing of—"

"I know, and me too."

"We've been married a long time, you'd think we'd know how to handle these things . . ." She smiled brightly, a little too brightly maybe, the way people do when they're using the smile to cover what's beneath, and I smiled back.

When we got to the airport, it was only about seven-thirty and she offered to come in and have a cup of coffee with me while I waited for my shuttle flight. Remembering that Ann was to meet me at eight, I said that by the time we found a parking space and walked to the terminal the passengers would be boarding the plane. The fact was, I didn't want to introduce her to Ann at that moment. I wanted to keep reality and fantasy . . . although I wasn't really sure which deserved which description . . . my marriage or my notions about Ann . . .

We kissed, both stretched out and on the edge of tears. I said I had to hurry to buy my ticket, although I'd already bought a round trip one. I turned to give her a wave as I walked away from the car. She returned it, then headed for home, starting off much too fast, as she always did when she was upset. My last thought before she disappeared was of her getting into an accident, a thought that froze my stomach. Why in hell couldn't she even learn to drive a car right?

12

THERE WAS STILL time for a cup of coffee. As I sat down at a counter in the terminal I saw Ann step through a door about a hundred feet away and come toward me. She was wearing a dress of tan camel's hair with a bright scarf of orange silk tucked around the neck, and altogether she looked more like a chic model than an administrative assistant. She had that distinctive dancer's walk, light on her feet and graceful. Behind her was Harry Comstock, carrying an apparently new blue suitcase. Mr. Comstock's face registered obvious displeasure when he saw me.

"I'm glad you're early too," Ann said. "I hate running for planes."

"Come on, we've got to check your bag through," Comstock said.

"I thought you wanted a cup of coffee," she said to him.

"There isn't time." He put his hand on her arm and hustled her off.

I tried not to stare after them but when I glanced in their direction a moment later I saw them standing close together in what seemed a heated conversation, which didn't exactly upset me. Ann seemed to be trying to calm him down. They moved slowly toward the ticket counter, and after he'd put her suitcase on the scales and handed her the receipt, he put his hand on her arm again and led her toward the gate, before suddenly stopping and taking her in his arms. She seemed to accept this passively before stepping back, and they began talking again—arguing? When a loudspeaker announced that passengers could board the shuttle plane he grabbed her again, gave her a kiss and turned away, swinging his long arms and looking angry.

"Harry," she called after him. He didn't pause or look back before disappearing into the crowd.

I didn't want to rush up to her at that moment, but she waited for me at the gate as the passengers filed in ahead of us and I couldn't delay long.

"I'm sorry about that little display," she said. "Harry can be a bit of a problem."

I said nothing as we joined the line going into the plane. This time we got seats together.

"I'll be glad to get back to Washington," she said as she adjusted the seat belt to fit her slender waist. "For me, anyway, it's a lot more peaceful than home."

"For me too," I said, and our eyes met briefly, then we both looked away. Suddenly I felt fine as I buckled myself in beside her. One thing I knew for sure about Ann and myself . . . we *liked* each other and made each other feel good—a feat no doubt easier for friends than for married people or lovers.

I confess I hoped she would tell me more about Harry, especially if she was as exasperated with him as she appeared to be. After our plane taxied to the runway and took off, the engines were roaring too loud for conversation, and after they steadied down, she sat looking out the window at the city below.

"New York is so damn beautiful when you can get far enough above it," she said. "Even Brooklyn looks great down there."

"Especially the bridges," I said, leaning forward to look over her shoulder.

"If you're born in Brooklyn, those are pretty hard bridges to cross," she said. "You know what I mean?"

"I think so."

"I was twenty-five before I could afford my first apartment in Manhattan. Boy, I thought I'd really made it, but Brooklyn can pull you back."

"I guess any birthplace can . . ."

"Harry is mad at me," she said, sitting back. "God, I hate having people mad at me. I've known him since high school . . ."

"Why is he mad?"

"Because I'm going back to Washington. Because I left Brooklyn in the first place. Because he thinks I'm a snob and worse who doesn't care about anything except money—at least that's what he said."

"I'd guess he has more on his mind than that."

101 _

"Sure, he's mad because I won't marry him. He says I'm ruining his life. Do you think a woman can really do that?"

"Not by *not* marrying a man," I said with what I imagined was some telling wit.

"The first time he asked me to marry him we were both nineteen. When I turned him down he ran off and joined the army."

"Girls who say no are a great help to their country. They get more men to join up than the recruiting sergeants."

"That's no joke. Now Harry says he's going back to the army."

"I'm sure they'll be glad to have him."

"But I love Harry—I mean I'm still very fond of him. I don't want to see him do a thing like that. Can't a woman be fond of a man without being in love with him and wanting to marry him?"

"I don't see why not." My, I was being so wonderfully sage and understanding . . . as long as the drift was in the direction that pleased me . . .

"Of course that's not what Harry wants. He wants to *own* me. I don't want to be owned."

"Most people don't."

"But isn't that what marriage means to most people, owning each other?"

"That's a sort of complicated question—"

"Tell me about it."

Watch it, I tried to tell myself . . . "Well, maybe some people want to own without being owned . . ."

"I wouldn't want to own anybody."

"I guess it all depends on what one means by 'own.'"

"How do you mean it?"

"Right now I couldn't really say . . ."

She looked at me. "Did you have a bad weekend too?"

"I haven't thought about going back into the army, but come to think of it, it's not a bad idea. Maybe Harry and I can go marching off together."

"I'm sorry," she said, briefly touching my arm. "I knew as soon as I saw your face that you were having a bad time."

"Am I that transparent?"

"You just looked sort of gloomy."

"Please don't say *that.*"

"Why?"

"One of the clearly justified complaints that my wife has is that I act so damn gloomy too much of the time."

— 102

"You haven't been that way in Washington."

Betsy and Ann were, it struck me, seeing two entirely different people. Of course Betsy knew me much better than Ann did . . . but maybe I was like a chameleon, changing according to the woman I was with. What was the other name for a chameleon? Lizard. From which one might graduate to rat . . . Despite *that* gloomy thought I could say to her now with candor, "You keep making me feel cheerful, a peculiar state for me. I hope I can handle it."

"I'm glad I'm of use to someone, all I've done for Harry lately is make him mad."

"If you're leaving him, I can't exactly blame him."

She shrugged. "No question . . . love affairs are a lot easier to get into than out of. I suppose marriages are even worse . . ."

Her hand was resting on her knee next to mine. It was a small, graceful hand, fingers tapered like the rest of her—everything about Ann appeared to be finely designed. It was a pleasing hand, with clear-lacquered fingernails cut short enough for typing, and no rings. On an impulse I put mine over it. She glanced at me, perhaps surprised, but did not move it. After a minute she turned her hand over and clasped mine. We said nothing.

Soon the stewardess came to offer coffee. As Ann reached out to accept a cardboard cup, the soft tan material of her dress tightened across her small, well-shaped breasts. I looked away. When Ann smiled at me over the rim of her coffee cup after her first sip, her eyes were warm. No gloom and doom permitted. Like me, Ann had in her way fought for survival and no one had to tell her about trouble. Young as she was, she was clearly a woman who knew how to handle herself. It probably was my problem to imagine that she would be hurt or disappointed if I made a pass at her. If she didn't want me, she'd tell me so, and if she did, she would know how much—and how little—we could give each other.

After she finished her coffee, we went right on holding hands. I had never heard hand-holding described as an erotic art, nor as a significant means of communication, but the varying pressure of fingers, quiet smiles, said a great deal. Our hands, as it were, approved of each other, took pleasure in the sense of touch, and union; they seemed to be making love, all on their own. It was perhaps fortunate that we were sitting in a crowded, noisy plane, which made intimate conversation or further touching impossible.

That flight seemed brief. The sense of excitement we'd built lasted as we hurried into the Washington airport and stood in line to get her baggage, our hands still reaching for each other. As we drove toward our office in a taxi I almost kissed her, but we had a talkative driver who insisted on giving us the latest news about the Washington Redskins, leaving no moment of privacy.

THE BUSTLE OF our office on Monday morning hardly lessened our preoccupation with each other. We both felt energized and threw ourselves into our work. After going through piles of mail, I telephoned Dr. Harbringer, who had just returned from England, and arranged for Ann and me to fly to Windsor, Ohio that afternoon. We would see him the next morning.

"I'm awfully busy, but I'll certainly make time to do anything I can to help President Kennedy and Mr. Hopkins to set up this conference," Dr. Harbringer said in his deep voice. "It could be a very exciting project, and God knows, it's needed right now."

In the kingdom of Ralph Hopkins, every fund-raising dinner was "a very exciting project," but Harbringer sounded as though he really did attach importance to our plans, and why not? It's not every day that a president of the United States and a president of a great broadcasting company combine forces to devise a national program for better mental health. Somehow the excitement of working with them on such an enterprise got mixed up with the elation that Ann was making me feel, and the world suddenly seemed full of fantastic opportunities. I don't think I ever felt more self-confident.

My ebullience continued to grow that afternoon when Ann and I boarded the plane for Cleveland, where we were to rent a car for the thirty-mile drive to Windsor. As it sometimes did unpredictably, the transportation department of United Broadcasting reserved first-class tickets for us, and we found ourselves almost alone in a luxurious compartment at the front of the plane. As soon as we sat down, our hands locked. After takeoff the stewardess busied herself with preparations for serving drinks, and the stout businessman who was our only fellow passenger sat five seats behind us with his face buried in a newspaper. As the plane's engines steadied at high altitude, the silence between us became tense. A man and a woman cannot, after all, sit holding hands forever without saying something—doing something. I leaned forward and kissed her gently on the lips. A mild approximation of what I felt like doing. We both sat frozen with our arms at awkward angles. I was surprised when she pulled back and said, "Damn it, I didn't want this to happen . . ."

"I'd be lying if I said that."

"I'm lying too, but I shouldn't be. I'm mixed up, Tom . . ."

We were both quiet for what seemed like a long while. Our hands remained locked, as though reassuring each other while all the reasons why we should stay apart marched through my mind and, I suspect, Ann's too. We seemed to be several people at the same time. With the hand-holding and the one restrained kiss, we were like teenage lovers (old style), but a more objective observer might have thought me just another middle-aged man in a gray flannel suit busily engaged in trying to start an affair with his assistant on a business trip. At least I didn't *feel* that way. Still, if I wasn't careful I'd start thinking of myself as the villain of a soap opera about marital infidelity, complete with scenes in which Betsy would slit her wrists when she found out the terrible truth, all my children would become juvenile delinquents and Ann would leave me for a younger man after laughing at my grand if unreal passions. Quite a parade of stereotypes, but each seemed to contain some aspect of truth. I was saved from further thoughts by the caress of her fingers on the back of my hand. Regardless of the rights and wrongs of the situation, I wanted her with an intensity that left little room for argument, and cared little for consequences. At least an honest desire swept away sentimentality and fear. I was going to start an affair with Ann if I possibly could, no matter what, or where it might lead. We'd reached that plateau, and it was a relief to face it. At least it was for me. What about her? I wanted to talk it out with her, but feared that she would think me ridiculous, that I would sound ridiculous. I told myself that if she wanted out from what was happening she could firmly put my hand down, pat it, and that would be the end of that. She didn't do it. Our hands seemed incapable of separating. The idea that the decision to continue this closeness or not was only fifty percent mine struck me almost as a revelation. The caress of her fingertips seemed an invitation, an acceptance of mine, or both.

We were sitting with our heads bowed. When I glanced at her, I saw that her face was quiet, her eyes closed—her hand, though, told me that she was far from asleep. I closed my eyes too now. Whatever questions had to be answered could wait while we enjoyed these minutes of what I can honestly call a sort of silent communion.

It was broken by the stewardess, who asked us what we wanted to drink. Ann ordered mineral water and lime and took her hand from mine to accept the glass. I wanted a martini, but knew that would call for a second, and this was obviously a bad time to get into the booze. A long night stretched ahead at the inn in Windsor, I'd better behave myself. I ordered mineral water too.

We sipped our drinks slowly and put the plastic glasses in the pockets in the backs of the seats ahead of us. Her hand was cold from the ice when I took it again in mine. Feeling awkward as a kid on his first movie date, I put my arm over the back of her seat and let it settle on her shoulders. She leaned toward me, appeared to rest comfortably with her cheek against my lapel. We closed our eyes again, but my senses had never been more wide-awake. There was the scent of her, faint but musky, a fragrance more subtle than any perfume. Under the wool of her camel's hair jacket, her shoulder felt warm in the palm of my hand. Her breathing sounded soft but irregular in my ear, quickening its rhythm as I squeezed her shoulder slightly. Opening my eyes, I glanced out the window of the plane and saw clouds on the horizon that had been turned by the setting sun into banks of fire. A single star glowed brightly.

"Look."

She turned and peered out the window.

"I keep forgetting how beautiful the world can be sometimes," she said, and came back to me with a sigh, letting her hand rest on my knee, squeezing it as I had squeezed her shoulder. We were already lovers—there was no more point in brooding over decisions to be made. In my life I had made fewer important decisions than I had liked to imagine . . . things tended to happen, and I sank or swam the best I could. There certainly hadn't been many moments like this. I too had kept forgetting how beautiful the world could be sometimes. This reminder . . . more a reawakening really . . . seemed worth any price.

13

It was a little after eight in the evening when we arrived in Cleveland and rented a Mercury for the drive to Windsor. Ann was a woman of small enthusiasms as well as big ones—she admired the luxuries of the sedan and said how nice it was to take even temporary possession of an automobile that looked brand-new. She even admired my driving skills as I threaded through traffic, following directions given by the man who had handed us the keys to the car. Such praise was still a novelty to me. Betsy and even my daughters were vocal backseat drivers, often entreating, or ordering, me to slow down, speed up, accelerate less jerkily. My mother and grandmother had also been rough on the driver. Actually I'd never had an accident, which was sort of a miracle, considering. Anyone who's had my time with backseat drivers can appreciate what a heady experience it was to have a woman actually praising the way I drove.

When we got to the turnpike to Windsor we sped along on the edge of the speed limit in companionable silence. It was a bright October evening with a hint of November chill in the air. The concrete road stretched ahead over the hills "like a ribbon of moonlight"—I remembered the quote from "The Highwayman," which was one of my favorite childhood poems. As we neared Windsor I felt the tension between us begin to develop. After the sense of closeness in the airplane it would be impossible to accompany her to her hotel room, as I had in Washington, and say a platonic goodnight. Like a honeymoon couple approaching their wedding night, we had created an inevitable finale, no matter what the mood of the moment might turn out to be. A few days ago this would have scared me, filling my head with forebodings of failure followed by embarrassment. But now when Ann let her hand drop to my thigh, all doubts retreated like shadows in the noonday sun.

Windsor turned out to be much like a New England college town, with the brick buildings of the Harbringer Clinic taking the place of a college. The Windsor Inn was surprisingly luxurious, with a heated swimming pool that glowed jade under a glass structure in the east wing. As we stepped from the car, we found the windy night fragrant with the smoke of autumn leaves, the ashes still smoldering in wire trash baskets by the curb, an aroma that took me back to the days of my youth in Connecticut.

The inn offered old-fashioned service. An elderly bellman in a plum-colored uniform met us at the front door and after taking our suitcases led us to the reception desk; the floor was so thickly carpeted that we walked in eerie silence. No one was in sight except the bellman and a clerk behind the desk who looked like a college boy and smiled at Ann with frank admiration. He had reservations for us, separate but adjoining rooms on the third floor. In the slow-moving elevator, Ann kept staring at her feet, her face tense. Maybe I'd assumed too much, and she was now looking to a difficult moment when she would have to turn me down without hurting my feelings too much. The bellman opened the door to her room first, a fairly large one furnished with fake early American antiques except for a king-sized bed beside a wall almost covered by a plate-glass mirror. That mirror I could have done without— and its unsparing reflection of myself in a wrinkled, travel-worn suit, hair windblown, face speckled by a stubble of beard turning gray.

"There's a connecting door," the bellman said, nodding toward it. "Do you want me to unlock it?"

"No, thank you," I said, still anxious that I was taking too much for granted . . . was I imagining it or did Ann look grateful . . . ?

"The dining room closed at eight, but room service can still bring you a sandwich and the bar's open downstairs," the bellman said.

"Nothing for me now," Ann said.

The bellman showed me to my room next door, which was identical to hers, and put my suitcase on a rack. After I'd given him two dollars, he gave an elaborate explanation of the heating, and air-conditioning system, *finally* walked back to the elevator, shutting my door behind him.

The room seemed to ring with silence. I wondered whether Ann was also standing in her own room, looking at herself in the mirror beside her enormous bed and wondering what to do next . . .

Instead of knocking at her door, I telephoned her. A total coward to the end.

"Tom," she said, sounding surprised and oddly faint. "This connection isn't very good—you sound as though this was a long-distance call."

"I'm about twenty feet away. I thought maybe we both need a few minutes to wash up. Then would you like to go downstairs and try that bar?"

"Sure, if you want, but I'd rather take a swim if they rent bathing suits. Are you too knocked out by the flight for that?"

"No . . . good idea," I said, although swimming was the last thing on my mind. The question of whether we were going to spend the night together had to be answered pretty damn soon. I figured I could manage a turn-down, somehow, but the not knowing was torture.

"I'll call and ask if they have any bathing suits," she said. "I'll get right back to you."

While I waited for her I hurriedly took my shaving kit from my suitcase and stripped to the waist, but before I could lather my face the telephone rang.

"They do have a few suits for guests," she said. "Do you want to go down and pick something out?"

"Give me two minutes."

It took me just about that to rid myself of the offending gray stubble and put on a fresh shirt. I hurried to her door, knocked.

"You look great," she said.

I tried to kiss her, but she pulled away.

"Not now," she said. "I feel all crazy inside. I need a good dunking to clear my head. Let's go . . ."

The desk clerk showed us to a closet where a variety of bathing suits hung on pegs. I found a pair of black trunks with a thirty-eight inch waist, but the only thing in Ann's small size was a white bikini with pictures of Donald Duck all over it—a natural for a teenager. With these in hand we followed the clerk to separate dressing and shower rooms near the pool.

"Bet I beat you into the water," Ann said as she went in to change.

I showered and changed quickly but when I walked out to the pool she was all ready, standing on the end of the highest springboard about twenty feet above the water. In a diver's pose with arms outstretched her slender figure was silhouetted against a floodlight overhead. When she saw me she jumped up, her feet coming down on the end of the springboard with a sharp crack, and sailed into the air, her arms spread in a good swan dive, her legs straight and toes together. For a moment she seemed to hang there at the peak of her arc, then plummeted and sliced cleanly into the water, hardly making a splash. I waited, expecting her head to bob up, but the jade surface remained glasslike. Worried, I started to run toward the edge to dive after her, then heard her laugh at the other end of the pool, where she had swum underwater.

"That was quite a dive," I said.

"Madison High's best about a hundred years ago . . . are you a good swimmer?"

"Fair."

"Race you the length of the pool."

She climbed out of the water, her white skin with its sprinkling of freckles at the neck and shoulders glistening. Her muscular thighs were slender as a boy's, her stomach board-flat, but her breasts were too full for that ridiculous bathing suit.

"What's the prize?" I asked.

"For me, the honor of Madison High . . . we take on all comers."

She got in position for a racing dive and I stood beside her.

"When I say *bang* that's the starting gun," she said. *"Bang."*

We launched ourselves. In college swimming had been my best sport, and a tall man should have an advantage over a short woman in the water, but I still had to do my best to keep ahead of her for the length of the pool, and before finishing got winded and quit, hanging on to the edge and panting.

"Are you all right?" she asked, turning over on her back to float.

"Hell no . . ."

"We've got to get you in shape. You have a fine big body, it's a sin to let it go . . ."

The compliment shook me almost as much as the last part of that sentence hurt.

"If you work out with me every morning before breakfast, you'll tighten up those muscles and get your wind back."

"I'll try—"

"You've got great shoulders. When you get about fifteen more pounds off I won't be able to keep my hands off you."

"I'll starve myself."

She laughed and swam away, doing a comic breaststroke, during which she appeared to be picking things out of the water and tossing them away.

"Did you ever see the East River crawl?"

"Did you ever really swim there?"

"Plenty of times. I beat all the boys across."

"It's a wonder the current didn't get you."

"You have to catch it at the change of tides—for about ten minutes the river is quiet as a pond."

She was a survivor, all right. After I got my wind back I swam over to the edge of the pool, climbed out and found that my shoulders already ached.

"Are you quitting?"

"I've had enough for tonight."

"One more dive and I'll come with you."

I watched as she climbed up the ladder to the springboard. She seemed to take the same sort of pleasure in motion that I'd noticed in my kids, working off excess energy instead of trying or needing to conserve strength. This time she executed a skillful jackknife. She was, I realized rather proudly, showing off for me. When she bobbed up at the far end of the pool I told her the truth . . . that she was one hell of a diver.

"Do you think I could make the Harvard team?" she asked as she climbed out of the water, her breasts nearly coming out of the skimpy top.

"They'd be lucky to have you."

"Can I help it if this Donald Duck thing is too small?"

"I'm not exactly complaining."

"I do feel silly in this thing . . . let's just wrap up in towels and carry our clothes to our rooms."

Her face was tense once again as we rode up in the elevator. At her door she felt in the pocket of her dress for her room key. Fumbling a moment at the lock, she opened the door and preceded me in, snapping on the lights.

"You can come in if you want," she said, her voice sounding suddenly flat. Or was it shy?

"You talked me into it," I said, trying to keep my tone light, but realizing my voice sounded strained. Nobody laughed.

She dropped her armful of clothes on an armchair. I put mine beside hers. My shoes slid to the floor, landing silently on the thick rug, which felt grainy under my bare feet. Tossing her towels in

111 _

the open bathroom door, she turned toward me, and suddenly there were no more decisions to make. Our embrace was silent and long. I fumbled with the button on the strap of her bikini which cut across her back, but the thing was so tight that I couldn't loosen it. Turning from me, she quickly pulled the top off and stepped out of the trunks, tossing them into the bathroom behind her. As she came toward me, she looked so splendid that for a moment I just stood there taking her in. There is no way to describe a woman like that, so much youth, grace, exuberant health, everything blossoming.

"I don't deserve you," I said, and meant it.

"You really think that, don't you?" she said, touching my face, running her fingertips over it.

I nodded, began to pull her toward me.

"Did it ever occur to you that I feel the same way about you?"

Comic relief, or intrusion, came rushing in as I tried to take my trunks off, got them caught around my ankles and damn near fell while I was standing on one foot trying to extricate myself. We both laughed, and then we moved toward each other, and I heard the sudden intake of her breath as our bodies met . . .

THERE IS OF course no way to describe what happened afterward except in physical terms, which do not get to the heart of the matter at all. All I can say is that I was not scared anymore, and all my old fears proved groundless. She seemed to have lent me her youth. Or brought my own back. For a while, anyway.

14

AFTERWARD WE BOTH fell into a profound sleep. I opened my eyes at three in the morning, feeling rested and as eager to explore as though I were waking up in a foreign land. My mind was racing. I needed to understand why this night with Ann had been so incredible . . . no matter how much I thought about it, sex and love still seemed to be essentially mysterious. Even the words were inadequate—"sex" sounding too cold, "love" too sentimental, much too soft for fierce passion, and even "passion" sounded too purple to be true. It seemed that no good words had been invented to describe the parts of the body that give the most delight. The clinical terms sounded as cold as an operating table, and the street slang was a desecration. Was there any other human experience which went so far beyond the limits of language?

For a long while I lay there trying to remember love poems or passages from novels that broke this barrier, but I couldn't think of any that came close. Descriptions of physical love always turned out to be so poetic that they evaded the act entirely, or they turned grotesque, disgusting, if they weren't saved by bawdy humor. Bodies, at their best, are instruments of communication, capable of transmitting the most complex mix of emotions, from basic lust to the most dizzying flights of the spirit . . . all right, but what had Ann and I been saying to each other that was so special?

She loved me, and I loved her—that seemed both simple and terribly, wonderfully complicated. Whatever it was she wanted in a man, at least she had the illusion of seeing it in me—and my apparent ability to please her so much I found as electrifying as it was a surprise. Betsy had found me lacking in many ways, even when we were young, and Maria had needed food and kindness more than love, but Ann seemed to crave what I was . . . And unless I wasn't hearing or feeling her right, she seemed surprised to find that I wanted her so much. We seemed to cure each other of an excess of humility that somehow had shadowed us both since earliest youth. In bed we celebrated and thanked each other. That was the message our bodies had to communicate, and they did not have to strain at all to make it clear . . .

I went back to a dreamless sleep and awoke at six-thirty, ironically the time for me to run to catch my commuting train, but our appointment with Dr. Harbringer wasn't until ten. I experienced a delicious sense of being at leisure. Beside me in the big bed, Ann was still asleep, one arm thrown across her face to shield her eyes from the sun which now shone through the window. The hotel in this small town was blessedly quiet, like an empty cathedral. For a long while I lay savoring this peace . . .

"Tom?" Ann said suddenly.

"Good morning."

"Thanks for not going back to your own room."

"Why would I do *that*?"

"I don't know. Anyway, it's nice to wake up and find you here."

She sat up and stretched, the sheet and blankets slipping to her waist, her body looking tawny in the blaze of sun. When I rolled over to kiss her, our bodies came together as though magnetized.

"Oh, a little morning fuck is very nice," she said.

"Yes."

"I'm sorry I said that."

"Why?"

"I don't know. Do you still think you love me?"

"Of course."

"Why?"

"As a matter of fact, I lay awake half the night thinking about that."

"It must be very hard to explain to yourself."

"Hardly. Deep thinker that I am, I figured out that we love each other because we love each other. I also admit that body of yours doesn't hurt."

"You don't know my weak points yet."

"Such as?"

"I'm not like you—for example, I never read anything—"

"How about all that stuff you keep quoting from encyclopedias?"

"That's about as far as I go. I can type, take shorthand and even spell okay, but I read *slow*—it takes me weeks to get through a book. At school they said I had a mild form of dyslexia."

"Nelson Rockefeller has that and he does all right."

"He can afford it. Dyslexia is a real disease. I never can get past the headlines in the newspapers. I don't *know* anything."

"I'd say somewhere you picked up a good deal of knowledge . . ."

"Mostly superficial. Maybe if you got me started . . . well, you'll find I don't know a damn thing—"

"Nobody who thinks she doesn't know anything is superficial. It's the superficial types who think they know it all."

"So a confession of ignorance is proof of knowledge? You're nice."

"And you talk too much," I said, and I kissed her.

"You fuck very good," she said. "Somehow I didn't expect that of a Harvard man . . . oh, God, I'm sorry, I don't know why I have to keep trying to sound so tough, when it's not how I feel . . ."

"You're still afraid of being serious, I guess. Can you really imagine that I could take you lightly?"

"Yes, no, please don't try to think ahead, and don't make me."

"At some point . . . well, we have to make plans—"

"What plans?" She jumped out of bed and wrapped the top sheet around herself like a toga. "Don't you think I know what's going to happen?"

"What?"

"You're a very responsible married man from Connecticut, and that's the worst kind. Husbands from Connecticut always go back to Connecticut. It's like they couldn't breathe anywhere else."

"We're going to work this out—"

"How? If you left your kids you'd be miserable. And I'm not in the business of being a homewrecker. At least that's one thing I've never done."

"My home wasn't exactly paradise before I met you."

"That's what they all say, before they go back to Connecticut."

"Come on, Ann . . . I'm trying to be serious . . . If this White House conference is a success I may be able to make enough money to get a divorce and support two households—"

"You don't have to support me."

"Good."

"Except I want to have a child. And of course another child is just what you've been hoping for . . ."

"With enough money—"

"It's not just *money.* I can live on almost nothing, but of course you can't. This whole thing is impossible anyway . . ."

"Nothing's impossible."

"Have you tried blowing in your own ear? Tom, I have no right to ask you to get a divorce anyway, or even to talk about having a child."

"Why not?"

"Because my history says I never stay with any man long. Ask Harry about that—I nearly drove him crazy. Every spring I fall in love with somebody new—"

"How come I happened in October?"

"Stop joking. I really am awful . . . I'm trying to warn you . . . let's just take it as it comes."

"Okay."

"I'm trying to be honest with you, Tom, and with myself."

"I understand that."

"Anyway, we have almost a year together before you have to go back to Connecticut, that is, if I don't get spring fever again."

"I'm going to do my best to cure you forever."

"Don't make any promises, people always break promises—"

"In that case I promise to leave you—"

"All right, promise me that and I'll promise you the same. We'll take reverse vows. That way we won't get our hopes all up, and if we break our promises, we won't be hurt."

Before I could think of a reasonable reply to *that,* she spread her sheet on the floor. "Come on, it's time for my exercising. If I quit that, it wouldn't be long before you'd stop thinking I was so damn *intelligent.* "

Lying down on her back, she started to do leg lifts.

"Of course you don't have to do this if you don't want," she said, "but it would do you a lot of good."

"I'd rather watch."

"There's nothing sexy about exercises."

"I wouldn't be too sure about that."

"Usually I wear leotards, but I didn't bring any with me."

"A pity . . ."

"Come down here and stretch your muscles."

— 116

Uneasily, I lay down beside her. The floor was very hard. I felt like a damn fool and said so.

"It's foolish *not* to exercise," she said. "When we go back to Washington I think I'll get you some leotards."

At least she smiled when she said it. I tried but thankfully failed to imagine myself in such a getup.

"Lie down flat," she ordered. "Just keep your right leg stiff and lift it a few inches off the floor."

"It hurts, damn it."

"You have to start gradually. In a few weeks it will be easy."

After the lifts, we rolled on our sides and moved our legs like scissors, or at least she did. My head was starting to ache and I was beginning to feel dizzy. The pain in my shoulder, which hadn't bothered me in bed, came back.

"I quit," I said, going limp on the floor. "I've already had more exercise in the last few hours than I've had in years."

"Tomorrow you'll be able to do it a little more."

"I doubt it."

"I know what you're thinking."

"What?"

"That if you can forgive me my dyslexia, I ought to be able to forgive you your flabby muscles, right?"

"My muscles aren't flabby, they're just tired."

"It's all in your mind. How can you be so good at fucking and so bad at this?"

"Because fucking is a lot more fun. It seems I'm a Calvinist turned hedonist."

"Aren't you interested in your health, in hanging on to life?"

"Now more than ever."

"Then you have to learn to live right, even when you go back to Connecticut . . . What's your blood pressure?"

"I don't know."

"You must have had it taken some time."

"It was a little too high, the doctor said I should watch it."

"Watching isn't going to help. You have to lose weight, and exercise is better for working out tensions than booze or food."

"I'm sure you're right, but why did I have to fall in love with a health nut?"

"I'm not the nut. You're the nut for wasting your body. I want you to live forever, you can't get mad for *that*."

I took a deep breath. The air did feel good in my lungs. "Every morning I'll exercise with you a little, and I'll even try to stick to your diet."

"Marvelous," she said. "You're saving me, and maybe you'll let me save you—"

"What am I *saving* you from?"

"Oh . . . an old bad notion that most men are shits or fools and that I'm not much more than a foolish little twit myself. Can you understand that?"

"Too well."

"Do you still really think you love me, dyslexia and all?"

"I'm sure of it."

"I've never had a Harvard man tell me that before. CCNY, NYU, even a Yalie once, but I never went really first class in the academic department."

"I'm glad you finally reached the top," I said with a smile.

"I'm not exactly a nice respectable girl, at least as most people figure those things. I guess you realize that now."

"Quit thinking about yourself like a tramp," I said suddenly. "That's worse for you than no exercise for me."

"How do you know I'm not a tramp?"

"You don't look like one, you don't sound like one, and I have *some* taste. How about trusting me a little?"

"You're so damn nice," she said, caressing my face. "You know, there really haven't been so scandalously many men. I guess I exaggerate because my grandmother kept yelling at me that there should be only one in a good girl's life—"

"My grandmother said the same thing about women. But who knows how they lived?"

"Grammy really did have only one man and she loved him very much. I don't know why I couldn't have been that way."

"Most of the people I know spend most of their lives loving no one."

"That's why I never got married. You know, a total of eleven men have asked me to get married—I think about half of them meant it."

"I'm sure more than that did."

"I just didn't want to get married, then fall out of love, and go all through my life living with someone I didn't love. That's what my mother and too many of her friends in Brooklyn did."

"It happens in Connecticut too."

She broke into my thoughts by jumping up and saying, "I'm *hungry*, let's get dressed and go down for breakfast."

She showered and dressed quicker than any woman I'd ever known. All her movements were quick with barely suppressed energy. She used no makeup, a little lipstick and did nothing to her thick, short curly hair beyond giving it a few quick brush strokes. In a business dress of dark gray flannel, her personality changed into the briskly efficient office assistant I'd first met. Before going downstairs to the dining room, she took out of her suitcase a biographical sketch of Dr. Harbringer that she had copied from *Who's Who* before leaving Washington. There wasn't too much of interest in it, except that he had studied at a lot of good universities, had served as a psychiatrist in the navy during World War II and had been married twice, having three children with each wife. Apparently some men did find the strength, and money, to start over again.

I was in such a euphoric mood and so hungry that our diet breakfast of cantaloupe, poached eggs, *no* bacon, black coffee and dry wheat toast actually tasted good. Apparently the senses can be awakened to all sorts of new appreciations. The delicate orange flesh I spooned from the ripe melon was more pleasing in color, texture and taste than any I could remember, and the coffee offered such a rich fragrance and flavor that I asked the waitress for the brand and was surprised to find it a familiar one.

"No wonder we're famished," Ann said. "We didn't even have any dinner last night. If you can make me forget to eat, you really must be a great lover."

I, of course, loved hearing that . . . nearly inflating my chest like a preening rooster. "Great lover?" Tom Rath? Well, Annie thought I'd been one for at least a night . . . so don't question it or you question her. Shut up and *enjoy* it . . . There was, I was sure, a visible new spring to my step as I walked out of that restaurant with Ann, perhaps the suggestion of a swagger . . . ?

Because we had plenty of time, Ann suggested that we walk, not drive, to the Harbringer Clinic, which was less than a half mile from the inn. It was a glorious October morning with red maple leaves swirling in the sunlight, the long grass on a nearby hillside shimmering in the wind like waves of gold. Ann seemed to dance along beside me, her arms and hands in motion almost as much as her legs and feet as she told me how good it was to be going to see a famous doctor on the president's business instead of sitting in an office making telephone calls to check out the résumés of prospective employees, which is what Ed Banks had had her doing before she came to work with me.

"This job is a privilege," she said with her special gamine grin. "I'd say that even if I hadn't spent the night with my handsome boss."

15

My exhilaration was an odd mood to take into a mental hospital, which, after all, was what the Harbringer Clinic was. Despite the collegelike appearance of the brick buildings and green lawns there was a gloom about the place that you had to feel as soon as you walked down a path and saw the glass-enclosed porch in which people were slumped in armchairs, staring out with heavy, expressionless faces. My mother had twice been hospitalized in a place like this for treatment of depression, and the unknowing terror I'd felt as a child when my grandmother had taken me to visit her still sometimes came back to me in nightmares. After those barbarous shock treatments my mother had barely recognized me, but always every inch a lady she had introduced me to her new friends, old people with dead eyes and smiles that were mostly grimaces. "These people are here to get better," my grandmother often said. "They'll all be as right as rain in a few weeks." Right as rain in a flood, I'd thought, but I smiled and kissed my mother's moist face before shaking the limp hands of the "friends" who sat on the porch with her, just like these people on the porch of the Harbringer Clinic.

The memory came and, thankfully, went fast as I walked into the front door of this new place with Ann at my side and presented myself to a kind-looking, gray-haired receptionist who directed us to Dr. Harbringer's office.

It was a large book-lined room suitable for a college dean. Dr. Harbringer himself turned out to be a tall tweedy man of about fifty who in manner and speech reminded me a little of President Eisenhower, whom I'd seen once while working with Hopkins in Washington. Harbringer too had that combination of strength,

121 —

humility and warmth which it was almost impossible not to like.

"Good morning," he said, standing up behind his paper-strewn desk. "I feel quite honored to be visited by representatives of Ralph Hopkins and, I presume, the president."

"Indirectly," I said as I took his big hand. "David McKay wanted us to consult with you."

"I've never actually met Mr. McKay, but I've had some good letters from him."

Harbringer dropped my hand and offered his to Ann.

"This is Ann McSoaring, my associate."

"I wish I had an associate like you," Harbringer said with his surprisingly close approximation of the Eisenhower grin. "There are too many gloomy faces around here."

Ann thanked him as he offered us chairs in front of his desk and we all sat down.

"Mr. McKay wrote me about the plans for a White House conference," he said, "and President Kennedy called me about it. I had the great good luck to know him a little during the war—just acquaintances, but I liked him."

I guessed he had to be careful not to imply that Kennedy had been a patient of his.

"The president apparently thinks very highly of you," I said.

"Well, at least he seems to want my ideas for this conference, even though they seem pretty radical to most people. I'm very grateful for that."

"Mr. Hopkins hopes you'll give them to us in detail. He'd come here himself but his schedule—"

"I understand. Hopkins and I have differed on a few issues but I'm glad to see that he's heading up this conference. If he can't get a good public hearing, no one can." Harbringer got up to pace behind his desk.

"Do you folks mind if I give you a little lecture?"

"That's what we came for," Ann said. "Do you mind if I take notes?"

"I can record it for you if you like."

"I'm sure that Mr. Hopkins will want to hear it, but I'd still like to take a few notes."

"That's good. Sometimes this damn machine doesn't work anyway."

He took a small tape recorder from a drawer, placed it on his desk and fiddled with the dials.

"To begin with," he said, sitting down, "I'm afraid I don't like the phrase 'mental health.' I don't know what the hell it means. Do you?" (He didn't wait for an answer.) "What we're really talking about is the reverse—mental illness. It's no abstraction—it's individuals who are damn sick. What we're talking about, to put it bluntly, is crazy people. I wish they could have a White House conference on 'crazy' people, but of course that kind of bluntness would offend everybody. Now, the big question is, who are these crazy people we're going to *confer* about? Who's suffering from a lack of this thing we call mental health? For starters, how many crazy people are there in this or any nation?"

"Are you talking about those who have been diagnosed as insane?" I asked.

"That would be a figure to start with, but God knows what it would turn out to be. It would depend on the definition of insanity, which is only a legal term, and on the ability of most doctors to diagnose craziness, which is questionable. I don't believe in statistics—most of them only make people think they know something they don't. Numbers can lie even more than words. All right, let's just say that there are millions who've been judged paranoid, manic depressive or schizophrenic, whatever those umbrella terms really mean. These poor souls are the ones we lock up and they're the ones most people think of when they hear the phrase 'mentally ill.' They should be only the start of a long list. How about the chronic drunks? They're easier to count. There must be close to ten million of them. How about the suicides?" Harbringer continued. "Usually they get counted as mentally ill only when they try to kill themselves and fail." He shook his head. "But who's suicidal and who isn't? Some fifty thousand people a year in this country are killed in automobile 'accidents' by suicidal, drunken or murderous drivers. Should the operators of those cars be added to our list? How about the people we call criminal, not insane, and lock up in jails instead of hospitals? Is a compulsive thief or sadistic murderer crazy? Drug addicts? Compulsive gamblers? Point is, the list of the mentally ill should obviously be much more comprehensive than it usually is. I'd even add compulsive workers, the ones we call workaholics, and their opposites, the people who can't work at all. The word 'disease' simply means a lack of ease, and I say that anybody who can't cope with life and find more joy than pain in it has a disease of some kind, mental if we can't find it in the body."

"You'd end up with a very long list."

"I'm afraid so. We're talking about a majority of the population, not a poor unfortunate minority. This is a key fact: most people in the world don't love life enough to work very hard at hanging on to it. Freud said it one way: the death wish is very strong. Thoreau said it another way: most people lead lives of quiet desperation. I say it a third way: most people are crazy. It means about the same thing."

"You paint a pretty bleak picture," I said.

"It must be faced. Among other things, it's the only thing which explains the willingness of so many people to go to war, even in this age when war is a fine mix of murder and suicide, the ultimate insanity. It explains why great nations spend so much of their energy on preparations for war instead of on cooperative efforts to solve basic problems, such as over-population, food shortages and the need to improve the quality of life for individuals in all sorts of ways."

"Do you want a White House Conference on Mental Health to focus on war?"

"Do you want to confer about all kinds of madness except the ultimate one?"

"This certainly is a new concept," I said.

"Why call it a conference on mental health? Why not a White House Conference on Survival? That's what we're talking about, isn't it, both for individuals and nations?"

"Yes," Annie said, moving her pencil rapidly over her pad. "Yes!"

"I'm glad I have been able to convince someone," Harbringer said with a grin.

"I don't mean to sound unconvinced," I said, "but what would a conference on survival be expected to say or do?"

"Perhaps it could start by stating some of these basic facts and declaring not only a national emergency, but a world emergency. It could ask other nations to hold summit conferences on survival. Is there any nation which doesn't care about that?"

"I don't think so, but what specific steps could all those conferences recommend?"

"I have a lot of ideas but I'm not going to try to spell them all out now—that would be the job of the conferences. Now I say only that you have to state a problem clearly before you can try to find solutions."

"Yes," Annie said. "I can understand that."

_ 124

"Harbringer smiled at her and then glanced at me. "What do you think Mr. Hopkins will think about all this?"

The phrase "pie-in-the-sky" leaped to my mind but I banished it.

"I can't speak for Mr. Hopkins, but the change from a conference to raise money for mental health to international conferences on survival could be fairly startling. Isn't there some danger that such conferences could degenerate into endless discussions like those on disarmament?"

"The problem with discussions of disarmament is that they seem to assume that nations must remain in eternal conflict, using one kind of weapon or another. As long as the peoples of the world hate and fear each other, of course they will insist on remaining armed to the teeth. We must look for ways to reduce the hate and the fear."

"How could that be done?"

"Don't you realize that governments egg peoples into hating each other? It's not really natural for people to hate and fear people on the other side of the world whom they don't even know. If all the propaganda used to maintain hostility were used to build understanding and cooperation, maybe a start could be made."

"Yes," Annie said.

"Obviously the conferences would have to explore possibilities for many complex solutions to the basic problem of how to create peace," Harbringer continued. "I'm not going to try to spell them out here. The purpose of the conferences will be to dramatize the need for an all-out effort now before it's too late."

He paused before adding, "I know that all this will sound wildly impractical and impossibly idealistic to almost everybody, but what is the alternative? What is so practical and realistic about nuclear war, the end of the human race?"

Pacing back and forth behind his desk, Harbringer went on to suggest ways in which nations might work to understand each other. He made a point of the fact that Hitler had never visited Russia nor the United States before declaring war on them, and had no clear idea of their strengths. If the Japanese leaders had had the slightest understanding of the American character, they never would have attacked Pearl Harbor. The leaders of great nations should constantly visit each other, he said. There should also be massive exchanges of students and teachers, business and professional men, scientists and artists. We must achieve *understanding* if we are to overcome hate and fear, he kept saying, and we must realize that cooperation has to take the place of conflict in this nuclear age.

"If Mr. Hopkins thinks that all this is impossibly unrealistic," he concluded, "please insist that he answer this fundamental question for me: what does he suggest as an alternative?"

Harbringer then sat down, rubbed his eyes and smiled.

"Well, that's the essence of it," he said.

Ann finished recording his words with a flourish.

"Is that all?"

"Isn't it *enough?*" he asked with a smile.

"If I may say so, Dr. Harbringer, I've enjoyed just taking your words down—they make *sense.*"

"Thank you. I hope your Mr. Hopkins is half as enthusiastic."

Dr. Harbringer then gave me the tape from his recording machine. We shook hands with him, and he went down the corridor with us to the front door of the building.

Suddenly we found ourselves walking back to the hotel in that bright October sunshine that made the world seem much too splendid a place for talk of mass murder, suicide, craziness and the rest of it.

"The only trouble is that Hopkins is going to think he's just plain nuts," I said.

"We can't be sure of that yet. Maybe President Kennedy can convince him."

"Maybe . . ."

"*If* Hopkins won't go for this, how about us resigning and going to work for Harbringer? I've always wanted a cause."

There followed a brief silence during which I considered the consequences of so much idealism. Money, for example, or rather the lack of it.

"Anyway, maybe Hopkins will love the idea, it could put him in the shoes of a world statesman—"

"Or make him look like a flaming liberal? I don't know . . ."

"When will you call him?"

"Right now, but we better buy a recorder first so we can play him the tape over the phone."

"You mean buy one for using just once?"

"Are you worried about saving money for United Broadcasting?"

"It's my nature . . . the world may be about to blow up, but I'd worry about what we'd do with that damn recorder after we used it once."

"All *right,* we'll try to rent one and if, God forbid, we have to buy one, we'll wrap it up and give it to Hopkins personally. Okay?"

Before she could answer, I stopped there on the quiet street and kissed her full on the lips.

"You're wonderful," I said.

"Because I worry about a lousy tape recorder?"

"Because of everything. Your enthusiasm . . ."

"You don't know how good that makes me feel," she said.

"Maybe I do. After all, you do the same for me . . ."

16

THE ONLY SHOP in Windsor that had the recorders offered only expensive models. That expense didn't matter when it came to expediting business for Ralph Hopkins apparently gave Annie a clearer sense of his power than all the trappings of his rank and office.

"Somehow I keep forgetting who we're working for," she said as we walked back from the store to the hotel with our purchase. "The guy can really have anything he wants, can't he?"

"All the tape recorders he can use."

She gave me a quick look. "What does he really want?"

"A lot of people ask that question. I'm not sure even he knows."

"What if he just turns this whole thing down and resigns if Kennedy insists on it?"

"Whatever else Ralph Hopkins is, he's too complicated to be predictable."

"Nothing's ever predictable, is it?"

I knew, of course, that she was talking about us. Where would we be if Hopkins resigned from the conference and left us without jobs . . . A man who was dead broke and had four children to support could hardly think about divorce, remarriage and starting life all over again . . . "We'll soon get some idea of what the old man thinks of all this," I said as I glanced at my watch. "If we hurry, we'll get him before he goes out to lunch."

MISS BANNERMAN, HOPKINS' executive secretary, put me through to him when I called.

"Did you see Harbringer?"

I told him we had and gave him a quick sketch of how he wanted to broaden the concept of the conference. I told him I'd rather he heard it in Harbringer's own words that we had on tape. Annie had already hooked up the machine and now turned it on, but Harbringer's deep voice sounded oddly tinny and disembodied in that hotel room, as though Mickey Mouse were trying to make great philosophical statements.

"The machine doesn't seem to be working too well," I said into the receiver. "Maybe you'd better let Ann read her notes."

"All right, but I don't see why he has to play with the phrase 'mental health,'" Hopkins grumbled. "Everyone knows what it means."

Ann sat on the edge of the bed, opened her pad, and I handed her the telephone.

"I think that Dr. Harbringer's message really began when he said, 'Who are these crazy people we're going to confer about?'"

She continued to read from her shorthand notes, her voice clear, brisk and unemotional at first but as she went along she couldn't manage to suppress her obvious admiration for Harbringer's words. Omitting Harbringer's criticism of television broadcasters, she ended with the question, "What does he suggest as an alternative?"

"He's talking about a whole new ball game," Hopkins said. "Damn Jack, why is he springing this on me . . . we'll have to sound around and get some of our good gray heads in on this decision."

Maybe I was selling him short, but I got the impression at the moment at least that he was thinking of Harbringer's plan as he would a script for a television show. How would it play in Peoria? Looking at Annie—was I trying to impress her with new-found integrity?—I said, "For what it's worth, I found Dr. Harbringer very impressive in person. I must admit that I left his office feeling that this could be something of a crusade—"

"Crusade? I'm not up on my ancient history. How did the real Crusades work out?"

I'd used the wrong term, and said so.

"Whatever, he's asking me to jump into one considerable controversy. If Jack pushes this, it will be very difficult for me to drop out, and if I stay in . . . it seems to me what he's really selling is pacifism, one-sided at that—"

"Maybe we should just concentrate on his word 'survival.'"

"'Better dead than red,' some people will say."

"Which is why somebody has to offer a better choice—"

"I see the good doctor's made one convert anyway . . . well, you better get back here, Tom, and argue the case with some of the people who'll tell me to stick to my own business or to fund raising. I want to debate this in private before I go to Jack."

"I'll catch the first plane back."

"Miss McSoaring can go back to Washington and hold the fort there. Before you leave have her type up her notes. I'll need to get a lot of opinions on this."

I wondered if he would resort to a public opinion poll, the way he did with some of the ideas for programs submitted to him. Market research. What's the public demand for survival? Demographic breakdowns . . . what do the people between the ages of twenty and forty with an annual income of more than thirty thousand dollars think of survival?

"I'll get the notes typed up, and I'll get back to New York as soon as I can," I said. "Miss McSoaring will go to Washington."

I'd put the telephone back on its cradle before I realized that the most immediate result of this call was the melancholy fact that Annie and I would have to part for a few days, maybe much longer if Hopkins resigned from the conference.

"Why can't I go to New York with you?" she asked.

"You heard the man . . . maybe it will be only a couple of days before I get back to you."

"I hope," she said, but I also knew she had a scary premonition, as I did, that the year we had hoped to spend together was not going to be ours.

"I told you we shouldn't try to think ahead," she finally said.

"Annie, what we've started we can't stop—"

"Until you go back to Connecticut and patch things up with Betsy—"

"No, we've gone too far, it wouldn't be any good for anybody to force something that's not there."

"Maybe." She took a timetable from her handbag and studied it. "The first plane you can catch in Cleveland would get you into New York at about midnight. I can't get to Washington before that, but if we leave here at about six tomorrow morning we can catch planes that will get us both in before noon. Would that be all right?"

"Either way is all right with me—"

"What do you mean? Is that what you think about having another night here with me?"

"I was figuring that either way we have the whole afternoon to ourselves."

"I'm greedy, Tom . . . I want as much time with you as I can get."

We went to bed then, not only to make love, which we did, but to hold and reassure each other that what we were both afraid of would not be allowed to happen . . .

LATER THAT AFTERNOON Annie got out of bed while I slept, borrowed a typewriter from the hotel manager and transcribed and edited her shorthand notes. It was a concise presentation of Dr. Harbringer's views. We went back to bed early and returned to that blessed state that was the opposite of loneliness, and for which I could find no adequate words. . . .

During the drive to Cleveland the next morning she was very quiet. I knew she was thinking that not only was I going to New York for at least a few days, but back to my wife and children in Connecticut at night. I tried to imagine how I'd feel if the situation were reversed . . . if she were married and now returning to a husband, daughters and son. Whether she was as capable as I was of jealousy I didn't know, but it seemed to me that I was asking and receiving considerably more from her than I was able to give—a total commitment in exchange for a partial, divided one. Life wasn't fair, as President Kennedy himself had once said. Well, this whole situation wasn't fair to anyone, to Annie, Betsy, my kids . . . even me. I was beginning to feel that in spite of all my good intentions I was cheating everyone, and sooner or later the cheater is likely to get cheated . . . The more I thought about going home, the more I wanted to see my children, but every time I looked at Annie the more painful the thought of our imminent parting became. I wanted to be in two places at the same time; be lover and father at the same time. Being split down the middle in such a circumstance was, of course, part of the punishment my Puritan forefathers had warned me to expect. "In Adam's fall we sinned all . . ." and so forth.

I had to remind myself that all was not lost. Ralph Hopkins still might be persuaded by President Kennedy, or even persuade himself, to stick with the White House conference in one form or another, and I might still have that year with Annie before we came to the time of hard decisions. I also ought to remember, I told myself, that I had never had a choice between a happy marriage and a love affair. The former just was no longer there . . .

As we stood in the Cleveland airport waiting for my plane, which was to leave an hour before hers, I tried to say some of this to Annie in a rush of words. She finally silenced me with a finger on my lips.

"Ride with it," she said. "I can and so can you."

Her words were repeated in my head as I sat down in the plane beside an empty seat. Tightening my seat belt, I put my head back and retreated into a sleep so deep that the stewardess had to wake me up when we landed in New York.

As soon as I returned to my office I called Miss Bannerman and asked her to tell Hopkins that I was on hand to see him at any time. I'd hoped he would call for me right away, but she said he'd scheduled a meeting with me and "some of the others" at his house on Sixty-third Street for eight that evening. In a way that was good news . . . the old man liked to hold important conferences in his home during hours when he and his top executives would not be constantly interrupted by the telephone.

I next put in a call to Betsy to tell her I was unexpectedly back in New York and would come home late that night. She didn't sound in the least upset.

"I'm glad we're going to get a chance to see you," she said. "I'm sorry I was bitchy on the way to the airport the other morning—"

"We both were on edge . . ."

"I've been thinking about some of the things you said, I *should* be more careful about money, I've decided not to charge any more, that's where I get in trouble . . . I'm trying, I want you to know that . . ."

She sounded so decent, damn it . . . this was a time when I'd have been glad to hear her gush over Bert Andrews. "How are the kids?" I said quickly.

"They're fine, of course they miss you . . . they're all at school now. How long are you going to be able to stay?"

"I don't know yet. I'll have to see what Hopkins has to say. A lot's going on with the conference—I'll tell you all about it when I see you tonight."

"Hurry home soon as you can. I love you, in spite of everything, it's true . . ."

"Me too," I said automatically. The words were half-meant, which made me feel a traitor—and something of a coward—to both Betsy and Annie. But this was no time to blurt out that I'd fallen in love with my assistant and wanted to start a new life with her. When would honesty demand that confession? When and how could it best be combined with kindness to Betsy, if that wasn't a hypocritical word when a man was planning to leave his wife of twenty-two years? What would I do when Betsy wanted to celebrate my homecoming by going to bed tonight? A man who sleeps with two women inside of forty-eight hours can't very reasonably demand fidelity from either of them, at least not for long. In spite of this self-evident truth, I still raged when I thought of any man except me making love to Annie *or* Betsy. The realization that my position was ridiculous didn't change what I felt. But this was no time to brood on such things. There was my meeting with Hopkins tonight, and I had copies of Annie's report on Harbringer's plan made and sent to Hopkins for advance distribution to his advisers.

I suspected I knew pretty well how the discussion would go. The executives of United Broadcasting weren't stupid. They would recognize the truth in much that Harbringer had said, but they would also believe that a White House Conference on Survival would get a lot of people upset, which wasn't how they made friends and won rating points.

Suddenly there seemed some humor in my presuming to be able to help straighten out these men while I was busily making my own life such a mess. Well, I did have one qualification that I thought Harbringer would approve: I wanted to live as long as possible . . . I'd probably need a lifetime to work out a solution to my own problems . . .

The one with Hopkins, it suddenly occurred to me, might be much simpler. The conference could be broken down into a dozen or more separate forums to discuss different kinds of mental illness. At least some of Dr. Harbringer's list of crazinesses could be used effectively—Hopkins would see greater public appeal in discussions of drug and alcohol abuse, fatal driving habits and all the rest than in the more traditional definition of mental disease. Harbringer could be given one committee to discuss war, "the ultimate madness," and with Kennedy's help might stir up a lot of support. If Harbringer's efforts backfired and stirred up too much opposition, Hopkins could point out that every successful conference needed one good controversy. His risks would be cut way down.

So, I thought, change the name of the conference to "The White House Conference on Mental Health—A Matter of Survival." And somewhere in my draft I could say, "For millions of people, the search for mental health is a matter of personal survival, but in this era it is also a question of national and even world survival. Nothing can destroy humanity but itself . . ." The next step was to put my thoughts into a memorandum I could give to Hopkins and his advisers when they were looking for some kind of a compromise. When I was through I telephoned Annie in Washington and read what I had to her.

"Great," she said. "You've turned the whole thing into something the old man can probably swallow."

"Keep your fingers crossed."

There was a pause before she said, "I'm still not sure I didn't just dream Windsor, Ohio."

"Everything *else* is a dream." A pretty facile line, Tom, but damn it, I meant it.

"When do you think you'll get back to Washington?"

"I don't know yet—maybe tomorrow, if everything goes well with Hopkins. I'm going to see him at eight tonight."

I of course knew she was thinking that I'd be going home to wife and children after that. All that she said, after a moment of silence, was, "Good luck."

There was a click and she was gone, and suddenly I wished I lived in China when a man could take two wives, or in Nigeria, where, as I'd heard, it could still be done. A sunny picture of a compound in Africa with Annie, Betsy and the children all happily helping me thatch a roof for our new home blossomed in my perverse mind as I went out for an early dinner.

17

AT SEVEN-THIRTY I began my walk from Rockefeller Center up Fifth Avenue to Hopkins' house on Sixty-third Street. Although I'd worked for the man more than ten years I still felt nervous every time I had an appointment with him. I thought of him as a sort of monarch, an immensely wealthy one who was worth half a billion dollars, according to *Forbes* magazine. Sometimes I tried to visualize all that money in silver coins stacked up higher than the United Broadcasting building itself, the tallest tower in Rockefeller Center.

What did Hopkins really think of me? I wondered. If he had enough confidence in me he could give me a top job in his public relations department or recommend me for one in any of the companies or charitable foundations he helped direct. My financial problems could be relieved with one telephone call. On the other hand he could drop me as an afterthought. If I played my hand decently tonight, conceivably he might make me staff director of the White House conference and let me keep some sort of advisory job with him to supplement my government salary—such arrangements weren't unheard of. I might come out of such a deal with thirty thousand or more a year. Dream on.

My relationship with Hopkins tended to be even more confusing because he was so friendly in at least superficial ways. It was Hopkins' way to conceal his power—the opposite of an army general who tries to symbolize power as well as wield it. Hopkins always called me Tom, stood up to shake hands when I came into his office, asked about the family's health, complimented me, gave me hearty slaps on the back. He could also let me tote his briefcase when we were boarding a plane. After I had worked on one of his speeches late at night he often offered me a drink and chatted about baseball or the difficulty of raising kids, but if I ever brought up the subject of a raise he'd give me a look as though I'd committed a major social gaffe. I believed he had some respect for my intelligence, my integrity, my ability to get along pretty well with people, but push come to shove, I was mostly one of thousands of men in gray flannel suits who probably would never break out of the ranks. I'd better find some way to change his mind. What I'd gotten myself into would take more than gray flannel and good names to resolve.

Walking up Fifth Avenue one entered the country of money . . . the mannequins in the store windows disported evening dresses and furs for women who didn't need to worry about household budgets—a diamond necklace in Tiffany's window would cost more than I could earn in ten years. Never before had I resented or even been interested in this kind of luxury, but now I had a sudden image of Annie in a sparkling evening gown with a coat of white ermine and I wished I were rich enough to give Betsy a diamond necklace as a sort of going-away present when the split-up finally came—she deserved something more than alimony checks for twenty-two years of marriage to me. Of course neither of them would want such showy stuff . . .

Back to Ralph Hopkins. There were only two worms in the fine apple of a career that Hopkins had grown for himself. Few people outside the world of big business knew him well enough to recognize his name, and those who were familiar with his accomplishments thought of him mostly as a driving money-maker or "the king of the wasteland," pandering to the lowest common denominator among the tastes of the public. No matter how many symphonies or art shows he put on the air, they couldn't drown out the cackle of the laugh machines that applauded his comedy shows or the sound of screeching tires and gunfire of the car chases on the tube. Even his long service as chairman of the National Foundation for Mental Health had failed to shine up his public image. The chairmanship of a White House committee on mental health couldn't help much, but his friend Neil McElroy had gone from such a post to secretary of defense and had even been mentioned as "presidential material." Maybe such dreams danced in Hopkins' head, and just maybe they weren't all that unrealistic if he forged a meaningful link with the Kennedy clan. After all, Hopkins had a good deal to offer the Kennedys. He controlled a great television and radio network, not only as its president but as a major stock-holder. He could offer massive publicity and generate contributions to campaign funds. In return, a cabinet post was a strong possibility, and if he made a spectacular success of that, anything could happen. But now Kennedy had perhaps given him, by his lights, a curveball. How to handle it? I hoped I had the answer in my briefcase.

I turned onto Sixty-third Street. Hopkins was a man who tended to judge an idea as much by its advocate as by its content. He listened to people who had built successful careers for themselves. How would I make out if judged by that standard?

In my anxiety I walked fast and arrived at the iron gate in front of his house eight minutes early. Despite Hopkins' attempts at informality, no one arrived for appointments at his house either early or late. I saw two chauffeur-driven Cadillacs, one gray, one black, standing by the curb nearby. Probably the other participants in this meeting were waiting in them. Turning back toward Fifth Avenue, I ambled along. The houses on both sides of the street offered the ultimate luxury of single-family, two- or three-story structures in a city of apartment houses and skyscrapers. Built of brick, brownstone or marble, they squatted like small-town banks, with bars at the lower windows to keep out intruders. Even the dogs that were walked by uniformed maids or chauffeurs looked snooty and pranced alertly, as though they sniffed money. Nobody on this street had to tell his wife to economize. It wasn't that I hated the rich, I wanted to become one of them. To pretend otherwise would make me a complete hypocrite . . . and there was material enough in my life for that just now.

Promptly at eight I approached the black gate. Two men from the Cadillacs converged there at the same time. One was Harry Robinson, a stocky gray-haired man who looked more like some distinguished professor than the director of a network public relations department. The other was B. F. Henderson, who went only by his initials; I had no idea what his first name was. He was a tall, aristocratic-appearing man of about my own age who recently had ascended to the vice-presidency in charge of advertising and who was most often talked about as the next president of the company when Hopkins retired. B. F. Henderson was one man who would love to see Hopkins go to Washington, and stay there.

Before we all had time to do more than nod at each other, Hopkins' houseman let us in. They both called him by name,

Lester, and commented on the coolness of the October evening with the same studied show of democratic friendliness to lowly subordinates that their boss displayed by example. Lester led us through a small, marble-floored foyer where a set of five broad, red-carpeted stairs led to a living room at a slightly higher level. At the head of these Ralph Hopkins waited to greet us. Except for his face, which radiated intense vitality despite his sixty-five years, he was, superficially, less impressive-appearing than most of his assistants. Short, thin and a little stooped, he wore gray flannel slacks and a navy-blue jacket with a maroon bowtie on his button-down white shirt.

"Thanks so much for coming over," he began as he so often did. "I don't like to ask you to give up your evening for meetings like this, but things do come up and sometimes it's good to just sit down and relax and chat about it."

He shook hands with each of us, calling Henderson just "B" instead of "B.F.," asking Robinson about the progress of a daughter at Radcliffe and giving me a comradely slap on the shoulder. Ushering us into the living room, which looked like a luxuriously furnished library, he stepped aside to let us all through the door first. Waiting for us in a large leather armchair was Herbert Mannerheim, the executive vice-president of United Broadcasting, and the only man there who considered himself an independent power with no need to please Hopkins or anyone else. A huge man, he was famous for financial wizardries. Apparently he and Hopkins had had dinner to discuss the business at hand in private before more general conversation. Mannerheim was cradling a snifter of brandy in one rather puffed hand and a demitasse of coffee in the other. He greeted us with a perfunctory smile that did nothing to soften the arrogance of his face. I had no reason except his looks to dislike him, but I thought him wise to operate almost entirely behind the scenes at the company, as he did. If the cartoonists had wanted a man to show as king of the so-called television wasteland, they wouldn't have had to exaggerate his features.

We sat around a marble-topped coffee table and Lester served drinks, including another brandy for Mannerheim, whose ability to drink a great deal without fuzzing his mind was famous in the company.

"Herb and I have been talking over some of this business about the White House conference," Hopkins began. "Did all of you get the memorandum on Dr. Harbringer that Tom prepared for us?"

Nods all around.

"It's fairly startling," Hopkins continued blandly. "Jack Kennedy came close to the brink of war last year during the Cuban missile crisis. I guess he was looking for long-range solutions to the problem, but I don't think he'd connected them up with this mental health project until after my appointment had been announced. Somewhere along the line this man Dr. Harbringer, who apparently has known him for a long time, got in touch with him and sold him on the idea of tying the two subjects together. This is a big change and could get me into some troubled waters . . ."

There followed a good deal of careful back and forth talk, and finally I heard what I'd been hoping for . . .

"Tom, do you have any ideas on this?"

"There is a compromise solution," I said, and went on to describe my plan for dividing the conference into many committees, only one of which would discuss the controversial subject of war as the ultimate madness.

"Nine tenths of your conference would be on more or less routine medical stuff, including alcoholism and all the rest," I said. "Political controversy would be a minor part of the whole, but we wouldn't refuse to talk about it."

"I think you may have something there," Hopkins said.

"It's a good idea," Mannerheim added. "Take it and run with it."

"Let me think about it for a while," Hopkins said, "but I think we're on the right track."

He got up and slapped me on the back. After that, his ritual of ending the meeting did not take long—everyone was tired by that time. When I got out in the cold air and hailed a cab to take me to Grand Central Station I felt in a mood to celebrate. The White House conference would go on according to my compromise. And Hopkins was not a man to let such service go unrewarded. I might not have only the pleasure of doing my bit to save the world from craziness; I might get rich enough from it to solve my personal problems at the same time.

What more could a man ask?

18

WHEN I GOT to Grand Central Station I could have caught the nine-forty-three to South Bay if I'd run, but I wanted first to phone Annie and I realized that it would be hard to find the privacy for that once I returned home. At a newsstand I changed a five-dollar bill and hurried to a coin booth. After the hotel operator in Washington put me through to Annie's room, the telephone buzzed for what seemed a long while and my well-honed jealousy surfaced again. Was she lonely enough to go looking for a new friend? I was much relieved when she answered somewhat breathlessly, "Hello!"

"It's me—"

"Tom, I was hoping you'd call but I gave up and was taking a shower. I didn't hear the phone ringing till I turned the water off."

I pictured her standing by the bedside table wrapped only in a towel and felt a rush of desire strong enough to drive everything else from my mind. However complex my other feelings for Annie were, they now had that overpowering undercurrent.

"I wish I were there," I said. "I miss you like hell."

"Me too. Did you see Hopkins?"

"Yes. I think he bought my plan."

"Terrific, I knew he would. Well . . . hurry home," she said, the word "home" suddenly sounding with its double meaning in our ears. "I'll be waiting for you. My clock seems stopped and it won't start again till you get back here."

Then she was gone, maybe imagining my other homecoming tonight . . . I should call Betsy and tell her that I was catching the ten-sixteen but I needed a drink first. When I was in Washington with Annie I hardly touched the booze, but the routine of life in

New York and South Bay had always seemed to demand a dose of alcohol. A martini in the station bar was definitely in order to calm my nerves enough for what lay ahead. From straight arrow to the stereotyped role of the two-timing husband . . . In the movies and on television shows, the part was played either as light comedy or soap opera. My experience fitted neither. Annie's lover, Betsy's husband . . . geography helped keep the two separate, but for how long? Sooner or later there'd be an accounting, but not to-night . . .

Two martinis provided some insulation, and I even managed to sound cheerful when I called Betsy.

"I'll meet you at the station," she said, "and the kids will wait up. Pete has some good news he wants to tell you himself."

I walked to a newsstand to buy something to read on the train. Standing in front of a magazine rack, I saw as though for the first time the great number of covers depicting partially clad young women in provocative poses, their faces smiling under the camera lights in imitation of desire. How many middle-aged men considered the body of a young woman only a distant memory or part of this garish fantasy? Better to be split as I was than to be one of them.

I picked up a copy of the good gray New York *Times* and hurried to board my train. The stuffy atmosphere of the New Haven cars seemed to return me to an earlier self, and as I sank down into a sagging blue-upholstered seat I felt as though I were being caught in a familiar trap, from which I had only briefly escaped. Just before the train started with a jerk, a harried, rumpled-looking man dashed aboard and dropped into a seat across the aisle from me, where he leaned forward resting his head on his arm on the back of the chair in front of him while he tried to catch his breath. For a moment he looked as though he were praying in a church. When he finally sat back I recognized the gray face as belonging to Ben Richardson, who seemed as much a part of this late train as the sagging blue seats. I remembered that Ben had suffered two heart attacks, but nothing could make him slow down, and I wondered now what was making him rush so hard toward his grave. Was he afraid his business would collapse if he didn't work until ten o'clock at night or, like me, did he have a complicated love life that held him in the city until the last train to South Bay? His worn but still handsome face looked distraught as he closed his eyes and finally slept with his lips slightly parted in a way that made him look especially vulnerable. For a little while at least, something finally was slowing poor Ben down.

I'd felt so full of beans for the past few days that I could easily *imagine* myself as twenty years old, if I didn't look in the mirror, but now the two martinis were taking effect and I felt very tired. Putting my head back, I too slept, protecting my eyes from the light and perhaps from some unexpected blow by resting with my forearm across my face.

As SOON AS I stepped down from the train in South Bay I saw our new station wagon waiting for me. The doors opened and my three children ran toward me, followed by Betsy. Janey reached me first with a big hug, and they all pressed around me in as fine a display of affection as any returning father could wish. (In my case it was, for obvious reasons, a matter of mixed feelings . . .)

"Tell him your news now," Betsy told Pete.

"Oh, it's not so much—"

"Tell him!" Betsy said.

"I wrote a report on my foot of earth and I got an *A* plus . . ."

"More than that," Betsy said, "Mr. Belasco thinks it's so good that he's submitting it to a state contest."

"Looks like you're going to be famous," I said.

"Not yet," he said very seriously. "I have a long ways to go . . ."

We all piled into the car and I drove home. They had left the big Victorian house ablaze with light, making it look as welcoming as it had when I was a boy coming home late from school. The embers of a fire were glowing in the living room fireplace, and as soon as he took his coat off Pete went to the cellar for more logs, something he'd apparently learned to do since my departure. Barbara hung her parka in a closet near the front door and stood in front of a hall mirror smoothing back her long brown hair. In a tweed skirt and snug brown sweater she looked startlingly like Annie, a thought that definitely was freighted with mixed feelings. I was grateful when Betsy went into the kitchen and poured a scotch for both of us. Betsy, wearing a cotton so-called house frock . . . after twenty-two years of marriage she didn't get all dressed up to greet me, why should she? . . . looked tired . . . as tired, I told myself, as any forty-two-year-old suburban housewife meeting her husband on the late train from the city. She also looked nice, and dearly familiar . . . Janey followed her from the kitchen with a plate of Edam cheese and crackers.

We were sitting by the fire when Betsy said, "Janey, show dad your new riding clothes."

"Now?"

"In the morning you'll have to be hurrying off to school—"

"They're really *neat,* dad."

She went upstairs and in a few minutes was back, all dressed up in her new regalia—brown boots, whipcord britches and tweed jacket complete with a black derbylike riding hat. The only trouble was that that rig had not been designed for my sweet-faced butterball and I shuddered at the thought of her trying to cling to the back of a runaway horse. Why the hell did my mind always rush to such images of disaster . . . ?

"You look great," I said.

"Bert says he'll start giving me lessons in jumping pretty soon."

She was not strong enough for lessons in jumping, and, of course, mention of Bert Andrews jolted me, as it always did. Well, don't make an issue of it now, for God's sake . . .

"I don't know about that, honey, but you sure look every inch a horsewoman." My lie was rewarded by a wonderful smile. I put my arms around her and gave her a hug, whirling her around.

"Okay, bed," Betsy said. "It's nice to have dad home but you still have to get up in time for school."

"How long are you going to be here?" Barbara asked.

"I don't know yet . . . I'll be around for a few days at least . . ."

Barbara kissed me on the cheek then, an unusual display of affection from her, and led the other two upstairs. If somebody had to fall in love with horses, I wished it could have been Barbara— she had the lithe strength and grace a rider needed, but of course she was much more interested in boys and motorcycles, more dangerous steeds. Strange in a way . . . my daughters liked hazardous activities, while my son seemed content with his microscope and fishing trips. Proving sexual stereotypes were just that . . . stereotypes . . . ? I also thought how my love for my children seemed so often to express itself in worry, a built-in weakness of mine.

"The children seem to be doing pretty well," Betsy said, refilling our glasses. "Janey seems to like Dr. Richter. I don't know whether it's him or the horses, but she seems to be coming out of herself . . ."

"Good. How about the lady?"

"Barbara? Well, she's seeing more of that Gordy than I like, but

I can't see that we can do much about it. After all, she's almost seventeen. Alice Richardson has the opposite worry—her daughter Judy doesn't seem to be interested in boys at all, and none of them seems interested in her."

"I doubt if Barbara will ever have that problem."

There was a pause while we sat on the couch sipping our drinks. "How's the conference going?"

I felt a little the way I used to when I came home on leave from the army and she'd try to get me to tell her about the war. Except now it was Annie that made me reluctant to talk, not the tepid wars of the mental health campaign.

"It's going okay . . ."

"How's your assistant working out?"

Was war being declared? "She's very efficient, thank God."

"How lucky for you . . . Have you made any friends in Washington? I imagine it gets lonely for you down there."

"I'm pretty well caught up in the work, I don't have much time to worry about it."

"That's nice. I feel the same about our rehearsals . . . they make the evenings go by . . ."

I nodded, smiled, feeling like an idiot . . . worse.

"Do you still think it will be a year before your assignment is over?"

"Something like that."

Silence. What the hell was she thinking? Was she suspicious? Glad?

"At least you're here tonight," was what she said, and moved closer to me. I put my arms around her shoulders, not too sure what we were doing.

"Have you missed me?" she asked.

I kissed her, felt her trying to respond with more passion than either of us felt. She wanted to do the right thing, she knew how a wife should greet her returning husband, but knowing and feeling weren't the same thing . . .

"Let's go to bed," she said a bit too brightly.

I made love to her more uninhibitedly than I had in a long time . . . in part to make up for my infidelities—past, present and future . . .

"Maybe you ought to go away more often," she said.

She slept, I couldn't. How could I leave my wife, my three children and this old house I'd grown up in . . . but how could I ever give up Annie? I thought of her waiting for me in Washington, felt fresh desire in spite of having just had sex with my wife . . . had sex, not made love . . . ? I needed her strength too, her steady approval. Clearly, when you came right down to it, I was a very old familiar story indeed. I was a man who wanted it both ways, wanted my wife and family and my lady love too. I was the quintessential double-standard man, wasn't I? Did worrying about it on a sleepless night make me somehow less cynical? Did feeling guilty make me less so? But good old New England Calvinist guilt was built-in for the likes of me. Too easy . . . ?

The grandfather clock in the living room that had come down in my family for three generations boomed a solitary note—one-thirty in the morning. I should go back to my commuting schedule and get up at six-thirty the next day to catch the seven-twenty-eight —I heard the sound of . . . someone walking downstairs? Did I imagine it? But there were only small rugs on the ancient floor-planks of the living room, the sound of someone walking down there was unmistakable. As I sat upright in bed it continued, stopped, then started again, apparently retreating toward the kitchen.

One of the kids having trouble sleeping, gone downstairs to raid the refrigerator? But when I got out of bed and walked to the head of the stairs I saw there was no light on down there. The children would feel no need to stumble around in the dark to make a midnight snack. I walked down the hall and peered into their rooms. In a shaft of moonlight Barbara looked like a sleeping princess. Janey lay on her side curled up almost in the fetal position, and Pete had gone to sleep in his blue jeans and T-shirt, half-covered by a blanket. I went back to our room and in the dim light of the moon saw the mound of Betsy on the bed, heard her slow breathing. All present and accounted for. Standing still in the darkness, I listened, hearing only my own breathing. Then there was a small scraping sound as if someone had stumbled into a chair. More footsteps. Someone definitely in the living room.

I felt tempted to snap on the lights, call out, "Who's there?" But if it was an armed thief he might attack. Somehow that seemed too melodramatic, until I remembered that Betsy had read about criminals coming out from the city to find easy pickings in the suburbs. The intruder or intruders downstairs didn't sound too professional, to judge by the heavy tread and the stumbling against furniture. Maybe he was drunk or on drugs, or maybe he was some

145 _

local amateur who knew I was usually away from home. If so, the son of a bitch had chosen the wrong night. I walked to my bedside table, found the key to my tackle box in the closet, where I'd hidden Betsy's automatic and my old Colt .45.

My fingers fumbled nervously with the lock, found the reassuring rough grain of the pistol, slid in an ammunition clip and cocked the gun. At least I knew my own house in the dark better than any damned junkie, or whatever he was . . . The second floor was carpeted wall-to-wall, which let me move around silently. My old paratrooper experience behind enemy lines was going to come in handy . . .

In the hallway outside my room I stood still and listened again, the Colt cradled in my arm. The house seemed to buzz with silence. Maybe the thief had got what he wanted, a bottle of booze, maybe, and had left. Barbara had been traveling with a lot of fairly scruffy kids lately. It wouldn't be too surprising if one of them broke into the house to raid the liquor cabinet. It was also possible that I'd misinterpreted the sounds. If a stray dog had managed to find its way in, as one had a few years ago, it might have thumped around down there making sounds like a man's footsteps . . . Well, was I going down or was I going to stand there all night? I heard another footstep, no question, it came almost as a relief. At least the situation was clear now.

What was there for a person to steal down there anyway? My grandmother's silver, the television and hi-fi sets, no more—it would be better to lose them than to shoot down a man in my own living room and risk my own life and my family's. The real time to fight would be if the intruder, or intruders, came upstairs. I'd have plenty of warning because those old stairs creaked . . .

The grandfather clock now announced with reverberating tones that it was two A.M.

I remembered that there was a back stairway leading from the kitchen to the other end of this hall on the opposite side of the house. An intruder who somehow knew the layout could use that and come at me from the rear while I waited at the head of the front stairs. All right, a remote possibility, but still, the door to the back stairway had a bolt that was usually left open. I should slide it shut. Walking on the carpeted floor, I passed the children's rooms and was about to lock the back door when I heard someone coming up the narrow stairs. I thought of holding the door shut, but then he would go downstairs again and maybe come up the other way. At least I now knew exactly where he was. Running my hand along the wall, I retreated a few steps and found the switch to the hall light, leaving my fingertips on it, waiting for the door to open before turning it on. Both the intruder and I would be blinded by that first flash of light, but he would be the one surprised. My pistol was loaded, cocked, safety catch off. I pointed it toward the door in the darkness and waited while the footsteps came closer. If in the first glimpse of him I saw that he carried a gun, I would shoot to kill before he had a chance to fire at me. I heard the knob turn and the creak of the hinges as the old door was shoved open. I gave him time to step into the hall and present a full target. Then I snapped on the light. In the sudden glare I saw a disheveled young man with bushy hair and something glinting in his right hand. I nearly fired before I realized that what he was carrying was a *beer bottle.*

"Don't move."

"What the—?" and in his panic he dropped the beer bottle, which foamed on the rug.

"Put your damned hands up—"

"Mr. Rath, don't you recognize me? It's Gordy—"

"What the *hell* are you doing here this time of night?"

"I just had to see Babs, she told me not to come tonight but I had to see her. All kinds of stuff is coming down."

Doors flew open down the hall, and Gordy and I were surrounded by Barbara, Betsy and Janey, with Pete sleepily bringing up the rear. Barbara was wearing a nightgown, Betsy was standing with her arms folded across her black negligee. Only Janey in a white flannel nightdress and Pete, still in his blue jeans and T-shirt, looked respectable and reasonably invulnerable—I wore rumpled undershorts, I now had time to realize. A threatening sight indeed.

"Gordy, I *told* you not to come tonight," Barbara said, and then, turning to me, added, "Daddy, what are you doing with that gun—?"

"I damn near killed this little son of a bitch with it."

"Daddy, you wouldn't really shoot Gordy, would you?" Janey asked.

"For heaven's sake, put that thing down," Betsy said. "It's crazy to stand here, waving a gun like that."

"I'm not *waving* it. Gordy, what the hell are *you* doing, sneaking around this house in the middle of the night?"

A ridiculous question. Obviously the little bastard was sneaking into my daughter's room, as he no doubt had done before, judging by his knowledge of the back stairs.

"I just wanted to talk to her," he said, slurring the words. He was drunk, on drugs or both.

"Barbara, go to your room and get dressed," I said to her, barely able to control myself. "I'll talk to you later. Gordy, you get the hell out of here. If I ever find you in my house again I'll turn you over to the cops for molesting a minor if I can keep hold of my temper long enough to do that."

"Tom, calm down," Betsy said. "There's no point in—"

"No *point*? Do you know what your daughter's been doing? How can you be so goddamn calm?"

"Oh, *daddy*," Janey said in pain, echoed by Barbara.

"Barbara, go put something on, your father told you," Betsy said. "We'll all go downstairs and talk this over—"

"I don't want to talk to Gordy here quietly or any other way," I said. "Get *out* of here."

"I wasn't doing nothing—"

"Get *out* before I bounce you off the wall—"

"Wait a minute," Betsy said. "How did you get here, Gordy?"

"My cycle—I left it out on the street."

"Have you been drinking?"

"Not much," he said defiantly, pronouncing the word "mush."

"I don't think you're in any shape to drive a motorcycle or to talk," Betsy said. "Go to the bedroom downstairs and turn in. We'll discuss all this in the morning."

"Wait a minute," I said to her. "This little . . . breaks into our house in the middle of the night and you're going to treat him like an honored guest?"

"Would you order a drunken boy out on a motorcycle in the middle of the night—?"

"I hope he drives the damn thing up a tree—"

"How would you feel in the morning when you read about that in the newspapers?"

"Great."

"Oh, daddy!" Janey said in more pain.

"Were you really going to shoot him?" Pete asked, piping up for the first time.

"You're damn right—"

"Tom, will you please stop acting like a crazy man? Put that gun away and let's start talking about this reasonably—"

"I'm not going to talk to dad about anything tonight," Barbara said, coming to the door of her room in a bathrobe. "I don't have to talk to a crazy man—"

"You come here and we'll have this out."

Wordlessly she shut the door. When I tried to open it, I found it locked.

"Come *out,*" I roared, shaking the knob.

No answer.

"Tom, go put some clothes on if you want to talk," Betsy said. "I will too."

She headed toward our bedroom. Gordy took this opportunity to turn and run down the back stairs. I headed for our bedroom and at the door met Betsy coming out, tying the belt of her blue flannel bathrobe.

"Janey, you go back to bed," she said. "You too, Pete. Nothing more is going to happen tonight, there's nothing to worry about."

"Is dad still mad at you and Barbara?" Janey asked.

"No—he's just a little upset."

A *little* . . . I couldn't find my bathrobe. As I pulled on my pants and my shirt I finally saw what a damn fool I'd made of myself, but the discovery that my daughter was apparently sleeping with this punk in my own house, without, it seemed, even arousing the wrath of my wife, still infuriated me. How could Betsy be so serene about all this? Didn't she care?

Of course the realization that I was hardly in a position to play the righteous Puritan parent . . . if example meant anything . . . did not improve my temper.

I found Betsy waiting for me alone in the kitchen.

"Do you want coffee or scotch?" she said.

"Scotch. Make it a double."

The thought occurred to me that I better get back to Annie before my family drove me into complete alcoholism.

"Talk soft," Betsy said. "The kids are all trying to get back to sleep."

"Is that damn Gordy really in our guest room?"

"He passed out on the bed without even taking off his shoes."

"Are you planning to give him breakfast in bed in the morning?"

"I don't like him but I do feel sorry for him. His parents separated, he really doesn't have any family—"

"I'll cry for him . . . do you really want him for a son-in-law?"

"Barbara isn't thinking about marriage, she's too smart for that—"

"What is she going to do if she gets pregnant?"

"I don't think that will happen—"

"You think they just go up to her room to talk?"

"No, I'm not a fool, Tom, no matter what you think."

"I never called you that, don't let's get started on us now . . . Why are you so sure she won't get pregnant?"

"I talked to her about birth control."

"A lot of kids know about birth control in theory and still get pregnant."

"I don't think she will."

"Why?"

"I went beyond talk about birth control with her. We discussed the pill, but a lot of people are still afraid of the side effects. I took her to a gynecologist in Stamford and had a diaphragm fitted for her."

"You did *that* without even telling me?"

"You weren't here."

"You could have called me. You knew damn well I'd hate the idea—"

"Would you rather have her get in trouble?"

"You gave her permission, you gave her your blessing—"

"I did no such thing. We talked all about the emotional and psychological hazards of this—"

"So then she asks a drunken idiot up to her bed?"

"Gordy's going through a bad time right now—"

"What are you doing, playing mother to him?"

"He needs one. Look, the kid's father ran off and left without even paying child support and his mother is trying to make a living selling real estate, which she doesn't do very well. He's been trying to work at the Shell station and play in a rock band at night. Today the band dropped him—apparently they found a better guitarist."

"Tough, but I don't want to give him my daughter for a consolation prize."

"Tom, don't you remember what it was like to be young—?"

"I was never like that."

"You don't remember very well, do you?"

"I didn't drink like that when I was that boy's age and I didn't drop out of high school."

"No, you were luckier in lots of ways, but you needed a girl, didn't you?"

"I fell in love with you."

"What do you think Gordy thinks he's doing?"

"Barbara has to have more sense. You wouldn't have fallen for someone like that—"

"Need is need. You keep telling me to face reality, don't you?"

"Where do you think this thing will lead her?"

"Oh, I think she'll go on from Gordy to better boys and men, but I don't think either one of them has to be scarred."

"Her first big love affair at sixteen!"

"Well, that's when I had my first, wasn't it?"

"You were seventeen. We stayed together and got married."

"So we did."

"What does that mean?"

"What if we hadn't felt so scared and guilty? What if I'd had a mother I could talk to, somebody who told me how to take care of myself?"

"We were careful—"

"We didn't even know what we were doing. Don't you remember how terrified I was?"

"I loved you."

A beat. "And I loved you. I must have, or I would have felt even more guilty. That's why I talked to Barbara. I didn't want her to have to go through what I went through."

"At least I didn't break into your father's house at two in the morning!"

"Gordy didn't break in. The kids always leave the back door unlocked."

"I didn't *sneak* in."

"Never? Have you forgotten the cottage my family rented in Vermont that summer, the sleeping porch out back? . . . Look, Tom, I don't blame you, you were trying to protect us. I don't want to blame anyone. Most of all I don't want you to make Barbara feel as awful as my parents made me feel."

"You told me they never spoke to you about us."

"They were afraid to. That's the way things were then. Everything was unspeakable. I don't want it to be that way with Barbara."

"What do you want me to do, give her and this Gordy my blessings?"

"No, I realize you can't do that . . . maybe it's a good thing you're not going to be here . . ."

"You intend to just let them go up to her room whenever they want?"

"Where would they be safer? In the backseat of some car or in some back lot where he could take her on his motorcycle?"

"Can't we damn well tell them just to quit this?"

"Do you think that would work?"

"No . . ."

"It won't last long if we don't try to fight it. I know my daughter. She knows Gordy's problems as well as we do."

"Then why—"

"It's hard for us to realize, but he's something of a hero in her set."

"The rebel . . ."

"Not only that. He's independent. At least he supports himself. Compared to the kids in her high school he has a certain grown-up air. And he needs her. She never ran into that before."

"You make it all sound so reasonable."

"It doesn't have to be so ugly—"

"How about dangerous? Sixteen and with a boy like that? You can't just calmly talk it all away."

"What do you want to do?"

"Send her away to school somewhere."

"In the middle of the school year? And you think he wouldn't follow anywhere she went?"

"I suppose . . ."

"We couldn't afford a boarding school anyway and next year she'll be in college. She'll meet other boys there—"

"And ask them up to her room?"

"I honestly don't think she'll be promiscuous—"

"What do you call what she is now?"

"One boy? Is that your definition of promiscuity?"

"But by the time she's twenty if she keeps on like this—"

"Tom, the sexual revolution is more than a slogan. Especially with kids. Don't you know that? A girl doesn't have to marry the first boy she goes to bed with anymore. Do you think we should all sit around and mourn that?"

"No, but . . . to tell the truth, it scares me."

"It offends your sense of morality . . ."

"Well, it did give a lot of people a hold fast, something to steer by."

Tom Rath, husband and father, meant all that. What about

Annie McSoaring's lover? I poured myself another drink.

"I agree these are confusing times," Betsy said, "but I really don't think the good old days were so great either. At least not for girls . . ."

Suddenly I wondered whether her so calm and tolerant attitude toward Barbara's behavior extended to her own, or might even be an outgrowth of her own. If she was having an affair with Bert Andrews it would be consistent for her to be less strict with her daughter, especially if Barbara knew about it, as she damn well might if old Bert was around all the time. Maybe my homecoming had been more complicated than I thought, with all *three* of us feeling guilty, and determined not to . . . the fully liberated family!

What would happen if Betsy and I were as frank with each other about our own departures from convention as we were about Barbara's? I tried to imagine Betsy congratulating me about my freedom from guilt with Annie and my telling her I was glad that she had found Bert to assuage her loneliness while I was in Washington. When the White House Conference on Mental Health or Survival was over, maybe I could bring Annie home with me to share this house with my liberated family and Bert could move in. We would have a *ménage à quatre.* Of course the old Victorian mansion might prove a touch small for that, but we could add a new wing or two. With Annie, Bert and Tom all working, money should certainly be no problem. The kids would have plenty of *security* and all could go to college without worrying about scholarships. Was this the new age promised by the sexual revolution?

Of course I didn't think so and the whole satirical idea made me sick to my stomach. Such utopias could never work . . . people were people . . . jealous, and couldn't help feeling possessive about those they loved or wanted or both. I adored Annie but the thought of seeing Bert put his hand on my wife made me see red. Likewise, I suspected Betsy would view with less than equanimity Annie sitting on my knee, and Annie in turn would not serenely hand me over to her on the nights Betsy might prefer my bed to Bert's. The *ménage à quatre* would reach its climax when Bert started chasing Annie around the room and I threw him out the window. Curtain, no applause.

I couldn't even stand to think of my daughter with another male, which was at least partly why I'd been so stiff about morality. I'd have to get over some of that for my daughters, but I was damned if I was ready to have Bert Andrews come into this house and take over my whole family. I noted how my jealousy had turned back to him, when Betsy hadn't even mentioned his name since my return . . . oh yes, I'd been looking for reasons why she'd become so, by my lights, permissive toward Barbara . . .

"Maybe the old times weren't so great," I said, "but do you think that everyone nowadays is free to break the whole Ten Commandments?" God, what a stuffy comment.

"No, of *course* not."

I wondered whether there was a hint of mockery in her voice when she said that.

"Anyway, I'm glad we finally had this out about Barbara," she went on. "It hasn't been so easy, trying to help her handle her problems alone."

"I'm sure . . . I mean I'm sure you've done the best you could under the circumstances—"

"Just don't lecture her tomorrow. Give her a hug. She still needs your love, maybe more now than ever, when she can't help having some doubts about herself . . . It's been a hard night," she said, "but I think we understand each other better, don't we?"

Did we?

19

TIRED AS I was, I still couldn't sleep. Slowly it dawned on me that I had damn near killed an unarmed boy. In that first flash of the hall light, the beer bottle in his hand had looked like a gun. I was all ready to shoot first, ask questions later. My hand was already squeezing the trigger. If the pistol had been oiled more recently, it even might have fired before my vision cleared and my family came to the rescue. Still, any man who hears someone prowling around his house in the dead of night has a right to grab a gun and investigate, doesn't he? Is he entirely the fool, as I'd been made to feel? I began to feel angry at Betsy and Barbara all over again. After all, that I was guilty of adultery had nothing to do with the attempt I'd made to defend my family. I wasn't disqualified from the right and obligation to do that, was I? In the old days there never would have been any doubt about it . . . a father in my position would have thrown the boy out, not ensconced him in the damn guest room. He would have ordered his daughter never to see the young man again, and so forth. Mother would have backed up father. At least everyone would have known where he or she *stood*.

Of course the trouble with this wonderful program was that it wouldn't work. Barbara would go on seeing Gordy no matter what I said. Bringing Gordy into court would only make Barbara more defiant. And if I ordered my daughter out of my house . . . forget it. It would be a classic example of cutting off one's nose to spite one's face.

But what if Barbara got pregnant in spite of her damn diaphragm, a not unheard-of happening. I would be the one who would have to support her child or find some way to get a safe abortion for her, two possibilities I didn't even want to think about. While waiting to see if such calamities would fall on us I'd be expected to accept the presence of my daughter's lover in the house. If this made me double up my fists, I could shove them into my pockets and keep on smiling. My rising blood pressure would be my own problem. If I let myself be crushed like that I'd have no one to blame but myself. Later in their lives my daughters would have a right to look back and accuse me of being weak. Barbara had a *right* to know where I stood—no point in giving her some lying, weak-kneed kind of approval I didn't believe in or feel.

Barbara wasn't the only one who needed some kind of show of strength from her father. Someone had to have the guts to tell my darling Janey, in a gentle way, that a person had to be in fairly good shape to ride a horse safely, especially to learn how to jump. Nature isn't forgiving. The arms and legs of an overweight young girl don't have enough strength in proportion to the weight of her body to keep her in a saddle. And heavy people often don't fall right. If they land on their neck or shoulder they're much more in danger of breaking their bones than a lighter, more muscular person would be. Of course no matter how tactfully I might try to phrase it, Janey would hate me if I tried to tell her any of this, just as Barbara's eyes would blaze at me if I told her bluntly Gordy was out, she wasn't to see him, never invite him to the house. If a man wanted approval, it took strength to stand up to his daughters, especially if his wife seemed to take their side.

I should straighten everybody out in this house or walk out. Sure. You tell 'em, Tom . . .

It was three in the morning. I was too exhausted to think any more. It was the ultimate relief—escape—when the grandfather clock boomed its notes and I fell asleep.

AT SIX-THIRTY my familiar if half-forgotten alarm clock drilled into my ear. For the first time in a long while, I woke up with a hangover and the vague sense of unease that seems to go with it. Betsy was rushing around the house with her determined smile. There seemed something about our family that required us to start the day with more hysteria than was displayed by soldiers on the way to battle. Breakfast was rarely a peaceful meal in our home. For some reason our kids never could find clean clothes and kept yelling, "Ma, I can't find a shirt," or "Where are my socks?" And so forth.

"We've got to get things organized around here," I would shout as I tried to rescue the bacon without dripping grease on my suit.

On this particular morning the tension, not surprisingly, was worse than usual. Barbara was worried about getting *poor* Gordy up in time for his job at the Shell station. She actually took coffee to him in the guest room, emerging with his dirty blue jeans and T-shirt, which Betsy put in the washing machine. Lordy, Gordy, you do pretty good for yourself in this house.

"Do you have a razor I can borrow for Gordy?" Barbara asked me, and I found myself actually getting him one from my travel kit. Good old Gordy. God *damn.*

In the midst of all the hubbub, Pete sat at the table calmly studying his algebra book and Janey made the toast, her soft round face, her big brown eyes full of what struck me then as an ageless kind of wisdom. Maybe my darling Janey's problem was that she understood too much, was too sensitive to the feelings of Barbara, Gordy, her mother and even me. When I kissed her before grabbing my briefcase to hurry for my train, she gave me a brief but warm hug. "Don't worry, daddy—everything's going to be all *right.*"

"I love you," I said, and felt like I wanted to cry. I could never tell her not to ride a horse. Probably she would realize her own limitations soon enough—at least I could hope for that . . .

At the last moment Betsy couldn't find the car keys and dashed around looking for her handbag. By the time we got to the station wagon we were running late and I had to tell her I would rather miss my train than drive as though we were trying to win the Grand Prix. As things worked out, the train wasn't on time that morning either, and arrived at the platform just as we did.

I kissed her good-bye, and she asked, "Will you be home again before you have to go back to Washington?"

"I'll call you as soon as I know," I said, and hurried to join the crush of impeccably dressed men who were scrambling aboard. Sinking down in a chair, I sat back and closed my eyes. Peace. Connecticut commuters often complained about the long train rides they had to endure. Right now I wasn't one of them.

HOPKINS DID NOT telephone me, as I'd hoped, the moment I got into my office. I paced around my desk until almost noon, when he called.

"I just talked to President Kennedy about giving Dr. Harbringer one committee to run, while we organize others on the more conventional aspects of mental health. He bought it."

"*Good.*"

"He wants a detailed statement of purpose for the whole conference, and we can go ahead with the job of appointing the committee chairmen."

"Would you mind if I worked on that in Washington? It might be easier if David McKay and I worked out the statement of purpose and submitted it to you for approval rather than doing it the other way around."

"Good idea. Jack is in a hurry for us to get going. He'd like to hold a preliminary meeting of the key committee chairmen in Washington within a month, somewhere around the middle of November. It's important to build up some momentum on this."

"We'll do it."

"That's the spirit, Tom. I'm going to recommend you for the job of staff director. The job won't pay any more than you're already getting, but some sort of raise should be in order with this increase in responsibility. Of course you'll still be working on my speeches —I'll have to give more of them than ever . . . which should entitle you to some extra stipend. Perhaps I can continue you on half pay, in addition to your government salary. That sound fair?"

"Very fair, I'm grateful—"

"Don't talk about the arrangement to anyone—it could be misinterpreted. When I ask an associate to take a government appointment, I can't expect him to make a financial sacrifice, and you do have some increase due. You seem to have taken hold of this whole business very well."

"Thank you—"

"I know that working in Washington so long is difficult for a family man like you."

"With a project this important—"

"I appreciate that attitude, Tom. How's your family?"

". . . Fine, just fine . . ."

"Glad to hear it. You can have the bureau teletype me a copy of your statement of purpose when you work it out with McKay. I want to keep on top of this . . . well, thanks, Tom," and there was a sharp click as he hung up.

I felt like jumping into the air and clicking my heels. When I got my government appointment I'd be making close to thirty thousand dollars a year, a good deal more than I'd expected so soon.

From habit my first impulse was to call Betsy and tell her about the raise, but I also realized it wouldn't take effect for a while, could get her all excited for nothing . . . My next temptation was to call Annie, which somehow didn't give rise to all sorts of reservations. I could also tell her that I'd take the next shuttle plane to Washington. . . .

"Tom! Thanks for calling . . . sometimes I get all crazy worried that you'll get so involved in New York . . ."

She didn't mention Connecticut, she didn't have to.

"No danger of that . . . Hopkins just called, I'm going to catch the two o'clock shuttle to you—"

"Terrific!"

"There's more. It's kind of complicated and won't happen right away, but in effect he gave me a big raise."

"That doesn't surprise me, but it's wonderful."

"Annie, anything is possible now . . . it really is."

"That's kind of awesome, isn't it?"

"I just don't want you to think that no future is possible for us."

"You got me over that, but we have time to figure things out. Please don't feel rushed . . ."

I was grateful to her for saying that, but sensed that she was also asking me not to hurry her. As usual I wanted it both ways—I proceeding with due caution, she wanting me enough to abandon all common sense.

"I'll meet you at the airport," she said.

"You don't have to do that," I said in surprise, because no one had ever done that. South Bay was a long ways from LaGuardia.

"Of course I'll meet you," Annie said. "It's all part of my service as your assistant. Also, I can't wait to see you. Nothing much going on in the office and, hussy that I am, I intend to get you to take me straight back to the hotel."

ON THE SHUTTLE to Washington I tried to sleep, couldn't. Thanks to Annie's tagline, the short flight seemed almost unendurably long.

Usually I was among the last passengers to disembark from an airplane. The men who stood up and waited in the aisle as soon as the engines were silenced had always struck me as ridiculous, but on this afternoon I cleverly maneuvered myself to the head of the line by going to a restroom before we were supposed to unbuckle our seat belts, and I was standing by the door with my small

159 _

suitcase when it opened. Hurrying into the airport, I saw Annie pushing through a crowd at the gate and running toward me, a slender woman in a tweed skirt and gray cashmere sweater. I put my suitcase down. Her arms grabbed me as hard as mine encircled her and our mouths met with a shock of pleasure.

"I was afraid it wouldn't be like this," she said. "I had a nightmare about your coming back all distant and aloof, sorry you'd ever met me."

"Hardly . . ."

"Do you have baggage?"

"Just this," I said, holding up my small suitcase.

"Let's grab a taxi."

We all but ran through the crowded airport, dodging around knots of people.

"The Westminster Hotel," I said as soon as we jumped into a cab.

The driver didn't know where it was, and I wasn't familiar enough with the city to give him directions, but Annie told him to start driving toward the Washington Monument, where we would give him further instructions. And then she was in my arms, my fingers digging into the smooth muscles of her back under the cashmere and the scent of her filling the air. We drew back suddenly, conscious of the eyes of the driver in the rearview mirror. It took extraordinary discipline to sit there demurely with my arm around her shoulders as the cab sped around curves, pressing us together.

When we got to the hotel I gave the driver a five-dollar bill and without waiting for change grabbed my suitcase and followed Annie through the lobby, where old people sat in easy chairs and peered at us over the tops of their newspapers. A rotund woman with a miniature poodle in her arms got into the elevator with us, looked steadily at us as the elevator seemed to move with infuriating slowness toward the fifth floor.

Annie had her key out of the handbag as we stepped into the hall, but the lock on her door would not open right away and I had a vision of myself breaking through the panel. Finally we were in her room, embracing by the bed, the door slammed shut behind us. There was nothing exactly gentle about our feelings at this moment. Our breath came as hard as though we were fighting. We didn't try to tease this out . . .

Afterward a moment of profound peace. Stretched out on the

— 160

bed, our bodies coated with sweat, a slight breeze blowing from an open window, we felt deliciously cool at first, then chilled enough to pull a sheet over ourselves. We went to sleep holding hands.

When I woke up it was almost dark. Annie hadn't turned on a light. She was wearing a short terrycloth bathrobe, pouring hot water into a coffee maker that looked like a big hourglass. The fragrance of the freshly ground beans filled the room, and the electric coil glowed red, then slowly turned to gray. Except for the sound of distant traffic the room was still, until the kettle made a sharp click as Annie set it down.

I sat up. Hearing the bed creak, Annie turned toward me.

"Welcome back," she said with a smile. "You were sleeping so soundly that I almost got scared—I held my breath there for a second so I could hear yours."

"I've never felt better."

"Do you mind if I turn on a light? I was afraid it would wake you up."

"Go ahead . . . I want to look at you."

She touched a wall switch and I closed my eyes against the glare of an overhead lamp

"Good Lord, I scratched you," she said, coming to touch my shoulders where she had left some red marks.

"I'm not complaining . . . Annie, would you take off your robe? I like to look at you . . ."

She did and dropped it on a chair, then took two cups from a cupboard and filled them with the steaming coffee, adding milk from the refrigerator before bringing me one. She went back to the stove for her own, then sat near me on the edge of the bed.

"Last night I thought I'd go crazy lying here alone," she said. "I couldn't help it, kept thinking about you going home to your wife and kids. I knew I shouldn't, but I couldn't stop myself . . . It wasn't just ordinary jealousy, although I felt some of that. I also kept thinking how rough this . . . this situation must be on you. I know you, you must have felt torn apart . . ."

"Well, that's putting it a little strong . . ."

"Want to talk about it? We shouldn't have to fake anything with each other."

"I agree."

"Maybe it's none of my business, Tom, but I do want to know about your kids. I don't want to be walled off . . ."

"Well, everything's pretty messed up at home . . ." And then I told her the story of Barbara and Gordy, along the way having to laugh some at myself, but still angry at Gordy.

"It's really not such an unusual situation," Annie said. "If she's almost seventeen—"

"But the boy's no good . . ."

"I'm sure he doesn't appear that way to her."

"And Betsy is *helping* her. She even helped her to buy a diaphragm."

"Isn't that better than—"

"She's only sixteen years old!"

"What are you afraid will happen?"

"It's already happened. God knows what the kids at her school are saying about her. My daughter probably already has the reputation for being a round-heels."

"Is it your reputation you're worried about or hers?"

"Both."

"What do you want to do about this?"

"I'd like to kill Gordy, and I damn near did. Wouldn't any father feel the same?"

"Maybe, but I doubt if many brandished guns around—"

"What else am I supposed to do? Just wait passively till she comes to her senses and gets rid of him?"

"Not a bad idea—"

"God, I even gave him my razor this morning."

"All you can do is let nature take its course. This won't last long—"

"Maybe, but she'll get another boy and start in with him—"

"Is that what you want?"

"I *don't* want a promiscuous daughter."

"Do you think it's possible for a girl to be sexually active without being promiscuous?"

"You're defending her, you sound like my wife. Whose side are you on anyway?"

"No side, Tom, but I am a woman and I guess all of us have certain things in common . . . By the way, she's only had one relationship, why are you already calling her a round-heels?"

"I didn't call her that, the other kids will."

"Maybe kids who talk like that aren't so important."

"They can *hurt* her, Annie. My God, she's so vulnerable. She hasn't any idea how rough the world can be—"

"Maybe she's learning."

"And I'm supposed to do nothing while she wrecks her whole life—?"

"Do you think my whole life was wrecked when I was sixteen?"

"This hasn't got anything to do with you—"

"Maybe not, but I had my first love affair when I was sixteen and somehow I survived it."

I confess I didn't love hearing this, but what I said was, "You're different."

"How?"

"You weren't brought up in South Bay, Connecticut. Connecticut is no Samoa, believe me—"

"You're saying that Brooklyn is? Funny, I never saw the palm trees."

"You knew what you were doing, you'd been earning your own living for a long while—"

"You're saying I was poor and had to work . . . your darling daughter is *different?*"

"No, damn it . . . hey, I'm sorry, I'm not trying to get into a fight—"

"Then you'd better be careful. I'm trying to help you, Tom. You can't go around eating your guts out over this."

"My guts will survive, but—"

"So will your daughter if she has any of your strength, and I bet she does."

"You really think she'll be all right?"

"The odds favor her, so far as I can see."

"What do you think I should do, give her my blessing?"

"Just treat her kindly. Don't let her think you've given up on her."

"I don't think she gives much of a damn what I think."

"Oh, yes she does."

"Most of the time she just avoids me."

"That's what my father said to my mother about me."

"You had good reason, didn't you?"

"Sure, he wanted me to be a vestal virgin. He shouted and carried on something terrible whenever I stayed out late with a boy. He was always talking about how he wanted to kill the little bastard." She smiled.

"Annie, you're being pretty rough on me."

"You're being rough on yourself, *and* on your daughter. Believe me, I'm really trying to help. I love you, and I still love my father, and I'd bet your daughter loves you."

"I suppose you think I'm making a damn fool of myself."

"Fathers tend to do that. It seems to go with the territory."

"I probably left her feeling I was furious with her. I was, and I guess I still am—"

"Then fake it a little for her sake. She'll be grateful to you for it."

"How am I supposed to fake it?"

"Send her a present, a pretty scarf, a new sweater, anything to show you still *like* her."

"Did your father do that for you?"

"That was one thing he was good at. He didn't stay at home much, but I kept getting coconuts carved into monkeys' faces from all corners of the world."

"And that meant something to you?"

"I still have a whole row of those things in my apartment. If we were at home I'd give you one of them to send to Barbara."

"I'll send her a sweater and a scarf . . . will you help me pick them out?"

"What size is she?"

"Just about the same as you, come to think of it . . ."

"It will be easy then. I know a good discount house."

There was a pause while she refilled our cups.

"You feel better now?"

"Yes, matter of fact I do."

"I thought so—your fists aren't clenched."

20

WE MADE LOVE again then in more leisurely fashion, but afterward I couldn't sleep. Once Annie had gotten me started, I seemed to have a need to go on talking about my other kids.

I told her about Pete, his fine mind and ambition, along with my worry that he was already a workaholic at thirteen. I loved him, but somehow our relationship was nothing like that I thought a father and son should have. I never could hug him without feeling him withdraw into himself, and whenever I tried to talk to him about anything important I could see a faraway look come into his eyes and almost feel his muscles tense while he waited for me to get the intimacy over with as soon as possible. We were wary with each other. I sensed he felt he was somehow failing me and was trying to make up for it with his good grades at school. I wanted to put my arms around him, crush him against me, but we both would have been terribly embarrassed if I'd tried that.

Annie said very little, but her dark eyes said she was not only listening but *hearing* . . . When I got on the subject of Janey and tried to describe her, a heavy little girl in an English riding costume who somehow understood everything, just the sound of those words made me almost break down. Lying in bed next to me, Annie didn't try to calm me down, didn't tell me everything would be all right and I was silly to worry so much. What she did was put her arms around me, her fingers digging into my back as she realized my miseries, letting them shoot from me through her, like an electric current, a kind of shock treatment.

I started then about Mark, my son in Italy that I had never seen but who looked so much like me, as his photographs showed. It was always with me . . . this image of myself growing up in the

165 _

slums of Rome, a boy, now a young man so unlike my other children, street-smart and tough . . . the way I often felt myself underneath my gray flannel suit—an old paratrooper and veteran of Rockefeller Center who also knew a little something about how hard a man had to fight for survival. In some ways I felt closer to the son I had never seen than I did to what society called my legitimate children. Somehow I imagined that if Mark and I ever sat down together at a bar we would know each other as the same kind of person without need for too many words . . .

"Of course you must bring him over here," Annie was saying. "We'll set that up."

"But I keep thinking, what if he hates me on sight? He'd certainly have a right."

"I doubt if he will, though. He'll be able to compare what you've done for him with what most men have done for those kids they spawned and left behind. Maybe deep down your other kids can't help comparing you to some ideal of a father who gives them everything—all his time, understanding without any worries of his own. That's what I did to my father for a long while—I kept comparing him to an ideal he couldn't measure up to instead of being grateful for all those grinning coconuts he kept sending me from every port."

"I think maybe Betsy does that to me too, and maybe I do it to her," I said. "We keep comparing each other to some ideal and go on disappointing each other—"

"What's the matter?"

"I shouldn't be talking about Betsy."

"I hear tell that most men need to talk about their wives to the other woman . . ."

She smiled when she said it, but I of course immediately wondered if Annie was talking from experience rather than hearsay. I wanted all women to be virginal, except when they were with me . . . Still, I was grateful, too, that I could talk to Annie.

"Does it bother *you* when I talk about Betsy?"

"It might if you said she was the bitch of the world. That would start me to wondering what you'd say about me someday."

"I'm not going to say that. But sometimes I do have this anger, a real rage . . ."

"Why?"

"I'm not sure . . . sometimes she seems so . . . so damn helpless—"

"She seems to have raised three children fairly well."

"I know, but, well, this seems so damn indiscreet"—I winced a bit—"yes, sorry, even with you I can be embarrassed to talk about things that happened with my wife, or didn't happen . . . What I'm trying in my not very forthright way to say is that there's not the kind of sexual excitement and satisfaction, that, well, that we have. Just had . . . I'm not saying it's all her doing or lack of it, but I guarantee you there are no red marks on my shoulders afterward, no—"

"I wonder if I'd be able to do that for you after twenty years."

"You don't let me get away with anything, do you?"

"I guess I do play hard ball. Any other game would bore you, wouldn't it?"

"Sometimes, to stretch a metaphor, you make my hands sting, but the truth is that Betsy and I were never able to give each other what you and I have right now . . . When we were young we were too scared, and then the resentments built up. Last night when we were talking about Barbara and Gordy she said something about nowadays a girl doesn't have to marry the first boy she goes to bed with. I guess I thought she was implying that that was why she married me, I was the first and she'd have felt guilty not to have sanctioned it with marriage. Maybe she never loved me, maybe I never loved her—"

"Do you really believe that?"

"I don't know. We were pretty different when we met. I didn't have any real family and she did. I think I *needed* her a lot more than she did me."

"Why do you suppose she accepted you in the first place?"

"Maybe she'd never felt intense emotion about the opposite sex before and needed it, at least as an experiment . . . only in our day nice girls weren't allowed much experimentation. I think maybe she felt trapped."

"Didn't she ever wake up to find that maybe she'd been trapped into marriage with a very fine man?"

"I've never heard her use words like that about me, and I've never even thought them about myself."

"Tom, at least consider that she was capable of comparing—"

"I doubt Betsy had any man to compare me to, except her old man."

"What was he like?"

"Calm, aloof, at least on the outside. He was the kind of man who walked the line all his life and never stopped smiling, even when it led straight uphill to the edge of a cliff."

"What happened to him?"

"He made it big as a banker until the Depression hit, and then he just seemed to grow smaller and smaller until he melted away like the Cheshire Cat, with only the smile left."

"No wonder she loved him, and probably hated him too . . ."

There was a pause.

"I wish I knew why I'm so angry at her all the time," I said.

Annie made no reply.

"Of course maybe I have reason now . . ."

Still Annie was silent.

"I think she might be having an affair," I said.

"Oh?"

"Maybe she's not going to bed with the person, but it seems she can't talk about anybody else, and he's around all the time."

"What kind of a man is he?"

"I think she believes he's just what she wants. He makes money, lots of it, with no apparent strain, no visible worry. It's not just the luxury of money she wants, though she misses it because she was always used to it, but it's the sense of competence, of strength she admires . . . she doesn't see him for what he is—"

"What is he?"

"Well, you can consider the source, but to me he's a sharpie who married for money, used his wife's money to speculate in real estate when Connecticut land was cheap, and then got rid of her. He's maybe twelve years older than she is but he comes on strong as a ladies' man, playboy of the western world, well, Connecticut, anyway."

"You sure don't like him very much."

"Why should I? He's moving in on my wife, on my whole *family.* He's giving riding lessons to Janey. He got a microscope for Pete. He got Betsy a car at a big fat discount—"

"Some of that could be interpreted as less than sinister . . ."

"Damn it, whose side are you on, why do you keep making me ask you that?"

"You want me just to lie here and agree with you about everything? I'm a lover, not a yes-man."

"Fine, touché. But this guy has convinced Betsy that he's some kind of platonic friend, or this romantic figure who's really crazy

_ 168

about her but wouldn't do anything improper for the world . . . and that's *not* what's happening."

"What is?"

"He's the kind who'd just love to have a nice little affair with a neighbor's wife to add one more notch on his belt of conquests."

"You're real sure of that?"

"You're damn right I am. I'd like to put my hands around that little bastard's neck and squeeze until his eyes pop out."

I actually put my hands up and flexed them.

"Are you going to do that before or after you shoot Barbara's Gordy?"

"How about on the same day . . . I'll go out there and clean house . . . I'd really love to do that—"

"The law takes the fun out of everything."

"Is a man supposed to stand around smiling while his wife and daughter go to bed with . . . with bums?"

"What if they weren't bums? What if they were real outstanding, upright individuals? Would you like that better?"

"No such would mess around with my wife or daughter—"

"How would you like to meet my father? He's retired in Scotland, but he comes over once in a while, and he's still fiercely protective of me."

"You're not sixteen years old!" (Neither was Betsy.)

"He still wants to kill any man who takes advantage of me."

"Well, I respect him for that. So would I."

"That's nice. I'm just trying to sort all this out. You want to kill your wife's friend for moving in on her while you're away. How would Betsy feel about me? She wouldn't be a pistol-packing mama by any chance?"

"She might want to be, but she's nothing like that."

"I'm glad. I was getting kind of worried about you Connecticut people."

I had to smile, finally. "Annie, please don't make too much fun of me. I know I'm being outrageous, but I've been trying to tell you the way I *feel*, with no holds barred."

"And I appreciate that, but thank God you recognize the absurdity of what you're saying—"

"I'm afraid it's quite possible for me to know I'm absurd and to keep on being it."

"Well, so far, at least, you're not acting out the worst of it."

"But what I feel is tearing me up—"

"You don't look so torn up."

"Sometimes I feel like a man who's surrounded by strangers, except for you. I don't know my wife really—to tell the truth, I have no idea what kind of woman she really is. I don't know my children and can't even guess what kind of people they'll turn into. Damn it, I'm not even sure I know you. The only person I know at all is myself, and it appears I'm crazy. Anybody who wants to run around shooting people must be that, even if he never really does it, not in peacetime anyway."

"Maybe there's no such thing as peacetime until we're dead. Maybe that's the way it's supposed to be."

"And you still want to live forever?"

"Sure. I'm not as good at hate as you are."

"Annie, you're a moralist, the only naked moralist I ever saw!"

She laughed.

"Do you still think you really don't know me?" she asked, reaching out to caress me in some very sensitive places.

"I'm beginning to."

"So what do you think I am?"

For once I had the good sense to shut up, lie back, and show instead of tell.

21

A SESSION WITH Annie seemed to reinvigorate me, never mind all my endless internal roilings. The next morning I began the job of organizing the White House conference with more vigor than I'd ever shown or felt in an office. Almost everything went unbelievably well. I banged out a detailed statement of purpose for the conference with an organization plan that listed all the committees to study the various aspects of mental health, read it over the telephone for Dr. Harbringer, who said he understood the need for compromise and would welcome a chance to lead the group which would discuss war as the final insanity, a culmination of all murderous and suicidal impulses, and so forth. I sent copies of the documents by messenger to David McKay, with a note saying that Dr. Harbringer had already approved of them but that I wanted his opinion before sending them on to Ralph Hopkins.

As soon as the office closed Annie reminded me that I should buy a present for Barbara and offered to help pick one out. We chose a sweater of soft white lamb's wool for Barbara, an almost identical one for Janey and a Swiss army knife for Pete. When the clerk called in the number of my American Express card she found it was overdrawn.

"Damn Betsy," I said. "This always happens—"

"Can't you pay with a check?"

I was never certain of the state of my joint account with Betsy and anyway the clerk declined to take my personal check. My purchases had already been gift-wrapped.

"Don't worry about it," the clerk said with obvious annoyance and placed the parcels under the counter.

"This is silly," Annie said. "Use this."

She handed the clerk her own American Express card.

"I can't let you do that—"

"You can pay me back later. It's not a big deal."

"Annie, I owe you so much—"

"You don't *owe* me anything. Tom, this is a two-way deal. Please stop being so *grateful* . . . Come on, let's get these things wrapped for mailing. The post office isn't far from here."

Sending off the presents to my children made me feel *good*. Why hadn't I done it before?

Everything seemed to go miraculously right. The next morning I received a note from Miss Bannerman, Hopkins' executive secretary, with an unexpected check for eight hundred dollars from a digest magazine that was picking up one of the articles about mental health I'd written under Hopkins' by-line several months ago. The old man was pleased by this publicity, and as he often did when I got one of his articles into print, made the check out to me as a kind of bonus. Usually I turned windfalls over to Betsy, but this time I cashed the check myself. The crisp hundred-dollar bills in my wallet gave me a sense of power, but also a feeling of guilt because Betsy must be running into financial trouble again if she'd gone over the credit limit on our American Express cards. Before spending any of the money I called Betsy up and asked about her latest difficulties with the budget.

"Oh, I didn't want to worry you," she said, "but the dishwasher broke down and the repair man said it was so old that it wasn't worth fixing. Bert got me a builder's discount on a new one and I charged it because I just couldn't pay for it this month. Then there were some clothes the kids needed . . ."

I sent her three hundred dollars. With the remaining five hundred I paid back Annie and then set out to buy her my first gift. I shopped around before settling on an antique necklace of thin gold chains and a sparkling cluster of garnets, only semiprecious stones but they were as rich in color as rubies and were arranged in a spray designed to embellish the throat and breasts of a young woman. Wrapped in gold paper, it felt good in my coat pocket as I walked back to my office, and I could hardly wait to give it to Annie. I delayed, though, until we got back to our hotel and sat down to dinner, which she'd prepared in the kitchenette of her room.

"Here," I said with total lack of suave as I handed her the

package. "I've never been much on presents but I discovered a little thing—"

"You didn't have to—"

"That made it all the more necessary."

"*But* I'm glad you did. God, I love presents, I shouldn't admit that but I do. My God, it's magnificent," she said when she saw the necklace. "I have to put on the right dress for it. Please go to your room and come back in five minutes."

When I came back she was wearing a low-cut black dress. The necklace glowed in a crescent across the upper swell of her breasts, emphasizing the warm curves of her flesh. I found it almost unbearably erotic. I traced the path of that necklace with my lips while she stroked my head, and without my asking she slipped off the shoulder straps of her dress, letting the black silk fall to her waist. The beauty of her breasts bisected by those shining red stones . . . I carried her to the bed, wishing I could paint her with the skill of a Rubens while she lay there wearing nothing but that glittering necklace. Yes, I was, am, an inveterate romantic . . .

"I wish I could afford to give you presents like this every night," I said with a wry smile when we had finished making love.

"It's my turn to give you something next," she said as she put the necklace back in its leather box and put on her terrycloth bathrobe. "Do you have a sentimental attachment to this?"

She touched the thick stainless steel watch attached by a frayed leather strap to my wrist.

"Not really, it's just the kind of thing I've worn ever since the war . . ."

The next evening she presented me with a fancily wrapped leather box that turned out to contain a handsome gold watch with strap to match. No woman had ever bought an expensive gift for me before, possibly because I had always insisted on economy so much. We made love again, and if this was the effect of gift-giving, I could see why jewelers prospered, even in hard times.

Two days later David McKay called me.

"I like your statement of purpose and the organization plan," he said in that Boston accent that sounded so much like President Kennedy's. "I think we're really on the right track."

"Good."

"The president hasn't had time to go over the stuff in detail yet, but I gave him the gist of it and he approves. I have just a few changes I'd like to suggest. Can you come over here now?"

"Sure thing."

"Let's have lunch. We're going to be working together on this for a long time and we have a lot to talk about."

IT WAS SURPRISING how my spirits sagged even when I left her for little more than an hour. I knew that it was pretty extreme to be so dependent on a woman, but even a trip to the White House seemed to lose its excitement without her.

McKay greeted me with considerable friendliness in his cramped office and had only a few minor changes to suggest in the documents I'd sent him. The main thing he wanted to discuss was lists of possible members for the various committees and a date for their first meeting, November twentieth.

"That's pretty short notice, but the president wants to stop in and greet these people for a few minutes at least. He has to go to Texas right after that and he'll be all tied up for quite a while."

I assured McKay that I could organize the first meeting of the committees for the conference on November twentieth. I thought that McKay would take me to some dining room for staff members in the White House, but at a little after twelve he led me to his car, a gray Porsche roadster, and drove to a small French restaurant instead. Apparently he had finished our business discussion and this luncheon was a sort of reward for setting up the conference in a way he liked. Over martinis, a thirst for which returned to me as soon as I got away from Annie, he discussed our Harvard days, which was difficult since we had known each other hardly at all in Cambridge. Next he talked about the war, which he had spent mostly in Washington.

"Did Betsy come down here with you?" he finally asked.

"No, we didn't feel we should take the kids out of school."

"That's the way my wife feels," he said. "She really hates Washington and nothing can get her away from Boston for long."

There was a pause before he added with a grin, "A lot of us around here are temporary bachelors. It has its compensations, though, doesn't it?"

I immediately wondered if he'd sensed my relationship to Annie during our first visit to his office.

"I guess so," I said carefully.

"This can be a damn lonely town until you meet a few people.

I'm having a few friends up to my apartment tomorrow night. Would you like to come?"

"That's very kind of you, but I have an awful lot of work . . ."

"You can't work all the time. Bring that attractive assistant of yours if you like. We're not exactly a stuffy group."

Obviously he had set me down as a fellow ladies' man. Was there an underground of genteel adulterers who didn't need a special handshake because members recognized each other on sight? McKay was a big, hearty man with a kind of plummy face, and I didn't think he was making fun of me. He was offering me the camaraderie of men of the world, or at least his world. Anyway, who was I to disparage it, even if what Annie and I had was hardly a part of his suggestion of casual fun and games.

"We'd like to come, but I'll have to check my calendar," I said, leaving an out for Annie if she wanted it. "I'll let you know."

Somewhat to my surprise, Annie said she wanted to go. We should get to know McKay, she said, and anyway, she was curious about everything that went on in Washington. I called McKay to thank him for his invitation and he gave me an address that meant nothing to me at the time but turned out to be a fashionable apartment house in Georgetown.

At first glance the gathering of McKay's friends was little different from a South Bay cocktail party, except the women here were much younger than the men, good-looking almost without exception, and the men did most of the talking. McKay introduced Annie and me around his living room, where perhaps thirty people stood, glass in hand. Most of the men were aides to senators or big shots of some kind, with one congressman present. The women were mostly researchers or secretaries. To say that this was a conclave of men with their mistresses would have sounded melodramatic, but I guessed that this was what it was, and it was disillusioning simply because it was so boring, without any hint of anything secret, forbidden, exalted or in the least exciting. Such liaisons in this part of Washington were obviously as matter-of-fact as marriage itself, and in some ways less emotional . . . somehow I couldn't even imagine these people getting *angry* at each other. Perhaps it was only my mood, but I felt oddly deflated by all this. When these men went home they probably said good-bye to their mistresses as casually . . . indifferently . . . as they would greet their wives. Now they just stood around telling pretty much the same

175 —

jokes that advertising men in Connecticut would tell. I wanted to leave that place as soon as I could and sensed that Annie was feeling the same way. It wasn't so much being unable to belong to this group as being terrified that we someday might become a natural part of it. As more people crowded in we were able to escape without being noticed. Alone on the street, we walked holding hands until we could find a taxi, and still held hands in the back of the cab, as though to signify a pact that *we* never could allow ourselves to become jaded like those people we had left behind.

RALPH HOPKINS so much liked the documents David McKay had approved that he sent copies to all the people he was inviting to serve on the various committees and beyond, to his wife's circle of friends and business associates. When enthusiastic comments poured into his office his taste for the conference grew and he began spending a lot of time in Washington in his suite at the Mayflower Hotel to oversee preparations for the meeting on November twentieth. On the third of that month President Kennedy invited him to a dinner at the White House and introduced him to several senators whose approval was needed for the final plan and the funds with which to run it.

"We've got green lights all the way," Hopkins said to me the next morning. "We could go a long way with this, Tom."

I guessed that Kennedy had promised him some sort of cabinet post. The old man was so worked up that his usual gray pallor was suffused with pink and he paced a great deal while he talked to me. He was almost like a gambler on a hot roll with no expectations but to keep on making sevens. He accepted invitations to speak and requests for magazine articles that came to him now, and I was kept busy at my typewriter while Annie took care of the organizational arrangements. We were busier than ever, working until after midnight, but somehow we rarely seemed to get tired.

I remember everything in those early days of November as being a delight. When the hot, muggy days of a Washington fall turned chilly and we had long days of rain, Annie proclaimed the weather as great for exercising, and no matter how late she had worked the previous evening, she did her workout in her black leotard before an open window every morning at seven, a performance I liked to admire from the warmth of our bed. No matter how cold it was, she would leave that window about a quarter open all the time. We often shivered as we got undressed after a hard day's work, but the sudden shock of warmth we felt when our naked bodies came together under the covers was all the more delightful because of it, and the whistling of the wind around the sash in the darkness made us feel especially snug. There are a lot of advantages to a cold room.

The original plan was to have the fifty or so V.I.P.s who had agreed to serve on the committees for the conference meet for luncheon in the private dining room at the Mayflower Hotel, conduct business sessions during the afternoon in adjoining rooms and then conclude the proceedings in time for those who wanted to catch planes home that evening. It was hoped that President Kennedy would at least stop in to deliver a few brief words of greeting toward the end of the luncheon. Maybe Hopkins thought that this wasn't sufficient to honor the blue ribbon committees he had chosen and asked the president for more. However it occurred, a hurried change of plans was announced on November tenth: the business meetings on the twentieth would be followed by a reception for the committee members in the Red Room of the White House. Both the president and Jackie would be there.

"I'll arrange for you and . . . your assistant to get invitations," Hopkins said. "I know how hard you've both worked on this, and anyway I'd like to have you both handy. You never know what's going to come up."

Somehow he never managed to remember Annie's name and always referred to her as "your assistant." It occurred to me that he didn't allow himself really to *see* attractive young women who might prove an unwanted distraction.

"I get the idea that he thinks I'm sort of a good typewriter," Annie had told me once, but when she heard that he was arranging for her to be invited to the reception at the White House she forgave all.

For the great evening she wore her black silk cocktail dress and the garnet necklace. The men were as one in dark business suits. But not even pinstriped worsted could dim the splendor of President Kennedy, who strode into the room with that ebullient smile of his and those penetrating blue eyes that somehow could flash with humor even on the gravest occasions without diminishing his dignity. Jackie stood at his side in a gray silk sheath, her smile a touch forced, but her large dark eyes were luminous as always. They looked like a bridal couple, much too young to be royalty even in a tiny nation like Monaco, yet there was a kind of glory in their beauty, the glamor of monarchy without that vapid quality that so often goes with the unearned rank and purely ceremonial functions of modern royalty. Here was a man who still looked as lithe as a college boy but who in fact wielded the vast powers of the presidency of the United States.

I was not often awed by celebrities, many of whom I met in the course of my work, but President Kennedy did fascinate me. I still kept wondering how he got to sleep at night with all the problems of the world waiting on his decisions; how he found the courage to admit his mistakes and go on with his look of quiet confidence, as though there were no problems he couldn't eventually solve.

He gave a graceful talk of not more than two minutes about the importance of working to find cures for mental illness, saying that he thought it a good idea to include on the agenda the ultimate insanity of war, a phrase he uttered with dry understatement. After thanking everyone for helping him organize such a conference, he said that he had great hopes for the growth of such studies in the future as people of all nations realized that the enemy was man's inability to grasp the fact that he'd live with his fellow man or not at all. There he let it lie, and turned to shaking hands and chatting with the committee members.

"To tell the truth, I've had my doubts about him in the past," Dr. Harbringer said to me, "but I honestly believe he's got the makings of a great man."

Harbringer had been surprisingly silent at the meetings that afternoon, and I'd worried that he had lost some of his fire.

"He has a lot more time than most presidents have had," I said, another comment I was to remember later.

"I wonder what he'll do after his second term," Harbringer said. "He'll still just be in his early fifties."

"I've heard rumors that he'll be president of Harvard," I said.

"That would be a good spot for him. Anyway, Jack is apparently still willing to listen to me. Today he didn't have much time, but he said he'd see me as soon as he gets back from Dallas . . ."

After the reception that night, Hopkins was ebullient.

"You've done a fine job helping set this up," he said to me as I walked with him from the White House to his limousine. "We have an enormous project here that may go way beyond the White House conference."

"I hope so—"

"We have a lot to talk about, but I have to go back to New York for about a week. Why don't you take a couple of days off?"

My conscience, ever active if not always effective, told me I should go home to see my children, but while I rationalized that the preparations for the meeting had left me more tired than I'd realized, mostly it was that I didn't feel up to the emotional crisis a return to South Bay would inevitably involve.

So on the morning of November twenty-first Annie and I rented a car and decided to spend a day exploring the eastern shore of Maryland, which had been recommended to us by David McKay as a good place for a holiday. Perhaps because she had seldom ridden in cars during her childhood in Brooklyn, Annie loved to get out of the city and drive through the countryside. Although she'd visited Europe several times she had actually seen little of the United States outside of New York, and took great pleasure in the villages we passed on the shores of Chesapeake Bay with their fleets of skipjacks, little sloops that were used for dredging up oysters but which had clipper bows more handsome than the hulls of the surrounding yachts. We stopped at an inn with a fine view of the harbor in Oxford, Maryland, and after a dinner of fresh crab cakes and broiled bluefish decided to spend the night. From the window of our room we could see the afternoon light fade over the bay, turning the still waters into delicate shadings of misty rose and gray. Silhouetted against the sky we saw a great wavering *V* of Canadian geese, a late flight from the Arctic on their way south. When Annie opened the sash we could hear them calling to each other, a sound much too joyous to be called "gabbling," a song of the wild that echoed with excitement and the delight of winging together through that chill golden twilight. As they circled to land for the night in the nearby cornfields, we heard a shot which was followed by complete silence, and I pictured an explosion of blood in the sky.

"I don't see how anybody can shoot them," Annie said.

"At least it's getting too dark for the hunters now."

We left the window open, as she always liked to do, and went to bed early, finding warmth in each other's arms. After a while we could hear the geese start to murmur again and gradually build up to their pitch of excitement.

"They must have a great time," Annie said, "until they get shot."

"I've heard that they mate for life."

"Unlike humans? I'm sorry I said that!"

"Never mind."

"We still have almost a year at least . . ."

"More . . . I think the White House conference will be just the beginning. We'll have plenty of time to work things out . . ."

THE NEXT MORNING, November twenty-second, we had a leisurely breakfast and took a long walk around the edge of the harbor before starting back to Washington. While we were riding together we were much too deep in conversation, or companionable silence, to want the radio on. We drove slowly, keeping to the far right side of the road and letting the trucks roar by as we approached the city. We felt no warning, no sense of premonition as we rolled to a stop for a red light in the outskirts of Washington. Suddenly a taxi driver in the line of traffic beside us leaned out his window to shout at us. At first I thought he was yelling because he thought I'd been driving too slowly and I ignored him, but he raised his voice and I heard those incredible words . . . *"Kennedy has been shot."*

"What?"

"Kennedy has been shot, in Dallas . . ."

The light changed and the traffic began to move as though nothing unusual had happened. Annie turned on the radio, and we heard a voice say, "This is Dallas. President Kennedy has been shot in the head by a sniper. He is on the way to the hospital . . ."

I knew then that he was dead. I didn't know why, but there seemed a terrible inevitability about it, as though all great dreams were bound to end more suddenly than anybody ever expected. I had a vision of the young president's smiling, confident face suddenly obliterated by blood—during the war I'd seen men hit by rifle bullets, and that's the way it was.

"I can't believe it," Annie said. Her face went pale, her voice sounded dead. I parked the car at the side of the street and took her into my arms, her face cold against mine. For some reason we couldn't cry. I think we felt as though we too had been shot, that life was draining out of us too.

We went back to our hotel, where we lay in bed mesmerized by the flickering light of an old television set which we had hardly ever used. When we heard that the president had been declared dead we couldn't help thinking what this would mean for us . . . there would be no White House conference, not one that would involve Ralph Hopkins and us, anyway. That whole plan had been built on the close relationship between him and Jack Kennedy. Our dream of the future had been shot down with our young president. It seemed terribly wrong to think of all this at such a moment, but the realization that even the year we had been so confident of having together had now disintegrated like a broken promise was there, not to be pushed away. We would be called back to New York and I'd either have to ask Betsy for a divorce or try to say good-bye to Annie, or play out the dreary scenario of a man with a family in Connecticut and a woman in the city. The year of grace we'd hoped for was gone. As for my so-called financial future, if Hopkins retired, as he might well do now that his political ambitions had been shot down with Jack Kennedy, it might be impossible for me to find a decent job at United Broadcasting, and who knew about anywhere else?

We heard the radio announcer talking about Mrs. Kennedy's ordeal, the search for the assassin, and while we now did forget ourselves, the feeling of death in Dallas was still shared, as though we were all targets of the same unknown murderer.

I went out to a package store and brought back a quart of scotch. For the first time Annie and I got drunk together, or at least I tried to knock myself out while she sipped about two ounces and finally went to bed and cried into her pillow. We comforted each other clumsily and kept falling asleep, only to awake an hour or so later for more news bulletins. Forty-eight hours floated by. The story the television set told of Lee Harvey Oswald's capture after he had murdered a cop and his own murder the following day by Jack Ruby seemed to me to be part of a drunken dream. Oswald's soft face looked like a spoiled college freshman's, not a killer's, and when his expression contorted in his own death agony, I found myself feeling renewed horror. An announcer with a weirdly calm voice said Oswald had a Russian wife and had spent some time in Russia, but that this was no reason to assume that any international conspiracy was involved. There was also no reason to believe that Jack Ruby, the owner of a sleazy little strip joint, was part of any conspiracy, the announcer went on. Possibly both these men were simply crazy . . .

Maybe one weak crazy man had done it, and that's all there was to it, no rhyme nor reason. Drunkenly I wondered what Dr. Harbringer would think of this. The television set announced that our armed forces were on the alert and that other government officials were being closely guarded. Lyndon Johnson, a man whom I had always considered a rather old-fashioned stereotype of a Texas

181 —

cowboy, had already been sworn in as president, and Mrs. Kennedy, whom I had thought of as a bride or a debutante, had arrived in Washington with her skirt still soaked with blood. Surely I must be hallucinating after all that whiskey, or the whole world was going through an attack of delirium tremens. Finishing off the bottle, I went back to sleep.

"TOMMY?" ANNIE SAID.

I opened my eyes and saw her sitting on the edge of the bed, dressed in a gray skirt and navy-blue sweater, her face calm. She was holding out a cup of coffee.

"Please don't order another bottle," she said.

"Did I do that?"

"Twice."

"I'm sorry," I said, sitting up and holding my aching head. "I haven't done this since I got out of the army."

"How do you feel?"

"Don't ask. What day is it?"

"Monday, November twenty-fifth, four P.M."

"I should have gone down to the office."

"I did. Nothing happening, of course."

"Has Hopkins called?"

"Not yet. The whole Washington bureau and probably the whole company is going crazy trying to keep up with the news."

I took the coffee from her and sipped it.

"Do you want some aspirin?"

"A couple might help. Did I really drink three bottles?"

"You spilled most of one of them."

"That must have been a pleasure for you."

"I think I envied you. At least you were out of it for a while. When I drink I just get sick."

"You're better off," I said, and waited while she got me two aspirin tablets and a glass of water from the bathroom. I swallowed them and after a few minutes was able to stagger into the shower. I was standing there letting hot water cascade down my face and body when I heard the telephone ring. Annie answered it and ran to stick her head through the shower curtain.

"It's Hopkins," she said. "Can you take it?"

"Sure," I said, and hastily wrapping a towel around myself, hurried to the bedside table.

"Hello, Ralph?" I said.

"Hello, Tom . . ."

His voice sounded so dead that I hardly recognized it.

"We've all had a great shock, of course, so I won't say much. A tragedy, still unbelievable to me . . ."

"That's the way I feel."

"Nothing seems very important now, of course, but the White House conference is off. I doubt if Johnson will want it, and we couldn't work together anyway."

"I can understand that."

"I'm going to retire. I was going to do that anyway before this whole White House thing came up."

"Yes, sir . . ." I said, my heart sinking.

"I'm not sure what I'll do after that. Chairman of the board, but I don't know yet how active I'll want to be. I'm going to take a good long vacation. I have a little island down in the Bahamas I've hardly ever had a chance to visit."

"I'm sure the sun will do you good—"

"I don't know how long it will be before I get back. I guess it would be a good idea for you to come back to New York for reassignment. Your assistant too . . . Ed Banks will have something for her, but you better check in with Robinson in public relations . . . I'm sorry things didn't go the way we thought they would, but like they say, the best laid plans . . ."

"Yes, sir, I know . . ."

"You've helped me a lot over the years, Tom, and I hope things will go well for you. I'll be in touch when I get back. It's still possible that I might have some special work for you . . ."

"I hope so," I said, and meant it.

"Well, Tom, keep in touch . . ."

"What's the matter?" Annie asked, handing me another towel.

I forced myself to smile. "We're supposed to go back to New York and report for reassignment," I said. "Like the army."

"I guess there wasn't much else we could expect . . . Tommy, don't worry about me. You don't have to make great big decisions all of a sudden." She tried to smile. "We're just going to have to follow the yellow brick road and see where it leads."

"What the hell does that mean?"

"For starters, you're going to have to begin going home every night to take care of your family—"

"What about you? Us?"

"I'll have my apartment. We can see each other during the day—"

"I'm *not* going to say good-bye—"

"Of course not . . . we're just going to have to see how things work out . . ."

She was no longer smiling.

Back in my room the red light on my telephone was blinking and the hotel operator told me that my wife had called four times over the past two days. Of course Betsy would have tried to get in touch with me as soon as she heard of the president's death, and I should have telephoned her. I had no idea how I could explain my silence. Why not just say I'd gotten drunk? At least that would be credible. Even if not, to Betsy, acceptable. I'd have to put up a good front, as we often did for each other. My finger was unsteady as I dialed my home number.

"Tom," she said as soon as she heard my voice. "Where have you been?"

"It's been a madhouse around here, this whole city has been turned upside down. I've been working day and night . . ."

Thank God she didn't ask what in hell I'd been working at.

"It's so awful," she said. "Nobody around here knows what to think, but now that Johnson is president, I guess things will go on pretty much as before . . . won't they?"

Betsy liked to think that things somehow would always go on pretty much as before, no matter what happened. She didn't really believe that life in South Bay could ever be really disturbed. Ignorance, innocence, self-protection? I was never sure.

"Well, the White House conference is off. Hopkins is going to retire."

"That won't affect your job, will it?"

"It's the end of my job, but I suppose the company will try to fit me in somewhere else . . ."

"Will you be coming home soon?"

I heard no eagerness in that question. It sounded almost casual and I wondered suddenly whether my return might mean as complex a readjustment for her as it would for me. After all, she'd had freedom for the past two months, with no one to question her comings and goings with Bert Andrews or to raise hell about the liberties she'd given Barbara. In some ways I had been the ideal suburban husband, I found myself thinking—a monthly check in the mail without any tired, irritable and demanding man to go with it.

"I'll be coming home as soon as I can wind things up here," I said, giving myself as much time as possible.

"We'll all be so glad to see you," she said, perhaps forcing a note of enthusiasm.

"How are the kids?"

"Fine. The news about Kennedy hit them hard, but they're getting over it. Kids are resilient . . ."

"Where are they?"

"Pete's still at school—he's been working late on some kind of a science project. Janey has gone to the dentist but Barbara is here. Wait a second and I'll call her."

Barbara's voice was oddly like that of a disgruntled wife when she finally got on the wire.

"Dad, we've been trying to get in touch with you!"

"I've been tied up. I'll be coming home soon."

"When?"

She made the word ring with more alarm than happy anticipation.

"I'm not sure . . . did you ever get that sweater I sent you?"

"Oh . . . yes, and it fits fine. We all got our presents and we were going to write you but you know how it is . . ."

I did indeed.

"Well, I'll see you soon," I said hastily. "Give my love to everyone."

AFTER PUTTING ON a freshly pressed suit I went back to Annie's room. She had placed her suitcases on her bed and was packing.

"We don't have to go back tonight . . ."

"It's not going to do much good to hang around here," she said.

"We'll have to get out notices about the cancellation of the conference, all kinds of details."

"Nobody will want to hurry about that. Mr. Hopkins will probably handle it all from New York."

"We can't just walk out of the office here—"

"Nobody's down there—they took all the secretaries for the newsroom. There's nothing there now but empty desks."

"You really want to get back to New York, don't you?"

"It's over here, Tom—it's just *over*. I don't like hanging around in limbo . . ."

"You sound like you think it's over for us too."

"I didn't say that, and I don't mean that—nothing can change that fast."

"Death can do it," I said, feeling rotten.

"This isn't death, it's just change, and I've learned to accept that." She folded up her black silk cocktail dress and put it into a suitcase.

"But you really do think this is the end of us—"

"I know better than to predict. Have you ever found life to be predictable?"

"No."

"I don't want to count on anything and I don't want you to count on anything, good or bad. That's the only way I know how to live. Don't be so downhearted. So far, we're way ahead, aren't we?"

"I don't know . . ."

"The past two months haven't been so bad, have they?"

"Just the best in my life."

"Mine too. So why cry? They're a hell of a lot more than I ever expected when I came down to Washington."

"Please don't make it sound as though we're already past history."

"Tom . . . don't make promises. That way they can't be broken."

Her voice was firm, but there were tears in her eyes.

"We're going to be in the same city during the day, at least. Anything can happen. Maybe we'll grow apart, maybe things will break right for us. Whichever way it goes, we're going to survive. That's what you and I always do, isn't it?"

I tried to kiss her, and she held still for it, but that was as far as she would let herself go.

"Well . . . I have a million things to do. Damn it, I have to call the people in my apartment and get them out. At least I didn't give them a lease—"

"Can't you forget all that for a few minutes?"

"*No.* I'll go crazy if we just start pretending that nothing has happened. If we're going to have to start a new life, let's get on with it."

ON THE FLIGHT back to New York that evening we sat together silent as strangers, and though we held hands it was more a gesture of consolation. It was about nine when we reached LaGuardia Airport.

"I'll get a taxi," I said when we collected our luggage.

"Tom, I'm going out to Brooklyn to stay at my grandmother's house. My apartment isn't ready for me yet."

"Let's stay at a hotel. One last night—"

"You don't have to start talking like that," she said, touching my cheek gently. "If I know us, it wouldn't be our last night anyway."

"One more night, then."

"My grandmother is expecting me, I cailed her—"

"Tell her you changed plans—"

"I can't do that. Tom, we're back in New York. It's time for you to go home."

"Tomorrow will be—"

"Tomorrow we should start trying to line up our new jobs."

"There's no hurry."

"Do you like the way things are now?"

"*No.*"

"Then let's see what happens next."

I kissed her and she put both arms around my neck, hugging me so tight I felt her body imprinted on mine. Maybe that was the idea.

"This feels too much like a damn last farewell," I said.

"Just farewell to our Washington assignment. It was a wonderful trip, wasn't it?"

"I can't leave it at that. When will I see you again?"

"How about lunch day after tomorrow?"

"Why not tomorrow?"

"I have to see about my apartment. I'll meet you the next day. How about twelve-thirty at the Jardin Français restaurant? It's on Fifty-third near Sixth Avenue. It's a quiet little place, no one's likely to see us—"

"I don't give a *damn* about that."

"Take it easy, Tom . . . if we're going to do a bad thing, let's do it well."

"Don't be a smart ass."

With a smile she piled her small suitcases onto her large one, which had wheels built into its bottom, and started rolling the pile toward the taxi stand.

"I'll take those," I said.

"You've got your own—I can manage, Tom."

Carrying my suitcases, I followed her to her taxi and kissed her once more as she got in, a quick embrace, and then she was gone.

187 —

 *   *   *

THERE WAS ALWAYS something about Grand Central Station
that I sometimes thought of as a final home. I'd been going in and
out of that place all my life, rushing between home and office along
with crowds of people who always looked as though they knew
exactly where they were going. In Grand Central there was no time
for regret or hope—one just got on with one's business. The
omniscient men who answered questions in the information booth
were not really oracles who could tell a man whether he should go
home or not—all they could do was read a timetable. I knew the
schedule of all the trains that went to Connecticut by heart anyway.
In Grand Central I was a native, a commuter who was more at
home in this natural habitat than at either end of the railroad line.
In the bar nearest Track 35 everything was familiar, even the flimsy
toothpick that speared the olive in my martini. No surprises here.
This was a world that never changed no matter who was president
of the United States or what bewilderments filled the world outside
this marble temple.

I still had a hangover. The first martini helped and called for a
second, but it seemed necessary now to draw the line between
madness and sanity. Pushing myself away from the bar, I went to
a telephone and called home. Barbara answered, sounding surprised.

"We didn't think you were coming home tonight," she said.
"Mom's at a rehearsal . . ."

"If she gets back in time, ask her to meet the train that gets in
at eleven-twenty. If she isn't there I'll catch a taxi."

"Gordy can meet you—"

"*Gordy?* On his motorcycle?"

"He has a car now," she answered with studied dignity. "We'll
both be glad to meet you."

"Thanks," I said, and fought back an impulse to return to the
bar for another martini.

As I walked down the aisle of the last train to South Bay looking
for a seat I saw my old friend Ben Richardson, looking more tired
and gaunt than ever, obviously ill, his face sunken, and I still
wondered what on earth drove this man to work so late in New
York regardless of his health. Were his bills piling up at home, his
advertising agency on the brink of failure?

"Sit down, Tom," he said, moving a newspaper from the chair
beside him. "How are Betsy and the kids?"

"Fine. How's Alice?"

"Good."

Obviously he still had not noticed that I had been gone the last two months. Nothing had changed for him. Putting his head back, he went to sleep, as he always did on this trip, his breath coming irregularly through slightly parted gray lips. The thought hit me that he quite possibly might die on this train. Every year or so some commuter had a heart attack and was hurried off to an ambulance at the next stop by the conductors. The old phrase "killed in action" returned to me; also "bravery beyond the call of duty." The New Haven Railroad should issue campaign ribbons to men like Ben Richardson and bury them with his fellow men in gray flannel suits, standing at attention while someone played "Taps" and fired a last volley of blank cartridges. If I tried to forget about Annie, how long would it be before I qualified for a death caused by boredom, strain and frustration?

I realized that Annie expected me to forget about her before long—she was already setting up her defenses for that, and I could hardly blame her. That's what usually happened. A man went to Washington on a business trip, had a fling, came down to earth as soon as he returned home. There would be a few embarrassed lunches in New York, maybe a rendezvous or two at a hotel, but in the end the strain of a "double life" would be too much for the man, and the woman would realize that there really was nothing in it for her. Before long she would meet someone else who had more to offer. The fling in Washington would not seem very important in retrospect, just one of those things that happened to people, a pleasant memory that would be increasingly tinged by guilt and regret as time wore on . . . Well, maybe them but not us . . . The future was never predictable, like she'd said. Maybe that was one truth we could hang on to . . .

A rusty Volkswagen van was waiting in South Bay. Barbara jumped out of it to greet me. Dressed in tweed skirt and green sweater, she looked like Annie in the dim lights of the station platform, or in other transmutations of memory, like Maria in Rome, or like Betsy herself long ago, when she had come running to meet me at South Station in Boston during the days before I was sent overseas and still got ten-day leaves. I had to jerk myself back to my middle-aged present and accept that this was my daughter, that she was at least as afraid as she was eager to see me, because she knew I disapproved of the young man she claimed she belonged to now. I was a father, not a lover, and a father is a man who has all the responsibilities of a lover without any right to demand anything in return. A man has to be unselfish to be a good father, calm and strong. They call it maturity, and if a man doesn't have it, he'd better fake it. And like bravery in war, the pretense can turn into reality.

"Hello, dad," she said, giving me a hug that wasn't much more than a touch on each shoulder and a peck on the cheek. "Mother is running late tonight—they're having dress rehearsal, and isn't Gordy's van neat?"

Gordy got out of the van to help with my suitcases. Uncertain of his reception but apparently trying hard to please, he shook my hand hard and displayed his strength by carrying my two suitcases under one arm while he opened the rear door of his disreputable vehicle. In sneakers, blue jeans and a brown leather jacket, his tall thin figure, which was crowned by a mop of dark hair, seemed to me like a stereotype of a teenage rebel, but there was also an intensity in his craggy face that made him look much older than the boys in Barbara's high school class.

"Thanks for meeting me," I said, "it's hard to get a taxi this time of night."

He got behind the wheel while Barbara and I crowded into the front seat. The back of the van contained a mattress covered by an old army blanket. In my day, as they say, we didn't have cars with beds like this, but the cramped quarters of the old sedans hadn't really hampered us much. I couldn't help thinking of my daughter and this boy going at it in this car, and hated the thought. Child psychology books said be an understanding father . . . well, I sure as hell understood, too much. What was the father of a sixteen-year-old girl supposed to do nowadays—just look up at the moon and say nothing?

That's all I felt I could do that night. As we turned into our driveway I saw that almost every light in every room was on, a welcoming sight maybe, but also proof that I had been away—who else worried about the electric bill and went around snapping lights off as though I loved the dark. Gordy carried my suitcases in. As soon as I stepped through the front door I was enveloped by a familiar fragrance, a slightly musty smell—Betsy never liked to leave windows open, she hated drafts. There was the scent of the lemon oil she used to polish my grandmother's furniture. There was also a faintly sour odor that was explained when Janey came running to meet me, holding a mongrel puppy in her arms.

"This is Bonkers," Barbara said. "We didn't want to tell you about her until you saw her. Mother says we can keep her if you don't say no."

The puppy growled at me.

"We can, can't we?" Janey said, hugging the dog, which now began to lick her face.

"Gordy gave her to us," Barbara said firmly.

I looked at the animal. It was an exceptionally ugly bitch, maybe part Airedale, part some smaller canine that left it with disproportionately short legs and a long tail.

"If the pound had to take her back, they'd kill her," Barbara said. "Gordy saved her life." She looked directly at me when she said it. Eyeball to eyeball, so to speak, with my sixteen-year-old daughter, and barely inside the house. Welcome home, traveler.

Ordinarily I liked dogs, but I hated this one on sight, for obvious reasons. Nonetheless, if I didn't want to play the part of a black-hearted villain in my own house I'd better go along.

"*Please* say we can keep her!" Janey implored.

"You can keep her," I said.

At least, if not a hero, I was now a nonvillain. Janey put the dog on the floor and ran to hug me while Barbara patted me on the back as though she were consoling me. "Oh, dad, thank you so much, I just knew you'd be nice about this."

Damn right she did. In any case, excited by this display, the dog stood quivering at our feet and peed.

"She's not quite housetrained yet but she's learning fast," Janey said, and ran to get a handful of paper towels. The dog followed her, wagging its ridiculously long tail and yapping full-throat.

"We call her Bonkers because she's a little crazy," Barbara said. "She was locked up in the pound for weeks before Gordy rescued her. I guess it made her a little neurotic."

"She just needs love," Janey said, scooping up the dog in one arm while she mopped up the pool with the other.

"Where's Pete?" I asked.

"He went up to bed," Janey said. "He hates Bonkers and Bonkers hates him."

I felt a sudden rush of affection for my son, a chip off the old block if there ever was one, but I wished that he'd waited up.

"He wants you to go up and see him—he said to wake him up," Janey said, reading the disappointment on my face.

I went upstairs to Pete's room. The boy had gone to sleep in his pajama bottoms, half covered by his blanket, his desk light on. His shoulders still looked thin, delicate, almost feminine, but his arms looked strong and his face, outlined against the pillow, was ruggedly masculine with a kind of dignity in repose. He was sleeping heavily and didn't stir when I said softly, "Hi, Pete, I'm home."

It was, after all, midnight and he had to get up early for school. Deciding not to waken him, I covered him, brushed his forehead with my lips and put the light out. I met the girls on the stairs. Janey was still carrying the dog.

"Gordy's left," Barbara said. "We're going to turn in."

"Mother will probably be home before long," Janey added, "but she told us not to worry if she was late—this is their first real dress rehearsal."

"Where is it?" I said.

"Uncle Bert's house—they've fixed up a regular stage over there. They have to rehearse the play a lot."

Was Janey acting a little too defensive? For Betsy? Maybe she sensed that her mother was spending too much time with Bert and that there might be tension in the house now that I'd come back. She buried her face in the neck of the dog, perhaps getting more comfort there than she'd ever been able to find with us humans.

"Good night," I said, kissed her lightly on the cheek, getting another growl from Bonkers in return. I walked to the kitchen and poured myself a glass of scotch . . . "The booze isn't good for you," Annie had said. "Among other things it makes you put on weight. One shot has eighty calories and then it makes you hungry . . ."

While I had been with her, I'd lost fifteen pounds, enough to make me need new suits, but before long I'd probably be bursting my waistband again. The grandfather clock boomed out twelve strokes, like a prelude to doom—I had never been able to understand why those old clockmakers had contrived such lugubrious tones, but then again, maybe they were suitable for marking the passage of time, of life. Carrying my glass of scotch I went back to the living room and sat down on the couch.

Maybe it was wrong to surprise Betsy by coming home earlier than she'd expected. From her spontaneous reaction when she first saw me I might be able to judge how she really felt about my being back—an unfair advantage, if unplanned. The truth was that Annie had pushed me out of her life, or seemed to have, more abruptly than I'd expected. I wondered where Annie was now and what she was thinking. Maybe she had got in touch with Harry Comstock, who was probably still hanging around Brooklyn despite his threat to go back into the army. He would sure be glad to have her back, and she probably needed someone to lean on now. My fists tightened. Now I wanted to kill Harry Comstock—my hit list kept getting longer.

But my glass was empty. I poured another scotch, my last if I had any sense—things were bad enough without having Betsy come home to find a besotted husband waiting for her. If we had a boozy argument, God knew what could come out. Well, why not? Why not be honest and spread all the cards out on the table right now? . . . "I'm sorry to tell you this but I'm in love with another woman," I might start, like a mellow-voiced actor in a soap opera with organ music in the background. "Do you want a divorce?" she'd ask sooner or later. "Yes, you can have the house and, say, two-thirds of my income, do you think you can get by on that?" "Two-thirds?" "Of course I may not have any income for long, you don't understand about United Broadcasting—" "Explain it," she might say. "The ghost writer of a man who's retired is a ghost in more ways than one." "Surely you exaggerate, you always see the gloomy side of everything—" "You don't understand UBC. They tend to fire men in their forties if they haven't already done something brilliant. Younger men supposedly have more energy, go along better with change. It's cheaper to give a man severance pay than to keep him until he can get a pension, but they're clever there too . . . They can keep giving you pointless nonjobs until you quit, or just let you sit in an office with nothing to do until your self-respect gets the better of you and you walk out. They can advise you that for your own good you should start looking for a job outside the company, and so forth. But it's no picnic for a man my age to find something new in New York. They have clubs for unemployed executives . . ."

The imagined dialogue . . . monologue, really . . . made me gag. Now we were coming down to hard cases: I was a man who wanted to support two women, but wasn't sure he would have a thing to give even one. I had three children to feed and educate, plus a boy overseas, at a time when my so-called career was in obvious crisis, but all I could do was fantasize about going off with a younger woman who made no secret of the fact that she wanted a child of her own before she was too old to have one.

My only chance to make a new life for myself and Annie was

somehow to damn near double my income. At the moment that seemed impossible. This hardly seemed a time to ask for a divorce. Even if Annie would have me after I was free, should I tie her to a man who already had more dependents than he could support and a future that was clear as the straight scotch in my glass . . . ?

No, it seemed unarguable that now was not the time to rock boats. My kids needed me—that much was sure. A father was needed to help Barbara realize that her future would have to hold more than Gordy if she didn't want to live in a rusty van for the rest of her life, and how could I even contemplate the prospect of leaving Janey to the dogs, so to speak? Pete *seemed* self-sufficient, but of course he wasn't and this was no time for his father to run out on him. I had duty here . . .

"Don't feel you have to make any big decisions," Annie had said. "We'll just have to follow the yellow brick road and see where it leads. Nothing is predictable . . ."

The clock struck twelve-thirty, and then, in almost no time at all, one. How long did these damn rehearsals take? It seemed unlikely that the cast would hang around Bert's place this late on a weekday night. Likely Betsy and Bert were having a few drinks to mourn my imminent return, even a last fling . . . ?

I could not get straight in my mind whether Betsy was having an affair with Bert. In spite of my own infidelity, the very idea of her being unfaithful still infuriated me. I scorned the double standard, but in practice I seemed to need the dear old thing. The image of Betsy in Bert's arms caused me such rage that I had to convince myself that I was imagining things, that I was too suspicious, that Betsy was too good a person for *that*.

On the other hand there was a certain logic, even symmetry in our reacting to a long separation from each other in similar fashion. Maybe she went to Bert as inevitably as I had gone to Annie. Maybe *she* had been looking forward to a year of grace in which everything could somehow be worked out, and the sudden news of my imminent return could have left her in a state as difficult as my own.

If so, what next? If one of us had the courage to admit the truth, the other would probably do likewise. We could have a grand double confession with mutual forgiveness. If we both wanted divorce and remarriage . . . she could move into Bert's big house with Barbara, Janey and Pete while I paid child support I could afford—if we sold this house my grandmother had left me we would have a fund for college tuition. If I could hang on to a reasonably good job I could keep maybe ten grand a year for myself and move into Annie's apartment without becoming dependent on her . . . The children could visit us often and though the change would of course be hard for them they would at least see that both their parents were happy, well, and still cared about them. Maybe the addition, officially, of Bert and Annie in their lives would bring them new kinds of strength that Betsy and I had never been able to provide . . . Betsy would have the luxurious life she'd always, I felt, expected as some sort of divine right and I'd have Annie to make life a delight even in a one-room apartment. Happy endings!

Also a pipe dream, far too good to be true. I got up to pace around the living room. Bert Andrews was not Mr. Wonderful. He had long been celebrating his own divorce by doing his best to make himself into a sort of playboy. It was possible that Bert was already tired of seeing Betsy so much and was relieved to know I was coming home. Maybe he and Betsy would see each other in secret from time to time, as I was hoping to visit Annie, until their affair tapered off, as I worried that Annie expected ours to do. Damn . . . if Betsy had to have an affair, why couldn't she have picked a better man than Bert Andrews?

At least I hadn't stolen another man's wife—which is funny to think of now but at the time, in my self-justifying state, seemed an important moral distinction. Also, willy-nilly, I still felt protective toward Betsy. She would be badly hurt when old Bert dropped her, as according to my fantasy scenario I was sure he would.

The clock struck two. Where *was* Betsy anyway? As if I didn't know . . .

In no time at all, two-thirty. I poured myself another scotch. The ice tray was frozen into the refrigerator and I was trying to yank it out when I saw headlights turn into the driveway. I walked out on the porch to greet her. She was still wearing her Blanche costume, a flowing dress of white cotton, and she had thrown a ski parka over her shoulders. Her hair was knotted at the back of her head, and she was fumbling in her handbag for her key. In the glow of the porch light her face looked pale and tired.

"Hello, Betsy . . ."

Her head jerked back.

"Tom! I didn't think—"

"I guess not."

"I'm glad to see you . . ."

She came up the steps and embraced me, her lips cool and taut against mine.

"A nice surprise," she said, stepping back.

"I caught an earlier plane," I said, and followed her inside.

"Did you have trouble finding a taxi at the station? You could have called me at Bert's. Didn't the kids tell you where I was?"

"Yes, but I didn't want to bother you—"

"I would have liked an excuse to leave. We had a dress rehearsal and it went badly. I don't know what we're going to do. I'm not getting my part right. Bert was awfully nice about it, but I really think I should quit. Do you want a drink?"

"I just got one. I'll fix one for you."

We sat on the couch, glasses in hand.

"We kept running through it over and over again, but each time I got worse. I'm afraid I've bitten off more than I can chew. I'm not really an actress. I know the lines but I just can't seem to get the emotion into them. Everybody's worked so hard and I'm just letting them all down . . ."

She began to cry.

"They can get somebody else for the part—"

"No, Bert won't let me give up. He says I'm getting better and all I need is more time."

"When are you supposed to open?"

"Next Friday night. Marcia Underwood's my understudy, and damn it, she doesn't even know her lines!"

"Don't worry, you'll get through it. Who expects much of an amateur performance?"

"Don't say that! What about Bert's dreams? Now I'm going to make a fool of myself. And of Bert!"

She pulled away from me to take a sip of scotch. Tears were streaming down her face.

"We have to take whatever we have to take," I said, somewhat pompously, I guess.

"Bert says that all talented people get jittery sometimes. He's sure I'll be great on opening night."

"And so you will be."

"And if I'm not?"

"Life is risky—"

"God, don't you have any confidence in me?"

"Relax, Betsy. You're going to be great."

"Do you really believe that? God, I'm exhausted. I have to get some sleep."

"I'm tired too," I said, with some relief.

The stairs were too narrow for me to help her up, but she did appear exhausted and I was ready to catch her if she fell. In our room we undressed in the dark and toppled into bed nude. Her body felt soft and dry when she rolled toward me to give me a goodnight embrace.

"It's good to have you home, Tommy," she said.

Almost immediately she went to sleep, her breath coming with a bronchial rasp that alarmed me. The room felt too hot and there was a musty smell left by the untrained puppy. I slept but almost immediately awoke in a panic, feeling lost in the darkness. For a few seconds I didn't know where I was, and when my mind cleared I was as bewildered as I had ever been in my life.

22

AT SIX-THIRTY I awoke, ready to catch my commuter train. Though there was no rush to start looking for a new job at United Broadcasting, I felt an urgent need to solve my problems quickly. In spite of too much whiskey and too little sleep, I felt alert, like a soldier in combat, scared yet too tensed up to be tired.

The usual pandemonium of breakfast grated on my nerves, and I wondered for the hundredth time why a family could not start the day with some order and peace. Perhaps the basic fault was mine —what had I provided in the way of discipline and leadership?

"Kids, let's do something to make our mornings better," I said.

"What?" Janey asked.

"To start with, lay out your clothes for the next day before you go to bed—then there won't be so much screaming about socks and underwear."

"We'd just have to do the screaming at night," Barbara said.

"And I don't want you doing your homework at the breakfast table. Don't leave it till the last moment. And don't ask for something different to eat—this isn't a restaurant."

"But dear, this isn't the army either," Betsy said.

Pete said nothing. After a casual greeting, he had buried his nose into a biology book, occasionally sipping hot chocolate. My family's indifference to my attempts to create order out of chaos infuriated me. When it came to paying the bills, I was the head of the family, all right, but no one seemed to respect me or believe I could make life tolerable for all. The puppy, which kept frisking around and yapping while the girls slipped it bits of food under the table, was the last straw. The children cared more about that damn dog than about me. I blew up. I told them to shut up the animal in another room while we ate. If they didn't learn to treat me better, I thought bitterly, then they shouldn't be surprised if I walked out. If a daughter got the impression that her father was willing to put up with endless irritations, what would her expectations of most men be?

Well, this was no time to start reforming my family, and besides, I had to run for my train. Seated in the railroad car with the New York *Times* on my lap, I wondered whether I would see Annie in the United Broadcasting Building, even though we didn't have a date until the next day. Maybe she would stop in at my office, or I could visit the personnel department for a few words with Ed Banks. The hope of seeing her bucked me up and I tried not to think what my life would be like without her.

IN THE LOBBY of the United Broadcasting Company B. F. Henderson, the vice-president who was in line to succeed Ralph Hopkins, strode by me. As soon as he stepped into the elevator, the operator slid the door shut and immediately started up—a perk of the president of the corporation. Hopkins had enjoyed it if only to decline it—unless he was in a hurry, he always gestured to the operator to leave the door open until the car was full. Henderson did not do this and with a dozen other people I had to wait for the next car. It was ridiculous to resent this, but it was an instant sign of change.

Another change was visible when I walked past the open door of the president's office on the way to my own cubicle. Miss Bannerman, who had been Hopkins' executive secretary for twenty years, was no longer sitting behind her desk. In her place was a much younger and prettier woman. Probably Miss Bannerman had retired along with Hopkins. Maybe it was a time for the changing of the whole guard.

As soon as I got to my office, I called Harry Robinson, the director of public relations and probably my new boss. When I had been Hopkins' special assistant Robinson's secretary had always put me right through to him, but now she said he was busy and would call me back. When my telephone remained silent all morning, I began to suspect that I was being cut down to size. As a department head, Robinson may have been irritated that I had been close to Hopkins. Now he had a chance to show me who was boss.

Perhaps I was turning paranoid, but the truth was I had never liked Harry Robinson. He had risen in the company during the scandals about rigged quiz shows. Hopkins had chosen him as spokesman for the company during the televised hearings because he didn't look or sound like a slick public relations man. Rotund, tweedy and professorial, Robinson was good at acting the role of Mr. Integrity. People believed him when he said that only a few producers had staged quiz shows according to prepared scripts with predetermined winners—he and the officers of United Broadcasting had been as shocked as any viewer. Later Robinson was deft in handling accusations that violence on television fostered crime—he was an expert on the "catharsis theory," that violence on the screen actually helped to purge people of their hostility, and fostered mental health. He had four children and five grandchildren, he often said, and couldn't possibly defend any program that he thought harmful to the young. His office was filled with photographs of his children and his indomitably virtuous-looking wife. I thought him the worst kind of hypocrite. He scared me, because people I dislike usually dislike me, and now my career would depend on my ability to please Robinson.

WHILE WAITING FOR the call, I paced around my desk and fought off the temptation to stop in at the personnel office in hopes of catching a glimpse of Annie. This would be a bad mistake—she would be nervous applying for a new job and didn't need any extra emotional tension. She would probably want to steer clear of Hopkins' old guard, which I so clearly represented. At thirty she was less in danger of being fired than I was. Trying to stay in tune with the times, United Broadcasting was making an effort to promote women into executive positions. Annie's salary was only half of mine, but her future was probably far brighter.

At one I went out for lunch and held back on the martinis. Back in my office I read the afternoon papers and for the first time in my life read the Help Wanted columns. Most of the jobs listed called for pipefitters, registered nurses or advertising copy writers. Maybe I could learn to compose the lush kind of prose that sells perfumes, expensive booze and Cadillacs, but what agency would hire a forty-three-year-old specialist in writing dull speeches about mental health?

Suddenly my telephone rang. I pounced on it and the clipped voice of Robinson's secretary said he would try to fit me into his schedule if I cared to come in and wait. Hopkins himself had never treated his subordinates in such cavalier fashion, but I was in no position to quibble. I walked down the hall to the office of the director of public relations. The waiting room was furnished with early American antiques, lots of potted plants and original paintings by Norman Rockwell. No one else was there except for two motherly-looking secretaries. I read old copies of *Time* and *Life* for about an hour before I was told to go in.

Unlike Hopkins, Robinson did not stand up behind his desk to greet me or even attempt to be friendly.

"Sit down, Rath," he said, motioning with a pudgy hand toward an uncomfortable-looking chair. "Ralph said he hoped we could find a spot for you. There are no vacancies now in our regular organization, but I have a temporary assignment which might be right for you."

"I'd like to hear about it," I said.

"Let me give you some background. We always get a certain amount of complaints about sex and violence in our programming. In the last few days there's been a big upswing in mail and telephone calls. I relate it to the Kennedy assassination. People see all that violence on the tube and somehow they blame it on us."

"I understand."

"The cries for censorship are getting louder. I think the storm will die down in time, but meanwhile, we have to come up with some answer to it."

"What do you suggest, sir?"

"Self-censorship, of course. That's the only answer—industry-wide self-censorship."

"Hasn't that been tried before?"

"Sure, and of course it never works—everybody goes for the ratings sooner or later, but still nobody wants the government to step in. So I've been sounding out the brass of the other networks and the feeling is that we should get up an industry-wide committee."

"Sounds like a good idea."

"Just announcing the formation of the committee will show that we're concerned with the problem, that we *care*. It will look a hell of a lot better than if we do nothing."

"I agree with that."

"We can set up codes, standards of decency, all that. We know it's impossible to legislate taste, but a lot of people want us to try and there's no reason why we shouldn't keep them happy."

Robinson's cynicism surprised me. Ralph Hopkins had never admitted to anything less than bland idealism, but of course he had made Robinson the head of his public relations department. Now B. F. Henderson was setting a new style, a harder sell inside the company. Maybe it was a form of honesty.

"What would my part in all this be?" I asked.

"You've had a lot of experience in dealing with high-level committees. We'll need a lot of them here."

I nodded.

"We should have a central committee made up by the top brass in the networks. They should appoint advisory committees made up of all the people trying to tell us what to do: psychiatrists, P.T.A. leaders, Bible thumpers—we can flatter them all by asking for their advice."

"What are we going to do when we get it?"

"They won't find it any easier to agree on specific codes than we do. Let them argue among themselves. We'll take the position of respectfully listening to every point of view. We'll be encouraging discussion and psychological research. Hell, psychiatrists never agree on anything either."

"How do you see all this ending up?"

"We'll thank every group for its report and take it under advisement. When we issue our own report, we can point out that it's impossible to get complete agreement on all these issues, maybe make a pitch for fairness, giving the public what it wants, which we sure as hell are always busting our guts to do. The ratings give us the majority votes. The committee will provide us a way to channel minority complaints constructively."

"Who's going to be the chairman of the central committee?"

"I don't think that any network president really wants that job or wants any of the others to have it. We'll probably end up with an executive committee of brass and some big outside name for an executive director, maybe a retired college president."

"I'm still not sure where I fit in . . ."

"You'll be our representative. Every network will appoint a man on the working level to get all this started and really run it. None of the brass is going to want to give much time to it. Basically it's a P.R. job, and you'll be working for me."

There was nothing I wanted less than to spend the next year working on such a false enterprise. The thought of just setting up all those committees for show, writing up endless reports of their useless discussions, made me feel dead. In such a job I wouldn't even have the spur of personal ambition—if ever there was a dead end, this was it. When the whole damn charade finally ground to a halt, I'd be a little older, a little more tarnished, and also out of work.

"I was hoping I could find something more in the mainstream of the company business," I said.

"Maybe a spot will open up for you later if you work out, but here is where I want you to start. I have nothing else to offer you."

"What kind of salary do you have in mind for me?" I asked.

"The same as you've been getting."

"Mr. Hopkins intended to arrange a considerable increase for me when the White House conference got more organized . . ."

"I'm sorry, but those circumstances have all changed. I know several younger men who would be glad to jump at this opportunity for a lot less than twenty thousand dollars a year."

Well, at least it was a job—I was still on the company payroll. I still could pay the bills in South Bay for another year or two.

"If you feel that something else may open up for me, I'll be glad to start with this," I said, trying to be enthusiastic.

"I can't guarantee anything. If you have any reservations, then don't take this job. Maybe it's time you started to look around outside the company."

"I have no reservations—I'll give it my best."

"Fine! Start by putting down on paper a plan for the whole thing, based on what I've told you. Dress it up, of course. If I like it, I'll try to get agreement with the other networks and we'll pick it up from there."

I knew what that meant. We'd write plans for self-censorship, then swap them around among the other companies for revisions. It would be a project that people would like to say they were working on, but which no one would ever want to finish. It was the old Sisyphus game—pushing a huge rock up a hill, only to have it roll down again and again.

There was no point in feeling sorry for myself, I kept thinking as I returned to my office. I had tumbled from a job in which we had hoped to save the world to one which was completely meaningless; but few people I knew saw much point in the work they did, only the money they made. Advertising men, P.R. geniuses, real estate promoters—few of them could afford the luxury of idealism. At least my work would be easier than that of a coal miner or taxi driver. I would be paid outrageously well for words almost no one would read and absolutely no one would learn anything from. My satisfactions, if any, would come from my private life, the rewards of being a good father, the joys of suburban living . . .

Annie! Her name rang out in my mind like a cry for help. I needed to talk to her, to hear her say that the future was never predictable, that the unexpected was the only thing anyone could ever expect. I needed to feel her arms around me, to know that no matter how mad the world, we still could give each other such delight, payment for all pain, the boredom, the demands, the responsibilities and obligations of my life. Annie wouldn't stick with me now for long, but at least I would see her tomorrow, and maybe a few more times after that before our affair finally ended and she found someone else.

On the train to South Bay, I looked at the tired faces of my fellow commuters with curiosity. How did they find the courage to keep plodding from office to home day after day, year after year? Not many of them seemed to need the excitement of a love affair. They played golf or tennis, took their children on fishing trips, mowed their lawns, got high at cocktail parties, played bridge, read newspapers and magazines. Their desperations, their pleasures seemed so low-keyed that they hardly seemed alive at all; but maybe I was the only one in the car who felt he was dying, that life was beginning to ask more of me than I could give. What a ridiculous notion. I had four children to support, and for any decent man that was reason enough to go on. I had a nice house in Connecticut and a job that never made me sweat. I had a lot of great memories, I still had my health, and I had no excuse for this shameful loss of courage and hope. And I still had Annie, for a while at least . . .

Betsy met me at the station.

"Don't get mad at me, but I have another rehearsal tonight," she said. "We have to keep at it till we get it right."

"I understand," I said, and at that moment I did understand her need to escape the routine monotony of her life.

"What kind of a day did you have?" she asked.

"The company gave me a new job."

"I knew they would. What will you be doing?"

"Working on a committee for self-censorship—an industry-wide thing."

"Sounds exciting, and God knows it's needed."

— 204

"I guess so."

"Any chance for a raise?"

"Not very soon, I'm afraid."

"Did you ask?"

"I asked. No dice."

"Maybe Bert is right when he says you could do better with real estate. Would you talk with him?"

Perhaps that's the way it would end—Betsy's great and good friend would give me a job pushing land developments for him.

"I'm afraid that real estate isn't my line," I said.

She looked annoyed and we drove in silence the rest of the way home. Gordy's car was parked in our driveway.

"I left a pot roast on the stove," she said. "Sorry, but I have to run."

"Aren't you going to eat first?"

"Bert's giving a little supper for the cast and I'm too nervous to eat anyway."

She drove off, going too fast as usual. I had a sudden, hateful thought: if she finally killed herself in that damn car, then I really could start my life all over again. I didn't like myself for thinking that. And I didn't like myself for wanting to go into the kitchen and start with a double scotch—this constant urge to get clobbered had to stop. Besides, I didn't want to look hung over when I met Annie the next day.

THE CHILDREN GREETED me perfunctorily when I entered the house. Janey was giving the puppy a bath, Pete was doing his homework and Barbara was talking with Gordy in the kitchen. A place was set at the table for him; apparently he was eating most of his meals with us. What was I supposed to do about that? I was too confused to figure out how I should be a kindly but firm father. Gordy seemed so embarrassed by my presence that he ate quickly, as did Barbara.

"We're going out for a drive," she said as they got up.

"Wait a minute. Have you done your homework?"

"Oh, daddy, I don't have much!"

"I don't want you to leave until it's all done."

"We have to meet a friend—I'll be back early."

"Be back by nine."

"Oh, daddy—you don't have to set a curfew. I'm almost seventeen years old!"

"Okay, okay . . ."

She flounced out of the house, and the van soon sped away. I knew damn well she wouldn't be back early. In our family we had no punishment that meant a damn. If I cut off her allowance, Betsy or Janey would give her money. What I had in my own home was responsibility without authority. The army at least never did that to a man.

What kind of children were Betsy and I sacrificing ourselves for anyway? If they were spoiled or neurotic, we had only ourselves to blame. Maybe Betsy and I had already needed so much approval from the children that we were afraid to set firm guidelines, so who was I to act like an expert on the art of living?

"Do you want to walk the dog with me?" Janey asked.

I welcomed that. It was cold, but we walked the dog twice around the block. When we returned, Janey offered to help do the dishes, but I was in a martyr mood and told her to do her homework. While I was washing Gordy's plate, I wondered whether I had reached a low or high point in the annals of fatherhood.

Barbara did not come home until after eleven.

"Sorry we're late, but the car broke down," she said.

In my present ugly mood I didn't believe her.

"If you can't get back on time, then you're going to be grounded for a week," I said.

We both knew this was an empty threat. She would come and go as she pleased, and to hell with me.

"Oh, daddy!" she said in disgust and went up to her room.

I tried to read, but nothing held my interest. I turned on the television, watched a cops-and-robbers melodrama with lots of car chases and shootings, the very thing a self-censorship committee should disapprove. A stupid situation comedy followed, and I twisted the dial, looking for more violence. Maybe there was something in the catharsis theory after all—I had plenty of hostility in me that night to let out.

At twelve I got up and went to bed. I was too tired to worry about Betsy, or even to be jealous. There must be a sharp line of definition in a marriage when a husband goes to sleep without waiting up for his wife.

It was almost three when she got in, and to my surprise she was a little drunk.

"Bert said I did fine," she said as she collapsed into bed. "We had a little party afterward . . ."

I had never thought she stayed out so late just to practice her part. I wondered if she came alive with Bert as I did with Annie. Maybe she did whether they were sleeping together or not—a question that now seemed almost academic. With me longing for Annie, Betsy yearning for Bert and Barbara going off with Gordy, what the hell kind of a family were we anyway? If love made the world go around then our little group sure was spinning.

I dreamed of being young again and swimming in a pool with Annie—miraculously we were both children together, not old enough to see any complexities in love, a wish fulfillment if ever there was one. When my alarm clock rang, I showered, shined my shoes, and put on my best suit. I was going to see Annie today.

"Are you going to see Ralph Hopkins today?" Betsy asked.

"Ralph is in the Bahamas," I said. "I have a new boss."

"You look nice," she said, helping me straighten my tie.

"You look good too."

Maybe we both did for our age, maybe love really does add a special glow. It was a clear, beautiful morning with a sprinkling of new snow on the lawn. The day held much promise—and any man who wakes up feeling that has got to be one of the lucky ones.

23

ANNIE HAD SAID she would meet me at the Jardin Français at twelve-thirty. I went there at noon to make sure I could find the place. It was one of those little restaurants with potted ferns in the window and bottles of wine displayed on mats of green leaves. The weather was cold enough to frost the glass and the people inside seemed to be moving under water. I went in to reserve a table and was glad to find that it was not crowded. Gleaming copper sauce-pans decorated one wall and the tables were covered with red and white checkered cloths. In the middle of each was a crystal vase with a fresh rosebud, a touch that made me like the place. I checked my wallet to make sure I had enough money. I couldn't use my American Express card—Betsy was careful about checking the bill for charges that I could put on my expense account. I had twenty-three dollars, enough since Annie ate so little and never drank more than one glass of wine. The fact that I had to think about money, even for lunch, set me to brooding that I could do so little for Annie. If she were my daughter, I'd tell her she was crazy to be running around with a man like me. Sure, I loved her, but anyone who liked her enough to care about her future would regard me as a predator. If I were a nice man I'd go away now and let our Washington affair die a natural death. But I wasn't a nice guy. I was out for what I could get—I was too damn hungry to be moral. Facing this harsh truth helped my self-respect a little.

Too nervous to sit and wait for her to arrive, I walked around the block. At twenty minutes after twelve I stood outside the res-taurant, looking up the street. It was cold and as I stamped my feet and rubbed my hands, I was hit by a fear, almost a conviction, that she would not come. Why in hell should she? A fling with her boss on an exciting assignment to Washington was one thing, but a drawn-out affair with a married, middle-aged man in New York was something else. She had probably decided to ditch me now. Failing to show up even for our first New York date would be easier than an emotional farewell.

The street was crowded and I inspected every face that passed by me. How few good-looking women there were in New York or in the world, how desperate most people appeared! If I was unhappy, I had plenty of company. It was a rough, cold world; what right did I have to expect a beautiful young woman to come hurrying to me with the gift of herself?

Then I saw her in the middle of the street, running around the back of a taxi—she had approached on the other side of the street. She was wearing the camel's hair dress I liked so much, no overcoat, and she looked like a stylish mannequin that had suddenly been given life and released from long imprisonment in a store window; she moved with that kind of exuberance. I hurried toward her and we met at the curb, our arms around each other, her momentum spinning us as though we were dancing.

"I was afraid you wouldn't be here!" she cried. "Then I saw you standing there, looking like you'd just lost your best friend."

"I was afraid I'd lost you."

"Never!"

I kissed her with people jostling by on both sides.

"This isn't the way to conduct a discreet love affair," she said.

"I don't give a damn," but I let her go and followed her into the restaurant. It was now crowded and the headwaiter was busy with a group of chattering matrons in from the suburbs for a pretheater lunch.

"Are you really hungry?" Annie said.

"Not particularly."

"Let's go up to my apartment. I wasn't sure I'd have it today, but the people were really nice about moving out."

I followed her to Seventh Avenue, where she turned uptown, then west on Fifty-sixth Street. Her building was small, old but well-kept, just back of Carnegie Hall. A uniformed doorman doubled as an elevator operator. As we went up, I heard someone playing a piano on the third floor, and the sounds of a violin on the fifth.

"A lot of musicians live here," she said.

We got out on the seventh floor. She led the way down a hall with hardwood floors like those of a school.

"Don't expect much," she said as she stepped in and turned on a light. "I haven't had the place long enough to fix it up."

The apartment was one large rectangular room with a kitchenette built into a closet, two windows overlooking an airshaft, the only visible furniture a table and an armchair, no ornamentation of any kind. In other circumstances it might have looked bleak to me, but now it seemed to have a special quality, like a secret cave. No sound of traffic penetrated here, and except for the distant strains of music the silence was complete.

"The bed comes down from the wall," she said. "The best part is that it's rent-controlled. I can live here for almost nothing."

"Which is just about what I can give you," I said.

"What do you think you're supposed to give me?"

"Everything."

"That's a lovely old-fashioned way of looking at it. Tommy, we have to talk, but first let's take our clothes off. We always talk best naked."

She took the bed down from the wall and casually pulled the camel's hair dress over her head. As she walked toward the closet she looked so damn beautiful in her white cotton pants and bra that she scared me. I could brood all I wanted about my obligations to my wife and children, but Annie owned me. Whatever happened, I would do anything not to lose her.

"Do you realize how much power you have over me?" I said.

"Do you really think of me like that?"

Her arms looked like wings as she put her hands behind her back to unhook the bra.

"I can't help it," I said. "Now I understand how a woman can make a man rob a bank or commit a murder."

"Then you're lucky I'm not evil," she said as she stepped out of her pants. "I'm really not, you know, unless you think sex is bad. I'm afraid there's a little of that in you."

"Then make me enjoy it all the more," I said and tossed my clothes onto the chair.

We were good together, mysteriously great because we gave each other so much excitement with so little effort. Annie liked us to lie together on the bed six inches apart without touching or kissing until our desire became unbearable, and then we came together with a shock of unbelievable delight. At my age I did not try for more than one climax, but the years had given me a kind of staying power, which she admired. Holding her in my arms while she exhausted herself, I experienced the most sublime sensation of giving pleasure. And this she needed too. Instead of trying for a simultaneous climax in the early stages, she liked to rest for a few moments after tiring herself, give her full attention to caressing me and building me up to unbelievable heights, then join me in my final release. She collapsed in my arms, breathed "thank you" into my ear and went to sleep before I could even thank her.

At one-thirty I woke her up. "Will they give you a hard time if you're late getting back to your office?"

"I gave an excuse before I left—I'm moving back into my apartment. How about you?"

"Nobody's checking up on me these days."

She stretched luxuriously, arching her taut body in a way that almost inspired me to try to make love again.

"Then we can take a little more time," she said.

I brushed my lips over her breasts and kissed her gently on her lips.

"What are we going to do?" I said.

"In the long run?"

"Yes."

"What would you do if you could do anything you wanted?"

"There's no point in dreaming . . ."

"You have to have a dream before you can make a plan."

"I'd like to make enough money to support Betsy and the kids in style and have an apartment with you big enough for the children to visit any time they wanted."

"That should be possible if we work at it."

"How? Robinson has put me to work on a damn censorship committee. There's not going to be much money in that."

"Censorship!" she said, her eyes gleaming with amusement.

"Don't laugh. It's just about the worst job I can imagine—we're going to have to pretend to invent codes for self-censorship that nobody in the networks wants."

"Then maybe you'd better start looking for something else."

"What? Annie, I'm forty-three years old, for Christ's sake. No one has ever heard of me outside of Hopkins' office."

"The only thing you lack is self-confidence. That's kind of a charming trait in a man as big and bright as you, but don't let it hold you back."

"You know the business world. What do you think I should do?"

"Maybe you could start by counting your assets."

"Such as?"

"Intelligence, charm, integrity and a perfectly lovely cock."

She patted that exhausted soldier.

"I always thought it was too small," I said.

"See? You're always putting yourself down."

"Those assets wouldn't look too impressive on a résumé," I said.

"But ten years of working for Ralph Hopkins will."

"Now he's retired, no one will want his ghost."

"I wouldn't write him off just yet. He's going to be chairman of the board, isn't he?"

"Sure, but the general feeling is that he won't be very active. Henderson is already taking over everything."

"You know Hopkins better than anybody else. What do you think he'll do when he comes back?"

"He'll have to find something to keep him busy. When he said good-bye, he told me he might have something for me."

"What could that be?"

"Maybe he's thinking of writing his memoirs. He has a file full of notes."

"That could be a big opportunity for you."

"Ghostwriting the old man's memoirs? That wouldn't take six months."

"What if you could sell him on the idea of doing a full autobiography? A man that successful would want to leave some kind of record behind, wouldn't he?"

"God, who'd want to read the autobiography of a man who never did anything but make money all his life?"

"A lot of business people."

"Hopkins is too modest for that. He hates anything personal. But I might sell him on the idea of writing a company history. That's something he could really do."

"Now you're talking!"

"It would only take a year or two and there wouldn't be big money in it. If we did a company history, they'd put teams of researchers and writers on it. They'd probably end by getting a big name to put it all together."

"Not necessarily—Hopkins is used to dealing with you. You know his style."

"There's a chance."

"Do you mind if we push this idea a little farther?"

"How?"

"If you did a book for Hopkins, you'd get quite a reputation with insiders, even if he didn't give you written credit. There must be a hell of a lot of big businessmen who want to leave some kind of record behind. If you did a good job for Hopkins, you'd find them coming to you in droves."

"A sort of freelance ghost writer?"

"At a very high level. And if you got into biographies, you could leave the ghost part out."

"You may have something there, Annie."

"There are three things that could make it possible," she said, really warming up now. "You work well with big shots, and that's a special sort of skill. You use words well. And plenty of corporation presidents resent the fact that they're so anonymous, so quickly forgotten, no matter how rich they are. There has to be a demand for a man who could help those big shots put their story on paper."

"I wonder how much work like that would pay?"

"You'd be hitting ego—all those guys would want the best. We're talking about millionaires. If Hopkins gave you a good recommendation, you could name your own price—maybe a hundred grand for a year's work . . . and an extra twenty-five or so for your chief assistant."

She laughed.

"It's a beautiful dream," I said.

"And possible—it won't be a pipe dream if you work at it."

"You give me hope," I said, kissing her on the forehead. "I'll talk to Hopkins about it as soon as he gets back."

"Do you want a cup of coffee and some scrambled eggs? I just remembered that we're supposed to be having lunch."

"I'll grab a bite later. What are we going to do while we're waiting for all these great things to happen?"

"You could move in with me and give your salary to your family. But you won't do that till you can pay your share here."

"That's right."

"Frankly, I don't think you're ready to walk out and leave your wife. I'm not criticizing. Things like that have to happen in their own time—and I'll never push."

"I'm grateful for that, but if I had to make a choice now . . ."

"You'd be miserable. I don't want you feeling torn apart."

"But meanwhile . . ."

"Meanwhile, run along home every night and take care of your family. You can have lunch here with me whenever you want."

"That's no life for you!"

"It's no life for you either, but what's the choice?"

"I don't know . . ."

"You might as well face the truth: you can't say good-bye to your wife yet and you don't want to say good-bye to me. So you're stuck with both of us. Do you think you're the first man that ever happened to?"

"I'm beginning to feel very dirty."

"So life is dirty sometimes, isn't it? If we nobly gave each other up while you made up your mind, would that make you feel cleaner?"

"You know I can't do that."

"Okay. So we'll handle the situation as best we can. Sometimes you can work late and take me to dinner."

"But you're going to be alone here most of the time."

"You don't have to worry about me—I've been on my own a long time. My work is going well. I'm back to being Ed's assistant, but he's going to let me start interviewing job applicants, and I may get a raise. I still know enough people to get free theater tickets whenever I want them. I have lots of friends. I'm not going to be sitting here crying while I wait for you."

"I'll lose you if I keep you waiting too long," I said.

"That's the chance you'll have to take, just like I have to take the chance that you'll decide to stay out in Connecticut and be happy forever after. Look, I'm sorry if I sound tough . . ."

"I feel I'm doing everybody wrong and there's no way I can do right."

"Sometimes you can take life too seriously," she said, with a touch of exasperation. "Turn it around. You have a lovely family waiting for you out in Connecticut and you have me waiting to pounce on you whenever you want to come here. How lucky can you get?"

"I'll never be able to live with that long."

"I don't think you will, either. I'm an optimist. I think that eventually everything's going to work out fine. Meanwhile let's enjoy each day as it comes."

"I think you're a lot stronger than I am."

She gave me a long, shrewd look.

"Maybe in a few ways. Do you know what I think is bothering you?"

"Tell me."

"Words. You think of me as a mistress or a lover and that scares you because mistresses and lovers can be very demanding and unreliable. Those are a moralist's words and you're a moralist—that's one thing I love about you."

"You're right about that, I guess."

"Believe it or not, I'm also your friend. I want you to do right by your kids—I wouldn't have any use for you if you didn't. I even want you to do right by your wife. She sounds sort of kooky but nice, and after twenty years you sure as hell can't just walk out and leave her flat. I know how guilty and mixed-up you feel. Don't you think I sympathize with you for that?"

"I'm grateful."

"But I don't feel guilty for stealing you from her and I'll tell you why: I don't think she's been treating you right. I think I can take better care of you than she can. I think you need me just as much as I need you."

"I still don't really understand why you think you need me. There are thousands of young guys around who . . ."

"Show me one who cares about me as much as you do! Show me one who can talk to me the way you do and listen and try to understand. Why do you think the sex with us is so good?"

"Magic. Or is it that I have such a lovely cock?"

"All that," she said with a laugh, "and also, I think we both know when we're loved, really loved, totally adored, approved and accepted, just the way we are. You even make me feel you'd love me if I got fat. Go on, take a shower and get dressed. Go back to your censor's desk."

"Okay," I said, climbing out of bed.

"Do you want to come here for lunch tomorrow?"

"Wild horses wouldn't stop me—to coin a phrase."

"I'll just have an hour from now on. But one great hour a day is more than most people have to look forward to, isn't it?"

24

ANNIE HAD DONE everything she could to put my mind at ease, but I was enough of a Puritan to know that was not the way it was going to work for me. Out of deception, lies and double-dealing, no lasting good could possibly come. That was what I had been taught, and that was what I believed.

Still, there didn't seem much choice now, and in the short run Annie's strength and confidence helped me become a better husband and father. When Betsy explained that she had to attend another rehearsal right after dinner I genially told her I didn't mind at all.

"You're really being a brick about this," she said. "Monday the whole thing will be over. I promise I'll stay at home and make it all up to you."

That alarmed me a little, but I felt sure Bert Andrews would find another project to keep her busy. I still did not understand the nature of their friendship, affair or whatever it was, but it was clear they needed each other. Even though they were going to see each other that evening, he telephoned while we were having dinner. He sounded rather tense—maybe *his* conscience bothered him—but Betsy appeared guileless when she picked up the receiver. "Bert, I'm so glad you called. I've been thinking about what you said . . ."

She chatted like a teenager with him for twenty minutes while her dinner went cold.

"Ma's always on the phone with him. Or going over to his place," Pete said, perhaps to test my reaction.

Despite the gift of the microscope, Pete obviously disapproved of Andrews, but my daughters didn't.

"She is not!" Janey said.

"They're putting on a play!" Barbara added. "Do you have any idea how much work that is?"

Gordy, who was sharing our meal, started at me silently. I wondered if he thought I was a double fool about my wife, and it took all my self-control not to keep from setting him straight right then and there.

I don't know why I decided to tackle Barbara that very night. I guess I needed to straighten *somebody* out, and since it couldn't be Betsy or myself Barbara was the most suitable target. As soon as we finished our ice cream, Betsy hurried off to Bert's house and Barbara and Gordy headed toward his van. This time they didn't even give me the courtesy of saying they were going for a "little drive."

"Wait a minute, Barbara," I called after her. "I want to talk to you."

"What about?" she asked sharply.

"I think it's time we had a talk," I said.

"I'll say!" Pete muttered, tossed down his paper napkin and went up to his room in disgust.

"Daddy, don't give her a hard time," Janey said, her dark eyes suffering for all of us.

"Come out here if you want to talk," Barbara said from the kitchen.

"Let's go up to my room," I said.

"Oh, daddy!"

Barbara could pack enough scorn into those two words to set my teeth on edge.

"Please don't use that tone of voice with me," I said, trying to sound calm.

"We're in a hurry," she said. "We have to meet friends."

"Come up to my room first."

She and Gordy glared at me, and for a moment I thought they would defy me and roar off in the van.

"Why are you making such a big deal of this?" Barbara demanded.

"I'll explain when we get upstairs."

She sighed and walked toward me, her face so sullen that she no longer looked pretty. Gordy hesitated, then followed her.

"You stay out here," I said in what I hoped was like an army voice.

"Yes, sir," he said with an echo of mockery.

With her arms folded over her breasts, Barbara walked up the stairs to my room and I followed.

"Sit down," I said, gesturing toward a chair in front of Betsy's vanity table.

"Stop giving me orders! Can't I even stand if I want?"

"Yes, I suppose you can."

"So what do you want to talk about?"

"You. I love you very much, but I'm worried about you."

The words sounded phony even to me.

"I can take care of myself!" she cried. "I'm not a child anymore!"

"Barbs, you're not yet seventeen and besides . . ."

"Don't call me Barbs!" she said, stamping her foot.

It was a childhood name she had objected to from the age of twelve, though to me it still had an affectionate ring.

"All right, Barbara, let's stick to facts. No girl your age can take care of herself. You still need parents to support you."

"I could get a job!"

"That's doubtful."

"Do you want me to try?"

"No! I want you to finish school and go to college."

"That's what I'm trying to do!"

"I want to talk to you about Gordy . . ."

"You have no right to get involved in my personal life!" she said, her eyes blazing.

"I *am* involved. I'm your father, for God's sake!"

"That doesn't mean you have a right to get involved with my boyfriends. Have you talked to muth about this?"

"Yes. And I don't much like what she said."

Her face flushed.

"She had no right to talk to you about me!"

"You don't think a mother and father have a right to talk about their daughter?"

"Not about private things."

"Look, I'm not going to talk about what goes on between you and Gordy. I'm sorry it happened to you so young, but there's not much I can do about that now . . ."

"Then what do you want to talk about?"

"I'd like to talk about your future."

"I'm going to college next year. I'm getting good marks. Mr.

Stover says I can get into any one I want."

"Have you picked one yet?"

"Connecticut College."

"Why that one?"

"Gordy's going to get a job in New London."

"What kind of a job?"

"I don't know. He'll find something."

"Did he graduate from high school?"

"No, his father left home and he had to go to work."

"I see. Doesn't his mother work?"

"Yes, but she's awful and she's living with a horrible man. But Gordy can handle it. He's no child!"

I knew it was becoming an inquisition, but I couldn't help myself. "Do you plan to marry him?"

"We're not even talking about that yet."

"This may make you angry, but you'd better think about it—without a high school education, Gordy is going to have a hard time making a living in this world."

"All you care about is money! It's all you ever care about! You don't know anything at all about love!"

I didn't want to try to answer that one, not now anyway.

"Maybe every girl thinks that about her father," I said.

"It's true about you. I don't want to grow up to be like you and muth, worrying about money all the time."

"Do you want to live in a house, eat three times a day and send your kids to college?"

"I don't think I want to have kids with the world the way it is."

"I went right from college into a war. So did my father. It's lucky for you that we didn't give up."

"Overpopulation is the worst problem in the world. People can't go on having kids anymore."

"I'm not going to argue that now."

"Can I go?"

"Wait a minute. I suppose there are good things and bad things about falling in love when you're young as you are."

"There's nothing bad about it! You just make everything dirty!"

"I don't know why you think that."

"The way you look at me!"

"I'm worried about you!"

"*Why?*"

She stamped her foot again.

"You may not believe this, but when people fall in love at your age it usually doesn't last long. People your age go through a lot of changes."

"How old were you when you met muth?"

I didn't answer that.

"We've had our hard times," I said. "I think she wishes we had waited."

"We're not like the two of you."

"Maybe not, but it's statistically probable that couples your age won't stay together very long. You'll have a lot of heartbreak."

"Is that what you go by, statistical probabilities?"

"Sometimes it's wise to take them into account. Barbara, you can hate me for saying this, but you'll get tired of Gordy. He's nowhere near as intelligent as you, and he can't cope with the world. Maybe it's cruel to say it, but you'll meet much better young men at college."

"That will be up to me, won't it?"

"Sure, but you ought to realize that it can happen."

"Anything can happen! Do you think I don't know that?"

"I'm suggesting that you might live more cautiously. A breakup could be hard not only for you, but for Gordy. Cool it a little."

That advice sounded ridiculous as soon as I said it. Cool it a little . . .

"Yes, daddy," she said. "Can I go now?"

"I have one more thing to say. I don't want that boy living here."

"He's not living here!"

"He eats most of his meals here, and his van is always parked out back."

"He has nowhere else to go!"

"He's got a job, hasn't he?"

"He can't just eat in restaurants all the time. He doesn't make enough money for that."

"What's he going to do in New London?"

"He thinks he can get a better job there. He's learning to be a mechanic. And he's getting better with his guitar." For the first time she tried to smile at me.

"I wish him luck, but I don't think he should be living here. A girl of sixteen shouldn't have a live-in boyfriend."

"I'll be seventeen next month—"

"You'll still need some privacy, time to be alone, to see other friends. I'm not saying you can't have dates, but I don't want him around all the time."

"We need each other! Can't you understand that?"

It was beginning to sound like a soap opera, father versus daughter in a battle of clichés.

"The more you're together, the more you're going to think you need each other—until you suddenly get sick of it and have a big blow-up. That's what happens at your age. You're being reckless. I'm trying to help you be more careful."

The advice sounded totally sincere to my own ears, but what a hypocrite I felt. Had I applied it to my own raddled life? Of course, I said to myself, I was much older . . .

"I know you're trying to help," she said with strained patience. "Can I go now?"

"We still haven't resolved this."

"What do you want me to do?"

"Tell Gordy you can still go out together but I don't want him eating his meals in this house anymore or parking out back all night."

"Have you talked to muth about this?" she asked, her face pale.

"Not yet. The point is, Barbara, you have to exercise some restraint."

"She'd never be so mean!"

"I'm not being mean! It's not good for your reputation, having that boy hanging out here all the time."

"Is it my reputation or yours that you're worried about?"

My child had a serpent's sting in her.

"The whole family's, maybe . . ."

"Bullshit!"

"What does that mean?"

"If you don't know, never mind. Everybody talks about everybody in this damn town. It's a snake pit. You're lucky you can stay out of it most of the time."

So she knew about her mother and Bert, probably a lot more than I did. There was no reason for me to feel so angry, but the gossip must have wounded her.

"I guess we all do the best we can," I said wearily.

"Are you still telling me that I can't ask Gordy to dinner?"

"Not every night!"

"Are you going to ration us? How many times?"

"It would be normal to ask him to dinner a couple of times a week."

"Do they have statistical studies of things like that?"

"Barbs . . . Barbara, I'm asking you to have some common sense!"

"That's not always so easy, is it?" she said.

"No. We all have to do the best we can." What a feeble response, I thought.

"We're doing that!"

"I wish I could be more help to you. I don't know why we have to talk like enemies."

"I wish I could help you too," she said softly and I guessed that she felt sorry for me because of Bert. Sympathy from her was the last thing I expected or deserved, and it made my throat constrict. What the hell kind of father-daughter relationship would it be if I broke down in tears? Maybe a damn good therapeutic one, but neither of us was ready for that.

She looked as though she too were about to cry, but she turned suddenly and ran down the stairs. A moment later I heard the engine of the van cough into action and it growled out of the driveway in low gear. I lay down on the bed with my arm over my eyes. A few minutes later there was a knock at my door. It was Janey.

"Are you all right, dad?" she said.

"I'm fine."

"I'm going to take Bonkers for a walk. Would you like to come?"

We walked the dog around the block three times. It was a cold clear night with a starlit sky as bright as a dream of youth.

GORDY'S VAN RETURNED around ten that evening, and after leaving Barbara off, he drove off to spend the night somewhere else, a small victory for me, I supposed, but a forlorn one. Barbara went to bed without saying goodnight, and the others soon followed. Betsy wouldn't return from her rehearsal until very late, I guessed. The big house was so quiet that the humming of the oil burner in the basement seemed unusually loud.

My whole family was in bad trouble—there wasn't any point in denying that. My anger suddenly exploded at Betsy for behaving with Bert in a way that was causing gossip and upsetting the children. Why the hell couldn't she even run her damn affair right?

I knew I was being unjust. South Bay was a small town and

people would talk, even if she and Bert were only friends who were working together late to put on a play. Gossip in South Bay was no proof of guilt, and even if she had been caught up in a great romance during my absence, who was I to be so righteously indignant? The only difference was that I was able to get away to Washington and New York.

But what was going to happen now? Betsy wouldn't find it any easier to break up the family than I would, even if Bert were serious about her, which I doubted. Maybe he would find it amusing to go on meeting her at late "rehearsals" at his house—the little bastard was obviously trying to prove his masculinity with the liaison right under my nose. Never mind my own guilt, I still wanted to kill him —at least I wasn't taking another man's wife and messing up his children. But choking the little prick to death, as I kept imagining myself doing, wouldn't help. During the war I had killed seventeen men whom I had no reason to hate, but my wife's lover was protected by the law.

What was I getting excited about? I had to stay calm. If I did nothing, Bert and Betsy would continue their clandestine affair while I had lunches and a few late evenings with Annie in New York. They called that "open marriage," didn't they? If Betsy kept busy with Bert, then she wouldn't object if I spent most of my time, including weekends, "working late" in New York. There would be no divorce, no breakup of family routine, no division of money or property and I wouldn't have to support two households. Life could go on in this sleazy way. We could all be happy, happy, happy, with plenty of fucking and a nice, genial, permissive home for the kids.

But where did Annie figure in this solution? My head whirled— there seemed to be no way out. Even if I could make enough money to give Betsy everything she needed except a husband, I knew she didn't have the strength to be a single parent, as they called it. She'd let the kids do whatever they wanted, and in the long run even teenagers don't like that. With Bert in and out of the house she'd be a hell of an example for the children. With my much younger mistress in New York, I could safely deliver stern lectures on morality and common sense, and if the children grew more and more mixed up, I could safely blame my Betsy for the whole mess.

Barbara would run off with Gordy or someone like him. Pete would become a bookworm, and Janey would suffer for all of us, finding comfort in her dog, her horses and her psychiatrist. At

223 —

night with Annie I would sometimes cry, and she would comfort me until she discovered that some wounds can't be healed. One reason she loved me, she had said, was that she respected me for being so responsible. How long would it take for that light to go out of her eyes?

I couldn't sleep, I refused to let myself drink and I couldn't concentrate on a novel. I could walk in circles around the living room or stare at television, where the screen showed people roaring with laughter at pratfalls or shooting each other and dying bloodlessly without convulsions or wounded cries. The trouble with the damn tube was that it had already been censored too much, one way or another, and now glowed without hint of life. Well, anything like real life was too boring or too tough to take after a hard day's work.

Lights suddenly flashed in the driveway. Betsy was home earlier than I had expected—it was only about midnight. She had not taken off her stage makeup and the deep eye shadow and powder made her look oddly spectral.

"It's good to get home," she said, collapsing on the couch. "Sometimes I wonder why I wanted to be an actress anyway."

"Can I get you a drink?" I said.

"Make it a short one. Tomorrow's the big dress rehearsal. I hope I can get a good sleep."

I poured her a drink and another short one for myself.

"I had a talk with Barbara tonight," I said as I handed it to her.

"Oh? What about?"

"I said I didn't think Gordy should be hanging around here so much. It's not good for her to have him practically living here."

"I noticed his van was gone. Poor Gordy!"

"It's Barbs we have to be worried about."

"I'm too tired to do that now. There are all sorts of things we should talk about. But for the next two days I just have to concentrate on the play."

"Do you mind if I ask one question?"

"Ask."

"Do you intend to see Bert a great deal after this damn play is over?"

"Oh, I can't get into that tonight!"

"It's important to me," I said, unable to stop myself. "The kids have heard gossip. It troubles them."

"Did they say that to you?"

"Barbara didn't mean to, but she made it pretty clear."

"Well, you know South Bay. Bert and I have been together a lot. He's the director of the play and I'm the star . . . or trying to be."

"I just want to know if it's going to go on," I persisted.

"I've been worried about that," she said after swallowing her scotch. "Bert's really a great friend—I like him and I've learned to depend on him a lot. But you always get so tense and suspicious when I mention his name that I'm afraid even to ask him over for a drink."

"Shouldn't I be a little upset?"

"I'm not sleeping with him! Can't you believe that?"

"I will if you want, but if he's become a large part of your life, that really is almost academic, isn't it?"

"He likes me, Tom! He respects me. Believe it or not, he thinks I'm a charming and talented woman, and not so bad-looking in my way. He makes me feel good. Do you want me to apologize for liking that?"

"Do you think he loves you?"

"Maybe. Do you find that incredible?"

"Of course not, but as your husband I might find it alarming."

"I didn't say I love him!"

"Do you?"

"I like him. I'm alone here a lot, even when you're only in New York, and he always cheers me up. If I weren't married to you, if I didn't have three kids, I might fall in love with him. I just don't let myself do things like that!"

"How reliable do you think he is?"

"What do you mean by that?"

"Do you think he'd marry you if you divorced me?"

"I've never even thought of a thing like that! Why, have you?"

"If he makes you happy and I don't . . ."

"I always thought that sooner or later we'd work things out. Have you lost hope?"

"I'm just trying to find my way. Sometimes I get pretty confused . . ."

"I know I haven't been much of a wife to you lately. With all this going on . . ."

"I'm not complaining, but I worry about the kids. None of them seems happy."

"That's just the way kids are. They go through stages. So do we."

"I just hope that in the long run we can all figure out a better way to live."

"Can't we put this on ice and talk about it later—after I'm finished with the play?"

"If that's the way you want it."

"I'm not up to a lot of heavy talk now. I have to keep eighty-three pages of dialogue in my mind."

"I'm sorry I bothered you."

"And I'm sorry you're not happy, Tom. Damn it, maybe I've memorized too much Tennessee Williams, but I'm beginning to wonder whether anybody is really happy. Maybe we just have to live with that."

"We still have to keep trying."

"Not tonight," she said, heading for the stairs. "Let me sleep late tomorrow. Take the car and leave it at the station."

"Won't you need it?"

"Bert will drive me down to get it later on. Goodnight."

I felt that I had got the short end of that conversation. What had I accomplished by it? I did not want to go upstairs and lie down in bed beside her now, so I paced for another hour before going to our room. I found Betsy sleeping peacefully on her back with her arms stretched out at her sides, her palms open in a gesture of supplication. I stayed close to my edge of the bed and soon drifted into a dreamless sleep of the sort that only the innocent are supposed to enjoy.

As usual I woke up at six-thirty the next morning, but I had not had enough sleep and I felt tired and even more irritable than usual at such an hour.

My mood became worse when I went to drive to the station and found Gordy's van parked again by the garage. Returning to the kitchen, I said, "Barbara! Didn't I tell you to get that van out of here?"

"I told Gordy!" she said in surprise.

"Well I'm going to tell him in a way he won't forget. Is he sleeping in the damn thing?"

"I'll talk to him," she said. "Don't wake him up. Something must have happened."

"Something is damn well going to happen—" I said in a rage.

I went outside and banged on the side of the van with the flat of my hand.

"Gordy!" I shouted. "I want to talk to you!"

Barbara, in bathrobe and slippers, ran up beside me.

"Don't do this!" she shouted. "What's the matter with you?"

The back door of the van opened and Gordy stepped out. He was wearing the rumpled blue jeans and dirty T-shirt in which he had slept, and was hunched over against the cold.

"What's going on?" he said sleepily.

"Didn't Barbara tell you I didn't want you parked here all night?"

"Yes, she did, Mr. Rath, but let me explain . . ."

"To hell with your explanation!"

"Let him talk!" Barbara said.

"I need time to find a place," Gordy said. He was shivering, as was Barbara.

"You mean this is the only place in South Bay where you can park?" I yelled.

"Mr. Rath, let me try to explain it to you. I can't go to the garage where I work—the boss locks it up at night. I can't go home because my mother and I had a big fight. So last night I went to the parking lot behind the school. About one in the morning a cop knocks on my window with his damn stick, gives me a ticket and tells me to move on."

"So couldn't you park on any street?"

"There's a law against all-night parking in this town, Mr. Rath. With your station wagon, they wouldn't enforce it, but with his old van . . . I didn't want another ticket."

"So drive out in the country."

"That's right, Mr. Rath, but the state cops and the farmers can get you there. They don't like old vans and kids with long hair. Besides, I was cold last night. Barbara has been letting me hook up the electric heater in your garage."

He nodded toward the lawn and I saw that he had run a long extension cord through the wilted grass.

"I'm going to get a good sleeping bag," he said, "and I'll find some place where I can park, but I couldn't do it in the middle of the night . . . and I figured that you wouldn't mind giving me a little time."

"He needs a place where he can use a bathroom," Barbara said. "Can't you give him a break, dad?"

I was filled with pity, exasperation and a feeling of helplessness.

"All right, but I still don't want this van here every night," I said.

"I've got to run to catch my train."

"Thanks, sir," Gordy said in that respectful tone which held an echo of mockery.

I felt for sure this boy was conning Barbara and me, using his pathetic needs to get exactly what he wanted, a place to sleep, free food, free booze, free laundry service and my pretty daughter . . . not a bad deal, and not one from which he would be easily dislodged. Or was I being too cynical? I couldn't think about that now. At noon I was going to see Annie, in my black mood. Suddenly I felt exhausted, a strange burned-out sensation, and I wondered if she would expect me to make passionate love to her every day on cue. Meeting her for one rushed hour every day could turn into a burlesque, with both of us tearing off our clothes and hurling ourselves at each other, then dashing to take a shower in order to get back to work on time. What if we just didn't feel like making love? Would she be hurt if I suggested that we actually go out to lunch or that I was too old for all this passion? Would she fake ardor when she didn't feel it, just to please me, to stroke my ego? She had said that one great hour a day was more than most people could expect. But what if the stolen hour began to become tense and embarrassing, even boring after a while? Sooner or later this was bound to happen. Meeting a lover for one hour a day was such an artificial situation that it inevitably would lead to a crackup.

We should take each day as it came, she had said, we shouldn't feel rushed. Enjoy the present while waiting for the future to work itself out. I wondered if she could really teach me, infect me with her sunny optimism, her unshakable belief in a bright tomorrow.

25

ALMOST AS SOON as I got to my office Robinson called to ask how I was coming with the plans for the self-censorship committees. The few pages I had written lay crumpled in the wastepaper basket, but I said it was coming along fine and I'd have a preliminary draft ready for him that night. As soon as I hung up I began to write. If they wanted shit, I'd give it to them. One thing I could do was type fast.

At eleven-thirty I quit and went to the men's room to wash my face and comb my hair. Glancing at myself in the mirror, I thought I looked as tired and old as I felt, hardly the kind of lover a young woman like Annie could be expected to greet with a show of anticipation. I walked slowly to her apartment, timing my arrival for exactly noon. The doorman who doubled as elevator operator looked at me oddly—he obviously remembered me from the day before. We avoided each other's eyes as he took me up to the seventh floor.

Nervously I knocked at her door. There was no answer and I knocked again. Maybe she was changing her clothes, or perhaps she had decided not to come. I stood in the hall feeling bewildered, waited a minute, knocked again, then walked back toward the elevator. As I reached it the doors rumbled open and Annie stepped out of the car. She was wearing a gray flannel skirt with a black cashmere sweater and she was carrying two large grocery bags.

"Sorry I'm late," she said breathlessly, "but I thought you might like to have a really nice lunch this time."

I was too stunned to say anything.

As I took the bags from her, she stood on her toes and kissed me on the cheek.

"Poor dear, you look tired," she said. "Have you had a bad day?"

"It's been a little confusing."

"I'll get a key made for you," she said as she used hers to open the door.

I put the grocery bags down on a counter in the kitchenette. She began unpacking them.

"Do you like cold boiled lobster with mayonnaise?"

"Sounds great."

"That's all I've got, plus a green salad and a bottle of wine. Do you want coffee?"

"I'd love some."

I sat in the only armchair in the room while she set a small table with plates and moved a straight chair in a corner up to it.

"I had kind of a rough morning too," she said. "I interviewed my first job applicants today. My trouble is that I feel so sorry for the worst ones that I almost hire them."

The lobster and the salad tasted splendid, but we didn't talk much as we ate, and the silence began to feel strained.

"I think you have something on your mind," she said as she poured the coffee. "Did you have a rough time at home last night?"

"Sort of . . ."

"Do you mind if I ask about it?"

Once I got started, I had to tell her about my conversation with Betsy.

"I think she's sort of strangely innocent," I said. "I mean, she's seeing this guy Bert Andrews all the time and she admits that they're emotionally involved, but she says they're not really doing anything wrong and I believe her. There's a sort of childlike quality about her that I find very difficult to deal with. She's so damned helpless!"

"That's a wife's best weapon," Annie said.

"I don't think she's using it on purpose."

"Maybe she's exactly what she seems to be, but on the other hand . . . She's running around with a lawyer, isn't she? Maybe he's told her not to admit to adultery in any circumstances. Lawyers generally advise that, and for good reason."

"I honestly don't think she's capable of lying."

"Are you?"

"You know the answer to that."

"Then why not her? Anyone can lie in some circumstances."

"I know, but she's different."

"So a lot of husbands think. I'm not putting her down, but maybe she's more sophisticated than you think. And kinder."

"Kinder?"

"She might not want to hurt you. Does she have any idea that you're seeing me?"

"Impossible."

"Well, if she's not sure yet what she and her friend can work out, maybe she just wants to save you as much pain as possible. Only idiots feel they have to make blubbering confessions."

"I suppose so," I said, feeling rather peculiar because I had often been tempted to make a clean breast of everything with Betsy. Didn't Annie value honesty? Apparently she read my mind.

"There are times when being frank can be very cruel," she said. "I think mature people should carry their own guilt and not try to shove it off on someone else."

I let that sink in for a moment.

"A woman like her with three children and a husband would have to go into a thing like this very carefully if she had any sense. She wouldn't want to burn her bridges until she was sure she had somewhere to jump."

"Do you think she's really so cold-blooded?"

"Aren't we? Don't we all have to be at a time like this?"

"To tell the truth, I think I'm the most cold-blooded of us all," I said wretchedly.

"Aren't you being hard on yourself?"

"Last night I think I was deliberately trying to push her into Bert's arms. I was being deliberately Machiavellian about it. I don't think she'd even thought of marrying the guy until I suggested it."

"I doubt that you planned that."

"No, it just came out. I'd been thinking that the only way out was for us all was for her to marry him. Then all the financial problems would be solved."

"If she's going around with the guy, she's obviously thinking about that."

"But the idea of pushing her into it is horrible. I don't even like the guy. In the long run, I think he'd be bad for her and bad for my children."

"How well do you really know him?"

"I've known him all my life."

"But how well?"

"Not very . . ."

"Isn't it possible that he's a better guy than you think?"

"It's remotely possible."

"Don't you have to admit that you're prejudiced? No husband likes a man who pays a lot of attention to his wife. And you say he's made a lot of money?"

"A hell of a lot in South Bay."

"No one who's been having a hard time like you could help feeling envious about that. The success of childhood friends is what hurts the worst."

"He never went to war, never had any kids . . ."

"Does that damn him forever?"

"He married for money and then ditched his wife when he got rich."

"How can you be so sure that's the way it happened?"

"Why are you defending the little bastard?"

"He must have something nice about him if your wife likes him so much." Why was Annie so damn logical?

"He's sold her a bill of goods."

"What if you're wrong? People hardly ever turn out to be what we expect."

"Usually they turn out to be worse."

"Haven't you ever been surprised the other way?"

"Barely."

"Cynicism and pessimism don't make any more sense than cock-eyed optimism. A lot of bad things have been happening to you lately. Maybe by the law of averages it's time for a surprise to come along."

"I hope so. Damn, it won't be long before you get fed up with me because of my damn moods."

"I'll get you out of them."

She stood up, put her hands on my shoulders and kneaded the muscles there.

"You're tense as hell," she said, moving her fingers up to the cords of my neck. "What you need is a good massage. I'm going to give you one."

"Please, no . . ."

"Why not?"

"It would embarrass me."

"That's absurd."

She took the bed down from the wall.

"Take off your clothes and lie down. I know you don't feel like making love, but I'm going to prove that I can make you feel relaxed."

"Annie, you're making me feel more and more tense!"

"Will you admit that I know more than you about some things, like the power of a good massage?"

She loosened my tie, began unbuttoning my shirt, and there was nothing I could do but take off my clothes and lie down on the bed. Feeling more and more apprehensive, I pretended that I was asleep while she went into the bathroom, soon emerging in her terrycloth bathrobe with an armful of towels. She spread them out beside me on the bed.

"Roll over on these," she said. "Lie on your stomach."

Peeking over my shoulder, I saw her take a bottle of baby oil from the pocket of her bathrobe, pour some into her right palm and rub her hands together. Kneeling over me, she started at the back of my neck, her touch very gentle at first, but soon her fingers bit deeper, stopping just short of pain. My shoulders came next, then the small of my back, with long strokes that caressed my buttocks and thighs.

"This isn't making me relax," I said.

"Give me time."

"You have a very loving touch."

"I love you. Haven't you figured that out yet?"

"I'm beginning to get the message in the massage."

"Roll over on your back."

She started under my chin and soon worked down over my throat to my chest, her long strokes reaching lightly down to my belly and thighs.

"You're making me horny," I said.

"I thought I noticed some stirrings of life."

"Quit this and come to bed with me."

"This is massage time. I want to relax you, not tire you out."

"I'm not tired anymore!"

"Will you let me finish what I've started?"

"This is just one-way sex."

"Someday when I'm real tired, I'll ask you to do the same for me."

"I couldn't do it without trying to lay you."

"That always can be a temptation. Massage takes discipline."

"I don't want discipline right now!"

"You don't have to have it. I'll help you to come in a few minutes. That's when you'll really relax."

"You come with me. I won't do it unless you do."

"Want to bet?" she said, caressing my groin.

"This is indecent. At least take off that damn robe. I don't like to be naked alone!"

She took the robe off and tossed it to the foot of the bed.

"Now give me some of that oil," I said. "I want to do you."

"You're supposed to be completely passive. That's where the relaxation comes in."

"I can't be completely passive. You're giving me the shuddering shakes."

I reached up and pulled her down on me, our bodies fitting together with such sudden completeness that we both gasped with pleasure.

"Better," I said after a moment.

"Someday when you're really beat, let me finish you off the other way," she said. "Don't feel you always have to play the great lover."

Her face grew taut as we found the right rhythm.

"Just don't quit now," she gasped.

SHE ALWAYS DID make me feel I was a great lover, but any man could feel like a bedroom champion with her. I had been afraid our desire would fade as the first excitement of the affair wore off, but now I was more optimistic. Perhaps my Puritan forefathers were wrong when they preached that sexual obsession was both temporary and destructive. If Annie had been evil, it would have worked out that way for me, but as she had wryly pointed out, she wasn't. Our miraculous ability to give each other great pleasure welded us together and resolved all doubts. She owned me but I also owned her—I was beginning to realize that and it gave me the most incredible sense of security, something I had never had.

"We're home!" she whispered in my ear over and over again while her body throbbed with joy, and I felt she meant more than the celebration of sexual completion—I was her home and she was mine, a concept that, for us, had depthless emotional power.

Time played strange tricks on us. I had always thought that moments of pain were long, minutes of pleasure short, but our lovemaking sessions were so intense that I was always astonished when I glanced at my watch to discover that only half an hour had gone by, not half the morning, or afternoon or night. On that afternoon after my first massage, Annie wasn't even a minute late getting back to work.

"I'll see you tomorrow," I said as she kissed me good-bye, fresh from a shower, her skirt and dress unrumpled, a very respectable, almost severe-looking young businesswoman, without makeup and her hair cut short.

"You mean Monday, don't you?"

The realization that I had to spend three days without her came as a blow, and I guess the disappointment showed in my eyes.

"Call me when you can," she said. "I'll be at my grandmother's house in Brooklyn."

Taking a pad and pen from her handbag she scribbled a number and handed it to me.

"Let me give you my number," I said.

"You really don't want me to call, do you?"

"I'm not in prison yet. Just say you're Annie, my old assistant."

"I probably won't, but I'm glad to have the number," she said, and wrote it down.

After she had gone I took a quick shower and dressed. I felt refreshed and, as she had prophesied, fully relaxed. I no longer doubted Annie and I would have to get married soon. Debating the rights and wrongs of divorce seemed about as relevant as arguing about our need to breathe. The only problem was how to give the least possible pain to all the other people I loved.

26

ANNIE'S FEELING THAT only the unexpected can be expected, and that good things were bound to happen, was justified surprisingly soon. About an hour after I got back to my office, my telephone rang, and to my astonishment an overseas operator with an English accent said that she had a call for me from Mr. Ralph Hopkins on Ship Island in the Bahamas.

"Hello, Tom?" Hopkins broke in, his voice as hearty as ever.

"I'm glad to hear from you, sir."

"How would you like to come down here for a few days? I have a little work . . ."

Apparently this was radio telephone, and his voice faded away before it came back. "It won't be long."

"I'd like that very much, sir," I said.

"Has Robinson got you all tied up?" he asked, faintly again.

"Nothing important."

"Then fly down here. Go to Nassau and my little plane will pick you up. BOAC has a flight leaving Idlewild at three tomorrow afternoon. That too soon for you?"

"No sir, I'll be on that plane."

"Good. How's the family?"

"Fine, sir."

"Be glad to see you. Lots of sun and fish down here, but not a damn thing to do. Even this telephone is impossible and the mail . . ."

His voice faded away again before I heard him say good-bye.

I should have known that an obsessed man like Hopkins couldn't enjoy a vacation for long, but the fact that he needed me so soon offered at least temporary escape from the censorship job. Probably a speech or a magazine article to write, but I would have a chance to sell him on the idea of a book, which might start me on the grand plan Annie and I had devised. Suddenly I wished I had asked him if I could bring her along, but if he had wanted me to bring an assistant, he would have told me. I doubted whether the old man would disapprove if he discovered that Annie and I were lovers, unless he felt she was distracting me from his needs.

I called Annie and gave her the surprising news.

"Great!" she said. "Tom, I think we can count on two things. The old man will never quit working as long as he's alive, and he'll always need you."

"He needs that guy Lester, his houseman, too. I wouldn't count on anything big yet."

"You can sell him on the idea of doing a book. He really started this whole company, didn't he? He's Mr. Broadcasting, yet he's also the man nobody knows. He has an obligation to tell his story —it's part of this country's history."

"I wish you were coming with me. You could really make the pitch."

"You can do it a lot better than me—he'd never take me seriously. Tom, I don't know how you can tell him this, but for his own sake he has to do this book. Right now he has a terrible reputation. Despite his charity work, he's really known as the king of the wasteland, the man who turned the greatest medium for communication into an idiot box. Do you think he wants that on his tombstone?"

"I don't think I want to ask him that."

"You don't have to—he knows it. He has to tell his side of the story before he dies. No one can help him to do it better than you."

"I wish I could see you tonight and kick this around."

"Well, can't you?"

"Betsy's play is opening—it's her big night. I have an obligation to be there. The kids are going to sit with me."

"I understand. Tell her to break a leg. God help me, I mean that in more ways than one."

Almost as soon as I hung up, Betsy called me.

"Tom, can you be home tonight by seven at the latest?"

"I'll get in at six-thirty-two."

"Great. I left the car at the station. Please see that the kids get dinner, then take them to the high school at eight. I'm at Bert's house. We're running through the play one last time and the whole cast is going to get dressed here—there's no place at the school for that."

"I'll take care of everything."

"Thanks. I'm so nervous, I don't know what I'm going to do."

"They say even professionals get butterflies before a performance."

"Butterflies? I've got *buzzards*. Bert's got me on paregoric and Valium."

"Don't knock yourself out."

"I'm going to take a nap now. Tom, I know you think that amateur theatricals are silly, but this is terribly important to me. It's a great play and we're really trying to do a good job."

"There's nothing silly about that. Break a leg!"

"What?"

"That's an old theatrical expression. It means good luck."

"That's a funny way to say it. Actually, they've got me wearing a long skirt and I'm scared to death I'll trip."

"You'll make it. I bet you do fine."

"After the performance, there's a party for the cast and our friends at Bert's house. Of course you're invited. You can leave the kids off at home."

COMPARED TO BRIDGE or cocktail parties, amateur theatricals always seemed to have a terrible pathos about them. The actors worked so hard for so long for only one or two performances, a laudatory review in the local paper—no one ever panned amateurs—and a self-congratulatory cast party followed by plans for another play. I wished Betsy could find something more satisfying to fill her life. For a lot of people, amateur theatricals were an excuse for parties, but I sensed that Betsy was seeking a kind of self-fulfillment and recognition that the high school stage and the parties were not going to give her. Maybe the approval of Bert and her fellow players was enough, but I had an uneasy feeling that she would suffer a terrible letdown later, would be even less able to cope with life. And then there was my fear that Betsy would disintegrate when she learned I wanted to leave her. She had never given me any reason to believe she was weak, and it was probably egotistical for me to believe that she could not survive without me. Still, the image of her gulping paregoric and Valium before her performance scared me. She needed a success now, not a failure. If she made a fool of herself in front of her friends and neighbors, I wasn't sure she could handle it.

The high school auditorium was filled to capacity. The production of *A Streetcar Named Desire* had achieved some notoriety in South Bay because some of the church people and school board members had opposed it, and the town had turned out in force. A rumor that Tennessee Williams was actually going to be there spread, but no one saw the playwright in the audience.

Barbara, Gordy, Janey, Pete and I arrived early. The children looked embarrassed and tense. Betsy had given them copies of the play to read beforehand and had told me she didn't think they understood it, but I thought they did. I sensed they comprehended the dark currents of life better than most adults I knew.

A few minutes before the curtain went up, Bert came from backstage and took a seat in a row ahead of us. The production was his baby and he must be nervous, I thought, but he looked genial and confident. Seeing me, he waved and said, "Everything's going fine!" His ebullience was so genuine that I could see why Betsy and others liked the little bastard.

Finally the lights dimmed and the curtain went jerkily up, sticking a moment before it completed its ascent. Tony Morasco, who changed tires at the local Ford garage, came charging out in his role as Stanley Kowalski and bellowed, "Stella!" When the local minister's wife came down the spiral staircase in her slip, a lot of people laughed. I cursed them under my breath, embarrassed for Betsy, waiting in the wings to make her big entrance.

The audience quickly recovered from the shock of seeing their minister's wife hug the local garageman. When Betsy came on stage in a gauzy, flowing white dress, she looked so fragile and vulnerable that my throat constricted—she really was Blanche DuBois. Somehow Betsy had learned how to speak with a southern accent and she tossed her chin up with such pathetic gallantry that she got a burst of applause. With astonished relief, I realized that she was a much better actress than I had ever thought she could be.

But the play was pretty blah. Tony Morasco turned Stanley Kowalski into an amiable oaf and the minister's wife seemed much too prim to be Stella. But Betsy was really magnificent as Blanche, and many women in the audience dabbed at their eyes with tissues as she finally descended into madness and was led away. The applause was not exactly deafening, but it was enthusiastic and swelled when Betsy came out to take her curtain call. Gone was her look of fragility and vulnerability. In this moment of triumph she was radiant, and looked younger and prettier than she had in years. Suddenly Bert bounded up on the stage and presented her with a huge bouquet of red roses.

"Ladies and gentlemen," Betsy said, "I guess you all know this is Bert Andrews, our producer and director. If there was anything good in our performance, we owe it all to him!"

Bert interrupted her. "No director can take credit for the vibrant talent of an actress like this!"

She took a rose from her bouquet and handed it to him. He kissed it before putting it into his buttonhole, a phony gesture, but he carried it off with a certain air and bowed to the audience. The curtain went down, but the applause was loud enough to demand one more curtsy and bow from Betsy and Bert.

"Muth was good, wasn't she?" Barbara said as we walked out to the car.

"I'll say she was!"

"She's not really crazy like that, it's just the character she's playing," Janey said nervously.

"She's just a very good actress," I said.

"I thought that man Stanley Kowalski was a jerk," Pete growled.

"I know the guy," Gordy said. "He really is a jerk—he wasn't acting a damn bit."

That was the sum of the family criticism.

As ALWAYS, I felt negligent when I dropped off the children at our house, but there was no point in providing a chaperone for Barbara and Gordy.

"Do you mind if we have a few friends in?" Barbara asked.

The idea of an unsupervised teenage party still bothered me and I hesitated.

"It's early and we don't have to go to school tomorrow," she added.

"I don't want any drinking around here," I said.

"We won't do that, sir," Gordy said with his hint of mockery.

"We're old enough to have beer," Barbara said. "We're not kids anymore, dad!"

"We'll be careful," Janey said.

"I don't care what you do," Pete said. "I'm going to bed."

"A little beer for those sixteen or over is okay," I said to Barbara, "but keep the music down and the lights on."

"Afraid of what the neighbors might think?" Barbara asked sardonically.

"I'm thinking of you kids. And I don't want you out riding in any car or motorcycle."

"Yes, dad," Barbara said.

"And I want the party to end at midnight."

"Am I Cinderella?" she asked brightly.

"You're my daughter and I'm trying to teach you some common sense!"

"Yes, dad."

"We honestly will be careful," Janey said. Well, at least I could trust her.

I DROVE TO Bert's place. He had surrounded it with floodlights, and the big white house with its flagstone terraces overlooking the river was impressive. I figured a couple of hundred thousand dollars had gone into converting the old gristmill into a showcase home. The beauty of the site lent a dramatic flair to the colonial architecture. Everything was kept freshly painted and trimmed by the professional crew that worked on Bert's housing developments. His spread made our Victorian house look shabby and stodgy, almost impoverished. I couldn't blame Betsy for admiring it. This was the kind of place she had been brought up to dream about, if not to own. It was what all nice Boston debutantes thought they deserved as a reward for their good breeding, beauty and charm.

The party was in high gear when I entered Bert's big, high-ceilinged living room. A stereophonic sound system was booming out twist music, and a dozen couples were gyrating in the center of the polished parquet floor. The whole cast of the play was here with oddly assorted partners. Stella was dancing with her minister husband, who twisted away frantically, and Stanley Kowalski was prancing around with his wife, a tall, stout Italian woman who looked as though she could teach him manners. Bert was dancing with a woman in a black cocktail dress whose back was turned toward me, and for a moment I did not recognize Betsy. When she circled toward me, I saw that she was laughing and saucily twirling the end of a brass chain she wore around her waist. I had bought her that belt long ago as a birthday present, but had never seen her wear it with that dress. I had no idea that she even knew how to do the twist.

When she saw me, she waved and came toward me, still twisting and followed by Bert.

"You were great tonight!" I said. "I really mean that."

"I did get away with it, didn't I?"

"More than that—you were magnificent."

"I've been trying to tell her that, but she won't believe me," Bert said. "I can't make her believe how good she was."

"If I say I believe it, you'll stop telling me," she said.

Her face was flushed and her eye shadow was beginning to run, but she looked happier than I could ever remember.

"Let's all have a drink," Bert said. "It's time for a toast."

He turned the music down and went to a bar in a corner. Taking a magnum of champagne from a brass ice bucket, he filled a row of glasses and handed them out.

"We've already drunk to each other," he said. "Now let's drink to the husbands and wives of the cast. They're the people who really make sacrifices for art."

A cheer greeted this. Stella kissed the minister and Stanley's hefty wife bussed him while Betsy came up to me and gave me a hug.

"You really have been a brick!" she said.

"We figure this play was such a success, we have to go on to other things," Bert said. "We haven't figured out just what yet, but we hereby declare ourselves a repertory company that intends to put on three plays in the next year."

I wondered if he realized how bad the rest of the cast was, except for Betsy, and why he wanted to continue to work so hard with people who would never deserve more than a high school auditorium. Despite her talent, Betsy seemed trapped into eternal effort with almost no rewards.

"Do you mind, Tom?" she said. "Now I've got the bug, I can't just stop."

So there would be an endless round of late parties with Bert, and if I had intended to live the rest of my life with her this way, I would have minded. But under the circumstances, who was I to object? When I began to spend more time in New York, she could hardly complain. The people who would really suffer were the children. The thought of this made me angry. Something better than this crazy existence had to be worked out, but this was no time to talk about it.

"If you can find the time for all this . . ." I began.

"I'll *make* the time. The kids are getting older now."

"What is time for?" Bert asked. "As the years dwindle down, like the song says, we might as well do the things we want to do, and besides, the play's the thing, isn't it? The play's the thing!"

He was, I realized, a little drunk. After turning the music up, he asked Stella to dance.

"I don't really like champagne," Betsy said. "I'm going to switch to scotch. This is my night to howl, right?"

"It's your night, all right."

She went to the bar and took a Pinch bottle from a shelf.

"This is great stuff," she said. "Can I pour you one?"

"Not tonight—one of us has to drive home."

"Don't be stuffy! Can't you ever unwind?"

"I'm unwound enough."

"Do you think I drink too much?"

"Hardly ever," I said.

"I've been good, haven't I? But tonight I have to unwind. I really did Blanche right, didn't I?"

"Perfectly."

"Sometimes I think I *am* Blanche. That happens to actresses, you know. They really start to live the part."

"Isn't Blanche's part too sad to live?"

"Yeah, but old Blanche never let herself get bored to death. She never wasted much time vacuuming a house and chauffeuring kids all over town. I bet old Blanche hardly ever washed a dish in her life."

Probably not, I said to myself.

"She didn't worry about budgets. Do you know what old Blanche would say if you gave her hell about not sticking to a budget?"

"I can well imagine."

"Damn it, you're stuffy, Tom! You're old before your time. You just work, work, work and worry, worry, worry. What's the point of it?"

"Do you want me to stop?"

"At least stop the worry part. Bert never worries. He takes big risks in his business, but he never worries."

"That's admirable."

"He makes a lot of money too. Take a look at this house. He didn't inherit all this—he bought it and fixed it up."

"That's admirable," I repeated.

"The real estate boom is just beginning, he says. He could show you how to get into it. Why don't you ask him?"

"That's not my thing."

"You know what's the trouble with you? You're too proud! You like to mess around with noble causes as though you were a rich man. Don't you know there's no future in that?"

Before I could answer, Bert came toward us across the dance floor.

"Do you mind if I ask your wife to dance, Tom?" he said, and before I could answer, they were twisting away together.

I had a strong urge to get drunk. How else make the time go by at a boring party? I wasn't a good dancer and had never tried the twist. Maybe Annie would teach me someday—she was a professional dancer. With music like this, she would really fly, and I could imagine flying with her after a few lessons.

An hour went by slowly. Betsy and Bert came to the bar for more scotch and their dancing grew clumsy, but few people noticed and everyone was drinking a lot. I had no reason to criticize—they had a right to celebrate their opening night. I tried talking with the minister and some other people, but the music was so loud that conversation was almost impossible. I was grateful when Bert led us all into his dining room, where a stout black woman in a yellow uniform was laying out a fancy midnight supper.

"Lobster Newburg!" Betsy cried, filling a plate. "Hearts-of-palm salad! Strawberry shortcake! This is really the way to live!"

She sat down with me at a table overlooking the swirling river, which must have been beautiful under a moon, but the floodlights made it look harshly cold and dirty. The black woman brought us crystal goblets of Chablis.

"Aren't these beautiful glasses?" Betsy said, holding hers up to the light. "And look at these plates—they're real Spode."

"It's a classy act, all right," I said.

She ate hungrily for a few minutes and drank her wine.

"Do you want brandy or Irish coffee?" Bert came over to ask.

The Irish coffee was topped by whipped cream. Betsy wiped some off the tip of her nose with a lace-edged napkin. For a moment she stared through the window at the river, where dead leaves revolved in whirlpools. Her face looked pale and suddenly she stood up.

"Tom, I don't feel so good," she said shakily. "I want to go home."

She started walking fast toward the front door. I followed and Bert caught up with us in the middle of the living room.

"What's the matter?" he said.

"She doesn't feel well," I said. Betsy, with her hand clamped over her mouth, looked at him wildly.

"Come into my room and lie down," he said, taking her arm.

"She wants to go home," I said.

"Let her lie down here, then." He continued to tug at her arm while she made for the front door.

"Bert, let her alone," I said. "I'm going to take her home."

"My room is closer," he insisted.

Probably he was right, but he still hung on to her arm, and my reaction was instinctive—I put my hand on his shoulder and gave him a shove which sent him reeling. If he hadn't drunk so much he wouldn't have stumbled, but he did a real pratfall.

"Bert!" she cried, rushing to him.

"I'm all right," he said with dignity as he stood up, and then he glared at me. "I was just trying to help!"

"I know you were and I'm sorry," I said.

Betsy turned suddenly and made for the front door.

"Sorry!" I repeated and followed her.

She ran to the parking lot across the road and was sick to her stomach, leaning her head against our station wagon. I gave her my handkerchief.

"I didn't want to be sick in there," she said. "Oh, I've made such a fool of myself!"

"Nobody except Bert saw us leave."

"Why did you have to hit him?"

"I didn't hit him. I just gave him a little shove and he was so damn drunk he fell down."

"Oh, that's terrible! After all he's done for us!"

"I apologized. Hell, he'll probably have a few more drinks. He won't remember any of it in the morning."

"I want to die," she said.

I couldn't think of what to say to that. She got into the front seat and sat hunched forward, her hands covering her face, her forehead resting against the dashboard. I got behind the wheel and drove home.

Our driveway was crowded with jalopies. I parked on the frozen lawn. Few lights were on in the house, but the sound of rock music was loud.

"The kids are having a party," I said. "You wait here until I go in and check things out."

The dimly lit room was crowded with teenagers, some on the couch, most entwined together on the floor. The television set had been tuned to a test pattern and glowed silently. I snapped on the light in the hall but was careful not to turn on the one in the big room. A girl I had never seen before was sitting on the couch hastily buttoning her shirt. The glowing ends of cigarettes quickly disappeared into beer bottles. The room was full of odd-smelling smoke. Marijuana, I guessed.

"Dad, you have no right to come busting in on us like this!" Barbara said furiously.

"Sorry about that. The party's over. Everybody out."

"You can't do this to me!" Barbara yelled.

"We weren't doing anything wrong, Mr. Rath!" Gordy said.

"Out!"

"Daddy, you can at least be polite!"

"Where are Janey and Pete?"

"They both went to bed."

"Thank God someone has some sense."

Carrying their beer bottles, the teenagers filed out the front door and piled into their cars.

"I don't like the idea of people using drugs in my house," I said to Barbara.

"Drugs! A couple of the guys brought a few joints!"

"I don't want that stuff around here. You could bring the cops down on us."

"And what would the neighbors say?"

"Go to your room."

"Where's muth?"

"She's in the car. Don't bother her now."

I went back to the station wagon. Betsy was feeling weak and I put my arm around her to help her up the porch stairs. She headed immediately for the downstairs bathroom and was sick again.

"If I drank like that, you'd raise holy hell with me," Barbara said, leaning over the stairs.

"Leave your mother alone. Go up to bed!"

"You must be drunk too, or you wouldn't have yelled at us like that. Don't you know that pot is better for you than booze?"

"I haven't had a drop. Now, if you don't go to your room, you're going to get the first real spanking you've ever had in your life," I said. "It's long overdue."

"You're crazy," she said, but beat a hasty retreat.

When Betsy came out of the bathroom, I helped her up the stairs and gave her a glass of water before she collapsed fully clothed on our bed. Ignoring her protests, I undressed her.

"Everything is such a terrible mess," she groaned and immediately went to sleep. I took off my clothes, put on my pajamas and lay down beside her. There was no reason to be shocked that she had drunk herself silly, but still I had a terrible feeling that if I left, before long the whole house would explode.

27

THE NEXT MORNING I woke up early out of habit, tried to get back to sleep, but couldn't. Betsy lay on her stomach, her face buried in her pillow as though she were crying. She was so motionless and silent that I was suddenly frightened and held my own breath to listen for hers. She was alive, all right—her breathing was as soft and regular as that of a child.

At three o'clock I would have to catch a plane at Idlewild for Nassau. United Broadcasting Company would have a ticket waiting for me at the BOAC desk in the terminal. All I had to do now was pack some summer clothes and get myself to the South Bay railroad station at twelve thirty-five.

I had just filled my suitcase when Pete came to the door. Seeing that his mother was still asleep, he whispered, "Could I talk to you, dad?"

I walked to the kitchen with him and put water on to boil.

"Are you going to be busy this morning?" he asked.

"Not that I know of . . ."

"Could you drive me around for an hour or so? I have a project . . ."

He wanted to take samples of water from the nearby ponds, bays and rivers for analysis, see how they differed in every measurable way. He had a big box full of bottles.

"Fine," I said, "but let's have breakfast first."

Barbara and Janey were still asleep and I had a rare opportunity to be alone with my son. As he sat hunched over his cornflakes, he seemed lost in his own thoughts, as he so often was. Unlike the other members of his family, Pete almost never liked to talk. Silence did not embarrass him as it did me.

"I have to fly down to the Bahamas this afternoon," I said.

"Oh?"

"Mr. Hopkins has some work for me to do. He's taking a vacation on an island he owns. I don't know how long I'll be gone—maybe only two or three days."

"Could you take one of my bottles and bring me a sample of the water? They say it's fantastically clear."

"Sure I could."

"They don't have rivers down there to run silt into the sea and there's no mud—just sand and coral."

"I see."

"They don't have any industrial waste either. I guess the population isn't big enough to give much of a sewage problem."

"The water must be very pure," I said.

"High in salt, though, with all that evaporation in the hot sun. It'll make an interesting contrast to water from Long Island Sound."

He took a sip of his cocoa and lapsed back into silence.

We dressed as though we were going fishing, in heavy windbreakers and rubber boots. He wanted to take his first sample from Norwalk Harbor, and as we drove there, my mind filled up with questions which I could not ask him. What did he really think of his mother's performance as Blanche DuBois? What did he think of Bert? Was he hurt by the rumors about him and Betsy? What did he think of Gordy?

Maybe these were subjects he didn't want to think about, or perhaps he was already like Ralph Hopkins and found the emotional problems of others less interesting than his work. I wondered if he had ever fallen in love. Of course he wasn't quite fourteen years, but when I was that age I was already smitten by the pretty girls in my school and became infatuated with a different one every month.

I wondered if Pete was troubled by sex, by masturbation guilt. I had tried to bring up our children in the modern way, answering all their questions about sex factually and clinically. Pete had once asked where babies came from, then lost interest. Of course he knew more about biology than I did, but had anyone tried to explain to him the urgency of human emotions?

Clearly it was my duty as his father to broach the subject, even though this did not seem the best time for a heart to heart.

"Pete, you're growing up awfully fast," I said as I drove through the streets of Norwalk, "and we've never really had a chance to talk about the problems which come with maturity."

"You mean sex?"

"Well, yes," I said, surprised.

"What's the problem?"

"I guess the problem is that God or nature makes us ready for sex somewhere around the age of twelve or thirteen, but our society doesn't really make marriage possible for a man until he's capable of making a living. For maybe ten or fifteen years, a boy or man has a tremendous urge for intercourse, but no legitimate way to handle it."

"There's nothing wrong with masturbation," he said. "Everybody does it."

"I'm glad you realize that."

"Everybody knows that. Even girls do it. Monkeys too."

"It's a natural release," I agreed.

"And anyway, people don't have to get married anymore just to screw. A lot of kids at school already do it."

"That's awful!"

"Why? Unless you're crazy, you don't have to get a girl pregnant, and venereal diseases can be cured easily these days."

"There can be emotional problems," I pointed out. I was fast losing the upper hand.

"Maybe for some people, but not for others. You can't make generalities about sex—you can't make generalities about *anything*."

"That's true," I said, "but for sensitive people . . ."

"You don't have to worry about me," he said. "I'm not very sensitive, I guess."

"Have you fallen in love yet?" I asked

"Do you mean, have I screwed anybody?"

"That's not what I asked."

"I'm not ready for that stuff yet. I have too much work to do. I guess I sublimate."

He paused.

"I'm not queer," he added. "I like to look at tits, but I don't have time for screwing around. I'd rather sublimate."

"That's a good way to handle it," I said.

"Old Barbara and Gordy sure aren't sublimating much, are they?"

"What do you think of that?"

He shrugged.

"I don't see why she picks a jerk like him. Gordy's nice enough, but he's not much smarter than Bonkers. He doesn't know *any-thing.*"

"What do you think of Bert Andrews?" I asked before I could stop myself.

He shrugged again.

"Bert's smart enough about some things, I guess, but he's awfully old, isn't he? And I don't see why he and muth make such a big deal of that damn play."

"She was awfully good in it last night, don't you agree?"

"Sure, but what's it get her? She doesn't get paid, does she?"

"There's a saying, 'Art for art's sake.'"

"I know—like pure science. But pure science teaches you things that eventually can turn out to be useful. What does art do?"

"What if it just makes people feel good?"

"That play didn't make me feel good. That woman muth played was nuts—no wonder they had to take her away."

"You felt no compassion for her?"

"What good was she to anyone?"

The question chilled me.

"Your mind is very highly developed," I said. "The emotions take more time."

"Why are you mad at me?"

"I'm not . . ."

"I know when you're mad. My emotions are highly developed enough for that."

"I don't think we can scorn people just because they don't seem to be of any use to anyone. Maybe people are like art. They can exist for their own sake, and have to be respected."

"How can you respect a woman who messes up herself and everybody else?"

"You can pity her, can't you?"

"I pity people like starving kids more. I hate people who go around messing everybody up."

I wondered if he would hate me and his mother when we finally got divorced—if we ever found the courage to do it. Probably. We would mess up our own children, even though in the long run we might be able to devise a saner life than this. I glanced at him and saw that he was attaching one of his bottles to a fishline to lower it from the wharf.

"This is pretty crude," he said. "Someday I'll figure out a way to take water samples at different depths."

WHEN WE GOT home about eleven, Pete hurried to his room to examine the water samples under his microscope and I went to my bedroom. I found Betsy getting dressed.

"I'm sorry as hell about last night," she said.

"Well, it's traditional for theater people to have a drop too much after opening night."

"Bert's being awfully nice about it. Look what just arrived."

She gestured toward a vase of sweetheart roses, baby's breath and forget-me-nots on her vanity table. It really took gall to send flowers to a wife while her husband was home, but that director-actress relationship could excuse anything.

"Very pretty," I said.

"Look at the card that came with it."

She had been holding it in her hand. It said, "To Blanche, from Tennessee Williams. I'm sorry I didn't behave very well last night, but everybody falls down once in a while."

"Cute," I said.

"I don't even remember much what happened—that booze hit me like a ton of bricks after all the Valium and paregoric."

"Nothing much happened. Look, I have to fly down to the Bahamas. Ralph Hopkins has some work for me to do. I never got a chance to tell you last night. I have to be at Idlewild to catch a plane at three."

"I'll drive you to the airport."

"I can catch a train that will get me into New York in time, and I can take a taxi to the airport. My expense account will cover it."

"I'll be glad to drive you. We need a little more time together."

I couldn't understand her at all. Despite her hangover, she insisted on repacking my bag.

"How long will you be gone?" she asked.

"Two or three days—I can't be sure."

"We'll miss you, but don't worry about us," she said. "We've learned to get along on our own."

Her smile looked simply bland, but then she was an actress.

During the drive to the airport I tried to concentrate on the road, though there wasn't much weekend traffic, and I didn't say much at first. I found comfort only in thinking about Annie, who at least loved me and asked nothing. How could her devotion be called anything but innocent? All right, people could say she was trying to steal another woman's husband, but she was also saving my life. If I had to live with a wife who was so infatuated with another man, how long could I endure? Money! Freedom had to be bought. If I could sell Hopkins on the idea of writing a book, he might take good financial care of me. Maybe, after the Bahamas, I'd be in a position to support two households. A home without a resident father would be tough on the children, but I had survived without a father from an early age, and a divorce would be more honest than running around behind each other's backs. Our children weren't stupid. Already they had picked up the gossip about their mother and soon would wonder about my long absences.

But meanwhile this masquerade had to continue, maybe for months. If a man was going to have an affair, he could at least do it discreetly. As Annie had said, if we're going to do a bad thing, we should at least do it well.

"I'm hoping that Hopkins is going to give me a long writing assignment," I said to Betsy.

"That's good. Any chance for a raise?"

"It's possible, but a lot of hurry-up work may be involved. It could keep me busy nights and weekends."

"At least you'll have something to do if I get involved with another play. I've been feeling guilty about that."

"I understand your need for self-expression," I said, glancing at her out of the corner of my eye.

She played it straight.

"I think that's absolutely wonderful of you," she said. "So few husbands would."

Maybe she was innocent after all, but so what? A wife in love with amateur theatricals was almost as bad as one who was catting around.

"I'm glad you appreciate me," I said, "but we have a problem. If we're both going to be away from home a lot, what about the kids?"

"We can take turns staying home," she said. "I won't have rehearsals every night."

"Not a solution," I said.

There was a moment of silence.

"Tom, are you seeing someone else?" she asked suddenly.

"What?"

"Are you interested in another woman?"

The temptation to make a clean breast of everything rose up in me, but as Annie had said, smart people never admit to adultery, and neither do kind people, not unless some mutual confession is made. Maybe Betsy was naive, but Bert was a smart lawyer. If she told him that I had admitted my guilt . . .

"Whatever makes you ask that?" I said.

"I don't know—you've been away from home so much, and you've seemed sort of preoccupied lately."

"It's just my work," I said.

"Do you still have that little assistant you told me about?"

"No—she was transferred back to the personnel department when we got back from Washington."

"You didn't tell me that."

"It didn't seem important."

"You usually talk a lot about the people in your office, but you've never talked about her, not since you hired her."

"There's nothing to talk about! She's not even working for me anymore!"

"Tommy, if you did get involved with her a little, I wouldn't be as shocked as I was about Maria. I've grown up a lot since then. I know it's hard for a man to be away from home a lot . . . and I realize I haven't been much of a wife to you lately."

"Do you want to talk about that?"

"I can't explain this theater thing and Bert. Words like 'self-expression' and 'self-fulfillment' sound phony as hell, but sometimes I just have to get out of the house and do something on my own. And I like Bert. He means a lot to me. I don't deny that."

"Do you ever think about divorcing me and marrying him?"

"Whatever gave you that idea? Bert and I have never talked about that. I don't know what I'd do without you. Besides, we couldn't do that to the kids."

"In the long run, maybe the best thing we can do for the kids is to make ourselves happy."

"Isn't that self-indulgent?"

"Not necessarily. It's hard for miserable parents to raise happy kids."

"Do you want a divorce, Tommy? Are you all that miserable?"

"I think we both have a great need to feel loved," I said. "I'm no longer sure we can do enough for each other."

"What would we do if we got divorced?"

"You might marry Bert. And if you didn't, I'd give you the house and enough money to let you live in it. And of course I'd pay child support."

"That wouldn't leave you much, would it?"

"Not the way things are. But I'm hoping like hell to make more sooner or later."

"I ought to be able to help. I hate the idea of selling real estate, but maybe I could do it."

"You wanted me to try that, remember?"

"I'm no good at dealing with money. You know that."

"You could learn . . ."

"You really want a divorce, don't you?"

"I'm just exploring all the possibilities."

"You already have somebody picked out! It *is* that little assistant of yours, isn't it?"

"Okay, she is my friend. She cares about me and I care about her."

"That's the important thing, isn't it? I'm not even going to ask if you're fucking her."

"Maybe it's about the same as with you and Bert."

"Except you know she wants to marry you, don't you?"

"Yeah, if it can be done without wrecking a lot of people."

"You won't wreck me! I'm strong! I can take care of the kids, get a job, everything—"

Her voice rose and broke. She looked down, covering her face with her hands, and her shoulders shook.

"Except I'm not really sure I can," she said and started to cry.

I stopped the car by the side of the road and put my arm around her shoulders.

"I'm going to keep on taking care of you," I said.

"You don't love me!" she said, pushing me off. "I won't let you take care of me!"

"Betsy, you can't have both me and Bert. That's what you've been trying to do, isn't it?"

"I don't have Bert! And now I don't have you! I don't have anybody!"

Her sobs grew worse.

"You still have me. I haven't gone anywhere yet."

"You can't have me and your assistant. That's what you've been trying to do, isn't it?"

"I guess we're both guilty."

"If I give up Bert, will you give her up?"

"Do you think we'd be happy that way?"

"No! I don't really have you anyway. You're hardly ever home. Even when you're there, you're all tied up inside yourself."

"Aren't we both guilty of that?"

"I've been more in love with the idea of being an actress than with Bert. Don't you realize that?"

"You're a very good one."

"He showed me how! He encouraged me! He didn't think I was just silly."

"I was stupid about that, Betsy."

"But I'm not really an actress, not a professional! I couldn't repeat the same part over and over again every night. I can't even stand the thought of doing Blanche one more time."

"Then be proud of one perfect performance."

"That's it. Do you think I could make a living at it? I'm too old to become an actress anyway—no one would hire me. You think I don't know that?"

"There's nothing wrong with being an amateur . . ."

"Except now I have to make money. I have to learn how to sell real estate."

"One way or another, I'll keep the money coming in."

"Remember when we used to say that money wasn't important?" She broke down in tears again. "When did you stop loving me?"

"I haven't really stopped," I said, and put my arms around her again.

"I've never stopped loving you," she said. "I know it's not the kind of love you want, but it's all I have."

"Nothing is your fault," I said.

"Sure it is! I never should have got so tied up with Bert . . . but do you know what he gives me?"

"I can guess."

"He thinks I'm marvelous just the way I am. He never gets mad at me. Every time I have a problem, he solves it. He's such fun to be with. He's always cheerful."

I'll bet, I thought, but didn't say it.

"But he never wants to get married again. His ex-wife gave him a terrible time. Anyway, he thinks he's much too old for me."

"So you have discussed this with him?"

"Only once, when you were away. He loves the kids—there's something wrong with him, he could never have any of his own. That's one thing that went wrong with his marriage—Paula never forgave him for that. But he's not impotent!"

"You're sure of that, are you?"

"All right! Are you sure your little assistant isn't frigid?"

"Reasonably."

"You *have* been fucking her, haven't you?"

"So when did *you* discover the little bastard isn't impotent?"

"We're both human. You were away a long time! I thought maybe it was just like with you and Maria. I didn't know you had *another* one! Somehow you always keep ahead of me."

"It's not a competition," I said, but my fists doubled up all the same.

"We didn't do it often—we were working on the play most of the time."

"Sure."

"When did you discover your little assistant isn't frigid?"

"Will you please stop calling her that? Her name is Ann McSoaring."

"She sounds like a damn airplane. Does she show you how to fly loop-the-loop?"

"Cut the sarcasm, Betsy. She does for me what Bert does for you. She thinks I'm marvelous. She never gets mad at me. Every time I have a problem, she solves it. And she's fun to be with. She's always cheerful. Okay?"

"But she's dying to marry you!"

"When and if we can."

"Bert wants to marry me, but he's afraid of taking on all that responsibility at his age. He has a bad heart, you know."

"It always seems to save him."

"What's that supposed to mean?"

"It kept him out of the war."

"He still feels terrible about that. Do you know how many war bonds he sold?"

"I'll give him my campaign ribbons. The little bastard can wear them on his Tyrolean hat instead of the chicken feathers."

"Stop talking about him like that!" she said, breaking into tears again. "He's the kindest man in the world . . . you can call him 'the little bastard' because he didn't go off and kill people during the war."

"Thank God we weren't all too nice for that."

"You don't know him, Tom! You don't really know him at all! Do you know the main reason why he doesn't want to marry me?"

"Tell me."

"He doesn't want to break up our family! He doesn't want to hurt the kids! He doesn't even want to hurt you!"

"Just let him try it."

"He's not afraid of you. He doesn't want to hurt anyone."

"Not as long as he can fuck my wife in his spare time. Doesn't he know I've shot men who never did anything to me at all?"

"Where does this woman Ann McSoaring live? I want to go shoot her!"

"Great, then we can both be happy in jail together. Maybe they'll put us in the same cell."

"Oh, Tommy, how did everything get so crazy?"

"I don't know," I said, rubbing my eyes.

"I hope you haven't got yourself all messed up. Isn't your airplane girl a lot younger than you?"

"About fourteen years . . ."

"Where does she come from?"

"Brooklyn."

"How did she get to be your assistant at the company? Was she a secretary?"

"She's been all sorts of things—a typist, a model, a dancer. That's the way she put herself through business college. She's supported herself since she was sixteen years old."

"I'm sure that's admirable, but a background like that . . ."

"Don't be a snob, Betsy."

"I'm not a snob, but people of different backgrounds can find it hard to make a good marriage. All kinds of experts say that."

"I'll be my own expert."

"Do you think she'll be good with the kids?"

"Yes, but I'm not talking about marrying her yet. I'm trying to do my best for you, the kids, for everyone."

"I won't stand in your way. Not for long . . ."

The word "suicide" suddenly flashed into my mind.

"Betsy, we have a problem, but I'm sure we can work it out for the good of everybody. I couldn't be happy for a minute if I knew you were miserable. We all care about each other. No one's evil here, not even Bert." I almost said Bert the bastard, but stopped in time. "Nobody wants to hurt anybody."

"But we all do it anyway, don't we?"

"Nobody can go through life without pain, but at least we're alive."

"We're alive, all right," she almost spat. "Too much!"

"Don't panic. I'm not rushing anything. Nobody has to do anything right away. When I get back we'll go on like before until we figure out what to do."

"Is she going to the Bahamas with you?"

"No. Honestly! This is strictly a business trip."

"Well, I guess it really doesn't make any difference. You'll see her as soon as you come home, right?"

"When I can. At least we won't have to lie to each other anymore."

"Maybe the lies were better . . ."

"They had to lead to this sooner or later. We're not the kind of people who could keep up that kind of shit for long."

"I'm going to need a lot of time to think," she said.

"So am I. This trip comes at a good time."

"What time is it?" she said with a start. "Are we going to miss your plane?"

"We can still make it," I said, and started driving fast.

Betsy sat tensely pale as I swerved in and out of traffic. If we got killed in an accident, I thought, our deaths would have been caused, at least indirectly, by adultery, and all my buried fears of punishment would be justified. Better to miss the plane and let Hopkins stew. I slowed down.

"How much time have we got?" Betsy asked.

"All we need, even if I have to wait for the next flight. Let's not turn this into an emergency. We're not falling from a plane with the ripcord sticking."

"But that's what it feels like," she said as we entered the airport.

"You'll always have me to count on. Nothing's going to change that."

She turned her tear-stained face to me and gave me a long, sorrowful look. "Those are great parting words," she said.

28

I was late but lucky; my flight had also been delayed. With half an hour to kill, I had a drink at a bar and sat worrying about Betsy until it occurred to me that I had time to call Annie and bring her up to date. Rough as things were for Betsy, they offered hope for Annie and me. Even while we were waiting for a divorce to be worked out, I wouldn't any longer have to invent excuses to keep me in New York. While getting a dollar's worth of change, I took from my wallet her Brooklyn telephone number and went off to find a telephone booth. Her number rang five times and I was about to give up when a man with a Brooklyn accent answered. "Hello!" He sounded angry and I was so startled that I said, "Who's this?"

"Harry Comstock," he bellowed. "Who are you?"

"Tom Rath," I said, trying to keep my voice even. "Is Annie there?"

"Annie doesn't live here anymore," he said, parodying the old song, and I realized that he was drunk. "She lives in Manhattan, she lives in Washington, but she don't live in Brooklyn very much."

"Where is she now?" I asked.

"She's in the cellar."

"The cellar? Will you tell her that I want to speak to her?"

"Annie!" I heard him shout. "Your gray flannel man is on the phone."

There was a jarring noise as he slammed the receiver down and the sound of his footsteps leaving the room before he shouted again. Then silence. The discovery that she was having a reunion with Harry Comstock fed all my paranoia. Was she still bound to this man she had loved for so many years?

Finally I heard her footsteps approaching the telephone.

"Tom?" she said, sounding surprised.

"I'm at the airport," I said, and then before I could stop myself, I added with heavy irony, "How's Harry?"

"Right now he's had too much beer," she said. "He actually did rejoin the army. They're about to send him to Germany."

"I didn't know you were going to see him," I said, sounding injured and knowing I was making a damn fool of myself.

"Tom, he lives right down the street. He's home on leave and of course he'd stop in."

"I'm sorry," I said. "I have no right . . ."

"He's just an old friend. You have no reason to be jealous."

She sounded to me like Betsy talking about Bert.

"I'm not jealous!" I said with considerable heat to make up for the fact that I was obviously just that.

"Then what's the matter? You sound upset."

While I was trying to decide what to say, a loudspeaker announced the imminent departure of my plane.

"I have to run," I said. "I just called to say I love you."

"I love you, too," she said, sounding puzzled.

"I'll call you as soon as I get back," I said. "Things are moving fast."

"What do you mean?"

I wanted to say that Betsy now knew all about her, that the road ahead was clear, but I was suffering from so many complex emotions that the words stuck in my throat. The loudspeaker again announced my flight.

"I've got to run," I said. "Plane's going."

"I love you," she said.

"I love you, too. What were you doing in the cellar?"

"Laundry," she said with a laugh. "Did you think I was burying a body?"

"Doing laundry is a hell of a way to spend your weekend."

"I'm trying to help poor Harry get packed. All he had was a foot locker of dirty laundry."

"That's generous of you," I said.

"Tom, we're practically brother and sister."

"Does he think of it that way?"

"He's learning to."

"Well, all right . . ."

"Don't worry. You have to learn to trust me."

"I know. I really have to run now. Everything's fine. I'll call you as soon as I get back."

I DASHED FOR my plane, arriving at the gate just in time. As I sank into my seat and buckled up, I felt acutely miserable. I was absurd to be so jealous, but why hadn't she said she was going to see Harry?

But then, why should she? I didn't really own her—nobody had a right to own anybody. If I was spending the weekend with Betsy, why shouldn't she see her old lover? And if I expected her never to see Harry again, wouldn't she have the right to ask me to say good-bye to Betsy forever? Impossible. I was being ridiculous.

A stewardess came around with drinks and I accepted a martini. Instead of calming me, the booze seemed to inflame my emotions. Maybe I had a right to be worried. If a woman did a man's laundry, she must still have a fairly intimate relationship with him . . . and I didn't go for that stuff about brother and sister. They were not that and they were not just old friends; they were former lovers, and their feelings still had to be explosive. The drama of Harry's departure for Germany had to create a highly charged atmosphere. Annie was so kind, so loving and so giving about sex that she might be tempted into giving the bastard one last night for old times' sake, a sweet charity fuck.

My fists doubled up—the second time today. If she did that, she would never tell me, she wouldn't want me to suffer because of her guilt—and besides, she had nothing but disdain for blubbering confessions.

One of two things was happening to me. Either I was denigrating Annie because of my insane jealousy, or I was becoming unusually perceptive about her character. When we first got together, she had told me about the former lovers. Every spring she had started a new affair, and Harry had been very patient. Maybe she would expect me to be patient, too.

I had to understand that she was a career girl, a former dancer and model, and still young. In this new era single women were not expected to defend their chastity like old-fashioned spinsters. If she was a beautiful virgin at thirty, most psychiatrists would judge her neurotic; she wouldn't have been able to give and take so much joy in bed with me. If I gloried in her uninhibited, lyrical sensuality and still expected her to have lived like a nun, I was nothing but an idiot. Wasn't the essence of love the ability to accept each other as we were, without recriminations? She loved me despite the fact that I had a wife, three children and an illegitimate son.

All very well, but the real question was whether she would stay faithful after we were married, after the first glow inevitably wore off. I knew what it was like to suspect my wife of sleeping with another man and finally to learn the truth. How would I feel if I had to go through all that again, if Annie needed somebody else to provide excitement? I would age faster than she. A trim young body calls for a trim young body—I couldn't ignore that fact of nature. Some women traded youth and good looks for money, power, security. Bert Andrews offered all this to Betsy—but what did I have to offer? A talent for understanding her, Annie had said; kindness, maybe, though I wasn't feeling too kind either to Betsy or Annie, and my knack for understanding was turning cynical and sour. Still, what were the real odds of Annie and me remaining happily married for long?

Yes, we shared a sexual obsession but this wouldn't last a lifetime, or whatever was left of my life. We came from different backgrounds—"two different worlds," as Betsy had hinted. Wouldn't all our differences—of taste, customs, standards—create more and more friction as the years went on?

And how many years did I have left? That was another question I didn't want to face. I called myself "middle-aged"; so what were my chances of living, say, to be eighty-six? My father had died at twenty-six. It had been an automobile accident, but I had always suspected that booze had set it up, booze and a suicidal impulse left over from the shell shock of World War I. Well, I hadn't inherited shell shock, and I was always fighting alcoholism, but the truth was that most of my male ancestors had died before fifty—only the women in my family lived long, my widowed mother being an exception. Life insurance actuaries didn't care for my family record and the doctors clucked over my blood pressure, my tendency toward overweight. What the hell right did I have to marry a bloomingly healthy woman who hoped to have a baby? What was I going to do, leave Annie a penniless young widow with an infant child? And I already had three—correction, four—children.

Though the cabin of the plane was cool, I was sweating. The stewardess offered me another martini and I took it. The martini was ice-cold, but made me sweat even more. Poor Betsy—she'd said she wouldn't stand in my way for long. She must have felt helpless. She had no idea of how to make a living and she didn't want to take money from a husband who no longer loved her. Bert was as scared of a second marriage as I was, and with the same good reason. Betsy was as young to him as Annie was to me, and besides, he had a bad heart. He didn't want to break up my family; now it would take more guts and love on his part to pick up the pieces at fifty-five. It was one thing to take my children on weekend jaunts, another to wrestle with the problems of Barbara and Gordy, or poor Janey's delicate emotions. Bert could easily find uncomplicated women to share his roadster and beautiful house for a night or two. Who could blame the little bastard if he copped out?

In my martini-soaked brain the scenario ran on. With her charm and looks Betsy would find some kind of job, maybe as a doctor's receptionist. And then, after Annie took off with a younger man, maybe Betsy and I would remarry—stranger things had happened. Jesus, why did we want to put ourselves, our children on this roller coaster? There was still time to stop.

Ah . . . but there was Annie, her dark eyes so full of hope and confidence in me. The quick intake of her breath when I kissed her, the memory of her whispering in my ear "We're home!" and all that meant. Could I forget her and resign myself to the dull comforts of South Bay for the rest of my life?

No—I could not give Annie up. Whether it was to be marriage or a life of deception, I could not give her up. Maybe that was why God or the fates had offered this trip to the Bahamas, a few days in which I could think my way out of this dilemma. One thing was sure: no matter which road I chose—continuing life with Betsy and seeing Annie on the sly, or marrying Annie—I would need money, lots of it. I was flying to see Ralph Hopkins, and whatever else he was he was a money man. In his manicured, pale hands he had held the invisible key to my future for the past ten years. I hadn't been able to persuade him to do much with it, but now was my big chance. Annie had been right about one thing: my writing skill and my ability to deal with important men. Those talents could be parlayed into a career that would let me support everyone I loved, no matter what road I took. Women loved strength, and in my generation, strength was money more than it was muscles.

That thought led me to remember Mark, my son in Italy, and the monthly checks that had so disturbed Betsy. Annie had said he could stay with her relatives in Brooklyn—a great idea, but I didn't want to bring him over until my own situation was clarified. My children didn't know he existed, and I didn't want to explain him along with the divorce—if that was going to happen. A young man brought up on the streets of Rome wouldn't be surprised to learn that his American father was feverishly trying to keep two women happy, but why face him until my own life was straightened out?

At least my course for the days ahead was clear: I would try to talk Hopkins into letting me help him write a book, either a company history or his autobiography. If that failed, I might not even have a job for long; the censorship committee thing was too feeble to last. As Annie had said, Hopkins would want to leave some record behind, some epitaph better than "king of the wasteland."

What would be my own epitaph?

"It really doesn't matter. Here goes nothing."

Those were the words I had repeated to myself when I stepped out of an airplane on combat jumps. I didn't like those words now —I no longer thought I was nothing, and life itself seemed to matter one hell of a lot. The final summation of the lives of most men is embodied in their children. What would mine grow up to be, and how would they remember their father?

With charity, I hoped. Then I mustered up the courage to refuse a third martini and tried to sleep. The engines of the plane droned like those of the bombers I had ridden so long ago. At least I wouldn't have to jump out of this thing with a gun.

29

THE PLANE LANDED at Nassau well after dark and in the middle of a tropical downpour. I was drenched by the time I walked into the terminal. At the door a boyish-looking man in wet khaki pants and shirt walked up to me. "Are you Mr. Rath?"

When I nodded, he said he was Tim Murphy, Mr. Hopkins' pilot, and because of the weather we were to spend the night in a hotel and fly to Ship Island in the morning.

The hotel at which he had made reservations was a large modern structure with balconies and windows almost overhanging the harbor. The luxury of my room made it seem all the more lonely. Annie would have loved the view of the freighters anchored nearby. After the rainstorm passed, the moon came out and silvered the sails of the native sloops that were tacking across the bay. I slid the curtains shut, changed my clothes and went downstairs to a cocktail lounge that was fitted out like the saloon of a passenger liner, complete with portholes. Tim Murphy was sitting at the bar surrounded by half a dozen women. The tourist season had not yet started and all the hookers or lonely shopgirls and secretaries obviously had to make do with slender pickings. Jovially he invited me to sit on a stool beside him, offered me a drink and introduced his admirers to me by their names.

"I have to have me a time whenever I get over here," he said. "Things are right quiet over on Ship Island."

I talked to a blonde with an English accent named Grace, who said she had come over from England two years ago to work as a ticket clerk for BOAC. She was pretty, with gray eyes, a narrow waist and a well-filled blouse. Lonely, bored and a little drunk, she asked me a lot of questions about New York, where she hoped to be transferred. When I bought her a drink, she asked if she could order a snack. She ended up with a seafood cocktail followed by a steak and French pastries. I ate little and signed the check, knowing it would go on my expense account. Talking to Grace somehow made me miss both Betsy and Annie more. Her nonstop questions about how much everything cost in New York got on my nerves.

"Are you married?" she asked suddenly.

"Yes," I said.

"I bet you don't let that bother you. No man is married when he's more than a hundred miles away from home, is he?"

She gave my leg a playful nudge under the table.

"If I came to New York, would you show me around?"

I guessed that the slightest show of interest would get her up to my room and that she would be better-looking in the nude than in her dowdy skirt and blouse. We could go to bed and try all the combinations of the flesh, but the prospect of that didn't cause a ripple of excitement in me. If I were perverse enough to try it, I would probably prove impotent; yet if I thought of Annie pouring baby oil into her hand, my whole body began to tingle.

"Hey," Grace said, waving her hand in front of my eyes. "Are you still there?"

"I'm here, all right."

"I asked if you'd show me around New York if I ever get there."

"I'm afraid I don't even live in New York," I said. "My home's in Connecticut. Thanks for your company. I've had a long day and need to get some sleep."

Before she could answer, I gave her a friendly pat on the shoulder and left the table. Up in my room I stood at the window, staring at the moonlit harbor and planning to bring Annie here someday. A good place for a honeymoon.

Alone in the huge bed I kept picturing Betsy with Bert and Annie with that bastard, Harry Comstock. Perhaps tonight both my women were cheating me and I was being double-cuckolded. If that was true, would I tell them both to go to hell?

No, in different ways I was the captive of both women, and I'd never be able to break away. I felt helpless, but if I didn't stop tossing and worrying, I'd be a wreck when I saw Ralph Hopkins in the morning. Untroubled by passion for any woman, Ralph always had a perfectly clear mind for business. How could I ever compete with that?

SHIP ISLAND TOOK about an hour to reach in Hopkins' twin-
engine Beechcraft. On the way we flew over the long, thin island
of Eleuthera, a barren strip of coral and sand.

"They call this the devil's backbone," Tim Murphy said. "Ship
Island is off the end of it—they should call it the devil's asshole."

From a distance of two miles, Hopkins' retreat looked like the
kind of "tropical paradise" one sees in advertisements for the
Bahamas tourist trade—palm trees, long, cream-colored beaches
laced by the surf, a crystal-clear sea that glittered in every shade
of blue, green, yellow, brown and purple. On a high knoll at the
southern end stood a large white building with low walls which
seemed to grow out of the surrounding bluffs. When Murphy set
the plane down on a landing strip of crushed coral on the other
end of the island and turned off the engines, I got an inkling of why
the place depressed him. Here was a desolate, almost uninhabited
island that Hopkins undoubtedly prized because of its privacy, but
the wind that kept the palm branches waving seemed to sigh with
loneliness. Nothing but empty beaches, and despite the cooling
breeze the morning sun beat down so mercilessly that I couldn't
imagine how anyone could live here.

A tall black man was waiting in a jeep with a blue and white
striped canopy and drove us the mile-long length of the almost
empty sand spit to Hopkins' house, which was surrounded by
terraces of tan concrete covered by white awnings. A gaunt black
woman in a uniform with a white apron opened a large plate-glass
door to admit us to a circular living room with long, low windows
instead of walls. The house was so strongly air-conditioned that
our shirts immediately felt cold against our sweating backs, but the
view of the multicolored shoals surrounding the knoll on which the
house had been built was spectacular. The glittering view dazzled
my eyes, and at first I did not see Ralph Hopkins lying in a white
wicker lounge chair beside an open fire that glowed on a hearth of
white bricks carved from coral. The air was so chilly that the flames
from the smoking driftwood looked and felt good. Hopkins was
dressed in his New York uniform—gray flannel slacks, white shirt,
maroon bowtie and navy-blue jacket.

"Hello, Tom!" he said heartily. "I'm so glad to see you! Pardon
me for not getting up—the doctor says I'm supposed to take it easy
for a while."

He held out his hand and gripped mine firmly. His skin was tan enough to look healthy, but he was so thin that his ice-blue eyes looked enormous. His short gray hair had been bleached by the sun, almost to pure white. The vitality, the almost boyish enthusiasm that had always illuminated his face, still shone there.

"It's good to see you, sir," I said and I meant it.

"We had a good flight, sir," Murphy said. "Are there any more runs you'd like me to make?"

"Not for now, Tim," Hopkins said. "You can take the boat out fishing if you want. I'm not going to use it for the next few days."

"Thank you, sir," Murphy said, gave a little salute and left.

"That's a good boy," Hopkins said, "but all he thinks about is fishing and the girls over in Nassau—every time I send him there it seems to rain so hard that he has to spend the night."

"It really did rain pretty hard yesterday," I said.

"I know, but that plane has every instrument money can buy, and no kind of weather can stop him from setting down in Nassau. But we have more important things to talk about. How have you been, Tom? How's your family?"

"Just fine, sir."

"You've lost a lot of weight, haven't you?"

"I've been trying to cut down."

"I have the opposite problem—the doctor wants me to gain. I had a little heart attack and lost my appetite."

"I'm sorry to hear that, sir," I said, though I was glad to hear that it wasn't cancer or a stroke.

"I'll be fit as a fiddle, as they say, before long. Meanwhile, I have to take it easy for a couple of months."

"This looks like a good place for a rest, sir."

"If you like to fish. Do you like fishing, Tom?"

"I guess I can take it or leave it, sir," I said with a smile.

"Thank God! I hate fishing, but there's nothing much else to do around here. Of course, the boat can take you over to Eleuthera if you like golf."

"I don't play much golf, sir."

"Neither do I. The doctor says I have to develop some new interests, some kind of damn hobby. Everybody tries to make me ashamed of the fact that I find my work the most interesting thing in the world. How do you feel about it? When you come right down to it, have you ever found anything more interesting than work?"

The truth was, I found women and children a lot more interesting than work, but this was not the time to explain that.

"No, sir," I replied.

"That's good. There's so much work to be done in the world that I can't see why grown men like to play so much. Even in this country—I mean America, not these damn islands—millions of people are sick and near-starving. With so much trouble all around us, how can we say that leisure is such a great thing? They sneer at the Protestant work ethic, but as long as there's so much human need, good men should work until they drop."

"That's an interesting philosophy, sir," I said and almost added, "Why don't you try writing a book?"

"It's not very fashionable these days," he went on. "Talking about work, what do you think of Robinson's self-censorship project?"

He had a way of throwing a tough question suddenly from left field. If that damn fool committee was one of his favorite projects, deriding it could be dangerous. Hopkins didn't like yes-men, but he did not long tolerate subordinates who disagreed with him on important issues. He also was quick to recognize fence-straddling tactics and to scorn them. Maybe he enjoyed putting me on the spot, testing me. Those ice-blue eyes of his weren't missing anything.

"To tell the truth, I'm not very enthusiastic about the self-censorship committee," I said.

"Why?"

He made the word sound like the flick of a whip.

"I'm sure that you know all the reasons, sir. The networks want censorship of any kind like a hole in the head. In the long run, pretense of any sort never works."

"That's true, but Robinson thinks we have to have some kind of sop to throw to our critics. His tactics might give us time to work out a better policy."

"Does it really take so much time to work out basic policy, sir?"

"No, it just takes courage, and maybe I've been short on that."

"How do you mean?"

"For years people have been calling me king of the wasteland, all that kind of nonsense, and I've never really tried to make a good defense."

"I'd love to try to help you work on that, sir."

"Well, the situation is simple enough. First of all, broadcasting is a business like any other. The stockholders put up the money to start it or to expand it, and they expect a fair return, the most they can get."

"That's reasonable."

"Sometimes stockholders seem greedy, but who are they, really? A lot of them are widows and old people who depend on us for their income. Universities have put a lot of our stock into their portfolios. Not all our stockholders are rich people trying to get richer, but even they have a right to get a fair return on their investment."

"Nobody can quarrel with that."

"Beyond that, we work on a much smaller profit margin than most people think. If we didn't keep the money coming in, we could easily go under. Plenty of big corporations do—they're all a lot more fragile than they look."

I nodded politely. I had always been a good listener.

"So we have to make money. To do that, we have to sell advertising, and to do that, we have to win an audience larger than our competitors are getting. We don't get paid for educating people or for telling them what they should want for their own good. This so-called wasteland is one of the purest forms of democracy there is—the public votes with the dial on their set, and if we don't give 'em what they want, they turn us off. If enough people do that, we fail."

Hopkins paused before adding, "That's clear enough, but now comes the rub, the big dichotomy, as the intellectuals say. I don't think anyone foresaw it, but it turns out that television is such a powerful medium that it affects people's lives in many ways. If we can change people's buying habits, maybe we can affect the way they vote, the way they think about all sorts of things. Maybe violence isn't good for people, despite the fact that they want it in their shows. Maybe this great new medium of communication should be used for improving people's minds, not just satisfying their appetites. Suddenly broadcasting isn't just a business anymore. It's a moral responsibility. We're asked to be half-pitchman, half-clergyman or teacher. The whole industry has a split personality and doesn't know where to go from here."

"Do you have an answer?" I asked, almost boldly.

"You bet I do, and it's not compromise. The United Broadcasting Company is going to go right on giving the public whatever it wants—within the limits of the law. The public is a better censor than any official or committee. People who think we'll end up with a Roman circus are selling the American public short."

He paused and grinned.

"I'd really stir up the animals if I came out and said that, wouldn't I?"

"There would be some criticism . . ."

"And some of it would be justified. *All* of television shouldn't be designed for the entertainment of a mass audience. The public should have a choice."

"How can that be arranged?"

"There should be one government network like the BBC. There should be many stations run by universities, foundations, religious organizations for the purpose of education, art, science, moral uplift—all those good things. It won't be long before the technology will give us a lot of new channels—all this will be possible. We must provide a great smorgasbord of the air, with something for everyone."

"That's quite a vision," I said.

"People will have to fight for it. If they don't, all the new channels will be farmed out to profit-making companies. Instead of getting diversity, we'll have more and more mass entertainment, and mass entertainment on television isn't different from tabloid newspapers, comic books, the old pulp magazines and the slicks that we drove out of business by taking their advertising. You can't make mass entertainment into something else—you can only offer other choices."

He paused, looking tired.

"Do you think you can make a good magazine article out of this, maybe something for *Harper's* or the *Atlantic*?"

"Yes, sir," I said and took a deep breath. "Maybe there's a better idea."

"What do you mean?"

"A magazine article would reach only a small audience, it would soon be forgotten . . ."

"It might start public discussion . . . I could follow it up with a few speeches."

"Yes, sir, but a book could have a lot more impact and would be a lasting record."

"That's an interesting idea," he said, and there was a moment of silence during which I held my breath. "The trouble is, I don't think there's enough material here for a book."

"Your thoughts about the future of television might attract a lot more attention if they came as the climax to your story about the growth of United Broadcasting from a small group of little radio stations. Nobody could tell that story better than you. And if you don't write it down, it will never be told right. A book like that could be your monument."

"My monument, eh?" he said with a wry smile. "What will be written on it, 'Here lies the king of the wasteland'?"

"Not if you tell how the wasteland grew and how it could be changed!"

"Not changed—just ringed by a few gardens, perhaps. As long as the public wants sun and sand, there will still be plenty of that."

"A book would give you a chance to develop the idea and put it into the right context."

"I'm not sure I have the energy or the time for a book."

"You could dictate it into a tape recorder whenever you had an hour or so to spare. I'd take the whole project from there."

"You think you're up to that?"

"Absolutely."

"Have you ever written a book before?"

"No, sir, but you've never dictated one before. I've had a lot of practice in putting your words on paper."

"That's true enough," he said and there was another agonizing pause.

"I'm sure we could get a fine book out of this," I murmured.

Wearily he rubbed his eyes and forehead.

"Let me think about it."

I should have foreseen that—he never made snap decisions. At least this wasn't a turndown, but he sounded discouraged, as though the mere thought of a book tired him.

"I should be getting a little rest," he said, touching a button on the side of his lounge chair. "Mrs. Markham will show you to your room."

"Thank you," I said, and started to follow a frail old black woman who immediately appeared.

"She'll show you where you can swim and get you anything you need," Hopkins called after me.

"Thank you, sir," I said.

"A book would be an awful lot of work."

"That's true, but what's more important than writing an accurate record of a career like yours?"

"I'll think about it," he repeated.

"There's no rush, sir," I said, though I felt there was, both because of his failing health and my needs.

"I know. If you go swimming, take one of the housemen or Tim Murphy with you. People shouldn't go swimming alone from these beaches. There's a strong undertow. My wife wanted me to put in a pool, but why do you need a pool on an island surrounded by beaches?"

"I like the surf," I said, waited a moment, and when he did not answer followed Mrs. Markham down a long corridor like a passageway on an ocean liner.

My ROOM WAS even more luxurious than the one I had in the hotel, and it had the same effect of increasing my feeling of loneliness. A telephone stood on an antique table beside the king-size bed. My worries about Betsy and Annie mounted as I looked at it. Why did I have to wait until I got home to call them?

I telephoned Betsy first. The overseas operator connected me with South Bay surprisingly fast, but there was no answer at my house. This scared me, and thoughts of disaster raced through my head, but it was Sunday, and maybe Bert had taken the family out for a drive or to dinner. Then I dialed Annie's number in Brooklyn. A woman with a strong Italian accent answered, Annie's grandmother, probably. The connection was poor, and she apparently couldn't hear me well.

"Who is it?" she asked. "Who is it? Who do you want to be speaking to?"

"Annie!" I kept shouting desperately. "Is Annie there?"

"Annie's gone back to her apartment," she finally said and hung up abruptly, as though she were annoyed with me.

I called Annie's apartment but there was no answer. Maybe she was out with Harry Comstock, or attending a movie alone, hating solitude as much as I did. I stood at the window and stared out at the brilliantly colored sea and the strip of deserted beach, where there were not even footprints on the sand. If Annie were here, this island would be a paradise, but without her, it seemed like hell. I wondered how Hopkins had spent most of his life alone, worrying about business and moral responsibilities. Maybe his concern for the stockholders was an abstract form of love, unlike mine. If Annie were here, the privacy of the beach would seem the ultimate luxury.

— 274

Someone had put my suitcase on a rack near the bed. I started to unpack it and found that Betsy had put in my bathing trunks, a thoughtful touch. For twenty-two years she had been a good wife. She did not deserve to be dropped suddenly, but in truth hadn't we really deserted each other long ago? But what was the use of brooding, of wondering if Hopkins would want to go ahead with the book? Swimming was healthier, and if I didn't go in too deep I wouldn't need a lifeguard to protect me from the undertow.

The sun stunned me as I left the air-conditioned house, and the sea was so warm that it did not give much relief. Taking a walk on the hot beach might tire me enough to sleep until Hopkins called for me again. Plowing through that soft sand that was marked only by the feet of birds, I felt like Robinson Crusoe before he met his man Friday. Seagulls wheeled over my head with hoarse, lonely-sounding cries, and the booming surf and the sigh of the wind in the palm trees seemed to mingle with the laments of the birds into one melancholy song. I had a sickening premonition that Hopkins would turn down the book idea. I pictured myself returning home to find that Betsy and the kids had run off with Bert while Annie had decided to go to Germany with Harry Comstock. Alone, I would sit in the United Broadcasting building writing endless reports of the feckless self-censorship committee. Could God devise any worse punishment for my sins?

30

THE WALK EXHAUSTED me enough to put me to sleep when I got back to my room, but an hour later Mrs. Markham awoke me and asked if I wanted lunch.

"Am I to have lunch with Mr. Hopkins?" I asked.

"No, sir. He already done eat."

Why hadn't the old man asked me to his table? Maybe I had come on too strong about the book and had annoyed him. This upset me so much that it killed my appetite and I sent Mrs. Markham away.

I went swimming again in the afternoon, this time with a diving mask and snorkel. The water was as clear as air, and the rainbow-colored tropical fish seemed suspended in flight, miraculously held up by their tiny fins. Annie would have squealed with pleasure; Betsy was too scared of moray eels and sharks to venture beyond the curl of the surf. In my imagination I saw both women on the beach, Betsy in her sedate green bathing suit, Annie in the white Donald Duck bikini she had rented in Ohio. They were sitting there laughing together, my two wives, happy as sorority sisters with each other while they waited for me to decide which one I would make love to under the coconut trees. A honeymoon *à trois!* Maybe that's what I really wanted—I'd take them both without giving anything up. After all, the housework in South Bay would be much easier if they could share it.

Obviously the sun was driving me nuts. When I started to swim for shore, I felt the tug of the undertow, a moment of panic. If I was swept out to sea, Betsy would get enough life insurance to keep her going for a year or so, but Annie would receive nothing, not even a notification of my death, and there wouldn't even be an

obit in the newspapers—ghost writers didn't rate much space, even
in the publications that printed so many of their words. The first
part of my old litany sprang to my mind, "It really doesn't matter . . . ," but suddenly my future, no matter how rocky, did matter
to me, and I swam for the beach as though a shark were nipping
at my heels. Soon my toes touched sand. I plowed through the surf
with a sense of triumph, and ran with the same sense that I was the
first creature to emerge from the sea and stand up on his hind legs
like a man.

AT SIX-THIRTY Mrs. Markham told me that Hopkins would
expect me for dinner at seven. The old man had changed to a white
linen suit and was walking around his living room with sprightly
steps.

"Will you have a drink, Tom?" he asked jovially.

"A scotch, please," I said.

A black houseboy who didn't look more than sixteen years old
poured two at a bar built into the wall near the fireplace, and
served them on a tray.

"Did you have a swim?" Hopkins asked.

"I had a very nice swim," I said. "The fish are beautiful."

"Was the undertow bad?"

"No, sir," I said, loath to admit that I damn near got caught in
it.

"Is your room comfortable?" he persisted.

"Yes, sir, and it certainly has a gorgeous view."

"This is a nice house, all right. My wife talked me into building
it about ten years ago, but I hardly ever get down here."

"It certainly gives you a lot of privacy," I said.

Mrs. Markham announced dinner and led the way to an adjoining dining room that also had a terrific view, but by that time I was
sick of glittering sea colors, even though they now glowed in the
last rays of the sunset.

A tall black waiter in a white jacket served us a fruit cocktail,
followed by broiled grouper with carrots and brussels sprouts.
Hopkins toyed with his food before pushing his plate away.

"The grouper is fresh, but all these vegetables come from the
States," he said. "The people can't grow anything around here
except coconuts."

"Why not?" I politely asked.

"No fresh water, no good soil. The natives eat fish mostly."

There was a pause while he stared at the view.

I was tempted to ask, "What about the book?" but that would have been pushing it. He would bring it up in his own good time.

The waiter offered bowls of vanilla ice cream and strawberries, which we both declined.

"Shall we have our coffee in the living room?"

Here it comes, I thought. Now he's going to let me down easy.

He sat in an armchair, motioned me toward another, and took a panatela cigar from his breast pocket.

"Will you have one?" he asked.

"No, thank you, sir."

"I'm not supposed to have any, but I let myself have one a day."

He lit the cigar, blew out a cloud of smoke, puckering his lips as though he was ready to say no.

"About that book," he said abruptly, "are you thinking of it as an autobiography?"

"Yes, sir, and it could also be a company history."

"I wouldn't even know how to start a thing like that."

"Maybe you should start at the beginning, with your birth."

"Oh, I don't want to go into a lot of personal stuff. Nobody cares about that."

"But people do! Of course you could begin when you bought the company . . ."

"That was a funny decision," he said. "I almost didn't do it. You know, radio didn't seem much at the time. Nobody foresaw what it could become."

"Except you . . ."

"Hell, I had no idea it could be anywhere near this big. If I hadn't been born in Pittsburgh, I probably never would have got into it at all. Station KDKA in Pittsburgh was the first commercial station, back in nineteen twenty. I was only a kid then, just out of college. I was working for my father in the soap business. This big lanky Irishman, Brian Kerry, showed up at our office and asked if we wanted to advertise on the air. All I could think was that he was going to try to print something on the air. I figured he was crazy."

"But you soon learned better?"

"He showed me his station—it was like a ham set today, though of course the equipment was nowhere near as good. It was a novelty—up till then, people just thought of radio as something that ships in distress used at sea. I bought a few time spots and made up our commercial right then and there: 'Princess soap gives you a complexion like an English princess. Buy Princess soap at your nearest drugstore. It's the big pink bar with the blush in it.' "

"Wow," I said. "Did that sell a lot of soap?"

"Not much at first, because not many people had receivers, but it brought me a lot of mail from the few who did. Most of them hated that commercial. They weren't used to having their news interrupted. Mostly they broadcast news in those days. Those early loudspeakers made music sound like a squeaking mouse."

"How did you go from your first commercial to buying your first station?"

"In a few years everyone had a receiver and we gave most of our advertising to radio. I could see it was going to keep on getting bigger . . ."

He paused and looked into the distance.

"Our soap company was only a small family-owned enterprise," he went on. "I had two brothers, one older, one younger. There wasn't really room for the three of us when my father died. I decided I wanted to buy into a radio station, but banks didn't understand radio, and no one would lend me any money. After trying everywhere, I sold my stock in the family company to my brothers and bought into a small station up in Buffalo. The first year it damn near failed. I spent most of my time knocking on doors, trying to sell advertising. Many's the hour I've spent sitting in a waiting room, hoping to see the manager, but I'll tell you one thing: I learned something about salesmanship."

"That will make an interesting part of your story," I said.

"Do you really think anyone would be interested?" he asked with remarkable diffidence.

"They sure will if you tell them what you learned about sales-manship."

"That could be a book in itself."

"Include it here, then, and make it a long one."

"I was one of the first to give away time when we couldn't sell it. After a few free commercials, a company would find that orders would start coming in and we'd have their business from then on. Tactics like that work a lot better than charm. You don't really need a lot of charm to be a good salesman. And you don't have to be glib."

There was a note of pathos in this statement—perhaps he had always thought of himself as a man without charm, though he had developed his own style.

"Anyway," he continued, "my station finally did well and when I heard of this thing called a network in New York, a group of six stations, I bought into it. My family's soap business failed soon after that and my brothers were after me for loans."

I didn't ask whether he had given them money. His eyes were gleaming with such malignant satisfaction that I figured he had told them both to go to hell. There was more to this story than appeared on the surface.

"I think all this should go into your book," I said.

"I couldn't put any of that stuff in about my brothers!"

"Then tell as much as you feel like. There's no reason why you can't concentrate on the development of your business."

"My next problem was raising four hundred thousand dollars to buy out my partners in the network . . ."

"I wish we had a tape recorder here," I said.

"I'll send Tim into Nassau to get one tomorrow."

That's when I knew I had him hooked.

THE PROBLEM WAS that he got hooked all too well and soon became a reminiscence junkie—he couldn't stop talking. For a long time he had been alone on the island with no one to talk to except his employees and a personal physician who lived in a distant wing of the house and ate his meals with Tim Murphy, leaving Hopkins to dine alone until my arrival. In a deeper sense the old man had been alone all his life—he had never stripped himself naked mentally and spiritually with another person as Annie and I had done. Parlor psychologists had often accused Hopkins of being a repressed homosexual; perhaps there was an element of that in the relief he apparently found in his rush of words, a thinly veiled plea for understanding, for respect, if not for love. As Hopkins lay on his lounge chair and I sat nearby listening, we presented a tableau remarkably like that of a psychoanalyst and his patient.

To me, at least, his story was compelling, despite or even because of the fact that his life seemed so loveless. He never mentioned his wife, the young son he had lost in World War II, or his daughter, who had married three times. In his own view, his sixty-five years had been spent largely in combat, first with his brothers, who had taken over his family business, and later with his partners in the network and an endless list of competitors. He was, in essence, a battle-scarred general recounting his campaigns, his near-defeats, his many triumphs. He had a very good book in him, but I soon realized that getting it down on paper was going to be more difficult than I had imagined. He was incapable of starting at the beginning and dictating a long narrative—he jumped all over the place and often I had to guide him back to explore a sensitive area, like the rivalry with his brothers, which at first he didn't want to talk about, but later described with relish, as he did every other fight he had won. In rewriting and rearranging all this to produce some kind of order, I would have to make him sound less vindictive and mean-spirited—his story deserved some of the above-the-battle courtesy and fairness that he had shown in his dealings with people. It was clear that he depended on me to do that.

"You'll have to fix all this up, of course," he often said. "I'm just trying to rough out the story for you—we'll have to smooth it up."

I hoped that he would not try to smooth it up too much and make his book as bland as his public personality, but that was a problem we would have to work out as we went along. It soon became clear that this project was going to demand months of working closely together. He couldn't dictate into the tape recorder that Tim bought for him unless I was sitting by his side, giving him a face as well as a machine for an audience.

As far as my job prospects went, this was marvelous—the more he got into his own story the more important the book became to him, and the more dependent he grew on me. After talking almost nonstop for three days, except for brief rest periods, he sensed that I was getting restless.

"Stick with me on this, Tom," he said. "We can both go back to New York in a couple of months, but I want to use the time I have here to get most of this on tape. When we get home there will be so many interruptions . . ."

"Yes, sir, but I'd like to make arrangements to get the tapes you've already given me transcribed. I think we should start working with this on paper . . ."

"Bring a secretary down here," he said. "I'll have Tim bring in whatever equipment she needs."

A light dawned in my brain then.

"Would you mind if I brought down the assistant I had in Washington?" I asked. "She's more than a secretary, but we're going to need to check a lot of facts, and she can also copy edit while typing from the tapes.''

''By all means, bring her down,'' he said. ''She seemed to be a bright little thing.''

''I think I ought to go back to New York and talk to Ann about this,'' I said. ''She's started a new job with the personnel department.''

''Ed Banks will let her go,'' he said impatiently. ''Don't worry about financial arrangements. I want to get this book done and I'll do whatever's fair for both of you. Use the telephone! If you call at night, the connection is better.''

The one time I had tried to call both Betsy and Annie three days ago, they had both been out, and I had somehow been afraid to call again.

Radio telephone reception was at its worst while the sun was going down, Hopkins explained, but after dinner I said I had a bad headache, and leaving the old man alone with his tape recorder, I went to my room. Standing at the window, I watched the orange ball of the sun sink into the glittering, multicolored patchwork of the sea and waited for the momentary green flash of the tropics. The light on the ocean faded into darkness and a rising wind not only whispered in the palm trees and under the eaves of the house, but whistled and moaned, the loneliest sound I had ever heard. My hand trembled as I picked up the receiver and placed the call to South Bay. Somehow I had to know how things stood between Betsy and me before I called Annie.

''Hello?'' Betsy said.

Her voice was strong, her clipped, upper-class Boston accent echoing in that single word. I hadn't heard that tone in years.

''It's me,'' I said.

''Tom, I've been dying for you to call!''

''I did a couple of days ago and no one was home.''

''Oh, we've been over at Bert's house a lot. Tom, I have the most wonderful news!''

''What?''

''He wants to marry me! He really does!''

''Why, that's wonderful!'' I said. Was I truly having this conversation with my wife, whom I had loved for twenty-two years? Would she expect me to give her away to Bert at the wedding? It would be the perfect ironic finale.

"He thinks that one of us should go to Mexico for a divorce," she said. "He wants to regularize our situation as soon as we can."

"I do like that word." I hoped she didn't catch the sarcasm.

"Oh, Tommy, I'm so happy! Be happy for me! Can you?"

"I'm happy," I said, though my throat felt peculiar. "How are the kids? Have you told them yet?"

"I had to, Tom—I'm no good at keeping secrets. They're a little confused, but the girls like Bert, and Pete will come around. The only thing is, they're worried about you . . . and so am I."

"Don't worry about me," I said, sounding like an old song.

"Is this girl of yours really nice? It would be terrible if you had second thoughts now. Men often do, after an affair."

"She's nice," I said. "I have no second thoughts."

"Do you think the kids will like her?"

"Yes, but I doubt if things like this ever go smoothly, not at first . . ."

"No, but is she somebody they can respect? They're not really children anymore . . . I don't know—you were all alone in Washington. At times like that a man's judgment might not be so good."

"Betsy, you don't have to help me pick out a wife. I know what I'm doing."

"I hope so. I'm dying to meet her. I haven't told the children about her yet. That's why they're so worried about you. Janey especially. She said, 'We can't leave daddy all alone!' "

"What did you say to that?"

"I said you're the kind of man who will always be able to find a good woman . . . and that's true, but I hope you aren't moving too fast."

"Aren't you making decisions pretty quickly?"

"We've known Bert for twenty years! How long have you known your airplane girl?"

"Please stop calling her that!"

"I'm sorry. It's crazy, but I'm still a little jealous. Are you?"

"Yes, but I'm beginning to like your little bastard. At least he's man enough to follow through."

"He's a marvelous man, Tom! The two of you have always been jealous of each other—you because he made so much money and he because he always had a yen for me. Did you know that?"

"I think I'd sensed it."

"And he admires you, your war record, the way you've devoted yourself to the kids. I told him about Maria and Mark. He even admires us for the way we handled that."

"I guess we're very admirable people." Would this never end?

"We've gone through a hard time, but we'll straighten out. When are you coming home? There's so much to do!"

I told her I was a prisoner on a desert island and would remain one for at least two months.

"But the work is going great," I said.

"Do you think you'll get a raise?" she asked almost automatically.

"Probably."

"Gosh, I don't have to worry about that anymore, do I? Still, I like to think you won't have to worry about money so much. I love Bert for his own sweet self, but God, it will be good not to worry about budgets anymore!"

"No, you won't," I said, and I thought with astonishment that my financial troubles were probably over too. There'd be no alimony to pay. Child support, of course, but with Annie and me both working on a book that was bound to make money, my days of brooding about debts and college tuition were probably done. What a crazy result of adultery! My Puritan ancestors must be screaming in their graves.

"I bet you never thought we'd have a happy ending like this," Betsy said. "If your girl is as good as you think she is, we're all going to get everything we want, aren't we?"

"It looks that way," I said, but were we? What if both Betsy and I had gone off our rockers and were making some godawful mistake? Bert still might turn out to be the bastard I'd always thought he was and leave Betsy flat in a few years. And on what fine spring day would Annie tire of me and run off with a younger man? Maybe my outraged Puritan ancestors would still be vindicated.

"We're going to have to be careful," I said.

"Oh, Tommy, this is no time for gloom and doom! We have to take a chance!"

God, I must have bored her all those years.

"Is your girl coming down to your desert island?"

"That's being arranged. She's going to be my assistant again."

"Why don't you keep it that way until you're sure she'll be a good wife? After all, you haven't known her very long."

"Betsy, you don't have to run my life anymore!"

"I know, but we're talking about a stepmother for my children. They don't need a wicked stepmother!"

"She's not wicked!" I remembered Annie saying, "I'm not evil!"

"I'll take your word for it, but she did steal my husband."

"And Bert stole my wife!"

"But we both wanted to be stolen, didn't we? What went wrong with us, Tommy?"

"God, I wish I knew . . ."

"Did you ever love me the way you love your airplane girl?"

"When we were kids, but we were always so afraid then . . ."

"I was too scared to know what love was. I needed someone calm and secure. I guess I still do. I'm glad that Bert is older than I am."

Yes, and so did Annie need someone calm and secure, and I wondered if I could ever play that part.

"Maybe you and I were too much alike," I said to Betsy. "Maybe it's true that opposites attract . . ."

"I have no regrets," Betsy said. "We helped each other a lot, and we got three great kids from each other, didn't we?"

"We're going to have to be very careful with them."

"I know this is a terrible time for them, but they're stronger than we think. And Bert is going to be a good influence on their lives —I promise you that!"

"I think he might well be," I said, and on reflection, meant it.

"If your girl is as good as you think she is, she will be too. At least the kids will know that you and I are happy. As you said, how can miserable parents expect to raise happy kids? So I really want you to be happy, Tommy. Don't jump too fast into marriage. Look around a lot first."

"Thank you, mother . . ."

"I do feel a little like your mother, or maybe like your sister. I still love you, Tommy . . ."

"I still love you in my way. You don't have to marry Bert for money. My work is going great."

"I'm not marrying him just for money!"

"I just don't want to think I've driven you to it."

"And I don't want to think I've driven you into the arms of some floozie. At least you'll get to know her better on your desert island. That should be the acid test."

"We don't need any damn acid test! What makes you think I could fall for a floozie, damn it?"

"Aren't we at what they call the 'dangerous age'?"

"I can't think of any time in my life that wasn't dangerous."

"I'm just asking you to be careful. There's no need for you to get married just for the sake of the kids—Bert and I can take care of them fine. And they could visit you in New York."

"I'm not going to get married for the sake of anybody except me!"

"Is she very pretty, Tommy?"

"I think so."

"I won't ask if she's prettier than I was at her age. Is she prettier than your girl in Italy was?"

"I don't even remember Maria very well . . ."

"I always knew you thought she was prettier than me, more exciting, anyway. Sometimes you said her name in your sleep."

"Jesus, Betsy!"

"Bert thinks I'm the most exciting woman he ever met. He keeps saying that and I really think he believes it."

"You're a very beautiful woman, Betsy."

"I used to be. But of course, to Bert I'll always seem young . . ." There was a pause before she said, "Do you want to speak to the kids now?"

What would I say to Barbara, Janey and Pete right now? Don't worry about the divorce! I'm very happy for your mother, and I have a girl I'm going to marry soon . . .

"I think I better wait a while," I said. "I'm afraid we'd all get too emotional . . ."

"You're probably right. Wait until things have settled down a bit."

"Tell them that I was in a terrible hurry when I called, but that I'm okay and send them my love."

Saying this made me feel cowardly, but it was better than breaking into tears, which I would if I talked to them.

"I will," she said. "Good-bye, Tommy . . ."

Those were the key words, weren't they? Good-bye, Tommy . . .

"Good-bye, Betsy . . ."

So a marriage of twenty-two years came to an end. With a telephone call from the Bahamas to Connecticut. There was no reason for me to feel like crying. We were both going to get everything we wanted, weren't we?

31

BEFORE CALLING ANNIE, I stood at the window and stared at the starlit sea, trying to calm myself. The wind kept moaning around the house and was making the surf louder on the beach, storm sounds that seemed to orchestrate my confusion at a time when I should be delirious with relief and joy, when all my problems were solved. The truth was that I was afraid to call Annie. In my jealous insecurity I was afraid there would be no answer or that Harry Comstock was still with her and might even answer the telephone.

Would I ever learn to trust her? My crazy jealousy could eventually drive her away. But should I propose marriage to a woman whom, my intuition told me, I could not count on to stay with me for the rest of my life?

"We have to take a chance," Betsy had said.

But one could learn to be a cautious gambler. I did not have to ask Annie to marry me right away. Betsy was right about one thing —there was no reason to rush. I would invite Annie down here as my assistant, then see how things worked out. At the worst we'd have two good months, and there was no reason why she couldn't remain my assistant indefinitely. Then if she decided to leave me one fine spring day, there would be less heartbreak all around.

But wait. She wanted to have a child of her own. She loved me, she said, she wanted to live forever with me. It was a nice dream, but sifting through all the facets of her character and mine, what was a few months, a year to make sure that we could turn it into something absolutely right?

Decisively I picked up the telephone and gave the number of Annie's apartment to the overseas operator. Annie knew from the

Bahamian accent of the operator that I was on the wire.

"Tommy!" she said. "I was so hoping you'd call!"

"How are you, Annie?" I said, my voice sounding odd to my own ears.

"Fine, but dying for you! When are you coming home?"

"Not soon, but I have good news. Hopkins loves the idea of doing a book and is dictating day and night. He wants you to come down and be my assistant again."

"*Wonderful!*"

"Can you catch the BOAC plane that leaves for Nassau at three tomorrow afternoon?"

"You bet!"

"I'll meet you at the Nassau airport with Hopkins' pilot, then we'll go on to the island in his plane."

"I can't wait! What's it like down there?"

"It's a real desert island with an air-conditioned palace on it. When we're not working, we'll be as alone as Adam and Eve. Will you be able to stand that?"

"It sounds like heaven!"

"I guess it will be sort of an acid test . . ."

"What do you mean?"

"If I don't bore the hell out of you during two months on a desert island, maybe there's hope for us in the long run."

"I don't need any acid test, and I've always had hope. Haven't you?"

She sounded hurt.

"Of course, but damn it, I still sometimes think that things are too good to last."

"I'll get you over it. Once in every thousand years good things actually happen. Hopkins went for the idea of the book, didn't he?"

"Go for it? I can't get away from him."

"Then other good things can happen. Maybe you've had your share of rotten luck."

"Keep your fingers crossed," I said. "Knock on wood!"

"I'd rather pray," she said. "I'm half-Catholic and half-Pres-byterian, so I know two kinds of prayers and I'm going to use both of them, even if I haven't been in a church for years."

"I love you," I said in a rush.

"I love you, too. Sometimes I'm afraid you don't really believe that."

As if she had seen through me . . .

"I love the sound of your voice and that perfume of yours—I can almost smell you over the wire."

"I'm glad you think I smell good," she said with a laugh.

"I love the way you look, the way you walk. Jesus, you've got me ready to write Tin Pan Alley songs!"

"And I love everything about you. I'm not going to change, Tommy. Just because I've been looking for you for a long while doesn't mean I'm going to go on looking, now I've found you."

"I wish I knew what you've found. Have you really been dying to meet a middle-aged man in a gray flannel suit?"

"I'm not going to explain your own worth to you now, but when I get you on that desert island, I'll give you a few lessons you'll never forget."

We went on talking lovingly for ten more minutes before we could bring ourselves to say good-bye, but when I put the telephone down, I still felt that I had betrayed her, I had lied to her by omission; I had not told her that Betsy was getting a divorce and that I would soon be free to marry her. For the first time in my life, I was trying to play it smart, and though that seemed only common sense, it made me feel rotten. I needed the courage to hold out for a few more weeks until she could convince me or I could convince myself that I was wrong in believing that our love was too good to last because of its very intensity.

AFTER LUNCH WITH Hopkins the next day, Tim Murphy flew me to Nassau in time to buy an electric typewriter and stationery before Annie arrived.

"We could sure use a woman on the island," he said as we waited at the airport bar for her plane. "Is this assistant of yours private stock?"

"You'd better believe it!" I said.

"No harm in asking, is there?"

"I'm glad you did."

"You're lucky. Hopkins pays me good money, but if I have to sit over there on that rock much longer, I might try screwing a seagull. Either that or old Mrs. Markham—she's starting to look pretty good."

"Cheer up," I said, looking out the window at the sky. "It looks like rain tonight."

Actually, there was not a cloud in the azure sky, but he studied it carefully.

"Damned if you're not right!" he said. "I better make reservations for us at the hotel."

"I'd like to get the same room I had last time, or one like it."

"That's easy—the whole place will be empty until after the first of the year. The only trouble is that Hopkins gets weather reports. He's beginning to get a touch irritable about my spending so many nights here."

"Doesn't that plane need to have the oil filters changed?" I said. "If we go back there tonight, Hopkins will put me right back to work."

"Damn, I'm glad you reminded me about those oil filters! It will take me time to scrounge up replacements. No reason why we can't all sleep late in the morning . . ."

DESPITE THE GOOD weather, Annie's plane was almost an hour late. Trying to stay away from the bar, I paced back and forth in the airport until my feet hurt.

When the arrival of her flight was announced, I went outside and searched the cloudless sky. It was empty, but then the silver plane came skimming in from the sea, lower than I had expected. It landed with a bounce that scared me, but rolled smoothly to a spot about a hundred feet from the terminal building. The attendants pushed up a flight of aluminum stairs but it seemed a long while before the door finally opened. Annie was the first one out—she must have been standing at the head of the line of passengers, as I once had when I expected to meet her. She paused at the head of the stairs looking for me, a slender woman in a tan camel's hair dress, the one she knew I liked so much, with the wind from the sea ruffling her short, curly brown hair. I waved at her and shouted, "Annie!"

Seeing me, she flew down the steps with that incredible grace of hers, and came running toward me. I hurried to meet her, and suddenly she was in my arms with her warm dress under my fingertips. All thoughts of caution fled.

"Marry me!" I said.

AFTERWORD

I AM SIXTY-THREE years old now in 1983, and Annie is almost fifty. After twenty years, we are still married—a triumph in itself. Are we happy? Of course we are! All our children are happy, happy, happy too, and our grandchildren laugh all the time, with never a tear of sorrow. I wish I could say that, but who can?

I can say this, however: despite various troubles and one tragedy, I still love Annie and she makes me feel certain that she loves me. It's not fashionable to admit that—only in trashy novels do people keep on loving each other. The great authors of our time seem to concentrate on marital misery. I don't blame them—there is no conflict, no drama in contentment, and with the world as it is, there is something almost indecent in private felicity. When asked for his definition of happiness, Tennessee Williams said, "Insensitivity," and who can fault him?

So I'm almost relieved to admit that Annie and I are still miserable a lot, even though we are good to each other. Like most people, we get scared when we think about the future, and we have pressing problems to cope with. One benefit of being sixty-three is the ability to live in the past, to edit out the worst parts, leaving only the most glowing memories. When I have trouble getting to sleep, as I often do, I find relief by going back to those months that Annie and I spent on Hopkins' desert island, recording the old man's lonely, combative story during the days, and lying on moonlit beaches in the evenings. Even the whistling of the wind in the palm trees no longer sounded dismal—it seemed a song of delight.

We have had lots of great moments. I shall never forget Annie's exuberance when I told her on the island there was no reason why we couldn't have a child when we were married.

"Why wait?" she said. "Neither of us is getting any younger, and women my age hardly ever get pregnant right away unless they don't want to. Anyway, what do we care if people count the months?"

The realization that the act of love could now make a new life made her feel so exalted that she turned it almost into a pagan rite of phallic worship. She was afraid she had "waited too long," and she felt the more ardor we inspired in each other, the greater the chance for conception. I did not try to dissuade her. When our first month of strenuous effort failed, I wasn't that unhappy. As a man of forty-three, in my prime, I was prepared to go on forever, a fact she was quick to discern.

"You're just *enjoying* all this," she said indignantly.

"Aren't I supposed to?"

"Yes, but you're not supposed to prolong it. I bet you're holding your best sperms back. I'll get them out of you!"

She pounced upon me, pinning me to the bed; but there was nothing lighthearted about her quest for motherhood. When, about a month later, she found that she had conceived, she thanked me as though I had personally achieved a miracle, and for the next nine months, she did indeed glow with contentment despite her morning sickness.

That was a productive time in several ways. During the two months on the island, we finished enough of Hopkins' book to send a segment of it to a publisher in New York. Of course we knew that few editors would turn down an autobiography of the grand old man of broadcasting, or the king of the television wasteland, whichever way one chose to put it, but Hopkins was remarkably diffident while we waited for a verdict. When the president of a noted publishing company called to give his enthusiastic acceptance, the old man was so grateful that he gave us a healthy raise and cut me in for a share of the royalties. I had not yet told him that I was divorcing Betsy, whose welfare he kept asking about, or that Annie and I planned to get married. Since we spent every free minute on the beach or in my room, all the servants knew we were lovers, and Hopkins must have guessed; but this held as little interest for him as if I had suddenly taken up kite flying, as poor Tim Murphy finally did in his bored desperation.

THE MONTHS ON the island were shadowed only by my concern for my children. As usual, I overdid it. When Bert Andrews did

293 —

things, he did them well. During the Christmas vacation, he took the whole family to Mexico, where he arranged for Betsy's and my divorce while sunning on the beach at Acapulco. I got a postcard with a picture of a man in a sombrero riding a donkey. On the back was written in neat, small letters, "Hi! We're doing fine and hope you are well. Love you!—Janey."

It made me want to cry.

When Betsy and the children returned from Mexico, they moved into Bert's place and closed the Victorian house my grandmother had left me. According to the terms of the divorce agreement, it would eventually be sold, with the proceeds going into a trust fund for the education of the children. Bert said that real estate values were rising fast in South Bay, and that it would be wise to keep it off the market for a while. This would give Annie and me a chance to use it if we wanted to spend weekends with the children.

This I looked forward to with both longing and dread. I believed that Barbara, Janey and Pete would love Annie when they got to know her, but I feared they might be hostile at first.

"I don't want to go to Connecticut," Annie said while we were flying back to New York. "Meeting all the kids and Betsy and Bert at the same time would be too much—it would be awkward for all of us. I'd rather have the kids come into the city one at a time, for a short visit at first—not a whole weekend. Let's get to know each other gradually."

"Do you think we should get married before or after you meet them?" I asked.

"Better if they met me first. Do they know about me?"

"Betsy told them I have a friend. They know I couldn't stay alone long."

"Do you want them there when we get married?"

"They were there when Betsy and Bert got hitched in his house, but they don't need another emotional scene like that."

"Let's play it by ear," she said. "It will be a while before anybody can tell I'm pregnant."

WE DECIDED TO have Pete come into New York first, start with the youngest and work up. I thought the relationship between Annie and Pete might be less complicated than that between Annie and my daughters, with fewer echoes of complicated rivalries. Pete always gave the impression of being less emotional than Janey and Barbara.

The children understood when I told them over the phone that Annie wanted to meet them one at a time. I think the girls were relieved to know Pete was first—they would get a report on their future stepmother from him. Pete sounded casual when he agreed to spend the following Saturday with us.

"I'd like to do some shopping," he said. "I'm getting interested in playing the guitar, and I've saved some Christmas money. Do you suppose I could buy one?"

We met him in Grand Central Station, almost empty at ten o'clock on a Saturday morning. When he got off the train, I was surprised to see he had grown a lot—the cuffs of his blue jeans and ski jacket were too short. I wondered why Betsy hadn't bought him a new outfit, until I remembered he couldn't care less about clothes. As he walked slowly toward us, I seemed to see him through Annie's eyes, and her through his. Here was a gangling, fourteen-year-old with a curiously adult face, reserved, almost aloof, but he was clearly astonished by his first glimpse of Annie. She was so young, more like a college girl than a future stepmother. His bony body felt stiff when I gave him a hug.

"Pete, this is Annie," I said.

They shook hands with awkward formality.

"What should I call you?" he asked.

"How about 'Annie'?" she said with her merry smile. "I hear you want to buy a guitar. I know a store near here where we can begin looking."

"I want to get a Martin," he said decisively.

"That's a good choice," Annie said.

"Do you play the guitar?"

"I can pick a few chords, but I'm no Segovia," she said.

"Do you know about him? Bert has some of his records—that's what got me interested . . ."

"I heard him play once," she said. "He comes to Carnegie Hall every so often."

"What's he look like?"

"Little and old and very happy. Wouldn't you be if you could play a guitar like that?"

"I sure would, but I never will. I'm going to be a scientist. Music is just a hobby."

"Everybody needs a hobby," she said with a smile.

WE WALKED TO a music store on Forty-fifth Street. Pete strode so eagerly on his long, thin legs that I found it difficult to keep up with him, but Annie trotted between us with her dancing, effortless motion. Pete selected an instrument that cost almost a hundred dollars, and to my surprise took five twenty-dollar bills from his hip pocket to pay for it. Bert must have given him a bigger Christmas check than I ever had.

When the clerk handed him the guitar in its imitation leather case, Pete said, "I'm dying to play it. Where can we go?"

"My apartment isn't far from here," Annie said. "Do you mind walking?"

Pete seemed barely able to rein himself in as we walked across town. When we got to Sixth Avenue and headed uptown, he started to outdistance us.

"Do you want to run?" Annie asked, catching up to him.

"What?"

"Do you want to run these last few blocks?"

"I sure feel like it!"

"Then why not do it?" she said. "We'll meet you up there, Tom!"

Off she dashed with Pete loping along beside her, his guitar gripped firmly in his arms like a baby. That is a picture that has always stayed in my mind, one of my most treasured memories, the image of two people I loved laughing and running, dodging through the crowd on Sixth Avenue. A cop stared at them with heavy, questioning eyes, but then laughed too.

WE INVITED JANEY to come in the following Saturday, but she said she had a cold and Barbara came instead. Perhaps as a declaration of independence, or maybe because she needed someone to buttress her, she brought Gordy with her. My heart sank when I saw them coming down the platform in Grand Central Station toward us. They both wore tattered blue jeans and black leather jackets, and with their arms defiantly around each other they looked like a couple of juvenile delinquents.

I couldn't guess what Barbara thought of Annie. My older daughter suddenly seemed more than seventeen, and Annie looked so much younger than thirty that they appeared to be sisters. They were almost exactly the same size and had similar coloring. Immediately after the introductions, Gordy said, "I liked that guitar Pete bought. I thought I'd take a look around the store and see if I can find one like it."

"We'll show it to you," Annie said.

I wondered if he could afford it. When he got to the music shop, he lovingly examined several instruments before settling on an electric one priced at three hundred dollars.

"How about time payments?" he asked the clerk. "I'm a professional musician. If you let me have it, I can get a gig and pay for it in a few nights."

"I'm afraid we can't do that," the clerk said.

"I have a car I can put up for security," Gordy persisted. "I have the registration right here."

He took his wallet from his jacket pocket and showed the clerk a wilted piece of paper. While the boy argued aggressively and the clerk kept shaking his head, Annie led me to the other end of the store. "Let's lend the money to him," she whispered.

"He'll never pay it back," I said.

"So what? Loosen up! Surprise your daughter. If you're nice to him, she'll lose interest in him a hell of a lot sooner than if you give him a hard time."

Feeling self-conscious, I walked back to where Gordy and the clerk were now shouting at each other.

"I'll lend you the money, Gordy," I said.

I'll never forget the look of astonishment and relief that Gordy and Barbara turned on me. Suddenly I was their ally in a tough world, no longer their enemy, a new meaning of the word "father" for them. I didn't think this breakthrough would ease all the tensions between me and Barbara, but it was a start. We had lunch in a Chinese restaurant with the cheeriness of friends. Annie taught us to eat with chopsticks, and offered me an especially succulent little shrimp from her plate. A loving gesture that took Barbara by surprise—she wasn't used to seeing me receive attention from anyone, never mind a pretty girl who did not look much older than herself. In her eyes, I had always been a grim old fuddy-duddy who exasperated his own wife, and the image of me as a lover startled her even more than my generosity. The tableau of Annie offering me the shrimp between the tips of her chopsticks while my elder daughter's eyes widened stays in my memory as a moment of triumph. For the first time in years, I felt that on the face of my rebellious daughter I was finally seeing the dawn of respect.

I HAVE A LOT of happy memories to make up for the inevitable pains of life. Some of the situations I brooded about turned out fairly well. My biggest worry was still Janey. When she finally came into New York we went to the station with some trepidation; she had been the closest to me and might resent Annie the most.

The moment Janey stepped from the train, she seemed a figure of youthful tragedy. Her quilted ski jacket exaggerated the weight problem that tortured her so much, and as soon as she glanced at Annie her dark eyes looked stricken, as though this graceful woman were an enemy she could never hope to rival. I hugged Janey hard. Janey forced a smile when I introduced Annie.

"Is there any shopping you want to do? Or would you rather see a show?" I asked.

"I don't know . . ."

"Do you like Chinese food?" Annie asked.

"I'm supposed to be on a diet."

"So am I and so is your father," Annie said. "Horrible, isn't it?" Janey forced another smile.

"Would you like to go to the Bronx Zoo?" I asked desperately.

"Okay," she said and shrugged. "But it's kind of cold for that, isn't it?"

I wanted to give her something. I had an overpowering urge to give her a present that would demonstrate my continuity as her father, but what? A fine new coat or a party dress? No. Janey hated to buy clothes even more than did Pete. She was too old for toys, too young for jewelry. What did she need, what did she want?

Me, I thought, but now I had gone away with this good-looking woman at my side. At home in South Bay, Janey and I had often felt silently allied against the rest of the family, but now she was all alone. Her mother had Bert, Barbara had Gordy and Pete had his science books and guitar. Janey had only self-recrimination for being fat, and her dog Bonkers.

Suddenly I had an idea.

"Let's go to Annie's apartment and talk," I said. "We have a lot of things to figure out, and it's fun to make plans for a new life."

I knew Janey hated the apartment as soon as she saw it. It was so small that, in her eyes, it was clearly Annie's and mine exclusively. There were only two chairs and when Annie insisted on sitting on the floor, Janey seemed embarrassed. We ended up reclining on the rug.

"Annie, the first thing we have to do is to get a bigger apartment, so the kids can visit us," I said.

"I'm hoping I can make a deal with the super," she said. "How many bedrooms do you want?"

I had planned on two with a convertible couch in the living room, but we weren't broke anymore, and it occurred to me that Janey could have a room of her own with us.

"Could we find four bedrooms?" I asked.

"Not here, but I have a friend in the Eldorado building on Central Park West. They have a lot of huge apartments. Do you want to look?"

I saw Janey's eyes brighten.

"Could I come in whenever I wanted?" she asked.

"Sure. You could even live with us after the school year. Did your mother explain the divorce agreement to you?"

"She said you have joint custody, whatever that means."

"It means you can live with your mother and Bert or with Annie and me, whichever you want," I said. I hadn't even discussed this with Annie.

"I'd love to have you with us," Annie said quickly, "and I know how much your father would."

"I don't know how we could work that out, but I'd sure love to have a room at your place," Janey said. "Could it be a small one? My room at Bert's house is so big that I get lost in it. And I don't like the sound of that river running all the time."

A small room of her own with us—that was the gift that Janey wanted most. We inspected several apartments at the Eldorado that afternoon, and she looked disappointed when we decided to search further before signing a contract. Perhaps she feared we were just doing it for show, that we didn't really want her with us at all.

"No matter where we find an apartment, we'll have to furnish it," Annie said. "How would you like to go to Macy's, give us some idea of what you'd like in your room?"

"Could we buy something now?" Janey asked.

Janey obviously needed definite action, some guarantee of the future. When she admired a reproduction of a four-poster bed, we bought it on the spot and told the clerk to hold delivery.

"Is it mine now?" Janey asked as I signed the slip.

"You bet it is!" I said.

With childlike glee, Janey jumped on the bed and lay spread-eagled on her back.

"Look at me," she said. "I'm home!"

That's a picture I'll always treasure, Janey triumphant in Macy's furniture department; twenty years later, that bed still awaits her whenever she visits us.

THERE WERE THREE more people whom Annie had yet to meet: Betsy, Bert and Mark. I wanted us to settle down before I brought Mark over from Italy. I dreaded the thought of us all gathering around the dinner table, making cheery toasts to each other, Bert's idea of camaraderie. The trouble was that Betsy insisted we spend a Sunday with them.

"We have to show the kids we still love each other," she said. "It's the anger and hatred that hurt children more than the separation."

I admitted she was right and sensed that she and Annie had a lot of curiosity about each other. A few days after Janey visited us Annie and I agreed to come to South Bay the next Sunday afternoon.

"I'll meet you at the station," Betsy said, as she had said so many times before. "Just wear old clothes. Bert's made a skating rink on a pond out back. Does Annie skate?"

I figured Annie wouldn't want to fall on the ice in her present condition. We would enjoy watching.

That Sunday Annie put on a brightly colored Scotch plaid skirt and black cashmere sweater, which did not do much to hide her blossoming figure.

"You look great, but Betsy said to wear old clothes," I said.

"No woman would wear old clothes in a situation like this," Annie replied. "Betsy is going to look her best. Want to bet?"

We took the train to South Bay, a familiar journey for me, but the ride seemed long to Annie.

"I don't see how you stood this trip every morning and night for so long," she said.

On reflection, neither did I. Three hours a day on a railroad train. I must have been out of my mind.

AT THE STATION I looked around for the Ford station wagon that we had had to borrow money to buy. Instead Betsy pulled up in a new Cadillac convertible, yellow with shiny wire wheels and a white top.

"Maybe it's conspicuous consumption or whatever you want to call it, but Bert gave this thing to me and I love it," she said as we climbed in.

In one sense Betsy had gone home, back to the land of rich people, the country of her youth, where money wasn't a problem, and nobody worried about bills while they drove expensive cars which did not break down. Betsy was, as Annie had predicted, looking her best in custom-made blue jeans, a ruffled peasant blouse and a short fur coat of white beaver. It made Annie's wool overcoat look pretty drab, but there was a kind of reverse pathos in that; despite her clothes and spectacular car, the sweet bird of youth, to use a phrase from her favorite playwright, had eluded Betsy and there were lines of fatigue around her eyes. Still, she looked happy, and why shouldn't she?

"I'm so glad to meet you," she said to Annie, sounding very *grande dame*. "You're even prettier than I imagined, but I shouldn't be surprised, should I? Tom always had good taste in women, if I do say so myself."

"I can see that," Annie said with a smile and they both laughed, but we were all uncomfortable.

It seemed strange not to drive back to our old house; we took the route that led to Bert's place.

"It snowed a little this morning and the kids are helping Bert sweep off the skating rink," Betsy said. "You'll skate, won't you, Annie?"

"I'm afraid not," Annie said.

"I'm not much good at it myself," Betsy said, "but Bert's a real champion. He's teaching the kids, and I'm trying to keep up with them. He's a great teacher. What size skate do you wear?"

"I'm not sure," Annie said.

"What's your shoe size?" Betsy persisted.

"Seven."

"That's funny—same as mine. I just got new skates, but there's nothing wrong with my old pair. You've got to get on the ice and give it a try. Bert won't let you fall."

Annie merely smiled and said, "I'll enjoy watching the rest of you."

"Well, you'll skate, won't you, Tom? I was getting some stuff at our old house this morning and I put your skates in the back of the car."

I didn't know why she was so insistent about skating. Maybe this way she and Bert could demonstrate all their agility and grace. She knew damn well I was a lousy skater.

"I'll watch with Annie," I said, and saw the familiar look of frustration tighten Betsy's face. She had planned a skating party, but like so many of her plans it wasn't going to work out.

"Anyway, Bert's going to build a bonfire and we can roast hot-dogs," she said.

We drove the rest of the way in silence to Bert's beautiful house on the old millstream. Betsy turned off on a newly ploughed road that led to a pond behind the house, a shallow backwater of the river. Bert and my children had already built a bonfire, and the flames seemed to blaze directly up from the fresh snow. A brisk wind was swirling the smoke away and my children, in bright new orange ski clothes, were carrying armfuls of logs. In a red jacket and Tyrolean hat, Bert was taking the logs and tossing them into the fire. Bonkers was frisking around, waving her ridiculously long tail, and they were all laughing, having such a good time that I felt a surge of jealousy. Who the hell did that little bastard think he was, their father? I was willing to let him take my wife from me, but not my children.

As she rolled to a stop Betsy touched the horn of her new car to announce our arrival. It sounded a medley of trumpet notes. The children dropped their armfuls of wood and raced toward us, with Bert following briskly, despite his bad heart. When they were about twenty yards from us, the wind grabbed Bert's Tyrolean hat and sent it rolling over the snow. The children dashed after it, shouting, but Bonkers took the hat in her mouth and thinking that this was a fine game, kept on running in circles with everyone in pursuit.

"I'm going to kill that dog," Bert shouted in mock fury.

Betsy jumped out of the car to join the chase, as did Annie. I too joined in trying to catch the dog, which kept dodging us. It was a comic scene that came to a climax when Bonkers raced a yard in front of me. On impulse I tackled her, and found myself lying in the snow with her wet furry body in my arms, hugging her as though I loved her.

"Don't hurt her!" Janey shouted, running toward me.

I struggled to my feet and handed the dog to her.

The Tyrolean hat had fallen near the toe of my shoe, and I grabbed it before it flew away again.

"Your hat, sir!" I said, holding it out to Bert.

He put it on his bald head, deliberately cocking it at a ridiculous angle, and smiled.

"For this and much else I thank you, sir," he said. "Let's go into the house and have a drink."

We would never be good friends, we would always feel uncomfortable together, but how could anybody really dislike a little bastard like Bert?

"You might as well take the station wagon," Betsy said to me later that afternoon. "I left it in our old garage. And you can have any furniture you want—there's no place to put it here."

"We'll see what we can use," I said. "The rest we can sell with the house."

Instead of driving Annie and me back to the station that evening, she took us to our old house, which looked strangely dark against the moonlit sky.

"I loved meeting you, Ann," Betsy said. "I hope we can get together often."

"Me too," Annie said.

I wasn't sure whether they meant it, but I knew damn well that we would all meet at weddings and, God help us, funerals.

"Thanks for a grand day," I said and got out of the car. Annie followed, as did Betsy, somewhat to my surprise.

"Good-bye, Tommy!" she said, giving me a hug and kiss on the cheek. Then she turned to Annie and hugged her.

"I told the kids that our family wasn't breaking up—we're adding two great people to it, and I meant it," Betsy said.

Before we could say a word she jumped into her car and as always, when she got emotional, roared out of our driveway much too fast. Annie and I stood staring after the red taillights until they disappeared around a corner.

"I like her, but just how real is she?" Annie finally asked.

"I've never been sure," I said.

Enough heat had been left on in the Victorian house to prevent freezing, but it still felt cold and damp, with that musty smell which had clung to the rugs and curtains ever since I could remember. When I turned on the lights, I saw that Betsy had covered the furniture with sheets, a ghostly custom of my grandmother whenever we went away. The living room was unnaturally silent, and I realized that I missed the ticking of the grandfather clock. I adjusted its weights and set it going again. Then I started to fold up the sheets.

"This is a lovely room," Annie said.

"When we get a bigger apartment we can take whatever you like."

"Do you want much of it?"

Something about the tone of her voice made me stop and think. No, the truth was no, I didn't want a stick of this antique furniture. I had grown up in this house. I had seen both my parents and my grandmother sicken to death in it, and I had watched my first marriage die here. Now I wanted to walk out of this house without taking a single reminder of it with me. Perhaps that was wrong; the old place had sheltered me and my children for a long time, but I had had enough of it.

"I don't want any of this stuff," I said, "but I should give you the choice."

"I like antiques, but they're not really my style."

"Then we'll sell all the furniture with the house," I said with great relief.

The grandfather clock chose this moment to strike ten mournful notes.

"I never really liked that sound," I said. "It's like the tolling for the dead."

"We don't have to come back here, do we?"

"No, I guess not."

"Isn't there any little stuff you want?"

There were clothes, of course, but I was still losing weight and few of them would fit anymore. There were books I didn't feel like lugging around and a fancy camera I had never been able to master.

"There's my grandmother's silver," I said, remembering how she had always counted the spoons, knives and forks after the servants had polished them.

"Save that for your daughters," Annie said. "I'd rather have stainless steel."

"What if you have a daughter?"

"I'm going to have a son, I'm almost sure, and if I do have a daughter, she'll want stainless steel like me."

"I can't think of anything I want to take, except my old pistol,"

I said. "I don't really want that, but I shouldn't leave it here."

"You can't keep a gun in New York," she said. "Do you really need it?"

"I brought it home from the war, but it's not important anymore. I'll figure some way to get rid of it."

"Can't you sell it?"

"I suppose that technically I stole it from the army. I wouldn't want to leave it in some hock shop that might sell it to some crook."

The problem of the gun bothered me. I shouldn't leave it in an unoccupied house, where thieves might find it. During the war I had killed several men with that gun and this blood bond made me responsible for it.

"I don't want to worry about the damn thing anymore," I said. "I'll throw it in some pond near the parkway."

"Aren't they all frozen now?" she asked.

"Then I'll bury it in the cellar."

A grotesque idea, but I had to end my responsibility for that gun. In the cellar I took a shovel, found a spot where the concrete had crumbled and scooped out a deep hole. I felt guilty, as though I had just killed someone, but burying a gun was the opposite of murder, wasn't it? The Indians had buried the hatchet in a peace ceremony, and that's what I was doing.

When the grave was prepared we went upstairs to get the pistol from the tackle box in my closet. My glance and I think Annie's slid over the double bed in which I had sired three children and had spent so many sleepless nights. On my bureau were two silver-framed photographs, one of my father and mother, a handsome smiling couple standing together in a garden shortly after their marriage, and one of my grandmother when she was a young woman. Annie studied the photos as I took the pistol from its box and slipped the ammunition into my pocket.

"You'll want these pictures, won't you?" she asked.

"They always make me feel sad as hell."

"You should save them for your children."

"I'll ask Betsy to take care of that. She'll comb through this whole place before we sell it."

I went back down to the cellar, glad to have Annie accompany me on this strange errand. After making sure the gun was unloaded, I tossed it into the hole and smoothed it over. Then I walked to the other side of the cellar, found another weak spot in the concrete and buried the shells with the ammunition clip.

"We should say a few words over them," Annie said.

"Forever hold your peace. How's that?"

"Just right," she said and shivered. "Let's get out of here."

As we got into the station wagon I kissed Annie, held her tightly against me and felt an overpowering desire to make love to her. Her kisses were as urgent as mine.

"The backs of this thing fold down," I said after a moment.

"Can you start the engine and turn the heater on?"

"I better back the rear end out of the garage first."

"That's a good idea. What a hell of a way to die!"

"I can think of worse, but no way at all appeals to me right now."

After I had backed the exhaust pipe clear of the garage, I put the backseats down and we spread our overcoats on the smooth plastic surface before removing our clothes. At first it was cold, which increased the delight of each other's warmth, but by the time we wanted to rest the heater was working well. Moonlight glittered on the windows of the car and on the snow as the wind moaned around the eaves of the old carriage house, making us feel snug in each other's arms. When we finally dressed and steered the car out of the driveway, back toward New York, I really did feel I was starting a new life without regrets.

"Do you know what I'd like to do?" she said.

"What?"

"I'd like to go down to City Hall tomorrow and get married without any fuss."

"I'd hoped to arrange something a little better than that. Maybe we could get a minister to come up to the apartment and have a few flowers around."

"We're already married! I don't need any ceremony. All I want is a piece of paper to register what's already happened."

"Damn it, you still deserve a beautiful ceremony. I want to give it to you."

"How many people get married with the ceremony and not much else? We have everything else! How can we complain?"

It took a while to get the paperwork straightened out, but we were married in a drab office in the Municipal Building two weeks later. Curiously, I can scarcely remember the ceremony at all and neither can Annie. I think we regarded it as an unwelcome intrusion of necessity into poetry, and we forgot it as soon as we could.

*   *   *

Now I come to a memory that still causes me pain. As soon as we moved into our larger apartment, Annie said, "With all this space, we can ask Mark over any time you want."

"So soon?" I said.

"Don't you feel you've waited long enough?"

"I'm not sure what he'd do in the city, how long he'd want to stay." I wasn't ready for this.

"There's only one way to find out. I'm not trying to push you, but this has to be done."

"Yes—I want to do it."

"Let's get him over here before the baby comes—things will be too busy after that."

Annie's baby was due in September. Mark wrote that he could arrive in New York on June twenty-fourth, at the end of the spring term at his seminary in Rome. I sent him a round-trip ticket, explaining we would like him to stay until August, after which I would have a very busy schedule. I didn't provide details.

It struck me that now I had to explain Mark to my other children. At first I tried writing them a letter, but I couldn't make it come out right, and in mid-June asked all three to spend a weekend with us in our apartment. When we had gathered in the living room before dinner, I said, "I have something important I want to talk about. As you know, I was a soldier in the war . . ."

Before telling them about Maria I tried to explain, without going into detail, what it was like to feel that I was going to die in battle before I ever got home.

"Gosh, you must have been brave, dad!" Pete said.

Janey's dark, brooding eyes understood, and Barbara, I thought, was eyeing me quizzically, wondering why I was trying to make myself out a hero.

"When I finally got to Italy and most of the fighting was over in Europe, I found I was going to be sent to fight in Japan. It was then that I met a girl in Rome and fell sort of temporarily in love— everything seemed temporary in those days. Anyway, we had a child, a boy I didn't even hear about until after the war was over . . ."

"Gee, dad, you sure are full of surprises!" Barbara said.

"You mean I have a brother?" Pete said. "That's neat!"

Janey said nothing, but I felt she understood. She was crumpling a handkerchief, straightening it out, then crumpling it. When I finished she gave me a kiss on the cheek and hurried to her room, to her beloved four-poster bed. The other children said they wanted to go to the airport to meet Mark. Meeting so many people all at once might confuse him, I pointed out, and we'd have a family get-together later.

At four in the afternoon of a day I both anticipated and dreaded, Annie and I drove out to Kennedy Airport to meet the plane from Rome. Annie was heavy with child then, and as we waited for Mark's flight she sat in a waiting room near the gate where the passengers were supposed to disembark, but I was so nervous that I kept pacing back and forth in front of her. This was a moment I had never thought would happen, until Annie showed me the way. My emotions were chaotic—part guilt for having been so afraid of a close relationship with Mark, part stubborn pride for acknowledging a relationship that many veterans had denied or ignored, part fear that I was to be victimized, but mostly eagerness to see what kind of a man my first born had turned out to be.

Hundreds of passengers filed through that gate before I spied him. I recognized him immediately, a tall, thin, tense young man, almost the image of my army self, though his hair was darker than mine, his eyes were brown, and he was shorter than I. He recognized me at once, and we hurried toward each other, both of us too inhibited to run. I started to shake hands before mustering the courage to hug him, feeling him stiffen almost to attention.

"God, I'm glad to see you, Mark!" I said. "I should have done this years ago!"

"It is very kind of you," he said with a strong Italian accent. It was as though he had memorized the phrase from a book.

Annie came up behind me and I saw his look of surprise when I introduced this young, pregnant woman as my wife. To my astonishment and his, she started to talk very fast in Italian, her hands flying. His face softened to a delighted smile and they talked together for a minute before she gave him a hug and kissed him on the cheek. This time he did not stiffen, though he seemed embarrassed, awkward but pleased.

MARK CULTIVATED the habit of silence. At first I thought it was shyness, his difficulty with English, but he didn't talk much in Italian with Annie either, and he never did speak much, even when he got to know us better. I thought this was odd until I reflected that Pete, Janey and Barbara were just as reticent with us.

We collected his baggage, one small black cardboard suitcase, got into our car and started back to our apartment. There was dignity in his silence, but his face was expressive. He seemed impressed by the size of the Ford station wagon—a poor boy in the land of the rich—and he must have wondered where he fitted in. His blue serge suit was shiny and worn. My God, I'd been sending him only two hundred dollars a month and that had made me feel generous!

We had invited him to New York for a "visit," a word as tentative as we felt. His return ticket was in his pocket, but I suspected he might want to stay here, go to college or try to get a job. He probably wanted to look us and the situation over before making any plans, I guessed as I looked at his tense face. When he saw the skyline of Manhattan, he smiled and nodded but still he said nothing, and I respected his dignity.

When we installed him in the room we usually kept for Pete, he gave us a taut smile and said that he would like to lie down for a few minutes before dinner.

"What are we going to do with him?" I said to Annie in sudden panic. "We can't just sit around here!"

"We can take him to plays, show him the town . . ."

"He'll get tired of that. Do you suppose that he really wants to stay in this country?"

"Take it one step at a time," she said.

"He's an Italian citizen. Isn't there a quota or something?"

"It might be possible for you to recognize him legally as your son—we'd have to see a lawyer. Maybe Bert could help."

"God, he's the last person I want to get involved in this."

I began to worry about money. Hopkins had given us raises and his book was almost finished, but with all the child support, in addition to a new baby . . .

At dinner Mark nibbled at his steak and hardly touched the apple pie à la mode. After drinking half a cup of coffee, he again gave us his taut smile and said he was so tired he wanted to go to bed.

"Jet lag," Annie said after he had gone. "And of course, a very awkward situation for him."

"If he does want to stay here, I'm not sure he could get into a good college or find a good job," I said.

"All these things will work themselves out," she replied.

IT IS DIFFICULT to write this now, twenty years later. Mark stayed with us a month, always courteous, but shy and withdrawn.

When I finally screwed up the courage to ask him important questions, his answers were curt.

"How's your mother these days?" I said one morning when we were walking up Fifth Avenue together.

"Okay," he replied, but his expression told me not to press for more news.

Later I said, "We really ought to sit down and talk about your plans for the future . . ."

"I don't have any yet." Again his face begged me not to press.

Money was an awkward subject. He owned only his one frayed suit and suitcase of clothes, but he was too old to take to Brooks Brothers and outfit like a boy; he kept telling me that the two hundred dollars I sent him every month was enough. In this respect he was my son—any mention of money made him look tortured. After talking it over with Annie, I put five hundred dollars in an envelope and before dinner one night, when she was in the kitchen, I gave it to him.

"We'd like to help you out with your expenses," I said gruffly. His face flushed.

"Thank you," he mumbled. "I want to say . . ."

"You are my son, after all," I said. "We're going to have to talk about long-range plans."

"Do you mind if I don't go back to Italy right away? I'd like to see more of this country. I could hitchhike—it wouldn't cost anything. My permit is good for another two months and my ticket can be changed."

"I don't see any reason why not," I said, but the image of my son standing forlornly by the side of a road with his thumb out bothered me.

"In Europe we hitchhike all the time," he said. "I'd like to see California."

"I can give you enough money to take a bus," I said, and he didn't object.

HE WAS EAGER to get started, and I couldn't blame him. Sitting around the apartment all day or walking the streets of New York while Annie and I were at work must have bored him. There was forced gaiety when we took him to plays and showed him the city, which put a strain on all of us. The Sunday when Pete, Janey and Barbara came in to meet him was even worse. They were still kids, and Mark clearly was an adult, but not yet mature enough to know how to deal with people younger than himself. What did he have in common with these children in blue jeans and ski jackets, full of careless disdain for city clothes and manners? Mark was always meticulously neat, low-voiced and polite. Seeing my children through his eyes, I thought they looked unkempt and boisterous, except for Janey, who obviously shared his torment. The get-together was so strained that Annie and I took them all to the movies before driving the kids home and showing a little of Connecticut to Mark. He stared at the rolling hills and expensive mansions silently, perhaps comparing them to the poor but lively sections of Rome where he had been brought up. I couldn't tell whether he dreamed of getting rich in America, or just wanted to see as much of this strange country as possible before he went home.

We dropped the children at Bert's house without going in—introducing Mark to Betsy and Bert seemed an unnecessary piece of drama. On the drive back to New York, Mark's continuing silence began to seem like a kind of judgment, but that was absurd. What did I expect him to say about my family and America?

Two days later Mark left for California. I insisted on buying him a bus ticket to San Francisco, but he said that he preferred to hitchhike back, and planned to return to New York in time to catch his plane to Rome on September first. I gave him a package of traveler's checks and felt my conscience was clear, or as clear as I could make it. After seeing him off at the bus depot, Annie and I returned to our apartment with a sense of relief that we dared not admit, and it was not long before we had other things to think about. A week after Mark's departure my youngest one arrived, nine pounds of him, and Annie was lost in the ecstasy of her own motherhood.

A FEW DAYS after the birth of William, named after Annie's father, history took one of those unexpected turns which so often had jolted me out of my euphoria. In that terribly calm voice that radio and television reporters use to announce doom, our friendly anchorman at United Broadcasting told me, while I was trying to refresh my knowledge of diaper-changing, that North Vietnamese torpedo boats had attacked American destroyers in the Gulf of Tonkin. President Johnson had already ordered retaliatory air strikes. This sounded like war to me and when, five days later, Congress authorized the president to take all necessary steps to "maintain peace," I was sure of it.

This appeared to be one war that I could sit out. During the Korean War I could have been called up, but now I was definitely too old and, thank God, Pete was too young. I never thought of Mark in connection with Vietnam, I expected him to go home to Italy. So I was astonished when he telephoned me ten days later from Denver, and said he wanted to join the American army.

"You have to be an American citizen," I said. He had been talking to someone who thought immigrants might acquire citizenship by joining the army.

"Why do you want to join the army?" I asked, and to my astonishment I heard him say, "I always wanted to be an American soldier."

Had Maria told him glowing stories about the kindness of American soldiers? She had, I knew, a picture of me in my captain's uniform that a sidewalk photographer had taken during our brief month together. Maybe Mark had grown up thinking that the uniform was a wonderful thing to wear, a protection against poverty and defeat. Also, the army would provide an escape from the mean streets of Rome, show him where he fitted into America. It made a kind of sense.

When Mark returned to New York, I tried to talk him out of enlisting but it was useless. He ached to be an American soldier; the one thing he wanted from me was to help him get into the army as soon as possible.

God help me, I did help him. I asked Saul Bernstein, the lawyer who sent the checks to Maria, draw up the papers for "legitimizing" my son, and by the time this was done, it was easy to enlist in the army anyway. Mark kept hoboing around the country, paying us brief visits during the waiting period, and worked at odd jobs, washing dishes and climbing mountains with a tree surgeon in Oregon. I had not seen him for about a month when he suddenly showed up at our apartment in uniform. His personality seemed to have been transformed. Gone was the reticence, and he talked eagerly about training camp and his dream of going on to officer's candidate school. He was a young man who knew where he was going, a real American.

"I owe it all to you," he said, as though he were one of the Kennedy boys talking to his father.

Mark had a successful, if brief, career in the army. After basic training he was sent to Vietnam and after one tour of duty volunteered for another. Four years later he received a field promotion to lieutenant, and then he was killed in the Tet offensive. Conceived in one war, killed in another. I received a telegram from the war department, just like a regular father. His mother got ten thousand dollars of G.I. life insurance, an ironic blessing for her. That was that, the end of a chapter in my life which still fills me with such confused emotions that I can barely think of it. I'm glad I tried to help my bastard son, but if I had run away from the responsibility, as so many soldiers did, Mark would still be alive today in Rome. So much for good intentions . . .

The news of his death shook me harder than anything that had happened to me since the death of my parents. I got drunk as I had when John Kennedy was murdered, and it took me a lot longer to get out of the depths of despair. My conviction that the world was mad deepened. My father had been smashed by the First World War. I had survived the second only by the skin of my teeth. And now my son was killed, three generations of war in my own experience.

"Thanks a lot, all you great world statesmen!" I shouted. "Congratulations to all you fucking *realists* who run the world! My name is Wrath, however you want to spell it! People like me won't put up with bastards like you much longer!"

In vino veritas . . . sometimes, anyway. Annie applauded my performance and fetched me an aspirin.

Somewhere I read that all a man can do is try to create an island of order in a sea of chaos. I kept thinking of that while I was coming out of my long drunk. I clung to those words then, and now.

IT IS DECEMBER now, almost 1984, and at least we can say that George Orwell's predictions have been exaggerated. I am sixty-three years old and can find comfort in the fact that few of the predictions I made in my life came true. Twenty years ago I worried about being too old for love or much of anything else. Nowadays I don't look too different in the mirror, except for the white hair, and Annie says that makes me look distinguished. My arthritis aches enough to remind me that no one can enjoy good health forever. My children are no longer children. Pete, Janey and Barbara are in their thirties; and our William is nineteen, a sophomore at Columbia. It is tempting to say that my sons and daughters have all "turned out all right," as though they were cakes uniformly browned in an oven, but they wouldn't let me get away with that.

William seems the most troubled, despite the fact that he grew up with so little dissension at home. Maybe Annie and I spoiled him, but the era in which he is maturing is enough to confuse anyone, and I didn't give him a heritage of perfect mental health and serenity. He had his problems with booze and drugs in high school, and since the age of fifteen has always been in love with some wild-eyed girl who did not suffer the restraints or guilts that were imposed on teenagers in my youth. I have an idea that he makes love to more women on almost any weekend than I have kissed in sixty-three years. I don't envy him—he has never known more than the skin of a woman. Pete told me long ago not to make generalities about sex, so I cannot tell if some sort of sexual inflation is setting in for William, making him value each affair less because there are so many of them, or whether his capacity for love will grow. He is handsome in a lithe, dark-eyed way that makes him almost a masculine replica of his mother. He is bright, energetic and idealistic in his fashion. After cracking up two cars, he is learning to drive carefully. He tells me he is glad he fouled up in high school, that he got it out of his system before going to college. I pray a lot for him.

Pete followed the trajectory that he established early in his life and became a marine biologist, a professor at the University of California. He is still a workaholic, but was smart or lucky enough to marry a hard-working woman in his field. They have one child, a son, two years old. They wear blue jeans and T-shirts, and march in peace parades together, taking turns at carrying their son like a papoose in a leather shoulder sling.

Janey has never married, though I still have hopes that she will. She still fights obesity like a religious fanatic struggling with a demon. Annie has taught her about diet and exercise, and at thirty-five Janey is emerging as a well-proportioned, if still shy and diffident woman. God help her, she has inherited my love of words, and works as a staff writer on a news magazine. Her secret ambition is to write a novel, and she works at one in her spare time. It is, I suspect, a thinly disguised family history. She never shows me her manuscript, and to tell the truth I view the prospect of reading it with some trepidation, but there is nothing cruel about Janey. I suspect she will never finish her book because of a fear of hurting us, or of going so sentimental that she would lose all sense of reality.

In a worldly sense, Barbara is the most successful, or at least the richest, of my children. Gordy and his battered van are long gone from her life—shortly after she went to Connecticut College they lost interest in each other, and he drove out to California, where he disappeared as completely as though he had dropped over the edge of the world. Later on Bert talked Barbara into entering Yale Law School, from which she resigned to marry a fellow student, an ambitious young man who became Bert's understudy, and is gradually taking over his law practice and real estate empire. This makes Betsy happy—she and Barbara go to the same cocktail parties in South Bay, and are active together in amateur plays. Barbara and her husband have two daughters. Betsy is an active grandmother and Bert plays the part of the grandfather with dedication since he and Betsy live almost next door to Barbara. Though I love my descendants, such an arrangement would be too cozy for my taste, and for once I can't find it in my heart to be jealous.

BY NOW I come to the conclusion of this love story. Annie and I have had twenty good years together, almost as many as Betsy and I had. I feel I have lived two lives, one as a man in a gray flannel suit, the other as a guy in dungarees and a red shirt, a costume I affect some of the time, now that I'm a freelance writer, not a ghost.

We enjoyed five years of prosperity after Hopkins' autobiography came out. As Annie had predicted, other businessmen wanted me to help them write their stories or self-advertisements, but eventually I tired of that form of public relations and tried to survive as an independent biographer of big businessmen. Unfortunately, the pay for trying to tell the truth is not as steady as it is for subsidized puffery, and I soon discovered that I am no Boswell. Still, we always seem to get by.

I worry a lot about money—as do most people, even the rich—although that part of life rarely gets into books. Last year Annie and I moved from New York, where apartment rents seemed to double every year, to a fine old house in Orlando, Florida. We are not retiring—we are trying to start a new life in an easier climate, where everyone seems less tense. Annie works as my typist and researcher, but with all the children grown she needed an additional outlet for her energy, and started a school in our large "Florida room" to teach people to diet, exercise and dance. The strict regime that she practiced for years has made her at fifty an expert at keeping fit, and many housewives and career women come to learn her secrets. Pretty girls in brightly colored leotards swoop around our house, and middle-aged matrons in gym suits sweat through a class which Annie advertises as "Ballet for Klutzes." I don't see much of this because I spend most of my time closeted in my study at the opposite end of the house, but I enjoy Annie's school, if only because of the stories I hear about the dancers. Most of her pupils talk to Annie as though she were a psychoanalyst, and she tells me enough about them to make me realize the incredible complexity of people's lives today. The "sexual revolution" may be an improvement over the double standard, the repression, the guilt and hypocrisy of my youth, but I'm glad I never had to endure the singles bars, the one-night stands, the loneliness that so many younger people nowadays seem to suffer. Few of Annie's dancers or the men who accompany them have children. They say they don't want to contribute to the problem of overpopulation, that they are afraid of getting tied down. Most teenage children end up hating their parents anyway, one dancer said, so why go to so much expense to risk so much trouble?

"What good does having children do you?" a direct young woman asked me at a party Annie gave for her pupils. "After all, you hardly ever see them anymore."

I did not know what to answer. I enjoy telephone calls to and from my kids, but I miss them, and I had no good answer for a satirical friend of mine who once said he could sell a son- or daughter-service on tapes that would guarantee a cheery call without recriminations, no requests for money, for only a hundred dollars a year, an enormous saving when compared to the vast cost of raising a child.

It is hard to point to many tangible rewards of parenthood these days. In more primitive countries and times, parents expected their sons and daughters to take care of them in their old age, but most senior citizens I know would rather languish in a nursing home with government aid than inflict themselves on the strained budgets and the cramped households of their children or grandchildren. Since Annie and I have been self-employed we are working to save enough to sustain us when we cannot earn anymore. Like most members of my generation, the last thing we want is to go begging to our children.

Then why do I feel that it is a triumph to have brought five people into the world, and why am I even glad that Mark had a short life instead of none at all?

Selfishly, I can look back and say that despite the worries and anxieties, I have enjoyed being a father and a husband more than anything else I have accomplished. How else could I have spent my money and my time? Eight hours of work a day were always enough for me—Hopkins or no Hopkins. My private life was always more important to me than my career. I don't like sports, fishing bores me, and I couldn't possibly have had many love affairs—whenever I got involved with a woman, I never wanted to let her go, and even my one divorce damn near tore me apart. Perhaps because I didn't have a very easy childhood, I have always had a morbid dread of loneliness, and a family is the best answer ever invented to that. My children helped to heal that wound almost as much as the three women I loved.

I rarely see my children nowadays, but I am not tempted to become one of those old men who complain because their sons and daughters don't visit, write or call more often. My children have their lives and I have mine—it's natural for young animals of all kinds to take off as soon as they can survive by themselves. I helped them when they were young, and in return they gave me ample pleasure, but we don't need each other now, except in spirit. Of course it's easy for me to boast of independence, for I still have Annie, but even if we got bored with each other, there are all those dancing girls to liven things up in our house. When I leave my study to go into the kitchen for a cup of coffee, I often see Annie leading a class in tap dancing, or in the convolutions of jazz, and her exuberant movements at fifty still quicken my heartbeat. I know that married love is considered unfashionable, a kind of sentimentality that sickens sophisticated minds, but sometimes it happens, and it would be a lie to pretend anything else. My only regret is that at sixty-three I can't expect this to go on much longer, but if I live carefully, maybe I'll have a few years left. A panel of physicians on a recent television show solemnly proclaimed love to be good medicine for old people. Just how good, they didn't say —clearly it doesn't do much for arthritis, but I can at least dream of going on to be a hundred, and becoming the horniest centenarian in central Florida.

Those learned doctors also said that exercise, especially dancing, is good for limbering up aching joints. Annie is threatening to teach me to tap dance, a grotesque idea but still pleasing. I have always been too embarrassed by my clumsiness to take lessons from her, but if anyone can teach an old dog new tricks, Annie can.

I'll undoubtedly quit after a few classes, but in my imagination I'll still soar with her. At my age dreams can be almost as good as memories, and I have a vision of myself tapping up a flight of white stairs with her, like the star of an old-fashioned musical comedy, tapping away until I finally drop. *Exit dancing!*